MURDER IN LOS ANGELES

MURDER IN LOS ANGELES

WRITTEN BY JON L. BREEN
D. C. FONTANA   GEORGE FOX
WILLIAM CAMPBELL GAULT
M. R. HENDERSON   VINCENT McCONNOR
WILLIAM F. NOLAN   RAY RUSSELL
CONCEPT BY BILL ADLER
INTRODUCTORY NOTE BY
THOMAS CHASTAIN

WILLIAM MORROW AND COMPANY, INC.   NEW YORK

Library of Congress Cataloging-in-Publication Data

Murder in Los Angeles.

  Contents: Starstruck / by Jon L. Breen—Cut to—
murder / by D. C. Fontana—Return to Venice / by
George Fox—[etc.]
  1. Detective and mystery stories, American. 2. Los
Angeles (Calif.)—Fiction. I. Breen, Jon L., 1943–   .
II. Adler, Bill.
PS648.D4M86   1987   813'.0872'083279494   86-23644
ISBN 0-688-06684-4

Printed in the United States of America

First Edition

1 2 3 4 5 6 7 8 9 10

BOOK DESIGN BY JAYE ZIMET

INTRODUCTORY NOTE
THOMAS CHASTAIN

Over the years L.A., "The City of Angels," has served
as the setting for some notable murder mysteries, both
factual, such as *The Black Dahlia* and *Hillside Strangler* cases, and fictional, including the novels of Raymond Chandler and Ross Macdonald, among others
in both instances.

The city provides a physical setting almost perfectly suited to the requirements of fictional mysteries: Located at the edge of the continent, Los Angeles,
surrounded by ocean and mountain and desert, is as
symbolically sealed in as in the locked room of the
classic murder mystery.

Then there's the isolation of the canyons and beaches,
ideal for raising a reader's goose bumps, along with

the sudden fogs that can sweep in blindingly without warning even on a sunny day, and the rains and floods that can work so effectively as eerie atmosphere.

And, finally, there's the lure of climate attracting a potent mixture of individuals, from the gifted to the psychotic, all seeking a place in the sun, all interacting with one another.

Where is the mystery writer, even Edgar Allan Poe, who could create from imagination such an ideal environment for fictional skullduggery?

For the dedicated reader of murder mysteries, happily, the best writers in the genre—while they did not create the setting of L.A.—have wisely learned how to use it, including Chandler and MacDonald and the eight talented writers of this book.

Here is Los Angeles of the motion-picture and television worlds as well as the lonely canyons and deserted beaches and blinding rains. And most of all, here is a cross section of the people who commit, are victims of, bystanders at, or solve murders in L.A., written by eight top authors who know their city and their subject from first-hand observation and experience.

Thomas Chastain, who makes his home in New York City, has lived and worked in Hollywood.

CONTENTS

MURDER IN LOS ANGELES

STARSTRUCK
JON L. BREEN

The first stop on any tourist's Los Angeles itinerary is Hollywood Boulevard, once the mecca of stars and star-watchers, now a seedy thoroughfare whose glamour is preserved only in the memorabilia that fill its bookstores and in the Walk of Fame, whose 2,500 stars are embedded in the boulevard's pavement for fifteen blocks from Gower Street to Sycamore Avenue (as well as for three blocks along Vine Street). Several hundred stars remain empty and ready to immortalize hot new sensations or aging screen idols, although there have been cases where one of the latter has had to decline the honor for lack of the $3,000 fee for casting the star's name in bronze. In other ways, too, present reality does not always reflect past fame;

the star of W. C. Fields, for example, is now on the doorstep of an adult movie house. And sometimes the past behind some particular star may be even sinister, as in Jon L. Breen's "Starstruck."

QUITE a few people had seen the tall, bent figure in the gray raincoat staggering along Hollywood Boulevard that April morning. Police were able to glean quite a complete description of his activities. He'd crossed to the north side of the street at Cherokee and staggered eastward, past Whitley. As the figure lurched along, witnesses agreed, he was looking down at the sidewalk, muttering the names of the show-business personalities immortalized on the Hollywood Chamber of Commerce's Walk of Fame. "Clem McCarthy . . . Danny Kaye . . . Ruth Etting . . . Toby Wing . . . David Butler . . . Ozzie Nelson . . ."

But why didn't anybody help him? He obviously was in pain, he obviously was in trouble, yet no one had come to his aid.

"I thought he was just drunk or on drugs," said one of the passersby.

"Half the people you pass on Hollywood Boulevard are talking to themselves," said another.

"I was just glad he didn't stop in front of my window," a merchant admitted.

You see all kinds of weird people on Hollywood Boulevard. Gaudily dressed prostitutes of both sexes, plus hustlers of every other variety; street preachers, bag women, and discharged mental patients; drunks, derelicts, and beggars; adolescents dressed, dyed, and clipped in punk style, earphones shutting out the world; aging hippies in army fatigues; and an occasional nattily dressed octogenarian who might have belonged to the old Hollywood. And some disillusioned tourists who, once they've had a look at the footprints in front of Mann's Chinese Theatre and a walk around the third-rate wax museum, have trouble finding much glamour in the tacky souvenir shops, junk-food stands, video parlors, barber college, empty store fronts, and—unless they are bibliophiles—bookshops.

The figure in the raincoat had lurched along another half block after crossing Whitley and finally fallen on one of the stars, a star shinier than the others, having been dedicated only a few weeks before. When the man fell, his raincoat came open, and passersby could see the red bloodstain spreading on his chest. Then they called the police.

The man on the street had been shot, dying slowly with every painful step he took, and soon actor Trent Gordon's glittering new star was roped off as a crime scene.

"Who are all these people?" Detective Gary Holmes asked his partner. "Clem McCarthy?"

"Used to call the Kentucky Derby on the radio," said Detective Manny Gonzales.

"And Toby Wing? Who was he?"

"No idea." Manny wished his partner didn't have such an appetite for nonessentials.

Holmes read on. "James Dunn . . . Reed Hadley . . . John Forsythe . . . Helen Hayes . . . Basil Rathbone . . . Penny Singleton . . . Martha Raye." There the trail of occasional blood spatters stopped. Beyond Trent Gordon's star, the stars of Jack Warner, Bob Hope, Mickey Rooney, and others were half covered by a building-site fence.

"We've got ID," one of the technicians said. "His wallet says he was Howard Achitty. And look what else he was carrying. Isn't this a friend of yours?" He handed over a business card.

* * *

Rachel Hennings was relieved when Manny Gonzales told her, somewhat regretfully, that his visit to Vermilion's Bookshop constituted official business. She led him through her extensive stock of used and rare books to the easy chairs in the back of the shop. She offered a smile that tried to be warm and friendly without encouraging romantic advances. As Manny spoke, the smile faded.

"To put it simply, Rachel, we found a dead man on Hollywood Boulevard who had your business card in his pocket. Fellow named Howard Achitty." He briefly outlined the significant details.

"Yes, he was here yesterday," she confirmed. "A tall man? Late fifties? Distinguished-looking?"

"Tall, yes, and the age is about right, maybe a little older than that. He didn't look too distinguished when I saw him, though. He'd taken a slug in the chest from a distance of a few feet. After it happened, he managed to stumble along the boulevard at least a block and a half. We're not sure just where he collected the slug. Tell me about his visit here."

"He came at the height of the rainstorm, a little after four, I think. I remember him well, because I didn't have another customer all afternoon. When he came in, I thought he looked a little familiar. Maybe one of the regular customers Uncle Oscar had when I used to visit the shop as a child. And he had that look in his eye, as if Vermilion's once meant something important to him. Finally he walked up to the desk in front and said he was looking for a book. Then he looked at me for a long moment and didn't say anything."

"I can see his point."

She shrugged off the flattery. "Finally he asked me if I was old Oscar's niece, the one who inherited the store. I said I was. He said, 'We all used to come to

Oscar's to get out of the sun and keep this damned climate from drying out our brains.' I told him, 'Los Angeles never did that to anybody. It's just a nice place to live.' And he said, 'Don't tell me that. I need an explanation for why I never managed to rival Thomas Wolfe.' 'You were a writer?' I said. 'Sure, I was a writer. Weren't all of Oscar's customers writers?' " She shook her head sadly. "He was a nice guy."

"What book was he looking for?"

"It was the autobiography of Burton François, the director. I didn't have one in stock—I'd just sold one a few weeks ago, in fact. It was published only about fifteen years ago but has gotten to be a pretty scarce item. I asked him if he'd tried any of the public libraries or other bookshops, and he said nobody seemed to have a copy available. I even asked him if he knew François, if he might be able to get a copy from him personally. He sort of snorted at that and said, 'I don't trust any of those guys.' I wondered what he meant. Then I remembered that François was best known as a science-fiction director, and I thought my friend Blast-Off Meagher, who specializes in sf, might have the book. I gave him a call, and he did, said he'd hold it for my customer. Blast-Off asked me the customer's name, and that was when he told me he was Howard Achitty."

"Blast-Off Meagher," Manny said. "His shop's on Cherokee, just off Hollywood, right?" Rachel nodded. "Achitty might have been there just before he died. He came from that direction. But he sure didn't have a book on him. . . . Did he say anything else?"

"No—once I'd told him about Blast-Off, he went out in that rain with such enthusiasm you'd have thought he was Gene Kelly."

"Would he have been able to buy the book from Meagher yesterday after leaving here?"

Rachel thought a moment. "I doubt it. This was late afternoon, and I think Blast-Off closes at five."

"Then I'll bet that's where he was this morning. You've been a big help, Rachel. Uh, how about dinner tonight? We could talk some more about the case. You could be a kind of unofficial consultant."

She grinned at him, suspicious as always of any invitation from Manny Gonzales to be an "unofficial consultant." "The LAPD always has time to entertain gifted amateur detectives, huh? Why wait for tonight? I have more for you now. After he left, I took down one of my movie references to find out what the connection was between Howard Achitty and Burton François. Let me show you." She stretched to pull a large book down from a high shelf, giving Manny a pleasurable view of a few inches of skin between blouse and jeans. She opened the book on the round table between them and showed Manny the credits for a film called *Menace of the Solar System,* released in 1952.

"It was François's first feature, and Achitty wrote the screenplay," Rachel said. "Look who the male lead was."

"Sure enough, Trent Gordon," said Manny. "And now Achitty dies a day after he was looking for François's autobiography . . ."

"And chooses to fall on Gordon's star."

"Chooses? Maybe he just couldn't go any farther."

"It would be quite a coincidence, though, wouldn't it?"

"They do happen. What do you think, it's Ellery Queen time? A dying message? Rachel, in all the time I've worked homicide, *nobody* has given me a dying message."

"So you've been deprived. You said the witnesses

thought he was reading the stars. Maybe he was looking for the right one to flop down on. Maybe Gordon killed him."

"Maybe Bob Hope killed him, but he couldn't get that far."

Rachel made a face. "Don't tease your unofficial consultant."

"I just can't buy the dying-message bit," Manny said. "But we'll look into it. Was this a major picture? Gordon was a pretty big star at one time, wasn't he?"

"Not in movies," Rachel said. "In the early fifties, Trent Gordon was strictly a B star. He only became really famous when he made that TV western series."

"I thought he was a private eye."

"That was later. He had a cowboy show first."

"I never saw it. Never liked westerns, even as a kid. Did you ever see a smart Mexican in a western, Rachel? Truthfully now."

Rachel ignored the question. "What was the symbol on Gordon's Walk of Fame star?"

"Symbol?"

"They identify them according to what branch of show business they became famous in. There's a microphone, a movie camera, a record, a TV set . . ."

Manny nodded. "It was a TV set all right." He looked back at the credits. "Who else was in this picture? Audrey Vance . . ."

"I think she later married Burton François, but it didn't last."

"How cozy. You seem to know Hollywood gossip as well as you know books."

Rachel shrugged. "Can I help it if things stick in my mind?"

"Billy Hook," Manny read. "Song-and-dance man, wasn't he?"

"He'd have been a big star if they'd kept making musicals."

"And Guy Wheatley. He goes back a long way."

"He was in silents. You going to talk to all these people, Manny?"

Manny snorted. "If they're still alive, I may have Holmes do it. He's the one that's starstruck. No reason to think any of the others have any connection to Achitty's death, but I guess I have to follow up on Trent Gordon and Burton François. Had Achitty done anything since the sci-fi epic?"

"Don't let Blast-Off hear you call it sci fi," Rachel said. She reached down another reference tome, this one on screenwriters, found the Achitty entry, and handed the book across to Manny. "Mostly B movies through the late fifties, then lots of TV scripts into the middle seventies. Then his career seems to have petered out. I noticed he talked about his writing in the past tense."

"You didn't give me an answer about dinner," Manny said.

"Well—"

"Look, why don't you come with me to see Blast-Off Meagher? I mean, you know books and all this movie lore, and it's looking pretty important."

"I'm in business here, Manny. I can't just leave the shop."

The UCLA library school student Rachel had recently hired as a relief clerk chose that moment to enter through the front door and roar in a theatrical bass, "Your slave is here, Rachel. What is it today, shelve or study my cataloguing? Say shelve, please."

Rachel wasn't sorry her excuse for not accompanying Manny had disappeared. But she'd have to make it clear to him their relationship would be strictly professional.

* * *

Blast-Off Meagher greeted them amid a seeming chaos of hardbacks and paperbacks, pulps and digests, scripts and souvenirs, nearly all with some science-fictional connection. The seeming disorder contrasted sharply with the neatness of Vermilion's, but the elderly, bushy-bearded bookseller seemed to know where everything was, despite a visual handicap that seemed insurmountable for someone in the book business.

"Sure, he was here this morning, and I sold him the book."

"Are you sure it was Achitty?" Manny asked.

"He said he was, but you have to realize, I'm legally blind, so I can't describe the guy."

"What did his voice sound like?" Rachel asked.

Blast-Off considered for a moment. "He sounded a little like Johnny Carson. Under sedation."

Rachel nodded. "That's the same man."

"Was he alone?" Manny asked.

"No. I heard him talking to somebody as he entered the shop. The other person stayed near the doorway, and as Achitty left, he started talking again."

"Did the other person say anything?"

"Not a word."

"Do you know if it was a man or a woman?"

"Can't help you there. Wasn't close enough to smell anything, and to tell somebody's sex, I have to be very, very close." Blast-Off chuckled.

"What time was this?"

"I don't make the effort to look at my watch until near closing time. I guess it was ten-thirty or so. I hadn't been open for long."

"Did you hear anything after he left the shop?"

"Yeah. For what seemed like a half hour, somebody was playing rock music outside—a tape, I guess, or a car radio—loud enough to make the building shake. I was afraid if they didn't quit soon, I'd be legally deaf, too."

"You didn't hear a shot?"

"No, and I wouldn't have. That music would have drowned anything out."

Rachel said, "Blast-Off, what do you remember about a movie called *Menace of the Solar System?*"

"Interesting picture. Sort of a cult item. Some people in the sf field think it was one of the classic films of the 1950s. You have to realize that you can find sf fans who will make a case for every bug-eyed-monster movie made before 1960, so you can't take what all of them say too seriously. But I think *Menace of the Solar System* was probably a pretty good flick. It had one of the great movie robots in it, right up there with Robbie and C3PO. They called it Ishmael—a little pretentious, don't you think? Of course, Burton François at that time was your basic Hollywood boy wonder, and he was under a great deal of pressure to come up with a movie to justify his advance billing. He put together a great crew of technicians and special-effects people and a cast that was straight out of a B-movie stock company. But as I recall, there was some problem with the studio about his finished product, and I think they took it out of his hands and did some recutting on it. Of course, the picture did make a little bit of money, and Burton François went on to become a pretty successful director, if not quite the *Wunderkind* people expected back then."

"What do you know about that vacant store next to you?" Manny asked.

Blast-Off laughed. "There's been everything in there from a hair salon to a hamburger stand to an old-record store. Place is jinxed. Bad location, I guess."

"Do they often leave the door unlocked?"

"They've been careless about that, yes. You have to realize there's nothing in there to steal, but the boulevard freaks have all sorts of unsavory uses for an empty store—flophouse, needle academy, stolen-goods exchange, coed brothel—"

"If somebody fired a shot in that empty store, would you have heard it?"

Blast-Off shook his head. "Not with that rock music going, I wouldn't."

As they left, Rachel looked at the empty shop on the Hollywood Boulevard side of Blast-Off's. The doorway was slightly recessed into the building, and there was only enough window space to show no one was doing business there.

"The scene of the crime?" she asked.

Manny nodded. "I think so. It all figures. Achitty and his companion come out of Meagher's. He's anxious to have a look at the book. They duck into the doorway, see it's unlocked, go into the empty store to examine their treasure. Once they're out of public view, Achitty finds out his friend is not so friendly. The other guy—"

"It could have been a woman," Rachel pointed out. "Blast-Off said—"

"Sure, it could have been a woman. The other person shoots him, takes the book—"

"And Achitty goes lurching down toward the Boulevard. Why didn't the killer finish him off, make sure he was dead?"

Manny agreed that was a good point. "It doesn't look like a pro. Maybe once the shot was fired, the killer got so scared he—or she—just bolted. Well, we'll find out."

"What's next?" Rachel asked.

"How about some lunch? It's after one o'clock, and I

was going to meet Gary Holmes at my uncle's place."

Manny's uncle's place served some of the best Mexican food in Los Angeles, so Rachel found herself readily agreeing. It should get her off the hook for dinner.

Joining them at their table, Detective Gary Holmes roared, "Hey, I didn't know they let Mexicans in here!"

Manny winced at his partner's heavy-handed humor, but he knew it was benignly intended. "I didn't know they allowed WASPs either," he said in a lower voice. "Sit down and try to behave yourself." Thanks to its location on Fairfax Avenue, Tio Pedro's perhaps had the largest Jewish clientele of any Mexican restaurant in the world.

Holmes picked up the menu, knowing he could ignore the prices. "You're sure this stuff is all kosher?" he said, winking at Rachel.

"Shut up," Manny said. "We know where the crime was committed and a little bit of why. What have you got to show for the last couple hours?"

"I've identified most of the stars. Reed Hadley played Zorro in a serial and used to have a TV show called *Racket Squad*. But I still don't know who Toby Wing—"

"Can it, Gary. Did you get to talk with Trent Gordon?"

"Sure I did. Just caught him going out the door, on the way to the library, he said, to study his art. Quite a character. All the acting talent of Tab Hunter, but to talk to him you'd think he was Laurence Olivier or something. The guy does have a connection to Howard Achitty. Ever heard of a sci-fi flick called *Menace of the Solar System*?"

Manny glanced at Rachel. "I think I've heard of it, yeah."

"Well, the guy that directed it was Burton François. It was his first picture, and now he's a big-shot director. In the last couple of weeks, François has gotten the idea he wants to reshoot the ending of the flick."

"Reshoot the ending?" Rachel said. "But it was over thirty years ago."

"I know. But it seems the studio screwed up the picture, didn't release it the way François wanted it. I guess in those days the director didn't have diddly-squat to say about what they did with his flick. Now François is rich and does what he wants. He bought up all the rights to the flick from the studio. All the main actors are still alive. He wants to reshoot a new finish, with all the characters thirty years later, then rerelease the picture the way he wants it. Some idea, huh?"

"Yeah," said Manny. "Has anybody ever done that before?"

Rachel said, "I remember hearing that Orson Welles wanted to do something like that with *The Magnificent Ambersons,* but it never happened."

"Anyway," Gary Holmes continued, "François had scheduled a meeting of the main actors at his home in Beverly Hills tonight."

"Is the meeting still on?" Manny asked.

"As far as Gordon knows it is."

"Was Howard Achitty one of the people invited?"

"I asked, and Gordon wasn't sure. It seems likely."

"I wonder if Mr. Burton François would mind if we dropped in on this little meeting."

Realizing the hounds were on the scent and the unofficial consultant would only be in the way, Rachel begged off the reiterated dinner invitation and left the two policemen to their investigations. But she had a busy afternoon planned for herself. Back at Vermil-

MURDER IN LOS ANGELES

ion's, she first made a quick call to the Hollywood
Chamber of Commerce. She had an idea of the possible significance of Achitty's falling on Gordon's bright
new star.

She asked if any of the principals in *Menace of the
Solar System* or director François had stars in the
sidewalk. François did, she was told, but his star was
well up Vine Street, near the Huntington Hartford
Theatre, quite a distance from the scene of Achitty's
death. Guy Wheatley also rated a star, one of the first
to be implanted back in 1961, but it, too, was blocks
away from where Achitty had been found. Audrey
Vance and Billy Hook had never been honored.

Next she drove down to the Los Angeles Public Library, an ornately imposing building dating from 1926.
It was soon to be vacated for a long-needed expansion
and remodeling, for now the old library was little
changed, a historic landmark bursting its bounds.

The library's film book collection was located in the
Art and Music department on the second floor. As she'd
expected, the circulating copy of François's autobiography was not there, but there was a reference copy
she could peruse on the premises. She scanned through
it quickly, looking for references to *Menace of the Solar System* and its cast.

François had been born in 1925, which made him
just over sixty now and in his middle to late twenties
at the time of *Menace of the Solar System*. The most
recent of the volume's selection of photographs showed
a mildly boyish-looking man in his mid-forties. People
had always said François seemed too shy and retiring
a person to be a successful director, and the photographs seemed to bear that illusion out. It was difficult to imagine his controlling a movie set.

"Most of us were kids when we made that picture,"

François had written about *Menace of the Solar System,* "and we were positive it was going to be the greatest science-fiction picture ever made. In our original conception, it would have been. What most of the moviemakers of the fifties (and later) forgot was that science fiction is a literature of ideas, not of horrors, and that was what we were trying to reflect in our film. But it was the time of the witch-hunt, and it's hard for people looking back to realize just what the atmosphere of Hollywood was like in those days. We were all afraid of our own shadows. I was only a genius on Mondays, Wednesdays, and Fridays. On Tuesdays and Thursdays, I was a scared kid, afraid what I'd achieved to that point would crumble under my feet like the sand on the beach at Malibu. When I was told to make changes, lest I be thought a purveyor of Communist propaganda, which I absolutely was not, I made the changes readily like a good little studio hack."

There was disappointingly little detail about the making of the film and no elaboration on the reference to the Communist witch-hunt. What had anyone found Communistic in the original script of *Menace of the Solar System*? And what changes had been mandated? François was maddeningly silent on the point.

There was also little about the others involved in making the film.

"Howard Achitty was a gifted writer who knew what I wanted and could provide it, knew what the studio wanted and could provide that, too. We worked well together but never had the opportunity to do so again. . . .

"Trent Gordon seemed destined for a career as a B leading man along the lines of Kane Richmond or Robert Lowery. Television would bring him a popularity beyond anyone's wildest dreams—but maybe not beyond his own. . . .

"Billy Hook was a song-and-dance star that the gods of the studio, in their infinite wisdom, signed to a long-term contract just a week before they decided to shut down their musical unit. They put him in various projects, including our picture, and he wasn't happy. But he was going to a drama coach and did his best to bring himself up to snuff as a straight actor. He did a good job as the comic second lead in *Menace*. Later on he made a mint in real estate. . . .

"Guy Wheatley had long been one of the great movie villains, from a silent-picture career leering at Leatrice Joy and Lillian Gish. He'd been young then but always played middle-aged. Our *Menace* was one of the best parts he'd ever had, he said, and he played it to the hilt. . . .

"Audrey Vance was about the most beautiful creature I'd ever seen, and shortly after we finished *Menace* I married her. She'd been married before, and she loved to talk about her previous husband's habit of reading scripts in bed. Everything was funny to Audrey, both in bed and out, and we just didn't get along at all."

François had no more to say about his *Menace of the Solar System* coworkers. Discussing later films and actors, he was much more forthcoming.

The photo section was better than the text. It offered a picture of the film's most memorable set: the spaceship's improbably grand and roomy flight deck. Trent Gordon was startlingly handsome in his futuristic space uniform—when his private-eye show had gone off the air only ten or so years ago, he'd hardly looked any older. And yes, Audrey Vance had been a notable beauty, tall and blond, her long legs fully revealed in the standard fifties vision of feminine space attire. The diminutive Billy Hook, playing Gordon's sidekick, had the kind of face that would appeal to specialists in sad-clown portraits. And Guy Wheatley had a suitably evil countenance as the titular Menace.

The picture's renowned robot, Ishmael, not as cute as Robbie or C3PO but somehow more believable, was shown in one still with Trent Gordon. As Rachel was looking at it, a voice from over her shoulder said, "He was a terrible scene-stealer."

She nearly jumped a foot. Turning, she found herself looking into the face of Trent Gordon. The actor was still so matinee-idol handsome she immediately thought about facelifts.

"I'm sorry if I frightened you. Could I have a look at that book when you're finished with it, please?"

"Yes, certainly, I was nearly finished."

Gordon sat down. Some of the other readers, who had old-fashioned principles about silence in libraries, were glaring at him.

"It's terrible for the ego," he told her more softly. "I spend many afternoons among all these students of the film, and I'm rarely even asked for an autograph. I haven't seen you in here before."

The actor's knee had made tentative contact with Rachel's. She sensed he was more interested in her than in the book she was reading. She was a bit charmed in spite of herself, but not so charmed she wouldn't have made a swift exit if she hadn't had another motivation for cultivating him.

"That book's tough to track down these days. I didn't read it when it first came out, though I'm not one of those actors who never read books, only scripts. What's your interest in my old pal Burton François?"

The guy certainly had confidence in his irresistibility, quizzing a fellow library patron when it was clearly none of his damned business. Rachel could play along quite nicely. She manufactured a girlish blush.

"To be truthful, it's not Mr. François I'm interested in. I was really interested in you, Mr. Gordon. Professionally, I hasten to add," she said, not intending the disclaimer to be convincing. "I was doing research for an article I hoped to write for, uh, my college film journal about your career. That's why I was so startled to actually see you."

"Well, coincidences do happen. In fact, I'll let you in on another that I've been itching to tell somebody about. A man died today on Hollywood Boulevard. Murdered. And I may be the chief suspect."

Rachel widened her eyes like a Victorian ingenue. "Really?"

"Yes. And the reason I wanted to see the book . . ." He looked around. "We really shouldn't discuss this among all these serious students of the arts. That woman in the plaid looks as if she'd like to kill *me*. I presume you've read in there about the picture I made with François and that upstaging robot?"

"Of course. That's why I got the book."

"Then join me for a cup of coffee or a drink. If you're afraid of being in the company of a murder suspect, I assure you the itinerary is well-peopled and includes no dark alleys."

Rachel closed the book. "I'll be honored," she said.

At a little after four, Rachel was sipping a margarita with Trent Gordon in the bar of the newly refurbished Biltmore Hotel. On the short walk from the library, all his talk had been determinedly small and ingratiating. Rachel sensed the actor's interest was now about evenly divided between discussing the Achitty case and getting her into bed before the evening was over. Her own interest was concentrated in the first area.

"What I wanted to know," he said confidentially, "was whether François said anything in his book about the death of William Bingham."

"William Bingham? No, not a thing. Should he have?"

"That's debatable, but I'm not surprised he didn't. William Bingham was a very good actor. We were in a play together not far from here in the old Biltmore Theatre, years and years ago. Bingham had the misfortune of holding rather, um, advanced social views and signed his name to things a little too freely in the thirties and forties. To put it simply, he got himself blacklisted."

Rachel nodded. "I remember his name now. But why should François have mentioned his death?"

With the air of a magician producing a rabbit, Gordon said, "Bingham was found dead on the set of *Menace of the Solar System* one morning, that's why. He was lying at the controls of Burt's state-of-the-art movie spaceship. And he was murdered with a knife in his back. Don't look for that in the newspaper files, though—as far as they were concerned, he died in bed. The studios had a lot of influence in those days."

"It was covered up?"

"Quite successfully."

"Did the police . . . ?"

"Officially, the police knew nothing about it. Unofficially, well, I don't really know what strings the studio head might have pulled."

"What was Bingham doing on the set?"

"None of us knew. As a blacklisted Commie, he was a pariah on any movie lot. We'd all have been scared to death of any connection with him. Presumably, he got on the lot through some ruse, met somebody on our set, maybe threatened to blackmail him about something. That somebody killed him. Up until Bingham's death, the making of *Menace of the Solar System* had been pretty much left alone. After all, it was a B, a programmer, kids' matinee stuff, and the B directors had more freedom than the big guys as long as they stayed within schedule and budget. After Bingham died, a studio flunky was always there to watch the shooting. I think the studio head, who had built up an image of himself as a patriotic American compared to whom Howard Hughes was a fellow traveler, actually read the script and found some things that made him nervous. He demanded changes."

Gordon downed his drink and signaled for another. Rachel continued to nurse hers.

"Howard Achitty made the changes, but he wasn't happy about it any more than Burt François was. They weren't really political, either one of them, and there was no Commie propaganda in that script. Howard had a sort of obsession about what happened from then on. He used to mention it to me whenever I saw him, and I had to admit it made me nervous, though I was just as curious myself. I'm wondering if Howard might have found out something after all these years, something he shouldn't have." Trent Gordon paused reflectively. "The last time I saw him was just a few weeks ago. He showed up at the ceremonies when they dedicated my star on Hollywood Boulevard. And when he died this morning, he was lying on my star, almost as if he was fingering me for the murder, which I know he couldn't have been, because I didn't kill him."

Rachel was fighting back the urge to ask him questions about things she wasn't supposed to know, like

Achitty's search for the François autobiography and tonight's scheduled meeting of the *Menace* cast. Was that still on? she wondered.

"It must be thrilling to have a star on Hollywood Boulevard," she said, still the starstruck college journalist.

Gordon smirked. "It came at a good time for me, because my career isn't exactly booming at the moment. Who knows what might help it?"

"What is your next project?"

Gordon looked at his watch and reacted stagily. Charming, but no great actor. "Well, look at the time! I'd love to talk to you some more, Rachel. How about some dinner later?"

"Well, I—"

"That's settled then. I have a little engagement first, though. I wonder if you might like to accompany me. You might find it interesting."

"Where are you—uh, we going?" she asked.

"To the Beverly Hills home of Mr. Burton François!"

Rachel considered swooning on the spot but decided that would be overdoing it.

Beverly Hills was one of the least-changed places in Southern California. As Gordon's car turned off Santa Monica Boulevard onto one of the tree-lined residential streets, Rachel saw an elderly black man in pristine white coat leading what looked like a purebred Pomeranian on a leash. He could have been Rochester, and the year 1940.

François's house was only slightly larger and more luxurious-looking than the Beverly Hills average. As they walked up the driveway to the front door, Gordon dropped the name of the silent-film star who had originally built it. "Screening room's bigger than those in some of these four-screens-in-one movie houses you see nowadays—that was one reason Burt bought it."

Sure enough, a butler let them into the living room. Posters and movie memorabilia were everywhere, recounting not just François's career but the whole history of Hollywood.

"Mr. François will be down in a few minutes," the butler said, and bowed his way out like a refugee from *Masterpiece Theatre*. A tall, still-blond Audrey Vance sprang from the sofa, and she and Trent Gordon greeted each other in the best effusive show-biz fashion. The former Mrs. François was heavier, a bit puffy-faced, and making no apparent effort to deny middle age, but her legs were fine as ever and shown to good advantage in her short loose-fitting dress.

Gordon introduced Rachel, and Audrey gave her a friendly greeting.

"I didn't know I could bring a date," Audrey said kiddingly.

"Rachel is my newly appointed official biographer. She goes with me everywhere."

"What, everywhere?" Audrey said with a leer.

Rachel practiced her girlish simper, while saying to herself, No, not everywhere, in fact hardly anywhere.

The two old costars halted their arch dialogue briefly to agree how tragic it was about poor old Howard.

"You and he were pretty good friends, weren't you?" Gordon said.

Audrey said sadly, "Used to be. I haven't seen him in years. Make yourself and Rachel a drink, why don't you?" Audrey gestured to a well-stocked bar. "I'm a couple ahead of you."

"I could tell," Gordon said. "I thought you'd gone on the wagon."

"No fun on the wagon."

"What's your pleasure, Rachel?" Gordon asked.

"Just some ginger ale." The margaritas at the Biltmore had been plenty.

"Funny idea remaking that movie," Audrey said. "I think I'll enjoy it, if Burt actually gets it off the ground. Take a little work to get myself in shape, of course. I know I'm supposed to be thirty years older, but I don't want to let myself look *too* ridiculous. Trent, you'll have to be heavily made up to look thirty years older."

"The hell I will, Audrey. You know cowboys and private eyes and space heroes never grow old. Or any older than they can help. Anybody else here yet?"

"Guy's here."

"Really? How is he?"

"All things considered, pretty good. Burt's chauffeur drove him down from the Motion Picture Country House in Woodland Hills, and he'll be staying over. He went up to his room to rest." She turned to Rachel. "The man's eighty-five, would you believe it? A little bit frail, but he's kept up his instrument—"

"You've already tested his instrument?" Gordon asked.

"His voice, you bastard. He says he's still capable of working, and I believe him. Next to George Burns, he's a kid. Give me a refill, will you?"

Trent Gordon delivered Rachel's glass and took Audrey's.

Audrey said to Rachel, "Don't mind our kidding, honey. You know, and he won't mind my saying this, kidding is why I'm not still married to Burt François. He always takes everything *sooo* seriously, and me, I'd make a joke out of anything. He and his work were too serious to kid about. My other husband was an income tax auditor, and even he had more humor about his job than Burt. Billy Hook was the same sort of guy, so you can imagine I made things kind of uncomfortable on the set. Trent and Guy like a good joke, but they know when to put a lid on it. I never knew when to put a lid on anything—and don't you make any filthy cracks, Trent." She took the drink. "Thanks, honey."

"What did Mr. François have to change in the film to begin with?" Rachel asked.

Audrey Vance laughed uproariously. "That was so damn funny, and nobody else seemed to see the humor of it at all. You know who was supposed to be mouthing the Communist propaganda in that movie? Ishmael the talking robot, that's who. This bucket of bolts was the one who was supposed to be giving you the Marxist-Leninist line. Basically, all Burt and poor old Howard had to do was change the lines of the robot. It was the funniest thing I ever heard—it was like in a cartoon, Mickey Mouse or Bugs Bunny's a Communist, you know? According to Burt, it changed the whole picture, the whole vision they had for it, and Howard was never the same again. But I don't know. I thought it was funny. Nobody else did."

"It seems funny now, Audrey, I have to admit," said Trent Gordon. "But those were the days of McCarthy, don't forget."

"Charlie McCarthy?"

A voice from the doorway said, "That's the McCarthy Howard Achitty said he felt like when he had to rewrite those lines."

"Why, Burt," said Audrey Vance, "did you just make a joke?"

"Sorry to disappoint you," said Burton François. "He didn't laugh when he said it." The director walked into the room, his face somber. He was clearly older but still oddly boyish-looking. His voice was soft. He dropped wearily into a chair. "I ought to have called this off."

"Why call it off?" Gordon replied. "You should go ahead with it as a memorial to Howard."

"I just meant for today. You really need the work, don't you, Trent?"

"Hell, no, but I insisted to my agent I had to fit this in. Out of respect for you, Burt, and film history."

Audrey's giggle spoiled the effect.

Burton François looked pointedly at Rachel. "I don't believe I know you."

"She's with me," Gordon said with wolfish pride. "Rachel Hennings."

"Are you in pictures?"

"No," said Rachel, praying her cover wouldn't be blown. "I'm a reporter," she said, trying for an air of sophomoric self-importance.

"You expect to write about tonight?"

"I'm not here professionally. I mean, I'm writing about Trent, but if you want anything kept off the record . . ."

"I want everything kept off the record," he said, still in soft and measured tones. She sensed he was angry at Gordon for bringing her but too concerned about keeping the peace to ask her to leave. "What paper are you with?"

Trent Gordon gave her a conspiratorial wink. "The *Times*, wasn't it?" he said.

"That's right, the *Times*," she said, smiling at him gratefully.

The butler reappeared, escorting a little man who looked like a retired jockey who'd been catching up on his eating.

"Is that you in there, Billy?" Gordon said.

Billy Hook glared at him. "I can still do a back flip. Want to see me?"

"Please, no. I wouldn't want the responsibility."

The whole group performed the show-biz greeting rituals, but it didn't entirely clear the atmosphere.

"I remember now what a talent we all had for getting on one another's nerves," said Burton François. "In the interest of this project, maybe we should do our best to keep things friendly. Jacob, ask Mr. Wheatley if he's able to join us, will you?" The butler bowed out.

"We miss you out at the Colony, Burt," Billy Hook said.

"Malibu just isn't my style, I guess. I'm more a Beverly Hills person."

"I read a script about Malibu a while back," Gordon said. "It was called *Sandbags and Cocaine*. Great title, but it'll never get made."

A moment later, Guy Wheatley tottered into the room. He was as slow-moving and as fragile-looking as anyone Rachel had ever seen, and she would have estimated his life expectancy at five minutes. But when he spoke, it was in a booming baritone that could still project to the back row.

"You know when I worked last?" he roared. "It was a cigarette commercial. That'll tell you how long ago it was. There I was, a lifetime nonsmoker, sending young cowboys and beach bunnies to their deaths." He looked at Rachel. "What did you play in *Menace of the Solar System*? I don't remember any babes in arms in the picture, but you must have been awfully young."

Rachel smiled. "I'm not an actress. I'm just here on sufferance."

Wheatley peered at her. "You're lovely, you know that? Did you ever work for D. W. Griffith? Silly question, you couldn't have, but he'd have loved that face. Burt, isn't she a dead ringer for Miriam Cooper?"

"Who?" said Billy Hook.

"That's why I love you, Guy," said Audrey. "Only you refer to people I'm too young to remember."

"Then how do you know you're too young to remember her?" the old actor said slyly. "She could be somebody Burt and I met last week. How about it, Burt? Doesn't she?"

"A bit," said Burton François, who clearly knew Miriam Cooper at least from film, but was far less entranced by Rachel than Guy was. "Now that we're all here, why don't we get started? You all know why I wanted you to come, and I know you share my grief that Howard Achitty can't be here with us."

"What happened to him?" Guy Wheatley demanded.

"He, uh, died this morning. But that sad event has nothing to do with our purpose here. As you know, I want to provide *Menace of the Solar System* with a new ending. And before we talk about it, there's something I want you to see."

François led the group out of the living room and along a corridor, decorated on both sides with movie posters, to a towering pair of ornately carved doors.

"The ballroom," said Gordon.

"It *was* the ballroom," said François, "but I have made another use of it, as you'll see." The director was more animated now, obviously eager for their reaction to what he was going to show them. He opened the double doors and directed them in with a flourish.

Filling most of the room was the memorable set from *Menace of the Solar System,* the deck of the spaceship, all steel and flashing lights, dials and screens, buttons and levers. In the center of it all, the main controls, facing a screen that showed a continuous pattern of whizzing asteroids, was the captain's chair. To one side, as if awaiting human orders, was Ishmael himself, one of moviedom's three or four most celebrated robots, who had narrowly escaped being the first blacklisted machine.

For a moment no one spoke. Rachel found the sight enormously impressive and strangely moving, and it didn't have the associations for her that it must have had for the others. Glancing at Audrey Vance, she was surprised to see tears in the actress's eyes.

Billy Hook was the first to speak. "I hated it when I worked here, Burt, but now it's like coming home."

"When do we shoot the new finish?" Gordon asked. "And are we all still on the space voyage or what?"

"These things take time," François said. "But it's going to happen, I assure you. This is still early stages."

"Better get on it fast," said Guy Wheatley. "I could pass away anytime, you know, and I don't want a coffin-nail spot for my last professional engagement."

Audrey had to cover her face, and François seemed close to weeping himself. "I'll do my best, Guy. I really will do my best."

Rachel walked over to the seat at the control board. Surely she wasn't the only one thinking about the death of a certain William Bingham in this very chair. "How long have you had this set, Mr. François?"

"Several years. I acquired it and the robot—and the rights to the film—when they tore down the old Apex studio in Culver City. At the time, my motives were strictly sentimental, but then I got the idea of shooting a new ending, and since all my principals were alive and well . . ."

"Was this the seat where William Bingham died?" Rachel asked softly.

François's mild face changed dramatically. It had

been a dangerous thing to say, she knew. But surely there was safety in numbers—they weren't all going to murder her as a team effort.

"What the hell are you talking about? Who's been talking to you?"

"Do you know who killed Bingham? Did the same person kill Howard Achitty? You don't say much in your autobiography."

"I should have thrown you out of here as soon as I found out you were a reporter." François was talking in a low voice, as if to prevent anyone else from hearing their conversation, but it was no use.

"Who the hell is this dame, anyway?" said Billy Hook.

"She's a reporter," said François, "and she seems to want to stir up a lot of stuff better left unstirred."

Gordon said apologetically, "We've been kidding you, Burt. She's not with the *Times*—she's a college girl."

"And you told her all about William Bingham, did you, you stupid bastard?"

"That happened a long time ago, Burt. We don't have to be afraid of the witch-hunt anymore."

"Well, Howard Achitty just happened this morning. And there could be a connection."

"That's what I thought," Rachel said.

Trent Gordon stared at her. "What *you* thought? What do you know about it?"

"Right, Gordon," said Billy Hook. "Bring your latest piece of ass here and put us all in danger."

"Watch your language, Hook, or I'll roll you out of here like a beachball!" Gordon exploded. But the look he turned on Rachel wasn't friendly.

"You have more to lose than any of us, Trent," Burt said. "Howard died on your star. He could have been saying you killed him."

"I don't think so," said Rachel, anxious to defend

Gordon and gain at least one ally. "I think Achitty was looking for Trent's star and picked that spot to fall. But he wasn't trying to tell the police you killed him, Trent. He was trying to establish a connection between his death and *Menace of the Solar System.* He knew where your star was, and he didn't know the location of anybody else's. Or if he did, he knew they were too far away to get to."

Gordon shook his head. "You know more about all this than I do," he said.

"I wish we could come to some understanding here before the police arrive," François said.

"Police arrive?" Hook squeaked. "You're expecting the police?"

François shrugged. "A couple of L.A. detectives asked permission to drop in. I could hardly refuse them. I thought it was just routine. But if there's some connection with Bingham . . ."

"Bingham died in bed," said Hook. "He had no connection to our picture, and he was never on the set."

"But he was," said Rachel.

"Only if somebody tells them so. The case is closed. Hell, it was never even open. Why bring up Bingham now?"

"I don't believe in coincidental murders," said Rachel.

"You don't believe—and who are you to believe or not believe?" Billy Hook was turning red, and Audrey Vance put a hand on his arm to calm him down. He shook it off.

Rachel wondered why Hook was so much more wrought-up than the others. Was it just his nature, or was it something else?

"What did Bingham do for a living after he got blacklisted?" she asked.

Surprisingly, the answer came from Guy Wheatley.

"The poor bastard did what a lot of the poor bastards did. Writers could write for less money under other names, but that wasn't open to actors. But he could teach. He became an acting coach. Gave private lessons, of course. Very secret."

"Who was your acting coach, Mr. Hook?" Rachel asked.

"I don't have to answer that," he said.

"No, you don't. But if Bingham was your acting coach, the information can't hurt you now as it could have then."

"Can't it?"

"Not unless you killed him."

"Well, I didn't."

"But if he was on the set to meet you, you couldn't have admitted it, could you? Your own career would disappear from under you. Guilt by association. Isn't that right?"

Billy Hook stared at her. "I didn't kill him. He helped me. He was a wonderful man. I had no reason to kill him. He turned me from an out-of-work hoofer into some sort of actor. I didn't make it big, but I made enough dough and invested it well enough to buy me a place in the Colony. I'd love to know who killed him." He shrugged. "At the time, I didn't have the luxury to wonder. I just wanted his blacklisted ass out of that studio like everybody else. That's the kind of egocentric son of a bitch I am."

Audrey had broken away from the group and had her arm around the robot. "Ishmael, you old bolshevik," she said, "I do believe you're the only human being in the room. Burt, any chance of another drink?"

François looked disgusted. "That won't always work, Audrey."

"Well, it's always worth a try," she said in a subdued voice, starting to sound weepy again.

The butler appeared at the door of the spaceship-deck set. "Two gentlemen from the police are here, sir. They're Los Angeles, though, not Beverly Hills. Should I call . . . ?"

"Let them come in, Jacob," François said dispiritedly.

When Rachel saw the look on Manny Gonzales's face, the uncomfortable evening started to seem worth it. But she still had the feeling everybody in the room wanted to murder her.

"Rachel, what the hell are you doing here?"

"She's a policewoman, right?" said Trent Gordon. "That meeting at the library was no accident."

"She's Hollywood's own Miss Marple," Manny said icily.

That struck a nerve. Rachel said, "I'm the LAPD's unofficial consultant, and I'm about to solve a couple of murders."

Gary Holmes was grinning, at both her chutzpah and his partner's embarrassment.

"I told you I didn't do it," said Billy Hook. Visibly trying to calm himself, he said, "I'm ready to tell you everything I can, but I didn't do it."

"I'm not accusing you, Mr. Hook. I don't need to accuse anybody. Trent, I'm not a policewoman, but I'm not a college student either. I'm sorry I fooled you about that. I'm really a book dealer. I have a friend, another book dealer, who has a wild sense of humor that might appeal to you."

Manny was staring at her but said nothing.

Rachel took a deep breath and launched her bluff. "My friend Blast-Off Meagher likes to pretend he's blind. But he's not. He can see just as well as anybody here. He was the last person to see Howard Achitty alive except his murderer. And he also saw Achitty's companion. The one who stood waiting for him in the doorway of the shop, the one who killed him." She turned to Audrey Vance. "Blast-Off can identify you."

Audrey seemed to go pale, but she managed to counterfeit a laugh. "You're nuts. The old guy's blind as a bat."

"You do know him then?" said Manny softly.

"No, no, I never . . ." She started to slip, grabbed the robot for support. "Tell 'em, Ishmael," she said. "Tell 'em the truth."

"You've had too much to drink," François said, leading her from the robot.

"I haven't had enough," she retorted, still trying to laugh.

François tried to sit her in the captain's chair.

"No, not there," she said. "Please, not there."

Rachel felt drained. She'd been ready for Audrey to lunge at her in murderous fury, but the woman had no kill left in her.

Manny touched her shoulder. "She did it?"

Rachel nodded.

"Can you prove it?"

"That's your department. I'm just the consultant. Consultants lay the groundwork and go away."

Rachel made Manny and Gary omelettes in the apartment over Vermilion's. They'd told her not to bother, but she was happier doing something. Audrey had come around and confessed, and they'd practically had to force her to consult a lawyer.

While they ate, Rachel explained. "Achitty was convinced the changes in *Menace of the Solar System* ruined his career. He became obsessed with the Bingham killing and spent years wanting to solve a murder no one else even admitted had taken place. With the ceremony planting Trent Gordon's star and François's plan to reshoot the end of the movie, things got stirred up again. And somebody Achitty confided in—we'll probably never know who, maybe somebody at the studio who had been involved with the cover-up—tipped him off that there was a clue to the truth in François's old autobiography. Maybe Achitty had never read it, or maybe he was convinced it was worth a fresh look. He started to look for a copy, and the harder it got to find, the more convinced he was.

"In the course of looking for the book, he told the wrong person, Audrey Vance, the only person in the *Menace* group he thought he could trust. Remember his remark to me that he couldn't trust any of those 'guys'? Well, how about a non-guy? After he talked to me yesterday, he must have called her and arranged to go to Blast-Off's with her. He'd probably already tried to get a copy of the book from her, and she'd put him off. She probably didn't really believe there was any clue in the book to implicate her, but she met Achitty armed just in case. She may have suggested that they duck into the store next to Blast-Off's. So just in case there *was* something, she could do—what she did. When she realized Achitty was getting the point, she drew her gun and shot him, knowing the noise from the rock band or whatever it was outside would muffle the sound. I think she was shocked when she'd done it. She'd murdered once before, but it had been years ago, and I don't think she was really a killer."

"Save the bleeding-heart stuff," said Gary.

"Leave it to her lawyer," Manny said. "He'll probably get her off on an insanity plea."

"That may be fair enough," Rachel said. "She fled,

taking the book with her, not even waiting to see if Achitty was really dead. He lurched down the street in a semidaze, feeling good as dead, looking for the star that would at least connect his death with *Menace of the Solar System*. By the time we saw Audrey that night, she was her humorous self. But she was drinking, and Trent Gordon seemed surprised. He thought she'd given it up. But the events of the day had been enough to bring her back to it."

"The poor dear," said Gary.

"Look, I don't know how she could act that normal if she wasn't—sick!"

"Say that again. She couldn't act sane if she wasn't crazy? Is that it?"

Manny held up his hand. "Save the high school debate and tell me what clue Achitty was supposed to find in the autobiography."

"We know Audrey killed Bingham because she'd been married to him, unknown to anybody in Hollywood, and she knew her career could be ruined if it ever came out. When she saw him on the spaceship-deck set, she didn't know he'd come to see Billy Hook. She thought he'd come to blackmail her."

"Yeah, she told us that."

"She didn't deny she'd been married before, but her *official* ex-husband was a tax auditor. She told me that tonight. But there's a reference in François's book to a husband who liked to read scripts in bed. That doesn't fit a tax auditor, but it does fit an actor like William Bingham."

"That's it, the great clue?" said Manny in disbelief. "It also fits Clark Gable and Gary Cooper."

"Manny, to someone who knew all the circumstances—which only people on that picture did—it was enough to send him in the right direction."

"Why didn't anybody ever see it before?"

"It was the kind of thing you could miss if you weren't looking for it. There are all sorts of ways to investigate her background, given that clue, the same ones you'll be following."

They ate their omelettes in silence for a few moments. Then Gary Holmes said, "I guess they won't be finishing that movie now. Too bad for the old guy. He really wanted to work again. He's gay, you know."

Rachel looked up. The way Guy Wheatley had looked at her had struck her as decidedly, if inactively, heterosexual. "Why do you think he's gay?" she asked.

"Before we left, I asked if he could tell me who Toby Wing was, and he said Toby was one of the sexiest, most enchanting creatures he'd ever known. The old coot looked downright lustful when he talked about this guy Toby. Hey, what's so funny, Rachel?"

Rachel got up. "Oh, nothing. Excuse me while I go downstairs for one of my reference books. I think you deserve a look at Toby Wing, Gary. Besides, I want to look up Miriam Cooper."

CUT TO: MURDER

D. C. FONTANA

For all the jokes it has inspired since "Valley Girls" and "Valley Talk" swept the country a few years ago, the San Fernando Valley is where L.A.'s comfortable upper middle classes pursue the American dream. Bounded by the San Gabriel Mountains on the north and the Santa Monica Mountains on the south, the Valley, with its million and a half inhabitants and more than two hundred square miles of land, would be California's second-largest city if it were not part of Los Angeles. Some people would do almost anything to achieve or maintain the modest success that enables them to live there; in D. C. Fontana's "Cut To: Murder," one of them, instead, dies for his success.

* * *

ANNIE Rose Mayhew let herself into the brick-faced ranch-style house on Oak View Drive and swept open the living-room drapes first thing, the way she did every Thursday morning. It was overcast, typical of June when the offshore fog moved in overnight and crept sleepily over the Hollywood Hills into the San Fernando Valley. Because there was always less of it in the Valley, the fog would burn off by midmorning, and Encino would be in for another eighty-degree day.

Wodehouse, the black-and-white cat, uncurled himself from the couch and ran to her, crying urgently. "Well, what's up with you?" she asked, bending over to scratch his ears. Wodehouse wailed again and trotted a few steps toward the kitchen, his tail curled into a furry question mark.

Annie Rose hung her coat in the foyer closet and straightened her smart white dress. Mr. Neubauer wouldn't care if she wore jeans and an old shirt for her housekeeping chores, but Annie Rose felt a good appearance was important. Neubauer was her weekly regular, employing her to come in every Saturday, Tuesday, and Thursday.

Wodehouse cried again, and Annie Rose followed him back to the kitchen. The sink had two rinsed plates, cutlery, and two wineglasses stacked in it, plus some pots and a casserole dish. No coffee cups, she noticed. He must have gone off to the studio early as he did now and then and hadn't bothered about instant before he left.

"So that's it, huh? Ran out and forgot to feed you. Easy fixed, Woody."

The cat curled around her white shoes as she opened a cat-food tin and dished out half of it for him. Once he had his nose buried in the food, she put some coffee on to perk for herself.

Now for the tricky part, she thought. She pulled the vacuum cleaner from the big broom closet, plugged it into the hall outlet, and briskly moved it up and down the corridor outside the bedroom door. When she shut it down, she stood still and listened carefully. Not a sound. She rapped delicately on the door, waited, then opened it.

The bedroom was empty. No female overnighter. That was the one thing she didn't much like about cleaning for Mr. Neubauer. She just never knew when she'd wake up some sleeping beauty he had entertained the night before and left in the house when he went to the studio. Annie Rose frowned uncertainly. The bed was made. That wasn't like him. She shrugged and brought in the vacuum cleaner. Maybe the lady had made up the bed and left the house with him.

The coffee had perked by the time she finished vacuuming the bedroom, and she poured herself a cup. Wodehouse chirped with the little rolling purr he had when he was up to something, and she heard the *pong* of his claws on the bottom edge of a door. She carried the cup into the hall and found him lying on his side with one paw extended under the door of the den. There was just enough clearance for him to wriggle his paw through; and as he chirped again and pulled the paw back, she heard the *pong* of his extended claws catching the door.

"What you doin', Woody? You know you ain't supposed to mess with that door." Wodehouse was not allowed in the den, because Neubauer was afraid cat hair would ruin the computer. "Come on away from there." She reached down for the cat, but he flipped to his feet and rubbed his side against the doorframe. If he put his mind to it, Wodehouse could keep just out of her reach all day.

Annie Rose grunted and reached for the vacuum she had left in the hall. Might as well get this room done now. Balancing the coffee cup, she opened the door and stopped, blinking. All the lights were on. Then Wodehouse sprang back in fright as Annie Rose screamed and dropped the cup, splattering coffee on him.

Griffin Neubauer was sprawled on the carpet in front of the comfortable sofa, his dead eyes staring at her. A graceful Emmy statuette lay beside him, one wing broken, and its base covered in blood from Neubauer's crushed skull.

Homicide Detective Jack Baterman looked in on the crime-lab team and nodded to Archison, the medical examiner. The body had not yet been removed, and the Emmy still lay in the congealed puddle of blood on the thick carpet. Baterman had never heard of Griffin Neubauer, but Lieutenant Olden had sent him and Detective Tom Beldon out of the West Valley Division with the message that some TV writer-producer had been found murdered. Neubauer must have been pretty good to get an Emmy.

"That the weapon?" Baterman asked, indicating the broken statuette.

Archison nodded. "Looks like the murderer grabbed it around the body and hit him with the base. It would've been like using a hammer on him. The wing must've broken when it was dropped on the floor. It was wiped clean, by the way."

"Figures." Baterman looked around the den critically. It was a pleasant room decorated in cool blues and white and set up as an office. Every bit of wall space was covered with bookshelves, ceiling to floor. Baterman noticed that most of the books appeared to be nonfiction. The practical oak desk held a computer and several manuals in addition to the usual desk accessories. There was no printer, and Baterman couldn't see any disks. Maybe Neubauer was just learning how to operate the thing. There was an expensive stereo unit and a cabinet full of records set in one corner, but no television set or video tape recorder. Baterman remembered seeing an elaborate setup in the living room as he passed through. Neubauer apparently kept this room exclusively for work.

"Where's the maid who found him?"

"Kitchen."

Baterman nodded and left Beldon with them to take notes. The ambulance team waited in the hall to remove the body, and he slid past them to the sunny kitchen at the back of the house.

Annie Rose had stopped crying and sat at the kitchen table cradling a new cup of coffee in her hands. It bothered her that the police hadn't let her clean up the one she had dropped. Wodehouse had disappeared, probably cowering under the bed, afraid of all the strangers in the house. What was she going to do about him?

Baterman questioned her gently, gradually drawing out the information that she had worked for Neubauer for eight years, ever since his divorce. Neubauer had been a freelance television writer then, working exclusively at home on his old electric typewriter. Annie Rose had noticed he seemed to have less work, and less money, about four years ago. For a while he had to ask her to come in just once a week. Then he started writing scripts for *Street Heat,* and things were all right again. He even got a computer. Last year he had become the producer of the show.

"But I don't know who'd want to kill him. He never

harmed nobody. Why, he just lived for that show, workin' on it till all hours. 'Course, he has a few lady friends, but he never had no trouble with them. They always liked him, even after he stopped seein' them. They were always friends like."

"Which one of these 'friends' might've been here last night?" Baterman had seen the two sets of dishes stacked in the sink.

"I don't know. He's been seein' two ladies. Lucy Cates—he's known her a long time now—and a gal named Sue Best. She's new. But he'd have it written down in his planner book. He wrote everything down in there."

"Where would that be, Ms. Mayhew?"

"On his desk, or in his briefcase. He always had it with him. Said he just wouldn't know how to do without it." Annie Rose sobbed and dug a handkerchief out of her pocket to wipe away a trickle of tears. "I can't believe he's dead. Just can't."

Baterman patted her hand, and she smiled shakily at him. "You've been a lot of help, Ms. Mayhew. I'd like you to give your address and phone number to Detective Beldon, in case we need to ask you anything else. Then you can go home. Do you need a ride?"

She rubbed at her eyes with the handkerchief again and shook her head. "No sir. I got my own car. Can't get around the Valley without one, can you?" She paused and sniffed a couple of times, patting at her nose with the handkerchief. "Sir? What about Woody?"

"Who's Woody?"

"Wodehouse. Mr. Neubauer's cat. There'd be nobody to take care of him."

"I think we can arrange to have the animal shelter take him in."

Annie Rose indignantly surged out of her chair,

slapping her fist on the table in front of the startled Baterman. "You mean the *pound*? No sir! I won't stand for that. No sir. We raised him from a kitten, Mr. Neubauer and me, and I ain't havin' that. If it's all the same, I'll take him with me."

"I'm sure there's no problem, Ms. Mayhew. If the former Mrs. Neubauer doesn't want him . . ."

"*Huh*," Annie Rose snorted derisively. "She's a dog lover. It's all right then? I can take him? Woody's a smart cat."

Baterman nodded; and the woman beamed, pleased that she could do something for her dead boss. Baterman wished the smart cat could tell them who had murdered his owner.

Beldon had found the planning book in Neubauer's briefcase. It had been carefully gone over by the fingerprint boys, and only one set of prints—Neubauer's—was found on it. It was really an organizer with several sections in it for appointments, business expenses, addresses, notes, contacts, and projects. The appointments were carefully entered in a big, bold hand that Annie Rose identified as Neubauer's. The last entry for Wednesday night was: "7:30—dinner—house—Sue."

Sue Best was clearly disgruntled at being disturbed by the police before noon, even by a fairly young, good-looking cop like Beldon. She was a leggy, long-haired brunette wearing little more than a cut-off T-shirt and shorts. Even without makeup, she was a beauty. An actress, of course. With those looks, anything else would have been unthinkable. Beldon idly wondered if he had ever seen her in anything.

She was distraught when Beldon broke the news to her, breaking into a torrent of tears and gulping sobs. A little theatrical, Beldon caught himself thinking.

Then he realized what she was sobbing.

"I should've stayed. I should've stayed. . . ."

"Ms. Best, can you just tell me what happened last night? You had dinner with Mr. Neubauer?"

She seemed to catch herself up, gathering in the tears and smudging them away from her violet-blue eyes with the back of her hand. Her voice was unsteady, but she had a little story to tell.

"Griff asked me to dinner at the house. He likes— liked—to cook now and then. There's this chicken casserole he does—did, I mean. Oh, God!"

"Just take it slowly, Ms. Best."

She nodded and started again. "Okay. We had just finished dinner when he got a phone call. I didn't hear much of it. He took it in the den, and I was rinsing off the dishes, but he seemed mad. I heard him say he was busy tonight, and why couldn't it wait. He finally came out and said I'd have to go home. Someone was coming over for a meeting—important business—and he didn't know how long he'd be so I couldn't stay. I left right after that."

"What time was that?"

She shrugged her slim shoulders. "Maybe nine. I got here halfway through *Harrigan's Luck*. It takes about fifteen minutes for me to drive home from Griff's place, and I turned on the set when I got in."

"And you don't know who it was he talked to?"

"Not a clue. Oh." She giggled. "No pun intended."

"None noticed," Beldon replied dryly.

Baterman had been trying, unsuccessfully, to contact Lucy Cates and Iris Neubauer. When Beldon called in with Sue Best's information, he put him on the job of tracking down the women and headed for Universal Studios.

Universal's history went back to the silent days when Carl Laemmle had founded the company. The huge property that made up the modern studio formed a rough triangle that touched on the boundaries of Burbank, North Hollywood, and Studio City. It was, in fact, a small city in itself, having a fire department, security force, and post office with its own zip code.

Griffin Neubauer's office was an attractive five-room suite in one of the newer buildings on the big lot. The secretary, Nita Flowers, fielded her business from a desk adorned with a Merlin phone system and a computer identical to the one Neubauer had at home. Flowers herself was a tall, pencil-slim woman, somewhere in her thirties and calm as a rock. Even the news of her employer's death had only made her pause a moment before she reached for the phone, commenting crisply, "I'd better let everyone know."

The other offices in the suite belonged to Neubauer; his personal assistant, David Thinne; the associate producer, Les Everborn; and the current director, Edna Day. Baterman set himself up in Neubauer's spacious office to interview the staff. The first thing he noticed was the ever-present computer on the desk, which was as orderly as the one at the house. Again, there were no disks in sight, either on the desk or on the bookshelves behind it. Baterman knew enough about computers to understand this particular model recorded on floppy disks. So where were they?

Edna Day, a small brisk woman with the energy of a nuclear reactor, quickly established an alibi. She had had dinner at The Castaway in Burbank, celebrating her husband's birthday with four other friends, and they had been there until well after eleven. Les Everborn, too, could account for his whereabouts in a regular Wednesday-night poker game with three friends. Since the game had been at one of the other players' homes, the man's wife was an additional witness.

Edna Day hadn't even known Neubauer well. He had hired her to direct the current episode of *Street Heat* on the strength of recent credits and her availability. Everborn was new to the show, having been signed as associate producer shortly before series shooting started a month before. He was a former production manager and rode herd on the physical execution of the show. Neubauer had concentrated on the scripts and the choice of directors and actors, and he coordinated the post-production with Everborn. The two men hadn't clashed in their short association, and Everborn insisted he had enough to do at the studio. He never took work home with him.

Dave Thinne came in nervously and plunked down in the chair opposite Baterman behind the desk. He was young—Baterman guessed about twenty-one or -two at most—and of moderate height and build, dark eyes peering shyly out from behind large-framed glasses. He explained that he had met Griffin Neubauer a little over a year before when Neubauer had been a guest speaker at Thinne's evening writing class at Cal State Northridge. Neubauer had encouraged him, given him some pointers, and critiqued a script Thinne had finally gotten enough courage to ask him to read.

"He said the script had promise, but he recommended a complete rewrite," Thinne said. He smiled self-deprecatingly. "See, one of my problems was I didn't have any idea of how a film was produced. I was pumping gas during the day, taking the class at night, and writing in my spare time. Griff offered me this job—sort of a glorified gofer, but it's pretty good pay, and I'm getting on-the-job training in production."

"Generous of him."

"Yeah, but he was like that."

"When did you start here?"

"Oh, beginning of last June. The Writers Guild was on strike, and Griff was producing the show alone. He wanted someone to take routine chores off Nita's hands while she helped him with the production."

Baterman consulted his notebook briefly. "What about the associate producer he had then, Jason Tabor?"

"Yeah, he was a writer. With the Guild on strike, he couldn't work on scripts. Fact is, Griff had most of the scripts ready to go before the strike came down— enough to get through until fall if he had to—so Jason wouldn't have had much to do anyway. And that's the way it turned out. The strike was over by the end of June, and Jase moved on to another show when his option came up right after that."

Baterman leaned back in the chair thoughtfully. "So Griffin Neubauer pretty well ran this show alone except for you and Ms. Flowers and his production personnel."

"Yeah, that's right."

"Then why is it so many of the other shows I see on television have a long list of producers and associate producers and story editors and whatnot?"

Thinne smiled briefly and shifted in his chair. "Well, that's how it's done in TV most of the time now. See, Griff was an old-timer. He started back in the days when one producer and one associate producer and some damn good freelance writers were all you needed for a top-rated series. And decent actors and directors, of course." The boy moved forward on his chair, his hands clenched into fists in fierce enthusiasm. "And he proved you could *still* do it today. He took *Street Heat* out of the twenty ratings last season and moved it right up to the top ten."

"You must have admired him very much."

Thinne stared at Baterman briefly, then collected himself and pulled back shyly into the chair. "I thought he was a great writer."

It turned out Thinne couldn't prove he was at home watching television the night before. He was very earnest as he explained that he was watching *Midtown,* which was on at ten opposite *Street Heat.* "Everybody in the office here monitors what the competition has on, and then we discuss it the next day. It was Griff's idea. If it's any help, I can run down the *Midtown* show for you."

Baterman declined. A synopsis could be found in any *TV Guide,* and a VCR could tape the show in Thinne's absence. It was interesting that the approximate time of death had been pegged between ten and eleven, when *Street Heat* had been broadcast.

Nita Flowers confirmed that the practice of watching the competition had been scrupulously followed by the production staff. Everborn complained that it interfered with his poker, but even he stopped to watch. Flowers had also been home alone watching the third network show, *Cutter's Kingdom.*

"Do you usually watch reruns?" Baterman asked. One of his personal complaints about television was that by June there was little on besides reruns.

"No, but last night was different. It's a sweeps week, and all the shows try to have a new episode on to generate some solid ratings. Mr. Neubauer was rather annoyed that *Cutter* beat us in the time period at the beginning of the season, but we've been first since De-

cember. It may very well be these analysis sessions
were a help. There were a lot of script revisions after
we started doing it last July."

"How long have you worked for Neubauer, Ms.
Flowers?"

"One week short of eighteen months." She was
nothing if not precise. "He was signed as producer in
the middle of January last year. The nineteenth."

"Who did you work for before him?"

"I was secretary to Mr. Sayers and Mr. Ordway, who
produced *Street Heat* for five years." She straightened
back a stray wisp of hair that had wandered out onto
her forehead and waited for his next question. Everything about Nita Flowers was contained, cool. She
didn't seem to have any passion, at least none she displayed. Baterman found her difficult to read, but maybe
she was playing *Dragnet* with him, just giving him
"the facts."

"I take it they went on to another show?" She nodded. "At another studio?"

"No. Here. It's not doing as well as *Street Heat*."

"I see. Did it bother you that they didn't ask you to
go with them on the new project?"

She stared at him levelly and brushed back the er-
rant wisp of hair. "They did ask me. Mr. Neubauer
and Mr. Selbeck, the executive producer, offered me a
substantial pay raise to stay."

"So it was money and not loyalty that kept you on
the show—and no particular liking for Neubauer."

"Liking doesn't come into it, Detective Baterman.
Mr. Neubauer was a competent producer and writer.
He required that I be competent in what I was asked
to do. We both respected our separate contributions to
the show, and we worked very well together."

Baterman sighed and reached over to pat the computer console on the desk. "Tell me about these. Neubauer had one at the house, too. Are they connected?"

"By modem, you mean? No, we just use them as standard word processors. Mr. Neubauer didn't really like computers and only reluctantly learned the basics of how to operate one. He preferred an electric typewriter, but it's simply faster and easier to use computers now. There are a few shows that won't even accept scripts submitted on paper anymore. They have to be delivered on floppy disk."

"Where *are* the disks?"

She looked up, startled, her eyes flicking around the office. "Why . . . Mr. Neubauer always took his home so he could work on them there. Then he'd bring them back in the morning."

"He had a date last night. It's doubtful he intended to work on a script."

"I'm afraid that's not my business," she said coolly. "All I can tell you is, he *always* took the disks home with him."

"No exceptions."

"None I'm aware of."

"We didn't find any disks in his office or briefcase. Would you have copies?"

"Not of the script he was working on. He never gave me the disks until the script was done. I kept trying to educate him about backup copies in case of a loss of data, but he just never bothered." She frowned briefly. "Very careless, really."

"Was there anything about that script that could be controversial or provocative . . . ?"

"Enough for someone to kill him over it?" Flowers pushed out of her chair briskly. "Hardly. I'll show you the story outline if you like. We have that on file, and it was approved by the network."

Baterman followed Flowers into the front office, where she snapped open a file drawer and flicked through some folders. The homicide detective caught a glimpse of Thinne behind the half-closed door of an adjoining office. He was working at the amber-charactered CRT screen of another computer.

"Here we are." Flowers handed him a small sheaf of papers. "Synopsis and story outline of 'Highlining,' the script Mr. Neubauer was writing. You can keep that copy if you like, but I doubt you'll find anything at all suggestive in it."

Baterman tucked it away in his jacket pocket. "Thanks. I may have some more questions later."

"We'll be here." She shrugged.

"You mean the show stays in production despite Neubauer's death?"

She stared at him blankly. "Why not? Mr. Selbeck and Les Everborn can handle it quite capably until a new line producer is hired. It isn't as if one of the *actors* died." The phone shrilled on her desk, and she turned away to answer it.

Baterman glanced at the half-open door where Thinne's CRT screen still gleamed. He hesitated, then crossed to the small office and slipped quietly into the room. The young man was hunched over the keyboard, typing briskly. He was working on a script, but Baterman couldn't read it from his position by the door. He could make out that the style was irregular, phrases separated by dashes instead of commas, and the sentences by three dots instead of periods.

Thinne suddenly realized he was not alone and jerked around nervously. "Sorry," Baterman said. "Should've knocked."

"No problem. Was there something else?"

"Maybe." Baterman moved closer to the desk and

pulled the sheaf of papers from his pocket. "This script Neubauer was working on." He glanced at the title again. " 'Highlining.' Ms. Flowers says he would have taken the script disks home with him."

"That's right."

"He had a dinner date last night. Was it likely he'd have worked on the script?"

"I don't know. He might've, I guess."

"As his personal assistant, did you ever handle the disks?"

Thinne shook his head emphatically. "Not while he was still working on them. Nobody ever got them until Griff was finished with the final draft."

"Do you know where he would have kept the disks while he was home?"

"His den, I guess. I've only been to his house once. He had a few people over for drinks last Christmas. Griff was kind of solitary, never let anybody get too close, y'know?"

"Yes." Baterman gestured at the CRT screen. "I see you're working on a script."

Thinne glanced at it casually. "Yeah. It's my screenplay, the one Griff wanted me to rewrite. I work on it lunchtimes." He reached over to pick up half of a sandwich from a plate on the desk and took a healthy bite.

Baterman smiled and tossed Thinne a half-wave. "Hope you sell it." He moved away, but paused at the door to look back. Thinne, still chewing on his sandwich, had already turned back to the keyboard and rapidly typed "CUT TO:" at the end of a scene.

The executive producer of *Street Heat* was tall, still slim at fifty-plus, graying gracefully, urbane in a Savile Row suit. His office on the top floor of the building was an elegant reflection of himself—understated good taste. Baterman felt as though he should have had himself steamed and pressed before he came in.

Peter Selbeck was arrayed behind a massive, cluttered ornamental table, not a desk. No computer, Baterman noted. A pile of scripts stood on one side of the table, apparently unread as yet. A higher stack loomed on the other side, dog-eared and with little yellow memo slips sticking out between a number of pages.

One script lay open before Baterman, and he could see cryptic notes jotted on the page in tight, precise handwriting. Selbeck was shaking his head in bemusement, nudging a gold Cross pen around on the desk. "I still can't believe it," he said. "I just *can't* believe it. I talked to Griff yesterday before he left to go home. He was happy about the way the show was coming along for this season. He felt good about his new script. The best yet, he said." Selbeck stared out the window thoughtfully. "I can't believe it. Who'd want to kill a *writer*? An actor, yes. A director, maybe. But a writer . . ." He looked back at Baterman and shook his head. "No. And certainly not Griff Neubauer."

"Why not?" Baterman asked.

"Griff wasn't one of those Hemingway types or a firebrand always flying off the handle. He didn't even take up causes. He was a quiet man who had a way with words, that's all. I've known him for, oh, twenty-five years. The most aggressive thing I ever saw him do was take the mike at a Writers Guild strike meeting one time—and even then he was only seconding a majority opinion."

"If he was that innocuous, how did he attract the kind of lady friend my associate called an 'absolute fox'?"

Selbeck smiled and shook his head. "Griff was intelligent, articulate, and charming. Don't tell me you believe the myth that all the beautiful women out there only go for the handsome hunks."

"Don't tell me a show like *Street Heat* doesn't perpetuate the myth."

"*Touché*. But it's what people want to see."

"Why'd you hire Neubauer as producer? I hear he hit a bad patch a few years ago and wasn't doing too well."

Selbeck leaned back in his chair and twiddled the pen in his fingers. "I said we go back a long way. When I first met him, he was producing a half-hour western called *Frontier*."

"Never saw it."

Selbeck smiled wryly. "That was its problem—very few people did. But in those days, you had an order for twenty-six episodes with an option for thirteen more, and *somebody* had to write them. I was a new writer with a couple of credits, and I went in to pitch ideas to him. One of them interested him, and he gave me an assignment. Well, I pulled it off and everybody liked it, so I wound up writing another. In all, I did six before the network canceled the show. That was an important track record then, and those scripts led to a lot more assignments for me. Griff went back to freelancing himself, but if he heard of openings on shows, he'd let me know so I could go in to pitch some stories."

"So Neubauer gave you a break when you needed one."

"Exactly. So when I heard he'd been having some problems getting work, I suggested him as a writer for *Street Heat*. I don't interfere with my producers as long as the show is doing well, so I didn't push it. But I saw Griff's scripts come through several times, and they looked all right to me. Some nice ideas professionally handled."

"But why name him as producer?"

Selbeck shifted in his chair and snaked a three-ring notebook off a credenza behind him. He flipped it open on the table and pushed it toward Baterman. "Nielsen and Arbitron ratings week by week. Right now, *Street Heat* is holding at number five. Last year the show was hanging around in the twenties and sliding toward thirty. It had been on five years, being produced by the same two men and written by the same six or seven writers, with the exception of a few outsiders like Griff.

"I felt Sayers and Ordway were getting tired of the show themselves. They had made a pilot that sold to NBC and were making noises about moving over to produce that. Plus we were looking at the strong possibility of a Writers Guild strike in March, which meant that scripts for the new season would have to be commissioned and finished before the strike was called or the show would be hopelessly delayed in shooting. It's a hassle."

"Is that legal?"

"It is, and it's a sensible precaution. Nine times out of ten, the Writers Guild will strike when a contract can't be negotiated, and they stay out. That means no scripts, no writing of any kind, by Guild members."

"What about non-Guild writers?"

Selbeck's mouth tightened in distaste. "They'd be scabs. Anyway, I casually mentioned the problem to Griff, and he had some suggestions for getting some fresh ideas and new writers in on the scripts, giving it some new blood. I liked what he had to say, so I hired him. Actually, he succeeded far better than I ever imagined he would. The scripts were innovative, tough, exciting." He smiled wryly. "Sorry. I don't mean to sound like a *TV Guide* review, but the show improved and shot up in the ratings. It was all due to Griff. His *own* scripts got better—sharper, crisper, more daring plots. I've never seen anything like it. He was inspired."

Baterman looked up, frowning. "I got the impression he was kind of an old war-horse. Set in his ways."

"I think he had just gotten into the habit of writing what other producers wanted. Once he was in charge, he started delivering what *he* felt worked best. He won an Emmy, you know." Baterman flicked a look at him, but the way Selbeck went on indicated he didn't know that Emmy had been the murder weapon. "Back in 1969, he won it for a *Warlord* script."

"That was seventeen years ago," Baterman pointed out.

"Be that as it may," Selbeck snapped, "producing *Street Heat* gave Griff a chance to write his way again, and he saved the show. And if you can figure out why anyone would want to murder him, I'll give *you* an Emmy. I never met anyone who didn't like Griff Neubauer."

"He did."

Beldon called in with the information that he had located Lucy Cates. She was a film editor, working at the Burbank Studios on a Warner Brothers movie. She and her assistant editor had worked late in the cutting room the night before, as they had every night that week because of the film's close deadline. They had not left until ten-thirty and had had a drink together at the El Chiquito restaurant across the street from the studio before calling it a night. Ms. Cates had also told Beldon she had not spoken with Neubauer for at least a week because the movie had been occupying so much of her time.

"Her assistant backs her up on the late-night work. I can question the night bartender at the restaurant if you want. She says he knows her."

"Not necessary," Baterman grunted. "How'd she take it when you told her Neubauer was murdered?"

"Broke up pretty bad. She said she'd known him for six, seven years. They were pretty close once, but settled for being friends after a while. Said she didn't know anybody who didn't like him."

Baterman sighed and shook his head. "Yeah, nobody seems to. Okay, keep trying to get hold of the ex-wife. I've got an appointment with Neubauer's agent."

Tony Aiken's office was located near the Doheny end of the Sunset Strip, and Baterman had to fight late-afternoon traffic all the way from where Laurel Canyon dumped out onto Sunset. He parked on a narrow side street and walked two blocks to get to the small office building where Aiken had a ground-floor suite.

The Aiken Literary Agency was a three-person operation, consisting of Aiken, his junior partner, and their secretary, representing a stable of thirty-three writers. The agent had the look of a pouter pigeon, chesty and thin-legged, his careful grooming almost making up for his complete lack of hair.

Aiken made it clear that his junior partner would not have made an appointment with Neubauer. There were certain old clients, and Neubauer was one of them, who were represented exclusively by Aiken. He had built his small agency into one with a highly respected name by hustling over the years, always with absolute integrity. The fact that he was prosperous on ten percent commission indicated how well he had managed for his writers.

Aiken had been at home alone the night before while his wife visited with her sister in Santa Monica. He frankly admitted he had faked a stomachache to get out of the visit himself. The police had notified him of Neubauer's death that morning. Like the others, he seemed not yet able to fully assimilate the reality of Neubauer's murder.

"Thirty-two years next month I'm his agent," Aiken said. He ruefully ran his hand over his head. "I had a lot more hair then—but I never had a better client. I want you to know that. We made it in this business together. Griff stuck with me when I had a broom closet for an office and three unknown writers I was trying to sell. And he stuck with me after he made it and maybe didn't need me to get him into story meetings anymore."

"I understand he had some career problems a while back. About four years ago?"

"You heard about that." Aiken seemed uncomfortable. "Well, everybody has ups and downs in this business. Griff had been around a long time. I think some of these young producers figured he was over the hill. And he was proud, you see. He wanted assignments on the top shows. Well, most of those shows are pretty much staff-written, and they weren't interested in Griff. I couldn't even get them to look at his credit list. He wrote a few movie scripts, too, but I couldn't sell them. They were a little old-fashioned. It got pretty tight for him for a while. Pretty tight." He tilted his head, slipping an embarrassed look at Baterman. "He wouldn't like me saying this, but he took a job as a bartender for about a year—out in Pacoima, so he wasn't likely to run into someone he knew. That was a blow to his ego. He hadn't had to do anything but write for most of his adult life."

"I thought he got some assignments on *Street Heat*."

Aiken nodded slowly. "One here, one there. Not

enough to really get by on—not with his expenses. And he didn't especially like the producers. He complained they rewrote him, and he wasn't happy with the way the scripts turned out."

"He did take the job of producing the show when it was offered," Baterman pointed out.

"The state of his finances at the time, he'd have taken a job mud wrestling if it had been offered," Aiken said sourly. "But he proved out a winner, didn't he? The way he took hold of that series and pulled it up in the ratings. He showed them the kind of writer he was. Nobody's going to forget that soon—"

"I'm sure that's true, sir," Baterman interrupted delicately. "There's one thing I'm having some trouble with. You must know his work habits after all this time."

Aiken nodded. "I suppose so."

"His staff insists he would have taken home the computer disks he was working on, but we couldn't find them when we went over the house. I don't know if it's significant, but they seem to be the only things missing."

"Did you try his safe?"

Baterman sat upright as if he'd been hit with a cattle prod. "*Safe*? We didn't find any safe."

"Oh, it's in one of those heavy wooden end tables he has in the den. There's a tricky little catch you have to trip to get the cabinet open. It's not much of a secret. Griff liked to show the safe off to everybody who came to the house. I'm sure his lawyer would have the combination. Would you want his number?"

"Please," Baterman sighed.

When Baterman settled in Olden's office to run down what he had so far, it was well past the end of his shift. Beldon tapped at the door when he was almost done, and the lieutenant waved him in. Beldon flopped in a chair and listened as Baterman finished.

"Neubauer's lawyer has offices over in Glendale, but he's in San Francisco today on business. I had to slog all the way over there to convince his partner I had to have a number where I could reach him. They finally got hold of him, and he's coming down on an early flight in the morning. I'll meet him at the house at nine, and he'll open the safe."

Olden looked at Beldon. "What about Neubauer's ex-wife?"

The younger man pulled out his notebook, shaking his head. "Not much there. Iris Neubauer. She's a paralegal with a law firm in Woodland Hills. They've been divorced eight years—no children. It was amicable, she says. She got a pretty hefty alimony settlement, but Neubauer paid it on time and every penny, even when he had money problems a few years ago. They got together for dinner every few months, very friendly. She says Neubauer gave her a lot of encouragement when she decided to train as a paralegal." Beldon flipped the notebook shut. "*And* he even liked the guy she's going to marry next month."

Olden leaned back in his chair and tapped his fingers on the desk. "Not much to get hold of, is there?" He turned to Baterman. "You think there's anything on those disks?"

Baterman shrugged. "Probably just a script, but they're all we can see that's missing—out of sync. And they're probably in that safe. I just want to tie up loose ends." He frowned and shook his head. "I can't see a motive. Everybody liked him, they say. He had professional respect, especially recently. He was doing well financially again, and his personal relationships seemed to be happy. But." He paused. "But he got a phone call that made him angry. The implication was it was someone he knew professionally. Business, anyway. He made someone mad enough to bash his skull in. Just maybe the answer's in that safe."

The phone screamed next to the bed at three in the morning. Aline moaned, rolled over and grabbed for it. "Uh?" she grunted. She listened, then poked her husband. "You."

Baterman was already reaching for the receiver. "Baterman." He listened a moment and then, swearing, shoved the instrument back at Aline and swung his legs out of the bed.

"What?" she asked sleepily.

"Fire."

It took the fire company an hour and a half to knock down the blaze in the house on Oak View Drive. From his vantage point in the yard next door, Baterman could see the heart of the conflagration was in the den. When it was finally out, Baterman picked his way through the wreckage to the fire chief, flashing his badge and ID.

"I can smell the gasoline," Baterman said.

The fire chief nodded and wiped his grubby face, coughing a little from the heavy smoke that still eddied around them. "Pretty crude. A lot of the windows are gone, but I suppose that's how they got in."

"The owner was murdered Wednesday night."

"Saw the crime-scene sign on the door. You think they're connected?"

Baterman stared at the crisped books on the floor, the sodden remnants of the couch, the broken and seared wood of the end table that revealed the blackened safe it had hidden. "If it isn't, this is one hell of a coincidence."

* * *

Baterman found the house still steaming when he pulled up in front of it at quarter to nine. A couple of beat cops had been assigned to keep the place under surveillance. Closing the barn door too late, Baterman thought sourly. The Mercedes that cruised up behind his old Buick jerked to a halt, and its driver catapulted out to stare disbelievingly at the wreckage of the house.

"My God, what happened?"

Baterman got out of his car and pulled out his badge and ID as he approached the pudgy little man. "Mr. Lindell? I'm Homicide Detective Baterman. I have the warrant to open the safe."

"*What happened?*"

"You are Mr. Lindell?"

The little man nodded distractedly. "Yes. Yes, I am."

"Someone broke in and torched your late client's house last night," Baterman said. "I have a hunch it might have something to do with whatever is in his safe. And if it wasn't a damned good fireproof, there's probably not much left in it now."

"Oh." Lindell peered anxiously at Baterman. "Yes, I see. Well . . . we should open it right away then."

They turned and moved up the driveway together, Baterman holding out his badge to the young foot patrolman who stepped forward. The homicide detective made for the ruined house and stopped in confusion when Lindell walked on toward the garage in the rear of the property.

"Where're you going?"

"The safe."

"But—" Baterman blankly pointed toward the hulk of the house.

"Ah, no," the lawyer said with a negligent wave. "Griff liked to put people on to the one in the house, told them all about it."

The garage-door opener had been destroyed in the fire. Baterman and the young patrolman pulled the door open with brute force.

"The older Griff got, the more nervous he got about keeping anything valuable in the house," Lindell went on as the other two men struggled with the heavy door. "Even a neighborhood like this could have break-ins. And there are some things you just can't put in a safe deposit box. You have to have them where you can get at them."

The door finally swung up, revealing the beige Jaguar parked inside. Lindell moved around it to a corner of the garage and pushed aside a couple of heavy cartons, revealing the flat top of a safe set in the floor. He looked up at Baterman.

"Griff never did anything by halves. He had his safe in the house as a diversion. Anything that was really important was in here." He slid a leather-bound notebook from his inside breast pocket and consulted some figures, then bent down and worked the combination on the safe. On the fourth number, he turned the little handle, and the lid opened.

"May I?" Baterman said, but he was already reaching in—and pulling out four floppy disks.

"Any luck?" Olden asked when Baterman bustled back into the squad room.

"Don't know yet," Baterman replied. "Just about everything in Neubauer's safe was personal. Some cash, some jewelry, some unused traveler's checks. Except these." He laid down the floppy disks. "I need the use of an IBM PC and a computer operator who knows WordStar."

Olden shoved a phone toward Baterman. "Try Records. They have a bunch of computers down there."

The officer Baterman found knew her business.

Neubauer's WordStar disks were labeled "High1," "High2," and "High3." Officer Harmon sat down at a computer Records wasn't using, slipped in the first disk and the WordStar disk, and called up the program. Baterman hovered over her shoulder as she typed in the file name. The screen flickered as the letters formed up, and the opening paragraphs of a script became readable.

"This what you wanted?"

"I guess." Baterman frowned. He wasn't that familiar with scripts, but it looked fairly standard. The words on the screen set up an action opening for *Street Heat*. It read well, even excitingly; but it didn't seem unusual. It *was* Neubauer's style. Baterman had gotten one of his other scripts for comparison purposes. "How do you move it ahead?"

Harmon hit a couple of keys, and the lines scrolled upward on the screen. The scene progressed, introduced characters, dialogue. Still nothing unusual that Baterman could see. He gestured, and Harmon moved it ahead again.

They continued that way through the first disk. It ended partway through the second act. "There's a lot of room left on this disk," Harmon commented.

"Must've left room to rewrite," Baterman muttered. He shook his head in frustration. "Try the next one."

Harmon efficiently switched disks and called up the "High2" file. It was the expected continuation of the script, albeit the plot was starting to interest Baterman more than he wanted to admit. But, dammit, it *was* just a story. Midway through the disk, he found the answer—or at least the clue to it. He wasn't ready for it when it flashed on the screen as Harmon scrolled forward. It took a moment to register because Baterman was involved in reading the text. Then he realized exactly what he was looking at, and he *knew*.

* * *

Baterman, Beldon, and another plainclothes detective arrived at the *Street Heat* offices at eleven to arrest the murderer. Nita Flowers glanced up in surprise as they pushed into her office.

"Detective Baterman," she said coolly. "I didn't expect to see you back so soon." She stood up and smiled calmly at them.

Dave Thinne came out of his office with a clutch of papers in his hand. "Nita, these changes will have to go in—" He stopped and stared at the detectives. "Oh, hi."

Baterman nodded to the others, and they moved toward Thinne. The young man backed away, but not fast enough, and they caught him by each arm. "What is this?"

"You're under arrest on suspicion of the murder of Griffin Neubauer, Thinne." Baterman read him his rights over his protests of innocence, which the detectives ignored.

"Detective Baterman," Flowers said, "David couldn't have—"

"I'm afraid he did, Ms. Flowers." Baterman turned to Thinne. "When you torched Neubauer's den to melt the disks in his safe, you were on the wrong track. There never was anything in that safe. He had another one, in the garage. A backup. Looks like he finally took Ms. Flowers's advice—in a way."

Thinne's face went pale, and he stared at Baterman, shaking his head. "No."

Baterman held up a set of disks. "I can show you these, if you want." He smiled slightly. "They're copies, of course. But I'm sure you know what's on them. You have a distinctive style of writing, Thinne—all those dashes for commas and dots between sentences. Neubauer was just rewriting you slightly, smoothing out the words, putting in correct punctuation. But the script was yours, wasn't it?"

Thinne had stiffened, trying to glare Baterman down as the detective's voice droned out the facts. Finally, Thinne sagged and looked away, giving it up.

"They were all my scripts," he said quietly. "All his 'originals' on this show and all the rewrites of outside scripts were mine."

"That can't be!" Flowers exclaimed. "He turned in the disks to me after—"

"After I wrote them first, Nita!" Thinne snapped. "Didn't you notice how his writing *changed* from the way it was before I got here? Didn't you notice how it improved the show? Griff Neubauer wasn't the man who saved *Street Heat*. It was *me*."

"I don't understand," Flowers said lamely.

"He was blackmailing me."

"What could he possibly have on you, Thinne?" Baterman asked.

"I told you I showed him a script after he spoke at my writing class. It wasn't a movie as I said. It was a script for *Street Heat*. And he didn't think it needed rewrite. He thought it was brilliant. He offered to buy it, and I sold it."

"What's wrong with that?"

"Oh," Flowers said quietly.

Thinne smiled at her bitterly. "Yeah, you got it, Nita. You remember when I came in to see him. It was the middle of the Writers Guild strike, and by selling him my script, I was scabbing. I was so dumb, I didn't realize it. Then good ol' Griff told me I could be fined by the Guild for up to a hundred percent of what I was paid for the script if I was reported for scabbing. I could be barred from Guild membership. You have to be a Guild member in this town, or you never get to write anything more than industrial films or low-budget cheapies for non-union producers. He could blow the whistle on me—or I could go along with him and he'd cover for me."

"Wait a minute," Beldon said. "If you were scabbing by selling the script, wasn't *he* scabbing by buying it?"

"Sure. But who'd believe me? I was a gas station attendant, taking a writing course at night. He was a thirty-year man in the Guild, the Emmy winner, the guy with two, three hundred credits, the new producer of *Street Heat*. But he offered me a deal. If I came on as his 'personal assistant' and kept writing scripts, he'd help me later on. He'd give me legitimate script assignments. Of course, all the ones I did in the meantime he'd 'rewrite' and put his name on. And collect the big script fees. And the residuals. Selbeck gave him a job, but he was a clapped-out hack and scared to death because he knew it, and I was his savior. That's why you never saw the disks until Griff had a 'final draft,' Nita. He was busy polishing my stuff into his style."

Flowers had collapsed back into her chair, sitting in a sad little heap. "Is that why you killed him?" she asked quietly.

"No." Thinne shrugged off Baterman's surprised look, but his face tightened grimly. "A few days ago, I got fed up with his using me. I got brave enough to make a few discreet inquiries. I found out that I could have gone to the Guild and gotten a fair hearing. I found out they try each situation on a case-by-case basis, and there was a good chance I could have redeemed myself for making one stupid mistake out of ignorance. I'd face some penalties, and they might be heavy; but it would be better than what Griff was doing to me.

"I called him that night and told him I wanted to

see him about the script. He was mad about it, but he told me to come over. When I got there, I told him what I'd found out. Oh, he'd screwed me royally, kept me half out of my mind with fear, kept me practically in slavery so he could line his nest. He wasn't about to give me a break, and he'd got me so deep in crap I'd never dig my way out. And he admitted it. Said he'd paid *his* dues and now it was my turn.

"I don't know, I got so mad I just grabbed the Emmy off the shelf when he turned his back on me and I hit him. I think I hit him again when he was on the floor, but I knew he was dead already. I wiped away my fingerprints, but . . ." He shrugged.

"The one thing you couldn't wipe out was the disks which would incriminate you. Did he tell you they were in the safe?"

"Yeah. He laughed about it. I thought it had to be the one he'd shown us at Christmas. The bastard. He never told me anything that wasn't a lie."

Baterman pulled his handcuffs off his belt and snapped them open. Thinne hesitated and then slowly held out his hands to be cuffed. "All I wanted to do was write."

Baterman's mouth twisted in irony. "If this was *Dragnet,* Friday would say there's just one thing left for you to write."

Thinne stared at him blankly, uncomprehending.

Baterman sighed. "Fade-out."

RETURN TO VENICE
GEORGE FOX

When speculator Abbot Kinney decided to
create an American counterpart to Italy's Queen of the
Seas on the California beachfront, he went all the way,
not only imitating the architecture and the canals but
even importing two dozen gondolas (and gondoliers)
direct from the original. But the area began to deteri-
orate almost from the beginning, and all but four of
the canals were eventually paved over. During the sixties, Venice became a magnet for L.A.'s hippie contin-
gent. More recently the "revival" of bohemian Venice
has made for an unusually wide range of inhabitants,
from upwardly mobile yuppies to vagrants, as well as
elderly hangers-on from the area's earlier incarna-
tions. Yet, sometimes urban renewals bring back old

nightmares with them, as we see in George Fox's "Return to Venice."

THEY'VE brought the old place back, he thought as he gazed at the unexpected image on the TV, his thick, powerful fingers opening and closing on his knees. Then he realized that memory had failed him. In 1959, the exterior of the Westwind Diner had been a dingy gray; now the polished chrome walls gleamed like the blade of a virgin Hoffritz carving knife.

"Venice, California—Portrait of a Neighborhood in Change" was the name of the show, part of a news program he rarely watched. "Sometimes, going forward means returning to the past," said the voice of Charles Kuralt while the TV camera moved slowly over the Westwind's Art Deco facade. "A classic American diner . . . built in 1940 . . . abandoned and boarded up in 1959, a 'hopelessly outdated' victim of the fast-food phenomenon . . . now, twenty-nine years later, back on all its mundane, misunderstood glory . . ."

He had always suspected that this TV series was full of crap. When the camera moved inside the Westwind, he was sure of it. The jukebox was correctly positioned but the music coming from it was all wrong. Who in the hell had heard of the Beatles in 1959? It was the endless repetition of the Coasters' "Run Red Run" that had gotten on his nerves that final summer. What really offended him was the ferns and trailing vines suspended in clay pots over the booths—not to mention the food! He watched in disbelief as a smirking waiter served braised duck with pineapple and tofu sauce.

"Old-fangled architecture and new-fangled cuisine,"

Charles Kuralt declared in his smug, folksy tone. "It's all part of the American way. Sort of." The program went on to show faded black-and-white photos of the modest twenties-and-thirties-era bungalows that used to line the south end of Ocean Front Walk, superimpose color shots of the condominiums that had replaced them. "Is what Californians have gained better than what they've lost?" Charles Kuralt summed up. "Yes, say the developers and the yuppies. Others, including yours truly, say: *Maybe not.*"

He turned off the television with his remote control, slouched down in the Barcalounger, listened to rain pound against the living-room window. It had rained in Venice, too, but not as much as here. Moving the Barcalounger to full recline, he tried to nap, even though he wasn't tired. Why was seeing the resurrection of the Westwind so upsetting? Until tonight, he had assumed the diner had been torn down years ago. He had long since given up the notion of returning to Venice or anyplace else in Southern California.

He had started to doze off when he understood what was nagging at the back of his mind. The TV show hadn't mentioned the *real* reason why the Westwind Diner had closed, hadn't mentioned the girls who had forced him to kill them! And if the TV people didn't remember, then probably no one in Venice remembered either! If they had remembered, they'd have told the television people! He lurched forward, forcing the Barcalounger into the upright position.

It was finally safe to go home.

"You're what he has in mind," Dolores said excitedly. "I'm sure of it. Delicate features, small nose, kind of graceful neck, big boobs, no waist at *all*. Exactly the opposite of me!"

Sheila Ransom shook her head in annoyance. "Would I have to wear mesh hose and a bunny tail?"

"More like an old-fashioned kind of outfit," Dolores said, a self-deprecating smile breaking on her plump-cheeked face. "Anyway, when I realized I wasn't the right type, I made an appointment for you. Ten tomorrow morning, right after the breakfast rush."

"You *shouldn't* have, without asking me." Sheila sighed, going to the window of the tiny rented room she shared with Dolores Gaines, a fellow UCLA student. She gazed out at the weed-grown bank of the narrow canal that ran past the bungalow. She had forgotten to throw pieces of stale bread to the ducks that afternoon, and now, with the sun almost down, they had glided back to their nests in the cattail reeds. She always felt guilty when she neglected the ducks.

"What does 'ambience' mean?" Dolores asked.

"The atmosphere of a place, something like that. Why?"

"Mr. Whitt used the word all the time. That's why I figure he's gay. Ever notice gays like words that aren't quite American?"

"Don't change the subject," Sheila chided, trying to suppress a smile.

"And he tries too hard to look young. Most men who aren't gay finally give up, unless they sell real estate."

Sheila had never been able to resent her roommate's meddling for long. At least Dolores means well, she thought as she lay in bed that night. God knows I *do* need a real job. The occasional Office Temporaries gig she picked up barely paid for meals and rent—and next fall's tuition was due in two months. Sheila didn't want to hit her mother in Idaho for the money; Mom really couldn't afford it this year.

But why, she wondered, did the hostess in a place

like the Westwind Diner have to fit definite physical specifications? It didn't make sense.

He nervously started up the short stretch of Washington Street that lay between Pacific Avenue and Venice beach. At first, nothing seemed different; the flimsy one- or two-story buildings were painted in the same wan pastels as twenty-nine years ago. Then, with relief, he saw that only the exteriors were familiar. Most of the business names had changed. He felt like a tired dentist checking out two rows of freshly filled teeth.

Although he had been back in Venice for weeks, he had avoided Washington Street until tonight. In 1959, he had lived above a kosher butcher shop three blocks away. But the shop and its neighbors had given way to a towering apartment complex. Not that he'd been all that worried about 1959 merchants and their customers. Most of the elderly Jews who had monopolized the area east of Pacific Street, Charles Kuralt said on TV, had been forced out in the mid-seventies by explosive rises in real estate taxes. How many of them would still be alive today, anyway? he thought, recalling the graying men and women who had regularly bought the Westwind Diner's fifty-five-cent Earlybird Breakfast—two eggs any style, hash brown potatoes, toast, choice of half grapefruit or small orange juice, unlimited coffee.

It was the last hundred feet of Washington Street that had worried him. Nothing changed much close to the sea, he had learned long ago. The ultimate reassurance was provided by his first look at the brown-shingled building across the street from the Crab Shell restaurant. It had become the kind of beachfront saloon where everyone, including the help, wore prefaded denim shorts. In the old days, it had been the roughest bikers' bar in L.A., the sidewalk in front

crammed with Harley-Davidsons, its open doors ex-
uding the mixed odors of sweat, beer, and gasoline.
The bikers' women would roam nearby streets, looking for tricks, while their men drank. He recalled the
time, in a carport off the Speedway, that he had yanked
down a biker whore's greasy blue jeans, flinched in
disgust when he saw the butterfly tattoo on her left
inner thigh. Why would a woman do something like
that to herself? he had thought as his fingers tightened around her throat. . . .

Forcing the memory away, he went back to Pacific
Street, wandered north. He saw the main square ahead,
quickened his pace. The cluster of buildings, erected
at the turn of the century, was all that was left of
Venice's original downtown. At this hour, with the
streets almost deserted, the buildings looked much as
they had when he was young—white and stark above
ornate, colonnaded arcades, modeled on structures in
the Italian Venice. He halted at the corner of Pacific
and Windward, gazed at the St. Marks Hotel annex,
remembering the winter of 1958, when they had shot
a movie here. Every night, after the diner closed, he
had come to watch, his eyes riveted on the Star, hun-
grily studying her short, feathered, champagne-colored
hair and her fine-boned face. She had worn a peach
cashmere top, molded like a layer of extra skin over
her full breasts, made to seem even larger by the
patent-leather belt cinched around her tiny waist and
the tightness of her skirt. Again and again he had
watched her cross from Windward to the St. Marks.
The director, an immensely fat man, kept ordering her
to repeat the walk, even though she did it the same
way every time. The company worked until nearly
dawn, but he had patiently kept vigil behind the saw-

horse barricade, imagining how the Star must look *without* the pink cashmere top, his mouth dry. When the picture came out he sat through it at least a dozen times, even though the story didn't make sense and it was in black and white. Two years later, after he left Venice, he saw the Star in another movie, also in black and white—and in the very first scene she was lying in bed with one of those silly, blank-eyed actors whose chins are too big for the rest of their faces. She wore a brassiere with enormous white lace cups and a backstrap so tight that little ridges of perfect flesh spilled over the elastic. If they went this far so early, he thought, maybe later they'll show her without the bra. In color. It had never happened before, but there had to be a first time. Halfway through the picture, his hands excitedly opening and closing on his knees, he thought it *was* going to happen! The Star took a shower—but it turned out to be just another cheap Hollywood trick! You never saw *anything* except hands covering breasts and other important body parts, while fuzzy water poured down from the showerhead. Sometimes the girl in the shower didn't even *look* like the Star. Finally, a crazy lady stabbed her to death with a kitchen knife. He cringed at the sight; only once, in panic, had he killed with a knife. You didn't contaminate a fine blade with human blood! When he was sure that the Star wasn't coming back, he left the theater, trying to hide his rage. . . .

"You okay?"

He hadn't realized that he was shaking until he heard the woman's voice—at first, as if from a great distance. He regained control, saw a crudely pretty Mexican girl with the too-arrogant look of a nervous apprentice whore.

"I'm just fine," he said.

"You want to party?" she asked, smiling, the tips of her long fingernails caressing his fly.

For a few seconds, he thought about running away—but the past was too much with him tonight.

"Yes," he told the Mexican hooker, "I'd like to party."

"Where you off to?" Mrs. Drabinsky asked, interrupting her weed-pulling when she saw Sheila Ransom come out of the bungalow.

"I have a ten-o'clock job interview, Viola," Sheila told her landlady. "At the Westwind Diner."

Mrs. Drabinsky tossed a fistful of dandelions into Howland Canal, peered quizzically at Sheila through her thick glasses. "They've opened up *that* place?"

"Months ago."

The old woman shrugged. "I haven't gone past the Grand Canal for years. Just plain honky-tonk over toward the beach. I liked the Westwind, though. We all did in those days, especially the cheap breakfast. The owner got in trouble a couple of months before Mr. Drabinsky passed on."

"What kind of trouble?" Sheila asked, edging toward the dirt path that ran along the canal bank.

"Killed some people," Mrs. Drabinsky said vaguely. "Nice-looking fellow, too. Who'd have thought?"

Sheila moved along the path a little slower than usual, impeded by the high-heeled shoes she had put on for the interview. Canal banks weren't meant for any kind of shoes, except sneakers. The morning air was even quieter than usual. It had been the comforting silence of the canal area that had prompted her and Dolores to move to Venice after a tortured year in a UCLA dorm. The loudest sound you ever heard was auto tires rumbling over the roadbeds of the Dell Avenue bridges.

She crossed the Grand Canal footbridge and found herself in the *other* Venice, the one that Mrs. Drabinsky hated, an area filled with souvenir shops and shacks renting roller skates and canvas-roofed beachfront stalls that openly displayed counterfeit Gucci bags and Rolex watches. The restored Westwind Diner, located two blocks east of Pacific Avenue, stood out because it seemed so massively real and solid. Even the neighborhood's historic structures—the buildings in the main square—looked fake in comparison, like decaying movie sets.

Sheila entered the diner at precisely ten o'clock—and from her roommate's mocking description, instantly recognized Roger Whitt, the owner. He stood behind the cash register, using a print calculator to compare breakfast checks with register tapes, a slight frown on his pink, too-unlined face. Dolores was right—he'd had a lift. But the dye job on his thin hair wasn't bad, without the clotted look produced by the bottle-in-the-bathroom self-treatment used by most vain, aging men.

"Hello," she said. "I'm Sheila Ransom. I've come about the job."

He raised his head, stared at her through watery blue eyes for a full fifteen seconds. "You certainly *look* right," he said at last, hitting the calculator's off button. "We'll go in the back and have coffee and you can tell me about yourself."

Sheila cringed inwardly. Whenever a prospective employer asked her to tell about herself, she knew she would end up hearing more about *him* than she really wanted to know, usually while a hand nudged her knee. At this hour—the hiatus between breakfast and lunch rushes—the diner held few customers. Roger Whitt led Sheila to a rear corner booth, next to one of those huge, ugly jukeboxes with bubbles gurgling through layers of yellow, pink, and purple glass tubes.

To Sheila's amazement, he really did want to know about her—to an almost disturbing degree. She started with the basics: age twenty-three; single; in the fall would enter her senior year at UCLA, majoring in business communications. A sixtyish waitress put two cups of coffee in front of them, went away. Whitt paused to stir a packet of Nutra-Sweet into his coffee, then continued to ask questions. By the time she was done, she had told him about her childhood in Ketchum, Idaho; about her widowed mother, who ran the fashion shop at a Sun Valley ski lodge; about dozens of other things irrelevant to the job.

"You must think I'm pretty nosy," Roger Whitt said at last.

"Of course not," Sheila lied.

"You have to be careful when you're seeking ambience," he said earnestly, leaning toward her. "I only took over the Westwind in May. The previous owners restored the building materially, but they didn't know how to restore its *soul*. That's why they went broke. No ambience. And lousy food—that *nouvelle cuisine* garbage. I give the people solid, traditional American cooking. Nothing phony! And I want customers to feel it really is 1956 or '57 or one of the other *good* years! The position of evening hostess is yours, if you want it."

"I think I do," Sheila said.

"You already have a fifties look about you," Whitt rambled on. "With a new hairstyle and wardrobe, the illusion will be perfect. Pay is twelve dollars an hour."

"Could you excuse me for a moment, Mr. Whitt?"

"First door on the left, after the jukebox."

Sheila, who actually didn't need to use the ladies' room, entered it and lit a cigarette. Even here the past had been reproduced! The walls were covered with garish old movie posters: Sandra Dee and John Gavin in *Tammy Tell Me True* . . . Tony Curtis and Piper Laurie in *The Prince Who Was a Thief* . . . Charlton Heston, Janet Leigh, and Orson Welles in *Touch of Evil*. What had startled Sheila was the hourly wage Whitt had offered, more than twice the going rate for student part-time jobs. Something *had* to be wrong.

When she left the restroom, she had made up her mind to turn down the offer—and would have, if she hadn't encountered the waitress who served their coffee. The woman, who had a weathered, tough-warm face, lightly touched Sheila's arm and whispered: "He's not really nuts, honey. Just enthusiastic. The only reason he hired me was that I reminded him of Thelma Ritter!"

Although she had no idea who Thelma Ritter was, the waitress's words instantly relaxed her. After all, she thought, how could you ever be sure of a sane working environment in a place like Venice? She went back to the booth, accepted the job, agreed to meet Roger Whitt again the following morning. "Won't take long to buy the right clothes," he promised. "I know exactly what I need."

As she was leaving the Westwind Diner, an LAPD black-and-white raced by, siren screaming. It turned left on North Venice Boulevard, headed toward the beach.

Detective Sergeant Ray Chavez got out of the squad car, strode across Ocean Front Walk to the beach. His graying partner, Detective Walter Haas—nineteen years older and thirty-three pounds heavier than the lithe Chicano—followed at a measured pace.

The homicide scene had been marked off with yellow tapes stapled on flimsy poles driven into the sand. The strong breeze off the ocean caused the tapes to shiver like festive paper streamers at an outdoor birthday party. A couple of dozen gapers had positioned themselves around the site, but most beachgoers continued to sunbathe or play volleyball or rub oil on their bodies. Venice, Ray Chavez had discovered on earlier assignments, was inner-directed even by L.A. standards. "Inner-directed" was the department's latest euphemism for people too stupid, stoned, or emotionally inert to notice what was going on around them.

Ray Chavez stepped over the tape, looked down at the face and neck of the dead brown-skinned girl, the only visible parts of her body. The rest of it was covered with heaped sand. He remembered how when he and his little sister were children he had buried her in the same fashion, leaving just a giggling face exposed. It had been their favorite beach game.

"Who found her?" Chavez asked a young cop standing nearby.

"Couple of kids. The wind came up all of a sudden and blew away enough sand to show her nose and left cheek. They ran and told a lifeguard. He cleaned off the rest of her face."

Chavez went to one knee, peered more closely at the purple-turning-black bruises on the girl's throat.

"Looks Mexican," the young cop said.

"I already noticed," Ray Chavez replied coldly. "Did you find a purse, anything with identification?"

The cop shook his head.

A Frisbee sailed over the tape, landed inches from the body. Walter Haas, who had just caught up with his partner, snatched the plastic disk off the sand, flung it out to sea. They heard a distant siren, knew that the medical examiner's ambulance was on the way.

When the ambulance attendants had extracted the girl's corpse from the sand—more gingerly than if she had been injured but still alive—Chavez and Haas went to the Venice substation, located in the basement of the municipal beach pavilion. It lay less than a hundred yards from the homicide scene. They took a statement from the lifeguard who had uncovered the girl's face, then settled in to wait for the medical examiner's unofficial phoned-in report. With luck, they would get it within an hour.

"It happened before," Walt Haas said flatly. "Same MO. Girl strangled and covered with sand. On *this* beach."

Chavez sat up straighter on the steel folding chair. "When?"

Haas shrugged. "Before I joined the department."

"That's a *long* time ago, Walt."

"Pulled eight months in Venice when I was still in uniform. The old-timers used to talk about the girl on the beach, how they were right at the edge of nailing the creep who did it when he up and disappeared. Really pissed them off, even years later."

"We'll run it through the computer when we get back downtown."

"If the case is even *in* the computer," Walt Haas said with a rueful laugh. "You're right—it sure as hell was a long time ago!"

"Jesus Christ, can you still see your own feet?" Dolores Gaines gasped. She had come through the bedroom door just as Sheila was straining to fasten the last backstrap hook on her fifties-style extra-high-uplift brassiere—a Spandex-reinforced white lace number.

"Don't make me giggle," Sheila cried, sucking in her

already flat belly. "If you make me giggle I'll *never* do it."

Dolores hastened to her roommate, barely managed to get the last hook in place. "Where did you and Whitt find this antique—Frederick's of Hollywood?"

"Are you kidding?" Sheila exclaimed, finally giving way to laughter. "The most exclusive lingerie shop in San Marino! They really hang on to the past up there!"

Dolores at first matched Sheila's laughter—then realized that the changes in her friend went beyond wearing an obsolete undergarment. Sheila's once shoulder-length dark blond hair had been cut and layered, so that the lowest strands curled upward just below the ears; it had been tinted a lighter shade. She had already put on makeup for her first night as hostess at the Westwind Diner. Again, the changes managed to be subtle and startling at the same time: brows darkened and more arched; no mascara on the lower lashes, which made her pale hazel eyes look even larger, emphasized the almost Oriental highness of her cheekbones.

"The salon didn't dye my hair," Sheila said defensively, feeling the impact of Dolores's stare. "It's just a rinse."

"That old flake at the diner insisted on all this?"

Sheila nodded before pulling a peach-colored cashmere top over her head, wriggling her shoulders as she eased it down, tucked it into an equally form-fitting skirt. "Authentic?" she asked, fastening a black patent-leather belt around her waist.

"How would I know?" Dolores asked wryly. "I wasn't born until 1965."

"You *found* me the job!"

"I didn't figure you'd take to it so well," Dolores said. "When do you go on?"

"In about half an hour."

Dolores Gaines decided to drop her teasing tone. After all, she got a monthly allowance from her parents, worked only to provide herself with luxuries. Sheila, putting herself through an expensive university in an even more expensive city, had to take advantage of any break that came her way, even if it meant playing a thirty-year fashion throwback for a few hours every night.

Better just keep my mouth shut, she thought. What harm can come to her except being stared at on the street walking to and from work?

"Finally located it," Walter Haas said wearily, dropping a manila folder on Ray Chavez's desk at downtown LAPD headquarters. "References *were* in the computer but the jerk who programmed the outdated-file index got the suspect's name wrong—Considine instead of Constantine. Threw me off."

Chavez felt no sympathy for his partner. While Haas had spent the last day and a half rummaging through archives, Chavez had worked the street, finally identified the murdered girl as Elsa Morales, nineteen, an undocumented immigrant with one soliciting-for-prostitution arrest on her record.

"How did you spot the glitch?" Chavez asked.

Haas grimaced. "Did what I should have done to start with—called cops who worked Venice in the fifties. Finally found a man in a retirement home who remembered every detail. Trouble is he remembered every detail about *everything* else, too. Couldn't get off the phone for nearly an hour."

Chavez skimmed the sheaf of yellowing reports. Compared with modern superstars like the Night Stalker, the guy had been a bush-league serial killer—

four rape-murders spread over the summer of 1959. Like Haas, Chavez was immediately struck by the similarities between the first attack and the Elsa Morales homicide. The 1959 girl had been a teenage Chicana streetwalker; her body was discovered only a few hundred feet down the beach from Elsa's, been buried in the sand, even though no one could possibly have witnessed the killing; estimated time of death in both cases had been between midnight and 3:00 A.M.

"You may be on to something," Chavez conceded.

However, as he read further, the MO disintegrated. The next two murdered girls were also prostitutes—but not Latinas. Both had died in pay-by-the-half-hour motels on Lincoln Boulevard, far from the beach. The fourth victim—a motorcycle gang girl named Mary-Beth Kroll—really wrecked the pattern. Unlike the others, she had fought her attacker, so fiercely that her fingernails had broken off to the quick. She had lost the battle but, in death, provided physical evidence that identified her murderer. Her body lay for two days in the rear corner of an unused Venice carport before being discovered. This time homicide investigators found a solid lead near the curled-up corpse—a torn-off pocket flap from a purple madras sport jacket. And, with it, a half-used matchbook with a cover advertising the Westwind Diner.

The detectives went to the restaurant, intending to ask waitresses, busboys, and other floor personnel if they had noticed any suspicious-looking men on the day of Mary-Beth Kroll's murder—especially a man wearing a purple madras sport jacket. There were to be no interviews. The first person they spoke to—the cashier—told them that the owner, Jack Constantine, hadn't shown up for two days, that no one had been able to reach him on the telephone. And that he had worn a purple madras sport jacket on the night of the murder! The cops hurried to Constantine's apartment. When they got no answer to repeated rings, they broke in, found the flat unoccupied. However, a purple madras jacket with a missing pocket was discovered in a trash pail behind the building.

"They never caught him," Haas commented. "Main problem was that they couldn't find a single photograph of Constantine at any age. He hadn't been married, as far as anybody knew; lived alone. All that he cared about was his diner, stayed there from early morning to closing."

Trying to tune out Haas's voice, Chavez read the physical description of Jack Constantine compiled from statements given by the Westwind Diner's employees and regular customers. No one had mentioned any distinguishing features—tattoos or scars, even nervous mannerisms or a facial tic. Just that he was tall, powerfully built, had thick black hair and was in his late thirties or early forties.

Chavez slammed the folder shut, shook his head. "This maniac was about forty years old in 1959," he said sarcastically. "So, if he's still alive, he'd have to be pushing *seventy*! You expect me to believe that after all these years, he's tottered back to L.A. and started strangling girls again?"

"I've run into old men I wouldn't take on with anything short of a bazooka."

Chavez glanced irritably at his wristwatch, stood up. "We'll grab a quick dinner and head back to Venice. Couple of possibilities I want to check out in the *modern* world."

That afternoon Sheila Ransom had been shown her duties—which consisted of smiling pertly at arriving diners, plucking an appropriate number of menus from the stack next to the cash register, leading the customers to their booths, handing them the menus, saying in a cheery voice, "Enjoy yourselves." What Roger Whitt hadn't told her was how to gracefully come through the front door of the restaurant wearing sneakers and carrying spike-heeled shoes in a brown paper bag. Talk about undermining your ambience!

She went around to the rear of the diner, entered the kitchen. The half-dozen white-aproned workers, all but one of them Mexican, glanced up from stoves and chopping blocks in surprise. The Anglo—a stocky, broad-shouldered, red-haired man in his forties—studied her silently for a few seconds, then asked in a puzzled voice: "Want something, miss?"

"A place to change my shoes," she replied, sitting on a wooden chair, starting to unlace her Reeboks. "I live on Howland Canal. Just can't make it here on high heels, not unless I buy a new pair every couple of weeks."

"Uh-huh."

"I didn't introduce myself," she said, taking the pumps out of the paper bag, dropping in the sneakers. "I'm Sheila, the new night hostess."

The baffled expression left the man's not quite homely face, was replaced by a wry grin. "Mr. Whitt said last night he'd finally found a girl who fit the part. I'm Frank."

"You're the chef?"

"Head cook," he corrected. "Nineteen fifty-nine diners didn't have chefs. Authenticity all the way—that's Mr. Whitt's big rule."

Sheila slipped on the spike-heeled shoes, stood up, held out her hand. Frank the cook took it briefly, then drew back. "Better hit the ladies' room," he apologized, "unless you want to spend your first night on the job smelling like diced raw chicken livers."

"Don't be silly," Sheila said, pushing her way through the swinging door. She paused on the other side, sniffed her right palm, went to the ladies' room, washed her hands. She was surprised to see that the fifties movie posters were gone; the walls had been freshly painted a pale violet. I wonder why Whitt changed it, she thought idly as she wiped her hands on a genuine 1950s cloth roll towel.

And then she went to work, soon realizing that her new job wasn't going to be the pushover she had expected. She had heard that the Westwind's popularity had grown since Roger Whitt took over. Nevertheless, she was startled by the number of patrons already waiting for booths. By seven o'clock, they were actually lined up on the sidewalk outside—and this wasn't even the weekend!

The Westwind Diner, blocks from the beach, was the last restaurant Chavez and Haas checked out. They had gone from place to place all evening, questioning bartenders, waiters, other liquor and food workers, on the chance that they had spotted Elsa Morales in a man's company on the night of her murder. "Especially a much older man," Haas inevitably added, to Chavez's annoyance. But no one recognized the dead girl when shown her photograph.

Ray Chavez blinked in astonishment when he saw the red neon sign atop the old-fashioned chrome-walled diner. "It's still open?"

"*Re*opened," Haas corrected. "Jack Constantine owned the building and the ground it was on—and couldn't sell without putting himself in the gas chamber. So it sat padlocked and empty, piled up unpaid taxes until the city took title and turned it into a Department of Water and Power storage shed. Last year somebody bought the old dump and restored it. Now, with the fifties nostalgia crap, it's the hottest restaurant in Venice, been shown on TV and in national magazines. That must have bugged Constantine—seeing a business he'd walked away from now a big success. It'd bug *me*—and I'm sane."

Since it was past ten o'clock, the waiting line had disappeared. They went inside, Chavez's jaw dropping when he saw the girl standing by the cash register. "I always heard fifties women's clothes were frumpy," he murmured to Haas.

"Only to guys who didn't have any imagination."

Chavez took out his wallet, flipped it open to his badge, told the hostess that they wanted to speak to the manager. "Nothing's the matter," he said, noticing the alarm in her huge hazel eyes. "We're checking *all* the neighborhood restaurants."

Sheila summoned Roger Whitt, who took the detectives to his tiny office in the rear of the diner. Chavez explained that they were investigating the Elsa Morales murder, asked to speak to the waitresses and busboys, one at a time. "Might as well begin with the girl up front," he said.

Whitt shook his head. "No reason to, Sergeant. This is Sheila's first night."

"You look disappointed," Haas remarked when Whitt left them alone.

Their interviews were as unproductive as at the oceanfront bars and cafés. The last person to be futilely questioned was Roger Whitt himself. From the moment he met the man, Haas had been puzzled about his age. He had spotted the dyed hair and cosmetic surgery instantly, estimated that, despite the ridicu-

lous mask, the man had to be at least in his middle
sixties. "You ever heard of Jack Constantine?" he considered asking—then inwardly flinched. The notion
that Constantine might have changed his identity and
his face, bought back the diner he had abandoned
twenty-nine years ago, was like the phony revelations
at the end of the Charlie Chan movies he had loved
when he was a kid.

"You think we should check him out?" Ray Chavez
asked in an embarrassed tone when they were back
on the street.

"Can't do any harm," Haas said, relieved that his
partner had considered the same absurd possibility.

The tall, white-haired old man came into the Westwind Diner half an hour before closing. He wore an
outdated wide-lapeled tweed sport jacket, too small for
his thick upper body. "You still serving dinner?" he
asked in a husky growl.

"Yes, sir," Sheila said, providing the necessary smile,
even though she felt close to exhaustion. The main
cause was the spike-heeled shoes Roger Whitt had
bought for her. Sheila's mother had worn the same
damned style most of her life, still did on occasion.
Why wasn't she in a wheelchair by now? "Would you
prefer the counter or a booth?"

"Booth."

Sheila escorted the old man to a booth, started
handing him a menu, was waved away. "Already know
what I want," he said. "A bowl of chili and a cup of
decaffeinated coffee."

"I'm not supposed to accept orders," Sheila was about
to say—until she noticed the old man's eyes, the color
of cinder block worn down by decades of rotten weather.

"I'll pass it on," Sheila murmured, hurrying away.

"It's your first night, so you didn't know any better," grumbled the waitress who put the order on paper. "But from now on, give them the menu, no matter what! That way they can get up and leave and there's no trouble for anybody."

"I don't understand."

"We still get Venice people from way back when. They don't realize that a bowl of chili and a cup of coffee in here comes to nearly nine bucks, plus sales tax. Some of them go into shock. Or plain can't pay."

About twenty-five minutes later, picking up the last of the menus before closing, Sheila suddenly realized that the old man was gone, had somehow slipped by her without paying his check. She went to his booth, found a ten-dollar bill and two quarters under a saucer. The sour waitress, picking up the cash later, muttered angrily: "They *still* haven't moved up to even fifteen percent . . . stingy old farts."

Roger Whitt came out of his office, switched off the neon sign atop the Westwind Diner, took the money and credit card slips from the cash register, carried them back to the safe. The four waitresses on duty—Sheila had been introduced to them earlier but still couldn't match names and faces—muttered good night and wandered away into the darkness. Sheila was about to follow when she remembered her Reeboks. She went into the kitchen, found Frank the cook and his Mexican helpers still at work. Frank, his thick biceps taut, was moving a block of pumice in slow circles over a blackened grill.

"We're always the last to leave," he said when he saw her. "You live back at the canals?"

"On Howland." She found the paper bag containing her Reeboks, sat down, switched shoes.

"You walked to work?" he asked.

"Yes."

"Better drive from now on. Somebody killed a girl near here the night before last. Mr. Whitt told me the cops were in earlier, asking about her."

"I don't own a car," Sheila said. "My roommate does, but she's hardly ever home this early. Anyway, people who eat here have to park down around where I live. That's Venice!"

"Still, I'd feel better if someone saw you home." Frank the cook turned to a slightly built teenage kitchen helper. "Luis, go with her."

It wasn't at all what Sheila had expected him to say.

The silent Mexican youth escorted her across the Grand Canal footbridge, right to the front porch of Mrs. Drabinsky's bungalow, nodded a shy good night when she thanked him for his trouble. She entered the house as quietly as possible, knowing Viola would have been asleep for hours, went to the bedroom, saw that Dolores wasn't home yet. Her roommate had said earlier that she might go to a late movie in Westwood.

Sheila undressed, took off her ridiculous bra, thought about putting on pajamas, decided it would be too much trouble, collapsed into her bed, dozed off in seconds. She had fallen into a deep, dreamless sleep when she felt hands on her naked shoulders, awoke so suddenly that a shiver ran the length of her body. Staring down at her, face white and frightened, was Dolores Gaines.

"Someone is out there, watching our house!" Dolores whispered, releasing her grip.

Dolores had gotten back about ten minutes ago, having been forced to park blocks away. She had taken a short cut across a neighbor's backyard. "I just missed him by a few feet," she gasped. "He was standing under that pineapple palm next door, the one they never trim. I pretended I didn't see him, just kept on toward the bungalow. He stood there, not making a move or a sound. When I unlocked the front door, I looked fast toward the place where he had been. He was already gone."

Sheila got out of bed, put on a bathrobe. "What did he look like?"

"I couldn't tell," Dolores said with a helpless shrug. "Just a kind of big, black . . . thing! Should we call the police?"

"They wouldn't come, not if he didn't threaten you. And he's probably over the Grand Canal by now. Anyway, we're safe enough in here. King Kong couldn't bust in!"

Like most old-time Venice residents, Mrs. Drabinsky long ago had installed deadbolt locks on all the doors and covered the windows with steel grating.

Sheila managed to calm her friend, repeating the litany spoken by all women who were forced to live in dangerous places: Maybe you imagined it or he was a wino looking for a place to pass out or a neighbor walking his dog. At last, when Dolores was snoring, Sheila went back to her own bed, fell asleep for the second time that morning. But this time she did dream.

He never should have come back to Venice, but now that he had, he knew he was too old to start life over again a second time.

Of course, it was really the fault of the people that made that damned movie, allowing the Star with the champagne-colored hair to parade her cashmere-covered body across the main square over and over again. If the little Mexican whore hadn't shown up just as he was recalling the image, he probably never would have gone with her to the beach. It hadn't happened in years—unless you counted those worthless bitches in Spokane and Butte.

The Mexican whore had taken his money and, without even asking what he wanted, knelt in the sand, unzipped his pants. The 1959 girl had at least asked what he expected her to do for him! The anger returned, stronger than ever before. He clutched her long black hair with his left hand, yanked her up out of the sand, saw the fear in her dark eyes, choked off a scream with his right hand. "You're supposed to do what *I* want," he told her. "Not what you *think* I want. All you had to do was *ask*. . . ."

When the crimson haze passed from his vision, another ungrateful girl lay at his feet on Venice Beach. In 1959 he had scooped a hole in the sand with his bare hands, rolled her into it, covered her up, the way he had covered up the dead parakeet his mother had finally found at the bottom of the flour jar. Now he did it all over again, knowing that the body would be discovered anyway. But his hands, independent of his mind, continued to claw at the sand. . . .

For the next two days, he went about his usual routine, fearful that the police would remember the other time he strangled a Mexican whore and covered her with sand. But the newspapers didn't mention the other time and the TV didn't cover the killing at all. I was right, he thought, they've all forgotten.

Then, tonight, he realized that he *couldn't* run away, not after the flesh-and-blood vision that had appeared before him. She had come back from the past, almost exactly as he remembered. The new girl's face was a little different—a shade more fine-boned—but the hesitant smile had been identical, a teasing contrast to breasts so high and thrusting that they threatened to pierce the fabric of her peach cashmere top.

Despite his fear of the police, he knew that he would stay on in Venice. He had no choice.

After the first few nights, the routine at the Westwind Diner became bearable for Sheila Ransom. It had its rhythms, like any physical job, and she fell into them. She even got used to the silly clothes. Roger Whitt, once he was sure she was going to stay, provided new costumes, although they varied in only minor details—almond, beige, and pale-cocoa cashmere tops to spell the first garment. But at least she wouldn't end up spending a big chunk of her wages on dry cleaning and Woolite. And in one way, it was the most reassuring job she had ever held. Each night a kitchen helper walked her back to the bungalow on Howland Canal. "The other girls take the bus or carpool," Whitt had said, after learning that Frank the cook had insisted that Luis escort her home the night that police came to the diner. "Maybe there's a nut around. Maybe not. But there's no reason to take chances."

She even started to get used to the jukebox. The big current favorites were Chuck Berry's "Roll Over, Beethoven," the Platters' "Harbor Lights," and something really dreadful called "Run Red Run." She sometimes wanted to ask Mr. Whitt if at the end of the year he planned to move on to the Golden Oldies of 1960. She had a feeling he wouldn't.

To her surprise, the old man with cinder-block eyes turned up three or four nights a week, always ordering chili or a bacon cheeseburger or something else that could be quickly prepared and just as quickly eaten. A couple of times, when she wasn't busy, Sheila had tried to strike up a conversation, was dismissed with a grunt or a brusque nod. Seconds later, she would turn away from the front counter and catch his cold, wrinkle-shrouded eyes studying her.

"Don't worry about it," advised Jeanne, the Thelma Ritter look-alike. "This joint attracts dirty old men the way some places attract roaches. Either way, they're part of the job."

Sheila would have dismissed the old man from her thoughts if it hadn't been for Mrs. Drabinsky's eighty-fourth birthday. "We ought to do something for her," Dolores Gaines had said. "Not just a card and a box of chocolates. What about taking her to dinner at that place where you work? She used to go there a lot back in the fifties."

Since Mrs. Drabinsky's birthday fell on a Monday, Sheila's night off, the plan didn't thrill her. But she went along with it. Dolores always means well, she reminded herself again. "I don't like it over there," Mrs. Drabinsky said nervously when the two girls presented her with an orchid corsage. However, she allowed them to escort her across the Grand Canal. Once inside the Westwind Diner, she relaxed. "God knows the food is a lot better than it used to be," she said, chewing delicately at her last forkful of veal stewed with onions and mushrooms. "The last guy did his *own* cooking. Shouldn't have."

Mrs. Drabinsky went to the ladies' room, brushing past Roger Whitt as he came out of his office. He recognized Sheila, halted at their booth. That afternoon she had shampooed-out the blond rinse from her hair, tonight wore a loose-fitting skirt and sweater.

"You've changed back," he said.

"It's my day off, Mr. Whitt," Sheila said, surprised at the faint quiver of anger in her voice. "Tomorrow night I'll be what you pay me to be."

"We're taking our landlady out to dinner," Dolores cut in. "It's her birthday."

Roger Whitt nodded and went on his way.

Mrs. Drabinsky came out of the ladies' room, halted at a booth near the jukebox, spoke briefly to somebody. Because a partition blocked her view, Sheila couldn't see the booth's occupant.

"Who were you talking to?" Sheila asked the old woman when she returned to her seat.

"Man I thought I'd met a long time ago," Mrs. Drabinsky said wistfully. "Turned out he's never lived in Venice."

Dolores called for the bill, was informed by their waitress that Mr. Whitt had taken care of it. Sheila had figured he might. As they passed the cash register, she sneaked a look at the hostess, wondering what other fantasy Whitt might have brought to life. The girl had been in the back of the diner when they came in. Now, a warm smile on her dark red lips, she was greeting a newly arrived young couple. She had a tumbling mass of wavy auburn hair, framing an incandescently pale face highlighted by eyes so deep a blue that they verged on violet. Around her throat she wore a green gauze neckerchief, the ends trailing down the swelling front of her white angora sweater.

"Girl was the spitting image of Piper Laurie," Mrs. Drabinsky remarked when they reached the street. "I guess you kids wouldn't remember Piper Laurie. She used to make movies with camels and things."

The next morning, Sheila Ransom slept late. It was almost noon before, clad in a terry-cloth robe, she went into the kitchen, intending to heat up whatever was left in the coffee percolator. Usually, at this hour, Mrs. Drabinsky would be watching *The Young and the Restless*. Instead she sat at the zinc-topped kitchen table, going through a stack of old leather-covered scrapbooks.

"These were poor Mr. Drabinsky's books," she said, putting down the volume she was reading. "That last year, when he was in the wheelchair, he didn't have much to keep him busy, so he cut stuff out of the papers. . . . I'll make fresh coffee. I don't know how you and Dolores can drink that sludge."

Sheila's gaze drifted to the open scrapbook. STRANGLED BEAUTY BURIED ON BEACH was the banner headline on the largest clip. She sat down, picked up the book, began reading.

"Sex murders used to be big news back in the fifties," Mrs. Drabinsky said, measuring coffee into a paper filter. "Now nobody pays any attention. The *Herald-Examiner* ran just three or four paragraphs on that Venice girl who got buried in the sand a few weeks ago. On the same page as the horoscope. According to today's, I'm supposed to be on the lookout for new career opportunities."

Sheila leafed through page after page. Reporters had started calling the killer the Westwind Strangler after a girl named Mary-Beth Kroll was found dead in a Speedway carport. Evidence discovered at the scene pinpointed Jack Constantine, owner of the Westwind Diner, as the principal suspect, but no arrest was made. "He must have gotten home before he realized the poor kid had ripped off his pocket while fighting for her life," Detective Sergeant Otto W. Elwanger, head of the Homicide Department investigative team, had said. "Along with the marks she left on him, that meant he was in real trouble. So he ran. But we'll get him no matter where he tries to hide."

They never did get him, though, at least according to the last entry in Mr. Drabinsky's scrapbook, dated months later. A tiny headline read: WESTWIND STRANGLER HUNT STILL ON. Sheila closed the book.

"Why did you dig these out, Viola?" she asked.

"You're working at the place now. Brought it all back, I guess."

"Nothing else?"

"What else could there be?"

"Who was the man you spoke to at the diner last night? I couldn't see him. His back was to the booth partition."

"Already told you. One of those people you talk to once or twice and, for some reason, never forget."

Sheila hesitated, knowing that her suspicions were too silly to voice aloud. "Did he have thick white hair? Gray eyes?"

"Yeah. Why?"

Sheila faked a laugh. "An old man who looks like that has been coming into the Westwind a lot. He's a little scary."

"Old men try to look scary nowadays," Mrs. Drabinsky said. "Especially in places like Venice. They think it'll keep them from being beaten up and robbed on the street. Doesn't fool the gang kids, but they like to think it *might*. . . . Coffee's done."

Mrs. Drabinsky's veiled sarcasm forestalled Sheila's next question: What if Jack Constantine came back twenty-nine years after he murdered those girls? Would you recognize him?

She considered calling the police, giving them the old man's description, realized how ridiculous she would sound. He had done nothing except patronize the Westwind Diner, behave rudely, and stare at a hostess wearing 1959-style clothes. The cops would take the message, hang up, and laugh their heads off.

At downtown police headquarters, Sergeant Ray Chavez belatedly opened his mail, found the FBI background report on Roger Whitt, the elderly owner

of the Westwind Diner. In the weeks since the Elsa
Morales strangling, the case had shifted to the back
of his mind. He and Walter Haas had put in three
solid days on the investigation before the pressure of
newer murders had forced them to "readjust priori-
ties." That was the latest department phrase for ad-
mitting you weren't getting anyplace.

He scanned the report, tossed it on Walt Haas's desk.
"Until earlier this year, Whitt was manager of a French
restaurant in Portland, Oregon," he summarized as
Haas started to read the typewritten pages. "Before
that he worked as manager or headwaiter at other
Portland restaurants. He is sixty-eight years old, unmarried, and has no criminal record, at least in Portland."

"This only goes back to 1963," Haas noted. "What
did he do with the first forty years of his life?"

"If you keep reading you'll see that's being looked
into."

"By who?"

"The Royal Canadian Mounted Police. Whitt immigrated from Canada in '63."

Haas shook his head in frustration. "How long will
that take?"

"I don't know," Chavez said. "I've never had to deal
with the Royal Canadian Mounted Police until now.
Anyway, the stats don't figure. Four women were
strangled on or near Venice Beach during the summer of '59. The murders came, tops, three weeks apart.
A serial killer is predictable. He hits, gets off, does it
all over again when the tension grows unbearable. But
it's been well over a month since Elsa Morales died.
What *other* girl has been strangled?"

"None," Haas admitted.

"Then all we can do is figure we've got a one-shot

murder and a couple of far-out coincidences. And a lot of other cases to deal with."

Walter Haas nodded in defeat.

An unusually quiet afternoon—Dolores and a boyfriend were attending a nine-hour Toshiro Mifune film marathon at the Nuart Theatre—gave Sheila Ransom time to decide that her fear of the old man was not only unfounded but downright silly. At five o'clock— wearing the peach cashmere top, her hair freshly rinsed in that phony shade she hated—she went to work wearing Reeboks, carrying her spike-heeled shoes in a paper bag. "Sure this doesn't violate the Board of Health code?" Frank the cook asked when she switched shoes in the kitchen. She made her equally dumb ritual reply: "Not as long as I keep on my pantyhose." It had become a standing joke between them.

Despite her new sense of confidence, she was relieved that the old man didn't turn up that evening— and that no one played "Run Red Run" on the jukebox. The regular customers had started to favor Buddy Holly's "Raining in My Heart." It wasn't very good either, but at least she had heard of Buddy Holly. Why was it that the only old-time rock stars who stuck in your memory either died young on dope or died young in car or plane crashes?

I need a different job, she brooded just after eleven o'clock, while handing menus to a party of Iranians. Seconds later, clouds of greasy smoke spewed into the dining room.

The fire—started when a kitchen helper emptied a vat of still-hot cooking oil into a plastic-lined trash container—didn't amount to much, except for the fumes and odor. Frank the cook had yanked an extinguisher off the wall, doused the blaze in seconds. "You might as well go on home," Roger Whitt told Sheila after they guided the last gasping customers out the front door. "Unless I call, don't come in tomorrow night. Takes at least a day to clear out the smell of a grease fire."

Sheila started off toward the Grand Canal Bridge, suddenly remembered that she had left her Reeboks in the kitchen, decided not to go back for them. Frank and his helpers wouldn't want to be pestered by a girl trying to retrieve a pair of sneakers!

Frank Riordan picked up the scuffed Reeboks, fought the impulse to toss them into a garbage can. Only those stupid sneakers, for twenty or thirty seconds every night, had conflicted with the dream he had nurtured for nearly three decades, the dream that had kept him from killing again after he buried the Mexican whore in the sand. He wasn't afraid that the police might connect the whore's death with the old Westwind Strangler case; even if they did, they would start hunting for Jack Constantine. But another death could trigger a wider investigation, force him to again run away, cut him off from an almost perfect facsimile of the woman he had worshiped since he was an eighteen-year-old helper in this same kitchen.

"Girl with the big tits forgot her sneakers?" asked Luis, dumping detergent on floor tiles blackened by the fire.

Frank Riordan barely heard the kid's words. He again recalled his numb astonishment when she first came through the back door, even more beautiful than the Star who had again and again crossed Venice's main square, dressed in identical clothes, her hair glowing with a pale softness he wanted to reach out and catch with his hands, the way he had caught lightning bugs when he was a child, tightening his fist until the light went out. . . .

"Just went by one of those old movie posters on the ladies'-room wall," Roger Whitt said when Riordan asked him how he had chosen and costumed the new night hostess. "You told me you wanted real fifties ambience, Frank. You must have noticed them."

"I've never gone into the ladies' room," he said. "I'll take a look after closing."

"Too late. I had it repainted. Woman customer mentioned that *Tammy Tell Me True* came out in the early sixties. I didn't want anything around that wasn't authentic." Whitt caught the sudden, inexplicable anger in Frank Riordan's eyes, hastily added: "I hired a Piper Laurie, too."

"Then I guess you've done pretty good," Frank said, turning to go back into the kitchen.

It had been an even wiser move than he had thought to put the Westwind Diner in Whitt's name, although the bulk of the down payment on the then-failing diner had come from Frank Riordan's life savings. The two friends had worked for years in Portland restaurants—Whitt as a headwaiter, Riordan as a chef. "My place is in the kitchen," he had told Whitt when, after learning the Westwind was for sale, he had proposed their partnership. No one, not even the police, thought about the harried, invisible people who worked behind the scenes in a busy restaurant.

"Finish cleaning up tomorrow," Roger Whitt said wearily as he came through the kitchen door. "I've already sent the girls home."

Frank Riordan waited until the others had left before picking up Sheila's Reeboks and hurrying into the alley.

* * *

Sheila was approaching the Grand Canal bridge when she heard pounding footfalls behind her. Fear came, moving up from the pit of her stomach in a frigid wave. Suddenly she remembered the dark shape that Dolores had seen spying on the bungalow. She started to run, clumsily, on her spike-heeled shoes.

"You forgot your sneakers!" called a familiar voice.

She halted, laughed in relief, turned to see Frank the cook, holding a Reebok in either hand. "Thanks."

"Besides, what with the fire and all, I forgot to have somebody walk you home," he said. She didn't know his true reason for taking the precaution night after night. As long as one of the Mexican kids was with her, she would be safe from him. In all the years between watching the Star in the main square and seeing this girl enter his kitchen, he had never felt love for a woman, wasn't sure that it would act as a restraint on his physical needs. Now he was sure. He could handle it this time!

Leaning against the bridge rail, she replaced her spike-heeled shoes with the Reeboks. They walked side by side across the bridge, descended into the black shadows of the canal district.

He remembered the last time he had been here—the night he buried the final portions of Mr. Constantine. . . .

Frank Riordan had been astonished at the fight put up by the biker girl before she died. Her nails had clawed through the front of his shirt, dug deep gashes in his chest and upper arms—but, luckily, missed his face. To get to his room on Washington Street, he would have to pass through busy, lighted areas, expose his wounds to passersby. But the Westwind Diner could be reached through alleys and side streets seldom traveled at so late an hour. Since one of his jobs was brewing the morning coffee, he had a key to the back kitchen door.

He hadn't expected to find Mr. Constantine sitting in the kitchen, reading *The Saturday Evening Post.* Didn't the old fool ever go home? "What happened to you?" Mr. Constantine asked when he saw the blood-drenched shirt front. "Dog bit me," Frank Riordan gasped, knowing instantly that he wouldn't be believed. "Why didn't you go to an emergency room?" Mr. Constantine said suspiciously, standing up. "Why come here?" Tomorrow they will find the biker whore, Frank Riordan thought, and then Mr. Constantine will call the police. . . .

He lunged over to a counter, yanked a long blade from a wooden knife block, sank it into Mr. Constantine's chest, twisted—and, staring down at his employer's body a few seconds later, realized that he now had two deaths to cover up.

Later, he couldn't figure out how he conceived the plan so quickly. He knew he wasn't terribly smart—never had been—but it all came together in a frightened rush. Mr. Constantine was wearing his bright purple madras jacket, the one that the waitresses made fun of behind his back. He raised the body, removed the jacket. Then, putting on a stained white tunic from the laundry bin to hide his wounds, he bundled the jacket under his arm and wended his way back to the Speedway carport, where the dead girl still lay undiscovered. He tore off a side-pocket flap of the madras jacket, dropped it on the ground beside her, saw a Westwind Diner matchbook come with it. God is with me tonight, he thought as he scuttled off.

By dawn most of his work was done. He had crammed the madras jacket into a trash pail behind

Mr. Constantine's apartment building, only a block from the Westwind; returned to the diner; used meat-cutting utensils to reduce Mr. Constantine to manageable sections, placed in plastic bags and hidden in the walk-in freezer. Then he meticulously cleaned the white-tiled floor, started the breakfast coffee, just a few minutes later than on less eventful mornings.

Frank Riordan and Sheila Ransom passed a two-story redwood-walled house. Although weathered by the ocean winds, it was noticeably more modern than the bungalows on the canal. In 1959, the house had still been under construction. The last portions of Mr. Constantine, Frank Riordan estimated, lay buried a few feet in from the first-floor picture window.

Why did I run away afterward? he asked himself. I had nothing to fear! Nevertheless, the day that the Westwind Diner closed its doors, he had packed up and fled Venice. He had fooled everybody—even the police—and yet he had run away. . . .

"You're awfully quiet," Sheila said. "What are you thinking about?"

"Mistakes."

She laughed lightly. "We *all* do."

They had turned onto the Howland path, were approaching the Dell Avenue auto bridge. Frank the cook fell a few steps behind her. The instant she stepped under the bridge, she felt his hands grasp her upper arms. He swiveled her around to face him.

"You want to go out tomorrow night?" Frank asked. "The diner will be closed for cleaning, so we'll both have an evening off."

"I'd love to," Sheila said, "but my boyfriend is coming into town tomorrow."

Frank the cook smiled tightly. "Didn't realize . . .

Sorry. . . . Been going together long?"

"Years. He's studying medicine at the University of Idaho, so we don't see each other very often."

"Uh-huh . . . Better get you home now."

"I'll be fine from here on in. Thanks again."

He nodded good night and started back toward the Grand Canal.

Years, she had said. He knew what that meant! Tomorrow a nameless, faceless college boy would lie in bed with her! His hands and mouth would stroke and taste the breasts and belly and thighs that would be forever beyond his reach! She was just another whore after all! And he could do *nothing*!

He halted, recalling that no one had seen him pick up the Reeboks. No one had seen him leave the diner, catch up with her at the Grand Canal bridge. He could do what he needed to do, then strip the sneakers off her feet, return them to the restaurant. . . .

Sheila Ransom had paused on the east side of the Dell Avenue bridge, gazed into the dark, still canal waters, guiltily wishing she hadn't told Frank the cook that silly lie about the Idaho medical student. Of course, it sounded better than the truth—that she simply didn't care for older men.

And then Frank the cook appeared again—not noisily, as he had when he brought her the Reeboks. He was just *there,* like a patch of fog unexpectedly moving off the canal. She caught a glimpse of his twisted, enraged face as he tore away her peach cashmere top, ripped off her old-fashioned rubber-reinforced bra as easily as if it were a piece of Kleenex. His left hand closed gently around a breast; his right hand savagely tightened on her throat, cutting off a scream, forcing her to the ground. She felt consciousness start to slip away. . . .

Then she heard a strange noise, soft and brittle at the same time, like the sound of a badly spoiled stalk of celery being broken in half before someone crammed it into the garbage disposal. The weight of Frank's body was gone. Standing over her was the old man with cinder-block gray eyes. He removed his ancient tweed jacket, gently placed it over her naked upper body, said: "Take it easy now, miss. You'll be fine."

Frank the cook lay sprawled on the bank of Howland Canal, his head submerged in the murky water.

"Funny," the old man mused, mostly to himself, "if that kid from the department hadn't called, I'd never have known he'd come back. . . . Don't read the papers much anymore. . . . First night I went to the diner, I figured you'd be the one he'd go after, if it *was* him. . . . So I kept watch. . . ."

"Thank you," Sheila said, the first tears starting to run down her cheeks.

The old man picked her up like a child, cradled her head on his shoulder, carried her toward Mrs. Drabinsky's stucco bungalow.

"Who *are* you?" she sobbed.

"Chief Inspector Otto W. Elwanger, LAPD, retired," the old man said. "I came back, too."

THE KERMAN KILL
WILLIAM CAMPBELL GAULT

Beverly Hills became known as the home of the stars after Mary Pickford and Douglas Fairbanks moved there in 1920. Others soon followed, and to this day Beverly Hills remains a ghetto for the affluent, with its own police and fire departments and school system. The latter is one of the richest in the state, and keeps an investigator on staff to root out illegitimately enrolled pupils. Among those from acceptable addresses who went on to graduate from Beverly Hills High have been Richard Chamberlain, Carrie Fisher, André Previn, and Marlo Thomas. In "The Kerman Kill" by William Campbell Gault, a novice PI with the unlikely moniker of Pierre Apoyan is hired to trace a missing

Beverly Hills High student—or rather her mother's precious oriental rug, which seems to have disappeared with her. But in this privileged atmosphere, as Pierre discovers, it may not be the rug that counts so much as what the family has swept under it.

"PIERRE?" my Uncle Vartan asked. "Why Pierre? You were Pistol Pete Apoyan when you fought."

Sixteen amateur fights I'd had and won them all. Two professional fights I'd had and painfully decided it would not be my trade. I had followed that career with three years as an employee of the Arden Guard and Investigative Service in Santa Monica before deciding to branch out on my own.

We were in my uncle's rug store in Beverly Hills, a small store and not in the highest rent district, but a fine store. No machine-made imitation orientals for him, and *absolutely* no carpeting.

"You didn't change your name," I pointed out.

"Why would I?" he asked. "It is an honorable name and suited to my trade."

"And Pierre is not an honorable name?"

He signed. "Please do not misunderstand me. I adore your mother. But Pierre is a name for hairdressers and perfume manufacturers and those pirate merchants on Rodeo Drive. Don't your friends call you Pete?"

"My odar friends," I admitted. "Odar" means (roughly) non-Armenian. My mother is French, my father Armenian.

"Think!" he said. "Sam Spade. Mike Hammer. But Pierre?"

"Hercule Poirot," I said.

"What does that mean? Who is this Hercule Poirot? A friend?" He was frowning.

It was my turn to sigh. I said nothing. My Uncle Vartan is a stubborn man. He had four nephews, but I was his favorite. He had never married. He had come to this country as an infant with my father and their older brother. My father had sired one son and one daughter, my Uncle Sarkis three sons.

"You're so stubborn!" Uncle Vartan said.

The pot had just described the kettle. I shrugged.

He took a deep breath. "I suppose I am, too."

I nodded.

"Whatever," he said, "the decision is yours, no matter what name you decide to use."

The decision would be mine but the suggestion had been his. Tough private eye stories, fine rugs, and any attractive woman under sixty were what he cherished. His store had originally been a two-story duplex with a separate door and stairway to the second floor. That, he had suggested, would be a lucrative location for my office when I left Arden.

His reasoning was sound enough. He got the carriage trade; why wouldn't I? And he would finance the remodeling.

Why was I so stubborn?

"Don't sulk," he said.

"It's because of my mother," I explained. "She didn't like it when I was called Pistol Pete."

His smile was sad. "I know. But wouldn't Pistol Pierre have sounded worse?" He shook his head. "Lucky Pierre, always in the middle. I talked with the contractor last night. The remodeling should be finished by next Tuesday."

The second floor was large enough to include living quarters for me. Tonight I would tell my two roomies in our Pacific Palisades apartment that I would be deserting them at the end of the month. I drove out to

Westwood, where my mother and sister had a French pastry shop.

My sister, Adele, was behind the counter. My mother was in the back, smoking a cigarette. She is a chain smoker, my mother, the only nicotine addict in the family. She is a slim, trim, and testy forty-seven-year-old tiger.

"Well—?" she asked.

"We won," I told her. "It will be the Pierre Apoyan Investigative Service."

"*You* won," she corrected me. "You and Vartan. It wasn't *my* idea."

"Are there any croissants left?" I asked.

"On the shelf next to the oven." She shook her head. "That horny old bastard! All the nice women I found for him—"

"Who needs a cow when milk is cheap?" I asked.

"Don't be vulgar," she said. "And if you do, get some new jokes."

I buttered two croissants, poured myself a cup of coffee, and sat down across from her. I said, "The rumor I heard years ago is that Vartan came on to you before you met Dad."

"The rumor is true," she admitted. "But if I wanted to marry an adulterer I would have stayed in France."

"And then you never would have met Dad. You did okay, Ma."

"I sure as hell did. He's *all* man."

The thought came to me that if he were all man, the macho type, my first name would not be Pierre. I didn't voice the thought; I preferred to drink my coffee, not wear it.

She said, "I suppose that you'll be carrying a gun again in this new profession you and Vartan dreamed up?"

"Ma, at Arden, I carried a gun only when I worked guard duty. I *never* carried one when I did investigative work. This will not be guard duty."

She put out her cigarette and stood up. "That's something, I suppose. You're coming for dinner on Sunday, of course?"

"Of course," I said.

She went out to take over the counter. Adele came in to have a cup of coffee. She was born eight years after I was; she is twenty and romantically inclined. She has our mother's slim, dark beauty and our father's love of the theater. She was currently sharing quarters with an aspiring actor. My father was a still cameraman at Elysian Films.

"Mom looks angry," she said. "What did you two argue about this time?"

"My new office. Uncle Vartan is going to back me."

She shook her head. "What a waste! With your looks you'd be a cinch in films."

"Even prettier than your Ronnie?"

"Call it a tie," she said. "You don't like him, do you?"

Her Ronnie was an aspiring actor who called himself Ronnie Egan. His real name was Salvatore Martino. I shrugged.

"He's got another commercial coming up next week. And his agent thinks he might be able to work me into it."

"Great!" I said.

That gave him a three-year career total of four commercials. If he worked her in, it would be her second.

"Why don't you like him?"

"Honey, I only met him twice and I don't dislike him. Could we drop the subject?"

"Aagh!" she said. "You and Vartan, you two deserve each other. Bullheads!"

"People who live in glass houses," I pointed out, "should undress in the cellar."

She shook her head again. "You and Papa, you know all the corny old ones, don't you?"

"Guilty," I admitted. "Are you bringing Ronnie to dinner on Sunday?"

"Not this Sunday. We're going to a party at his agent's house. Ronnie wants me to meet him."

"I hope it works out. I'll hold my thumbs. I love you, sis."

"It's mutual," she said.

I kissed the top of her head and went out to my ancient Camaro. On the way to the apartment I stopped in Santa Monica and talked with my former boss at Arden.

I had served him well; he promised that if they ever had any commercial reason to invade my new baili-wick, and were short-handed, I would be their first choice for associate action.

The apartment I shared with two others in Pacific Palisades was on the crest of the road just before Sunset Boulevard curves and dips down to the sea.

My parents had bought a tract house here in the fifties for an exorbitant twenty-one thousand dollars. It was now worth enough to permit both of them to retire. But they enjoyed their work too much to consider that.

I will not immortalize my roomies' names in print. One of them was addicted to prime-time soap operas, the other changed his underwear and socks once a week, on Saturday, after his weekly shower.

When I told them, over our oven-warmed frozen TV dinners, that I would be leaving at the end of the month, they took it graciously. Dirty Underwear was currently courting a lunch-counter waitress who had been hoping to share an apartment. She would inherit my rollout bed—when she wasn't in his.

On Thursday morning my former boss phoned to tell me he had several credit investigations that needed immediate action and two operatives home with the flu. Was I available? I was.

Uncle Sarkis and I went shopping on Saturday for office and apartment furniture. Wholesale, of course. "Retail" is an obscene word to my Uncle Sarkis.

The clan was gathered on Sunday at my parents' house, all but Adele. Uncle Vartan and my father played tavlu (backgammon to you). My mother, Uncle Sarkis, his three sons, and I played twenty-five-cent-limit poker out on the patio. My mother won, as usual. I broke even; the others lost. I have often suspected that the Sunday gatherings my mother hosts are more financially motivated than familial.

My roommates told me Monday morning that I didn't have to wait until the end of the month; I could move anytime my place was ready. The waitress was aching to move in.

The remodeling was finished at noon on Tuesday, the furniture delivered in the afternoon. I moved in the next morning. All who passed on the street below would now be informed by the gilt letters on the new wide front window that the Pierre Apoyan Investigative Service was now open and ready to serve them.

There were many who passed on the street below in the next three hours, but not one came up the steps. There was no reason to expect that anyone would. Referrals and advertising were what brought the clients in. Arden was my only doubtful source for the first; my decision to open this office had come too late to make the deadline for an ad in the phone book yellow pages.

I consoled myself with the knowledge that there was no odor of sour socks in the room and I would not be subjected to the idiocies of prime-time soap opera. I read the *L.A. Times* all the way through to the classified pages.

It had been a tiring two days; I went into my small bedroom to nap around ten o'clock. It was noon when I came back to the here and now. I turned on my answering machine and went down to ask Vartan if I could take him to lunch.

He shook his head. "Not today. After your first case, you may buy. Today, lunch is on me."

He had not spent enough time in the old country to develop a taste for Armenian food. He had spent his formative years in New York and become addicted to Italian cuisine. We ate at La Famiglia on North Canon Drive.

He had whitefish poached in white wine, topped with capers and small bay shrimp. I had a Caesar salad.

Over our coffee, he asked, "Dull morning?"

I nodded. "There are bound to be a lot of them for a one-man office. I got in two days at Arden last week. I might get more when they're short-handed."

He studied me for a few seconds. Then, "I wasn't going to mention this. I don't want to get your hopes up. But I have a—a customer who might drop in this afternoon. It's about a rug I sold her. It has been stolen. For some reason, which she wouldn't tell me, she doesn't want to go to the police. I gave her your name."

He had hesitated before he had called her a customer. With his history, she could have been more than that. "Was it an expensive rug?" I asked.

"I got three thousand for it eight years ago. Only God knows what it's worth now. That was a sad day for me. It's an antique Kerman."

"Wasn't it insured?"

"Probably. But if she reported the loss to her insurance company they would insist she go to the police."

"Was anything else stolen?"

"Apparently not. The rug was all she mentioned."

That didn't make sense. A woman who could afford my uncle's antique oriental rugs must have some jewelry. That would be easier and safer to haul out of a house than a rug.

"I'd better get back to the office," I said.

"Don't get your hopes up," he warned me again. "I probably shouldn't have told you."

I checked my answering machine when I got back to the office. Nothing. I took out my contract forms and laid them on top of my desk and sat where I could watch the street below.

I decided, an hour later, that was sophomoric. The ghost of Sam Spade must have been sneering down at me.

She opened the door about twenty minutes later, a fairly tall, slim woman with jet-black hair, wearing black slacks and a white cashmere sweater. She could have been sixty or thirty; she had those high cheekbones which keep a face taut.

"Mr. Apoyan?" she asked.

I nodded.

"Your uncle reccomended you to me."

"He told me. But he didn't tell me your name."

"I asked him not to." She came over to sit in my client's chair. "It's Bishop, Mrs. Whitney Bishop. Did he tell you that I prefer not to have the police involved?"

"Yes. Was anything else stolen?"

She shook her head.

"That seems strange to me," I said. "Burglars don't

usually carry out anything big, anything suspicious enough to alert the neighbors."

"Our neighbors are well screened from view," she told me, "and I'm sure this was not a burglar." She paused. "I am almost certain it was my daughter. And *that* is why I don't want the police involved."

"It wasn't a rug too big for a woman to carry?"

She shook her head. "A three-by-five-foot antique Kerman."

I winced. "For three thousand dollars—?"

Her smile was dim. "You obviously don't have your uncle's knowledge of rugs. I was offered more than I care to mention for it only two months ago. My daughter is—adopted. She has been in trouble before. I have *almost* given up on her. We had a squabble the day my husband and I went down to visit friends in Rancho Santa Fe. When we came home the rug was gone and so was she."

I wondered if it was her daughter she wanted back or the rug. I decided that would be a cynical question to ask.

"We have an elaborate alarm system," she went on, "with a well-hidden turnoff in the house. It couldn't have been burglars." She stared bleakly past me. "She knows how much I love that rug. I feel that it was simply a vindictive act on her part. It has been a—troubled relationship."

"How old is she?" I asked.

"Seventeen."

"Does she know who her real parents are?"

"No. And neither do we. Why?"

"I thought she might have gone back to them. How about her friends?"

"We've talked with all of her friends that we know. There are a number of them we have never met." A pause. "And I am sure would not want to."

"You daughter's—acceptable friends might know of others," I suggested.

"Possibly," she admitted. "I'll give you a list of those we know well."

She told me her daughter's name was Janice and made out a list of her friends while I filled in the contract. She gave me a check, her unlisted phone number, and a picture of her daughter.

When she left, I went to the window and saw her climb into a sleek black Jaguar below. My hunch had been sound; this was the town that attracted the carriage trade.

I went downstairs to thank Vartan and tell him our next lunch would be on me at a restaurant of his choice.

"I look forward to it," he said. "She's quite a woman, isn't she?"

"That she is. Was she ever more than a customer to you?"

"We had a brief but meaningful relationship," he said coolly, "at a time when she was between husbands. But then she started talking marriage." He sighed.

"Uncle Vartan," I asked, "haven't you *ever* regretted the fact that you have no children to carry on your name?"

"Never," he said, and smiled. "You are all I need."

Two elderly female customers came in then and I went out with my list of names. It was a little after three o'clock; some of the kids should be home from school.

There were five names on the list, two girls and three boys, all students at Beverly Hills High. Only one of the girls was home. She had seen Janice at school on Friday, she told me, but not since. But that didn't mean she hadn't been at school Monday and Tuesday.

"She's not in any of my classes," she explained.

I showed her the list. "Could you tell me if any of these students are in any of her classes?"

"Not for sure. But Howard might be in her art appreciation class. They're both kind of—you know—"

"Artistic?" I asked.

"I suppose. You know—that weird stuff—"

"Avant-garde, abstract, cubist?"

She shrugged. "I guess, whatever *that* means. Janice and I were never really close."

From the one-story stone house of Miss Youknow, I drove to the two-story Colonial home of Howard Retzenbaum.

He was a tall thin youth with horn-rimmed glasses. He was wearing faded jeans and a light gray T-shirt with a darker gray reproduction of Pablo Picasso's *Woman's Head* emblazoned on his narrow chest.

Janice, he told me, had been in class on Friday, but not Monday or yesterday. "Has something happened to her?"

"I hope not. Do you know of any friends she has who don't go to your school?"

Only one, he told me, a boy named Leslie she had introduced him to several weeks ago. He had forgotten his last name. He tapped his forehead. "I remember she told me he worked at some Italian restaurant in town. He was a busboy there."

"La Famiglia?"

"No, no. That one on Santa Monica Boulevard."

"La Dolce Vita?"

He nodded. "That's the place. Would you tell her to phone me if you find her?"

I promised him I would and thanked him. The other two boys were not at home; they had baseball practice after school. I drove to La Dolce Vita.

They serve no luncheon trade. The manager was not in. The assistant manager looked at me suspiciously when I asked if a boy named Leslie worked there.

"Does he have a last name?"

"I'm sure he has. Most people do. But I don't happen to know it."

"Are you a police officer?"

I shook my head. "I am a licensed and bonded private investigator. My Uncle Vartan told me that Leslie is an employee here."

"Would that be Vartan Apoyan?"

"It would be and it is." I handed him my card.

He read it and smiled. "That's different. Leslie's last name is Denton. He's a student at UCLA and works from seven o'clock until closing." He gave me Leslie's phone number and address, and asked, "Is Pierre an Armenian name?"

"Quite often," I informed him coldly and left without thanking him.

The address was in Westwood and it was now almost five o'clock. I had no desire to buck the going-home traffic in this city of wheels. I drove to the office to phone Leslie.

He answered the phone. I told him I was a friend of Howard Retzenbaum's and we were worried about Janice. I explained that she hadn't been in school on Monday or Tuesday and her parents didn't know where she was.

"Are you also a friend of her parents?" he asked.
"No way!"

She had come to his place Friday afternoon, he told me, when her parents had left for Rancho Santa Fe. She had stayed over the weekend. But when he had come home from school on Tuesday she was gone.

"She didn't leave a note or anything?"

"No."

"She didn't, by chance, bring a three-foot-by-five-foot Kerman rug with her, did she?"

"Hell, no! Why?"

"According to a police officer I know in Beverly Hills, her parents think she stole it from the house. Did she come in a car?"

"No. A taxi. What in hell is going on? Are those creepy parents of hers trying to frame her?"

"Not if I can help it. Did she leave your place anytime during the weekend?"

"She did not. If you find her, will you let me know?"

I promised him I would.

I phoned Mrs. Whitney Bishop and asked her if Janice had been in the house Friday when they left for Rancho Santa Fe.

"No. She left several hours before that. My husband didn't get home from the office until five o'clock."

"Were there any servants in the house when you left?"

"We have no live-in servants, Mr. Apoyan."

"In that case," I said, "I think it is time for you to call the police and file a missing persons report. Janice was in Westwood from Friday afternoon until some time on Tuesday."

"Westwood? Was she with that Leslie Denton person?"

"She was. Do you know him?"

"Janice brought him to the house several times. Let me assure you, Mr. Apoyan, that he is a doubtful source of information. You know, of course, that he's gay."

That sounded like a non sequitur to me. I didn't point it out. I thought of telling her to go to hell. But a more reasonable (and mercenary) thought overruled it; rich bigots should pay for their bigotry.

"You want me to continue, then?" I asked.

"I certainly do. Have you considered the possibility that one of Leslie Denton's friends might have used her key and Janice told him where the turnoff switch is located?"

I hadn't thought of that.

"I thought of that," I explained, "but if that happened, I doubt if we could prove it. I don't want to waste your money, Mrs. Bishop."

"Don't you worry about that," she said. "You find my rug!"

Not her daughter; her rug. First things first. "I'll get right on it," I assured her.

I was warming some lahmajoons Sarkis's wife had given me last Sunday when I heard my office door open. I went out.

It was Cheryl, my current love, back from San Francisco, where she had gone to visit her mother.

"Welcome home!" I said. "How did you know I moved?"

"Adele told me. Are those lahmajoons I smell?"

I nodded. She came over to kiss me. She looked around the office, went through the open doorway, and inspected the apartment.

When she came back, she said, "And now we have this. Now we won't have to worry if your roommates are home, or mine. Do you think I should move in?"

"We'll see. What's in the brown bag?"

"Potato salad, a jar of big black olives, and two avocados."

"Welcome home again. You can make the coffee."

Over our meal I told her about my day, my lucky opening day in this high-priced town. I mentioned no names, only places.

It sounded like a classic British locked-room mystery, she thought and said. She is an addict of the genre.

"Except for the guy in Westwood," I pointed out. "Maybe one of his friends stole the rug."

Westwood was where she shared an apartment with two friends. "Does he have a name?" she asked.

I explained to her that that would be privileged information.

"I was planning to stay the night," she said, "until now."

"His name is Leslie Denton."

"Les Denton?" She shook her head. "Not in a zillion years! He is integrity incarnate."

"You're thinking of your idol, Len Deighton," I said.

"I am not! Les took the same night-school class that I did in restaurant management. We got to be very good friends. He works as a busboy at La Dolce Vita."

"I know. Were you vertical or horizontal friends?"

"Don't be vulgar, Petroff. Les is not heterosexual."

"Aren't you glad I am?"

"Not at the moment."

"Let's have some more wine," I suggested.

At nine o'clock she went down to her car to get her luggage. When she came back, she asked, "Are you tired?"

"Nope."

"Neither am I," she said. "Let's go to bed."

I was deep in a dream involving my high school sweetheart when the phone rang in my office. My bedside clock informed me that it was seven o'clock. The voice on the phone informed me that I was a lying bastard.

"Who is speaking, please?" I asked.

"Les Denton. Mr. Randisi at the restaurant gave me

your phone number. You told me you were a friend of Howard Retzenbaum's. Mr. Randisi told me you were a stinking private eye. You're working for the Bishops, aren't you?"

"Leslie," I said calmly, "I have a very good friend of yours who is here in the office right now. She will assure you that I am not a lying bastard and do not stink. I have to be devious at times. It is a requisite of my trade."

"What's her name?"

"Cheryl Pushkin. Hold the line. I'll put her on."

Cheryl was sitting up in bed. I told her Denton wanted to talk to her.

"Why? Who told him I was here?"

"I did. He wants a character reference."

"What?"

"Go!" I said. "And don't hang up when you're finished. I want to talk with him."

I was half dressed when she came back to tell me she had calmed him down and he would talk to me now.

I told him it was true that I was working for Mrs. Bishop. I added that getting her rug back was a minor concern to me; finding her daughter was my major concern and should be his, too. I told him I would be grateful for any help he could give me on this chivalrous quest.

"I shouldn't have gone off half-cocked," he admitted. "I have some friends who know Janice. I'll ask around."

"Thank you."

Cheryl was in the shower when I hung up. I started the coffee and went down the steps to pick up the *Times* at my front door.

A few minutes after I came back, she was in her robe, studying the contents of my fridge. "Only two eggs in here," she said, "and two strips of bacon."

"There are some frozen waffles in the freezer compartment."

"You can have those. I'll have bacon and eggs."

I didn't argue.

"You were moaning just before the phone rang," she said. "You were moaning 'Norah, Norah.' Who is Norah?"

"A dog I had when I was a kid. She was killed by a car."

She turned to stare at me doubtfully, but made no comment. Both her parents are Russian, a suspicious breed. Her father lived in San Diego, her mother in San Francisco, what they had called a trial separation. I suspected it was messing-around time in both cities.

She had decided in the night, she told me, to reside in Westwood for a while. I had the feeling she doubted my fidelity. She had suggested at one time that I could be a younger clone of Uncle Vartan.

She left and I sat. I had promised Mrs. Bishop that I would "get right on it." Where would I start? The three kids I had not questioned yesterday were now in school. And there was very little likelihood that they would have any useful information on the present whereabouts of Janice Bishop. Leslie Denton was my last best hope.

I took the *Times* and a cup of coffee out to the office and sat at my desk. Terrible Tony Tuscani, I read in the sports page, had outpointed Mike (the Hammer) Mulligan in a ten-round windup last night in Las Vegas. The writer thought Tony was a cinch to cop the middleweight crown. In my fifth amateur fight I had kayoed Tony halfway through the third round. Was I in the wrong trade?

And then the thought came to me that an antique Kerman was not the level of stolen merchandise one

would take to an ordinary fence. A burglar sophisti-
cated enough to outfox a complicated alarm system
should certainly know that. He would need to find a
buyer who knew about oriental rugs.

Uncle Vartan was on the phone when I went down.
When he had finished talking I voiced the thought I'd
had upstairs.

"It makes sense," he agreed. "So?"

"I thought, being in the trade, you might know of
one."

"I do," he said. "Ismet Bey. He has a small shop in
Santa Monica. He deals mostly in imitation orientals
and badly worn antiques. I have reason to know he
has occasionally bought stolen rugs."

"Why don't you phone him," I suggested, "and tell
him you have a customer who is looking for a three-
by-five Kerman?"

His face stiffened. "You are asking *me* to talk to
a Turk?"

I said lamely, "I didn't know he was a Turk."

"You know now," he said stiffly. "If you decide to
phone him use a different last name."

I looked him up in the phone book and called. A
woman answered. I asked for Ismet. She told me he
was not in at the moment and might not be in until
this afternoon. She identified herself as his wife and
asked if she could be of help.

"I certainly hope so," I said. "My wife and I have
been scouring the town for an antique Kerman. We
have been unsuccessful so far. Is it possible you
have one?"

"We haven't," she said. "But I am surprised to learn
you haven't found one. There must be a number of
stores that have at least one in stock. The better stores,
I mean, of course."

An honest woman married to a crooked Turk. I said,

"Not a three-by-five. We want it for the front hall."

"That might be more difficult," she said. "But Mr.—"

"Stein," I said. "Peter Stein."

"Mr. Stein," she continued, "my husband has quite often found hard-to-find rugs. Do you live in Santa Monica?"

"In Beverly Hills." I gave her my phone number. "If I'm not here, please leave a message on my answering machine."

"We will. I'll tell my husband as soon as he gets here. If you should find what you're looking for in the meantime—"

"I'll let you know immediately," I assured her.

I temporarily changed the name on my answering machine from Pierre Apoyan Investigative Service to a simple Peter. Both odars and kinsmen would recognize me by that name.

Back to sitting and waiting. I felt slightly guilty about sitting around when Mrs. Bishop was paying me by the hour. But only slightly. Mrs. Whitney Bishop would never make my favorite-persons list.

Uncle Vartan was born long after the Turkish massacre of his people. But he knew the brutal history of that time as surely as the young Jews know the history of the holocaust—from the survivors.

I read the rest of the news that interested me in the *Times* and drank another cup of coffee. I was staring down at the street below around noon when my door opened.

It was Cheryl. She must have been coming up as I was looking down. She had driven in for a sale at I. Magnin, she told me. "And as long as I was in the neighborhood—"

"You dropped in on your favorite person," I finished for her. "What's in the bag, something from Magnin's?"

"In a brown paper bag? Lox and bagels, my friend, and cream cheese. I noticed how low your larder was this morning. Did Les Denton phone you?"

I shook my head.

"I bumped into him in front of the UCLA library this morning," she said, "and gave him the old third degree. He swore to me that he and Janice were alone over the weekend, so she couldn't have given her house key to *anybody*. I was right, wasn't I?"

"I guess you were, Miss Marple. Tea or coffee?"

"Tea for me. I can't stay long. Robinson's is also having a sale."

"How exciting! Your mama must have given you a big fat check again when you were up in San Francisco."

"Don't be sarcastic! I stopped in downstairs and asked your uncle if you'd ever had a dog named Norah."

"And he confirmed it."

"Not quite. He said he thought you had but he wasn't sure. Of course, he probably can't even remember half the women he's—he's courted."

"Enough!" I said. "Lay off!"

"I'm sorry. Jealousy! That's adolescent, isn't it? It's vulgar and possessive."

"I guess."

"You're not very talkative today, are you?"

"Cheryl, there is a young girl out there somewhere who has run away from home. That, to me, is much more important than a sale at Robinson's or whether I ever had a dog named Norah. This is a dangerous town for seventeen-year-old runaways."

"You're right." She sighed. "How trivial can I get?"

"We all have our hang-ups," I said. "I love you just the way you are."

"And I you, Petroff. Do you think Janice is in some

kind of danger? Why would she leave Les's place without even leaving him a note?"

"*That* I don't know. And it scares me."

"You don't think she's—" She didn't finish.

"Dead? I have no way of knowing."

Five minutes after she left, I learned that Janice had still been alive yesterday. Les Denton phoned to tell me that a friend of his had seen her on the Santa Monica beach with an older man, but had not talked with her. According to the friend, the man she was with was tall and thin and frail, practically a skeleton.

"Thanks," I said.

"It's not the first time she's run away," he told me. "And there's a pattern to it."

"What kind of pattern?"

"Well, I could be reading more into it than there is. But I noticed that it was usually when her mother was out of town. Mrs. Bishop is quite a gadabout."

"Are you suggesting child molestation?"

"Only suggesting, Mr. Apoyan. I could be wrong."

And possibly right. "Thanks again," I said.

A troubled relationship is what Mrs. Bishop had called it. Did she know whereof she spoke? Mothers are often the last to know.

Ismet Bey phoned half an hour later to tell me he had located a three-by-five Kerman owned by a local dealer and had brought it to his shop. Could I drop in this afternoon?

I told him I could and would.

And now what? How much did I know about antique Kermans? Uncle Vartan would remember the rug he had sold, but he sure as hell wouldn't walk into the shop of Ismet Bey.

Maybe Mrs. Bishop? She could pose as my wife. I phoned her unlisted number. A woman answered, probably a servant. Mrs. Bishop, she told me, was shopping and wouldn't be home until six o'clock.

I did know a few things about rugs. I had worked for Uncle Vartan on Saturdays and during vacations when I was at UCLA.

I took the photograph of Janice with me and drove out to Santa Monica. Bey's store, like the building Vartan and I shared, was a converted house on Pico Boulevard, old and sagging. I parked in the three-car graveled parking lot next to his panel truck.

The interior was dim and musty. Mrs. Bey was not in sight. The fat rump of a broad, short, and bald man greeted me as I came in. He was bending over, piling some small rugs on the floor.

He rose and turned to face me. He had an olive complexion, big brown eyes, and the oily smile of a used-car salesman. "Mr. Stein?" he asked.

I nodded.

"This way, please," he said, and led me to the rear of the store. The rug was on a display rack, a pale tan creation, sadly thin and about as tightly woven as a fisherman's net.

"Mr. Bey," I said, "that is not a Kerman."

"Really? What is it, then?"

"It looks like an Ispahan to me, a cheap Ispahan."

He continued to smile. "It was only a test."

"I'm not following you. A test for what?"

He shrugged. "There have been some rumors around town. Some rumors about a very rare and expensive three-by-five Kerman that has been stolen. I thought you may have heard them."

What a cutie. "I haven't heard them," I said. And added, "But, of course, I don't have your contacts."

"I'm sure you don't. Maybe you should have. How much did you plan to spend on this rug you want, Mr. Stein?"

"Not as much as the rug you described would cost

me. But I have a rich friend who might be interested. He is not quite as—as ethical as I try to be."

"Perhaps that is why he is rich. All I can offer now is the hope that this rug will find its way to me. Could I have the name of your friend?"

I shook my head. "If the rug finds its way to you, phone me. I'll have him come here. I don't want to be involved."

"You won't need to be," he assured me. "And I'll see that you are recompensed. You were right about this rug. It is an Ispahan. If you have some friends who are not rich, I hope you will mention my name to them."

That would be the day. "I will," I said.

I drove to Arden from there, and the boss was in his office. I told him about my dialogue with Bey and suggested they keep an eye on his place. I pointed out that they could make some brownie points with the Santa Monica Police Department.

"Thank you, loyal ex-employee. We'll do that."

"In return, you might make some copies of this photograph and pass them out among the boys. She is a runaway girl who was last seen here on your beach."

"You've got a case already?"

"With my reputation, why not?"

"Is there some connection between the missing girl and the rug?"

"That, as you are well aware, would be privileged information."

"Dear God," he said, "the kid's turned honest! Wait here."

He went out to the copier and came back about five minutes later. He handed me the photo and a check for the two days I had worked for him last week and wished me well. The nice thing about the last is that I knew he meant it.

From there to the beach. I sat in the shade near the refreshment stand with the forlorn hope that the skeleton man and the runaway girl might come this way again.

Two hours, one ice cream cone, and two Cokes later I drove back to Beverly Hills. Uncle Vartan was alone in the shop. I went in and related to him my dialogue with Ismet Bey.

"That tawdry Turk," he said, "that bush-leaguer! He doesn't cater to that class of trade. He's dreaming a pipe dream."

"How much do you think that rug would bring today?" I asked.

"Pierre, I do not want to discuss that rug. As I told you before, that was a sad day, maybe the saddest day of my life."

Saddest to him could be translated into English as least lucrative. A chauffeured Rolls-Royce pulled up in front of the shop and an elegantly dressed couple headed for his doorway. I held the door open for them and went up my stairs to sit again.

I typed it all down in chronological order, the history of my first case in my own office, from the time Mrs. Whitney Bishop had walked in to my uncle's refusal to talk about the Kerman.

There had to be a pattern in there somewhere to a discerning eye. Either my eye was not discerning or there was no pattern.

Cheryl had called it right; my larder was low. I heated a package of frozen peas and ate them with two baloney sandwiches and the cream cheese left over from lunch.

There was, as usual, nothing worth watching on the

tube. I went back to read again the magic of the man my father had introduced me to when I was in my formative years, the sadly funny short stories of William Saroyan.

Where would I go tomorrow? What avenues of investigation were still unexplored? Unless the unlikely happened, a call from Ismet Bey, all I had left was a probably fruitless repeat of yesterday's surveillance of the Santa Monica beach.

I went to bed at nine o'clock, but couldn't sleep. I got up, poured three ounces of Tennessee whiskey into a tumbler, added a cube of ice, and sat and sipped. It was eleven o'clock before I was tired enough to sleep.

I drank what was left of the milk in the morning and decided to have breakfast in Santa Monica. I didn't take my swimming trunks; the day was not that warm.

Scrambled eggs and pork sausages, orange juice, toast, and coffee at Barney's Breakfast Bar fortified me for the gray day ahead.

Only the hardy were populating the beach. The others would come out if the overcast went away. I sat again on the bench next to the refreshment stand and reread Ralph Ellison's *Invisible Man*. It had seemed appropriate reading for the occasion.

I had been doing a lot of sitting on this case. I could understand now why my boss at Arden had piles.

Ten o'clock passed. So did eleven. About fifteen minutes after that a tall, thin figure appeared in the murky air at the far end of the beach. It was a man and he was heading this way.

Closer and clearer he came. He was wearing khaki trousers, a red-and-tan-checked flannel shirt, and a red nylon windbreaker. He nodded and smiled as he passed me. He bought a Coke at the stand and sat down at the other end of the bench.

I laid down my book.

"Ralph Ellison?" he said. "I had no idea he was still in print."

He was thin, he was haggard, and his eyes were dull. But skeleton had been too harsh a word. "He probably isn't," I said. "This is an old Signet paperback reprint. My father gave it to me when I was still in high school."

"I see. We picked a bad day for sun, didn't we?"

"That's not why I'm here," I told him. "I'm looking for a girl, a runaway girl. Do you come here often?"

He nodded. "Quite often."

I handed him the photograph of Janice. "Have you ever seen her here?"

He took a pair of wire-rimmed glasses from his shirt pocket and put them on to study the picture. "Oh, yes," he said. "Was it yesterday? No—Wednesday." He took a deep breath. "There are so many of them who come here. I talked with her. She told me she had come down from Oxnard and didn't have the fare to go home. I bought her a malt and a hot dog. She told me the fare to Oxnard was eight dollars and some cents. I've forgotten the exact amount. Anyway, I gave her a ten-dollar bill and made her promise that she would use it for the fare home."

"Do you do that often?"

"Not often enough. When I can afford it."

"She's not from Oxnard," I told him. "She's from Beverly Hills."

He stared at me. "She couldn't be! She was wearing a pair of patched jeans and a cheap, flimsy T-shirt."

"She's from Beverly Hills," I repeated. "Her parents are rich."

He smiled. "That little liar! She conned me. And what a sweet young thing she was."

"I hope 'was' isn't the definitive word," I said.

He closed his eyes and took another deep breath. He opened them and stared out at the sea.

I handed him my card. "If you see her again, would you phone me?"

"Of course. My name is Gerald Hopkins. I live at the Uphan Hotel. It's a—a place for what are currently called senior citizens."

"I know the place," I told him. "Let's hold our thumbs."

"Dear God, yes!" he said.

From there I drove to the store of the tawdry Turk. He was not there but his wife was, a short, thin, and dark-skinned woman. I told her my name.

She nodded. "Ismet told me you were here yesterday." Her smile was sad. "That man and his dreams! What cock-and-bull story did he tell you?"

"Some of it made sense. He tried to sell me an Ispahan."

"He didn't tell *me* that!"

"He also told me about some rumors he heard."

"Oh, yes! Rumors he has. Customers is what we need. Tell me, Mr. Stein, how can a man get so fat on rumors?"

"He's probably married to a good cook."

"*That* he is. Take my advice, and a grain of salt, when you listen to the rumors of my husband, Mr. Stein. He is a dreamer. It is the reason I married him. I, too, in my youth, was a dreamer. It is why we came to America many years ago."

Send these, the homeless, tempest-tost to me. I lift my lamp beside the golden door. . . .

I smiled at her. "Keep the faith!" I went out.

My next stop was the bank, where I deposited the checks from Mrs. Bishop and Arden and cashed a check for two hundred dollars.

From there to Vons in Santa Monica, where I stocked up on groceries, meat, and booze. Grocery markups in Beverly Hills my mother had warned me, were absurd. Only the vulgar rich could afford them.

Mrs. Bey might believe that all the rumors her husband heard were bogus. But the rumor he had voiced to me was too close to the truth to qualify as bogus. It was logical to assume that there were shenanigans he indulged in in the practice of his trade that he would not reveal to her. To a man of his ilk the golden door meant gold, and he was still looking for the door.

I put the groceries away when I got home and went out to check the answering machine. Zilch. I typed the happenings of the morning into the record. Nothing had changed; no pattern showed.

There was a remote chance that Bey might learn where the rug was now. That was what I was being paid to find. But, as I had told Les Denton, the girl was my major concern.

It wasn't likely that she was staying at the home of any of her classmates. Their parents certainly would have phoned Mrs. Bishop by now if she hadn't phoned them.

Which reminded me that I had something to report. I phoned the Bishop house and the lady was home. I told her Janice had been seen on the Santa Monica beach on Wednesday and that a man there had told me this morning that he had talked with her. She had lied to him, telling him that she lived in Oxnard.

"She's very adept at lying. Did you learn anything else?"

"Well, there was a rug dealer in Santa Monica who told me he had heard rumors about a three-by-five Kerman that had been stolen. I have no idea where he heard them."

"There could be a number of sources. My husband

has been asking several dealers we know if they have seen it. And, of course, many of my friends know about the loss."

"Isn't it possible they might inform the police?"

"Not if they want to remain my friends. And the dealers, too, have been warned. If Janice has been seen on the Santa Monica beach, the rug could also be in the area. I think that is where you should concentrate your search."

It was warm and the weatherman had promised us sunshine for tomorrow. Cheryl and I could spend a day on the beach at Mrs. Bishop's expense.

"I agree with you completely," I said.

I phoned her apartment and Cheryl was there. I asked her if she'd like to spend a day on the beach with me tomorrow.

"I'd love it!"

I told her about the groceries I had bought and asked if she'd like to come and I'd cook a dinner for us tonight.

"Petroff, I can't! We're going to the symphony concert at the pavilion tonight."

"Who is *we*?"

"My roommates and I. Who else? Would you like to interrogate one of them?"

"Of course not! Save the program for me so I can see what I missed."

"I sure as hell will, you suspicious bastard. What time tomorrow?"

"Around ten."

"I'll be waiting."

I made myself a martini before dinner and then grilled a big T-bone steak and had it with frozen creamed asparagus and shoestring potatoes (heated, natch) and finished it off with lemon sherbet and coffee.

I had left *Invisible Man* in the car. I reread my favorite novel, *The Great Gatsby,* after dinner, along with a few ounces of brandy.

And then to my lonely bed. All the characters I had met since Wednesday afternoon kept running through my mind. All the chasing I had done had netted me nothing of substance. Credit investigations were so much cleaner and easier. But, like my Uncle Vartan, I had never felt comfortable working under a boss.

Cheryl was waiting outside her apartment building next morning when I pulled up a little after ten. She climbed into the car and handed me a program.

"Put it away," I said. "I was only kidding last night."

"Like hell you were!" She put it in the glove compartment. "And how was your evening?"

"Lonely. I talked with the man Denton's friend saw with Janice on the beach. She told him she had come down from Oxnard. He gave her the bus fare to go back."

"To Oxnard? Why would anybody want to go back to *Oxnard?*"

"She claimed she lived there. Don't ask me why."

"Maybe the man lied."

"Why would he?"

"Either he lied or she lied. It's fifty-fifty, isn't it?"

"Cheryl, he had no reason to lie. He told me the whole story and he has helped other kids to go home again. He gave me his name and address. Mrs. Bishop told me yesterday afternoon that Janice was—she called her an adept liar."

"And she is a creep, according to Les. Maybe Janice had reason to lie to the old bag."

"A creep she is. A bag she ain't. Tell me, what are you wearing under that simple but undoubtedly expensive charcoal denim dress?"

"My swimsuit, of course. Don't get horny. It's too early in the day for that."

It was, unfortunately, a great day for the beach; the place was jammed. They flood in from the San Fernando Valley and Hollywood and Culver City and greater Los Angeles on the warm days. Very few of them come from Beverly Hills. Most of those people have their own private swimming pools. Maybe all of them.

We laughed and splashed and swam and built a sand castle, back to the days of our adolescence. We forgot for a while the missing Janice Bishop and the antique Kerman.

After the fun part we walked from end to end on the beach, scanning the crowd, earning my pay, hoping to find the girl.

No luck.

Cheryl said, "I'll make you that dinner tonight, if you want me to."

"I want you to."

"We may as well go right to your place," she said. "You can drop me off at the apartment tomorrow when you go to the weekly meeting of the clan. It won't be out of your way."

"Sound thinking," I agreed.

What she made for us was a soufflé, an entree soufflé, not a dessert soufflé. But it was light enough to rest easily on top of the garbage we had consumed at the beach.

The garbage on the tube, we both agreed, would demean our day. We went to bed early.

The overcast was back in the morning, almost a fog. We ate a hearty breakfast to replace the energy we had lost in the night.

I dropped her off at her apartment a little after one o'clock, and was the first to arrive at my parents' house. Adele was the second. She had brought her friend with her, Salvatore Martino, known in the trade as Ronnie Egan.

It was possible, I reasoned, that I could be as wrong about him as Mrs. Whitney Bishop had been about Leslie Denton. I suggested to him that we take a couple of beers out to the patio while my mother and Adele fussed around in the kitchen.

We yacked about this and that, mostly sports, and then he said, "I saw three of your amateur fights and both your pro fights. How come you quit after that?"

"If you saw my pro fights, you should understand why."

"Jesus, man, you were *way* overmatched! You were jobbed. I'll bet Sam made a bundle on both of those fights."

Sam Batisto had been my manager. I said, "I'm not following you. You mean you think Sam is a crook?"

He nodded. "And a double-crossing sleazeball. Hell, he's got Mafia cousins. He'd sell out his mother if the price was right."

That son of a bitch . . .

"Well, what the hell," he went on, "maybe the bastard did you a favor. That's a nasty, ugly game, and people are beginning to realize it. Have you noticed how many big bouts are staged in Vegas?"

"I've noticed." I changed the subject. "How did you make out with the commercial?"

"Great! My agent worked Adele into it. And the producer promised both of us more work. We're going to make it, Adele and I. But we can't get married until we do. You understand that, don't you?"

"Very well," I assured him. "Welcome to the clan."

My mother had gone Armenian this Sunday, chicken and pilaf. One of Sarkis's boys hadn't been able to attend; Salvatore took his place at the poker session.

That was a red-letter day! Salvatore was the big winner. And for the first time in history Mom was the big loser. I would like to say she took it graciously, but she didn't. We are a competitive clan.

"Nice guy," I said, when Adele and he had left.

She sniffed. "When he marries Adele, *then* he might be a nice guy."

"He told me they're going to get married as soon as they can afford to."

"We'll see," he said. "He could be another Vartan."

The day had stayed misty; the traffic on Sunset Boulevard was slow. I dawdled along, thinking back on the past few days, trying to find the key to the puzzle of the missing girl and the stolen Kerman. The key was the key; who had the key to the house and why had only the rug been stolen?

One thing was certain, the burglar knew the value of antique oriental rugs. But how would he know that particular rug was in the home of Whitney Bishop?

It was a restless night, filled with dreams I don't remember now. I tossed and turned and went to the toilet twice. A little after six o'clock I realized sleep was out of the question. I put the coffee on to perc and went down the steps to pick up the morning *Times*.

The story was on page one. Whitney Bishop, founder and senior partner of the brokerage firm of Bishop, Hope, and Nystrom, had been found dead in a deserted Brentwood service station. A local realtor had discovered the body when he had brought a potential buyer to the station on Sunday morning. Bishop had been stabbed to death. A loaded but unfired .32 caliber revolver had been found near the body.

According to his wife, Bishop had been nervous and irritable on Friday night. His secretary told the police that he had received a phone call on Friday afternoon and appeared agitated. On Saturday night, he had told his wife he was going to a board meeting at the Beverly Hills Country Club. When he hadn't come home by midnight, Mrs. Bishop had phoned the club. The club was closed; receiving no answer there, she had phoned the police.

When questioned about the revolver, she had stated that she remembered he had once owned a small-caliber pistol but she was almost sure it had been lost or stolen years ago.

A murdered husband. . . . And there was no mention in the piece about a missing daughter or a stolen rug. Considering how many of her friends knew about both, that was bound to come out.

When it did I could be in deep trouble for withholding information about the rug and the girl. But so could she for the same reason. And spreading those stories to the media could alert and scare off any seasoned burglar who had been looking forward to a buy-back deal. That was the slim hope I tried to hang on to.

I put the record of my involvement in the case under the mattress in my bedroom. I showered and shaved and put on my most conservative suit after breakfast and sat in my office chair, waiting for the police to arrive.

They didn't.

I thought back to all the people I had questioned in the past week. And then I realized there was one I hadn't.

I went down the stairs and asked Uncle Vartan if he had heard the sad news.

He nodded and yawned. He had heard it on the tube

last night, he told me. I had the feeling that he would not mourn the death of Whitney Bishop.

"You told me you went with Mrs. Bishop when she was between husbands. Who was her first?"

"A man named Duane Pressville, a former customer of mine."

"Do you have his address?"

"Not anymore. It has been years since I've seen him. What is this all about, Pierre?"

"I was thinking that it was possible he still had the key to the house they shared and would know where the alarm turnoff switch was hidden."

He stared at me. "And you think he stole the rug? That's crazy, Pierre! He was a very sharp buyer but completely honest." He paused. "And now you are thinking that he might be a murderer?"

"The murder and the rug might not be connected, " I pointed out. "Tell me, is he the man who bought the Kerman from you?"

"Yes," he said irritably. "And that's enough of this nonsense! I have work to do this morning, Pierre."

"Sorry," I said, and went up the stairs to look up Duane Pressville in the phone book. There were several Pressvilles in the book but only one Duane. His address was 332 Adonis Court.

I knew the street, a short dead-ender that led off San Vicente Boulevard. Into the Camaro, back on the hunt.

Adonis Court was an ancient neighborhood of small houses. It had resisted the influx of demolitions that had invaded the area when land prices soared. These were the older residents who had no serious economic pressures that would force them to sell out.

332 was a small frame house with a shingled roof and a small low porch in front of the door.

I went up to the porch and turned the old-fashioned crank that rang the bell inside the house.

The man who opened the door was tall and thin and haggard, the same man who had called himself Gerald Hopkins on the beach.

He smiled. "Mr. Apoyan! What brings you to my door?"

"I'm looking for a rug," I said. "An antique Kerman."

He frowned. "Did Victoria send you here?"

"Who is Victoria?"

"My former wife. What vindictive crusade is she on now? No matter what she might have told you, I bought that rug with my own money. It was *my* rug, until the divorce settlement."

"Why," I asked, "did you lie to me on the beach?"

He looked at me and past me. He sighed and said, "Come in."

The door opened directly into the living room. It was a room about fourteen feet wide and eighteen feet long. It was almost completely covered by a dark red oriental rug. It looked like a Bokhara to me.

The furniture was mostly dark mahogany, brightly polished, upholstered in well-worn velour.

"Sit down," he said.

I sat in an armchair, he on the sofa.

"Have you ever heard of Maksoud of Kashan?" he asked.

"I think so. Wasn't he a famous oriental rug weaver?"

He nodded. "The finest in all of Persia, now called Iran. But in his entire career, with all the associates he had working under him, he wove his name into only two of his rugs. One of them is in the British Museum. The other is the small Kerman I bought from your uncle. I remember now—you worked in his store on Saturdays, didn't you?"

I nodded.

"You weren't in the store that day this—this *ped-dler* brought in the Kerman. It was filthy! But far from being worn out. My eyes must be sharper than your uncle's. I saw the signature in the corner. I made the mistake of overplaying my hand; I offered him a thousand dollars for it, much more than it appeared to be worth. That must have made him suspicious. We dickered. When I finally offered him three thousand dollars he sold it to me."

"And I suppose he has resented you ever since that day."

He shrugged. "Probably. To tell you the truth, after he learned about the history of the rug I was ashamed to go back to the store."

"To tell the truth once again," I said, "where is your daughter? Where is Janice?"

"She is well and safe and far from here. She is back with her real parents, the parents who were too poor to keep her when she was born. I finally located them."

"You wouldn't want to tell me their name?"

"Not you, or anybody else. Not with the legal clout Victoria can afford. Do you want Janice to go back to that woman she complained to when her third father tried to molest her, that woman who called her a liar? I did some research on Bishop, too. He was fired by a Chicago brokerage firm for churning. He had one charge of child molestation dropped for insufficient evidence there. So he came out here and married money and started his own firm."

"And was stabbed to death Saturday night not far from here."

"I heard that on the radio this morning." His smile was cynical. "Are you going to the funeral?"

I shook my head. "According to the morning paper

he must have been carrying a gun. But he didn't fire it."

"The news report on this morning's radio station explained that," he told me. "The safety catch was on."

"I didn't hear it. What do you think that Kerman would bring today?"

"Fifty thousand, a hundred thousand, whatever the buyer would pay." He studied me. "Are you suggesting that the murder and the rug are connected?"

"You know I am. My theory is that Bishop got the call from the burglar on Friday and decided not to buy the rug, but to shoot the burglar."

"An interesting theory. Is there more to it?"

"Yes. The burglar then stabbed him—and found another buyer. Bishop might have reason other than penuriousness. He might have known the burglar knew his history."

He said wearily, "You're zeroing in, aren't you? You're beginning to sound like a detective."

"I am. A private investigator. I just opened my own office over uncle Vartan's store."

"You should have told me that when you came."

"You must have guessed that I was an investigator when we met on the beach. Why else would you have lied?"

He didn't answer.

"If Janice's real parents are still poor," I said, "fifty or a hundred thousand dollars should help to alleviate it."

He nodded. "If the burglar has found the right buyer. It should certainly help to send her to a first-rate college. And now I'm getting tired. It's time for my nap. I have leukemia, Pierre. My doctor has told me he doesn't know how many days I have before I sleep the big sleep. I know what you are thinking, and it could be true. I'm sure you are honor bound to take what I have told you to the police. I promise I will bear you no malice if you do. But you had better hurry."

"There is no need to hurry," I said. "Thank you for your cooperation, Mr. Pressville."

"And thank you for your courtesy," he said. "Give my regards to Vartan."

I didn't give his regards to Uncle Vartan. I didn't even tell him I had talked with his former customer. I had some thinking to do.

For three days I thought and wondered when the police would call. They never came. Mrs. Bishop sent me a check for the balance of my investigation along with an acerbic note that informed me she would certainly tell her many friends how unsuccessful I had been in searching for both her rug and her daughter.

I had no need to continue thinking on the fourth day. Duane Pressville was found dead in his house on Adonis Court by a concerned neighbor. I burned the records of that maiden quest.

DREAM HOUSE
M. R. HENDERSON

Just minutes from the honky-tonk urban charms of Sunset Boulevard is the lovely residential area known as the Hollywood Hills. With its lush vegetation, narrow, winding streets, cul-de-sacs, soft, refracted light, and charming views of the city below, the area resembles an Italian hill town. In the thirties and forties its quiet atmosphere lured many movie stars to build homes there. In recent times, however, one is more likely to see screenwriters and other young professionals as they perform the morning and evening California ritual known as "jogging." In this tale by M. R. Henderson we meet a young decorator named Ann who finds her "Dream House" in the Hills. Little does she know that her dream-house door opens onto a nightmare.

* * *

HIS breath made small, harsh sounds in the cool morning air. He wished he had gloves. His fingertips tingled as he flexed his hands. He didn't like damp weather. It was spring—it was supposed to be warm, not foggy and cold. He always thought of Los Angeles as warm sunshine, beach weather.

Had he been away that long or had he forgotten? Maybe he just never noticed before. His memories were of wonderful, hot, lazy days on the beach with Mara. He smiled, thinking of her. Mara loved the sun. Summer was her favorite season. They used to go to the beach often. They stretched out on a blanket on the hot sand, soaking up rays. When he closed his eyes, he could still feel Mara's smooth, bronzed skin under his palm as he spread oil on her back and legs.

He'd been searching for her since he got back. He'd gone to her house, but a fat, bald real estate agent told him he'd never heard of Mara De Long. The house had been on the market for months and had finally gone into escrow. The new owner would be moving in soon.

He didn't believe Mara had sold the house. It was such a perfect house for her, with floor-to-ceiling glass that was a showcase to display her beauty to the world. On a steep hillside near the summit of one of the dozens of twisting streets that climb into the Hollywood Hills from Sunset Boulevard, Mara's house reigned over a small canyon like a monarch, with Hollywood and Beverly Hills kneeling at her feet. Looking down from the balcony at night, lights twinkled like a procession of worshipers carrying candles in homage to their goddess. He didn't believe Mara would give up the house. He was sure the real estate man was lying. For days, he parked his car at various places along the road where he could watch the house through binoculars. For a long time it looked empty, but then one day a moving van pulled up and he watched two men carry furniture into the house.

Even then he didn't believe she was gone. She wouldn't move far, he was sure of that. She loved the neighborhood, its privacy and its history of old-time stars who'd lived there back in the thirties and forties. She'd never move away. So he kept his vigil until it was finally rewarded.

She was here. He'd seen her, up on the road that branched across the summit of the hill. The sight of her took his breath away. He'd been looking so long, he'd begun to wonder if he'd ever find her. Then suddenly, she was there. It was early morning. He'd been working the graveyard shift as dishwasher at the Starlight Club on Sunset Strip. It was a dumb, nothing kind of job, but it wasn't far from Mara's neighborhood, and it left his days free. He slept in snatches and spent every waking minute looking for Mara. Each day he drove up the steep road, slowing when he came to the hairpin curve that gave him his first glimpse of her house across the canyon, driving at a crawl around the long, U-shaped curve and past the house, then finishing the snaking climb to the road across the flat summit above. Often he stopped on the upper curves to look back at the house through the binoculars in the hope of seeing her. No matter what the fat real estate agent said, he would never believe Mara was gone.

One morning he made the drive in the predawn fog, not really expecting Mara to be out that early but too restless to sleep if he went back to his tiny furnished room. Mara hated early morning. She liked to sleep late, warm and cuddly, pressed against him. . . . But suddenly, there she was, jogging along in the wild purple sweatsuit he'd bought her for Christmas. It was only a glimpse, but there was no mistaking the lustrous blond hair caught up in a ponytail that bounced on her shoulder, no mistaking the slender figure, or her graceful stride that made running look so easy. He was still on the long curve approaching the top of the hill when he caught a glimpse of her on the flat stretch of the road above him. For a moment, he was too stunned to react.

When he finally gunned the car up the grade and maneuvered along the narrow road to the spot where he'd seen her, she was gone. He drove on past the bend where the road began a steep decline on the other side of the hill, then down more than a mile before he realized that somehow he had missed her. He turned around in a driveway and went back, taking time to explore two side streets that cut off the main road, but he didn't find her. If only he'd been quicker!

That night he quit his dishwashing job at the Starlite. He had enough money to last awhile, and he could always get another job when it ran out. It was much more important to find Mara. To find her and beg her to forgive him. He had never meant to make her angry, never meant to hurt her. He'd do anything if only she forgave him.

For a week, every morning he drove up the hill at dawn to look for her. And waited, sometimes until long after the neighborhood was stirring. He was careful not to park the car in the same spot each day. This was a neighborhood where suspicious activities alerted lurking Dobermans or were quickly reported to private security companies. This morning he parked half a mile down on the other side of the summit. Dressed in a blue jogging suit and Nikes, he loped uphill to the long exposed stretch of road that crossed the ridge, then slowed to a walk as he listened to the morning over the rasp of his own breathing. Only an occasional twitter of a bird broke the stillness. As he did every morning, he followed the street until it reached an empty lot surrounded by a four-foot wall. The gate had rusted off its hinges, and the concrete slab for the house that had never been built was cracked and choked with weeds. Thickets of bougainvillea that had been planted along the wall drooped over the road untended. Beyond the lot, the summit road began to drop downhill in a sweeping curve.

Mara would come today. He felt it inside—a knowing, a certainty that erased the confusion and doubts that sometimes clouded his mind. She would come today. He could count on it. He could always count on her.

She'd be surprised to see him at first. But all he needed was a chance to talk to her. He would beg her to forgive him so they could start over again. And she would. They'd make up, and everything would be the way it used to be. They'd go to the beach . . . have long nights together . . . they could go back to—

He cocked his head as he heard the faint, steady thump of running shoes hitting the asphalt. Quickly he pressed into the thicket, ignoring the spiny barbs of the bougainvillea that had grown wild. He curled and uncurled his toes inside the running shoes as his sweat began to cool. Hunching his shoulders, he flexed his hands nervously.

He caught a glimpse of motion, then a flash of purple. The purple jogging suit. An outrageous, bold color that demanded attention, like a brightly plumed bird flitting through the trees. In the faint predawn light, it looked almost black against her golden hair.

Thump . . . thump . . . thump . . . thump . . . Through the hazy screen of green and fuchsia, he had a clear view of the woman in purple. His breath quickened as he watched the rhythmic bounce of her breasts under the purple sweatshirt. His palms were wet and he clenched his fists as she came around the curve and headed toward him.

The steady rhythmic flap of her running shoes called his name: *Nick . . . Nick . . .* His hammering heartbeat pulsed loudly in his temples. When she was almost to him, he stepped out in front of her. She let out an astonished explosion of breath and tried to dodge past him, but the downhill grade had already given her too much momentum. She crashed into his outstretched arms. He grabbed her and held her close.

"Mara—"

Breathing hard, she tried to pull away from him, but he gripped her more tightly. She gulped air and clawed at his arms, trying to pry them loose. With a burst of effort, she twisted sideways suddenly and at the same time slammed her elbow into his middle. Air whooshed from his lungs, and, taken by surprise, Nick almost lost his grip. But before she could slip free, he clamped his hands around her throat. When she kicked and clawed, he brought his knee up sharply into her middle. She made a funny gurgling sound as her knees buckled, and her weight became heavy under his squeezing hands. Slowly, she went limp.

Nick stood supporting her weight, his hands still clenched around her throat, studying the features he had once thought beautiful. Her eyes were brown. He remembered them as blue. And her hair wasn't golden at all. It was a muddy shade streaked with gray. Most of all, her face wasn't pretty anymore. It was twisted and ugly. He realized it wasn't Mara at all. It was someone pretending to be her.

A burst of air escaped from his lungs. He'd forgotten about the cold until he took his hands away from her warm flesh. He stared at the crumpled figure in the purple jogging suit. Of course it wasn't Mara, he could see that now. How had he made such a mistake? His head ached and pain pressed behind his eyes.

The dream shimmered like a reflection in a pond. She was walking along a hot, dusty road, but she was cold. In the distance, a low rumbling sound rolled through the canyon, and she glanced upward in search of storm clouds. But the sky was cloudless and parched under the molten disk of sun. She shivered and hugged her arms around her body, riveting her gaze on the dust-covered, cracked asphalt. One step at a time. When she reached the house she would be safe.

The rumbling noise grew louder, and she tried to block it out by counting her footsteps on the pavement. One . . . two . . . A shadow fell across her path. Her glance shot up, and she saw the man blocking her way. He stood in the middle of the road, arms outstretched, fingers grasping. She couldn't see his face, only his gaping mouth screaming soundlessly. Terrified, she tried to run, but the walls of the canyon closed around her, trapping her and covering her in shadows. Cold sweat bathed her as the rumbling sound became an ominous roar, and the canyon walls began to undulate like a huge wave, wavering, then slowly collapsing toward her, breaking apart in slow motion to define individual bits of rock and grains of sand. Panicked now, she ran from the choking dust that enveloped her. Blinded, she sprawled headlong on the rough ground as sand poured over her, covering her as it formed her tomb.

Ann woke with a start. The blanket was tangled around her, and she struggled wildly. When it finally fell away, she shivered with the sudden chill of the cold room. For a moment, she was tempted to crawl back under the covers until their warmth banished the remnants of the nightmare, but even as she considered the idea, the alarm clock buzzed softly. Reaching to shut it off, Ann saw the slash of gray foggy morning beyond the sliding glass doors where the drapes didn't quite meet. She shivered, reminded of the dream that had wakened her.

It was the second time she'd had the dream. That in itself was frightening. She couldn't recall ever having dreamed the same dream, especially a terrifying one like this one. The first time she had it the night she moved into the new house, she chalked it up to exhaustion. After years of apartment living, she was so eager to settle in her own place, she'd pushed herself beyond the limits of her normal energy: unpacking her dishes and crystal and rewashing everything before arranging the kitchen cupboards, neatly putting away her clothes in closets and dressers so she didn't have to hunt for things, and most important—and exhausting—organizing the studio.

It was the studio that had cinched her decision to buy the property. She'd been looking at houses off and on for a year. She was desperate to escape the apartment she had outgrown as her decorating business expanded, but she refused to settle for anything ordinary simply because it gave her more space. She'd seen several places that were great but too far out of the price range she could afford. She told real estate agents how high she was willing to go, but they persisted in showing her more expensive properties. Show the highest-priced merchandise first; you can always come down. Selling houses wasn't any different from the way most decorators sold draperies and carpeting. Ann, however, prided herself on always considering the client's preferences first.

The brisk, snappy, no-nonsense woman from a small real estate office on Sunset Boulevard had been the first one who really listened to what Ann was saying. She didn't waste time with higher-priced houses or affordable dark, cavelike dwellings tucked in obscure canyons amid the Hollywood Hills. She had one listing that met Ann's needs: a light, airy hillside house with one large bedroom, one and a half baths, and an enclosed inside patio that had been converted to a studio/den by the former owner. It had a flagstone floor, greenhouse windows overlooking the canyon, and a skylighted roof. The house was in good condition even though it had stood empty for two years while it was tied up in the lengthy settlement of the former owner's estate. Did Ms. Laurie want to look at it?

Ann fell in love with the house at first sight. It was as if all the house hunting had been a process of elimination, clearly defining the impossible places in order to prepare her for the reward of perfection. She wandered through the rooms, mentally defining new color schemes, window treatments, placement of furniture. The real estate agent wisely left her to her thoughts and inspection. When Ann finally tore herself away with difficulty, she knew she couldn't let this one get away. She returned with the agent to the real estate office and signed a purchase agreement immediately.

From the first day, it was as if the house had been built for her, or at least that it had gotten tied up by legal red tape until she came along. Now after three weeks, she was still delighted with everything about it. She'd settled to living and working comfortably within its walls that were in no way confining. The sliding glass doors of the bedroom and living room and the greenhouse windows of the studio gave her a vista of the canyon falling away until it spilled into Hollywood and Beverly Hills. In the crystalline blue of smogless days, she could see the ocean in the distance and the hazy, dark hump of Catalina Island twenty-five miles offshore. Built on stilts in the years before fire regulations made it mandatory to close in "shelf" houses, the house overhung the canyon like a spider clinging to a web. Fronting the winding road that climbed the hill was a double carport and a small patio enclosed by a seven-foot-high redwood fence and gate. Ann had the house repainted from bright yellow to a soft green. Except for the front door, the portion of the house facing the outside patio was four-by-eight-foot panels of glass, with another sliding door that opened to the living room. If the house had been twice its size, it couldn't have been more spacious.

Whatever the studio had been used for previously, it was perfect for Ann's decorating business. She left the greenhouse windows and the skylight roof uncovered to take advantage of the working light all day. She arranged plants to soften the huge expanse of glass and designed a small conversation area in one corner where she could talk with clients. She installed comfortable chairs, a low table, and a lamp that cast soft light. A colorful Navajo rug coordinated the grouping. The rest of the flagstone she left uncovered. Her desk and work table occupied most of the space, and she used a large circle of Lucite atop decorative sawhorses for a side table to hold pieces of fabric, pictures, or art objects around which she was working.

Rubbing her arms, Ann threw aside the blanket and got up. She pulled open the drapes and saw the fog pressing against the city. It was unusual weather for

April, but a tropical storm off the coast of Baja had created the phenomenon the past few mornings. Close to the top of the hill, the house seemed to be above the fog layer, but she knew it was an illusion of light and distance. The sky was leaden, but in a few hours the fog would be blown away and the day would turn warm.

Shivering, she dressed quickly in a warm jogging suit, heavy socks, and running shoes. The route of her morning run was another bonus that had come with the house. It was a mile to the top of the hill and the flat stretch of road that ran along the summit. Each day she started out at a brisk walk, then hit her running stride across the flat and down the slight grade at the far end for a half mile before swinging around a cul-de-sac for the return lap. In all, it was a little over four miles and took an hour. A refreshing shower, breakfast, and she was ready for the day by eight. This morning she would finish the room layouts and decide how she was going to work around the bold colors Mrs. Hackmer, a new client, had chosen.

The house was still swathed in semidarkness, but Ann didn't turn on any lights as she went down the hall to the kitchen, where she poured herself a glass of orange juice, downed it, then pocketed her house-keys and let herself out. In the patio she took time for a quick series of stretches and knee-bends before she unlocked the gate and started up the road.

As she approached the summit, Ann quickened her pace to a steady jog. Papery eucalyptuses sighed softly in the breeze, and tendrils of fog swirled over the hill-top to be absorbed by the clouds. Ann found brisk mornings exhilarating and conducive to creative thinking. She had been searching for days for a way to mute the bold colors that were too stark for the house she was doing. Now the answer was all around her. Gray, the delicate mauve-gray of the fog. She could use it in large areas which could then be highlighted with Mrs. Hackmer's brilliant hues. Ann's taste ran more to pastels and Impressionists, but she had a talent for working within any client's demands.

The rhythmic slap of her Adidas echoed faintly between the houses that flanked most of the summit road. The first homes had been built along the ridge during the 1920s and 1930s by motion picture stars who craved privacy. The hilltop aeries were designed to satisfy the whims of each owner: swimming pools, saunas, screening rooms, bedrooms with mirrored ceilings and walls; English Tudor, Hollywood modern, quaint cottage, or garish opulence. Their isolated privacy had eventually been usurped by Southern California's real estate boom following World War II, and now other houses shouldered close like eager fans hoping to brush the stars. But the stories lived on, gossiped avidly or mentioned in passing by real estate agents who wanted to impress prospective buyers, but never completely forgotten. Mary Miles Minter . . . Joan Blondell . . . Dick Powell . . . Errol Flynn . . . Frank Sinatra . . . replaced in more recent years by ordinary people from many walks of life, some connected to the glamorous business that gave the Hollywood Hills their start, others ordinary people in ordinary jobs.

Ann knew a few of her "neighbors" by sight or to greet casually, but she'd had neither time nor inclination to socialize. And she'd lived in Los Angeles long enough to know that people who lived in the Hills still resented invasions of their privacy. That had not changed over the years.

She reached the bend of the road that marked the start of the downgrade. The bougainvillea that covered the stone wall around an astonishingly large lot that had never been developed caught Ann's attention. In the cool morning light, the flowers were the same shade of magenta as Mrs. Hackmer's swatch. It was dramatic against the soft gray morning. On the ground below the bush was another purple, slightly more red. It would be a perfect secondary color, Ann thought. Unconsciously, she stopped to study the new shade more closely. Yes, in the drapes. Reserve the deeper purple for accents where it wouldn't claim the eye totally. And bougainvillea prints on the walls to tie everything together.

Gazing at the splotch of reddish purple in the heavy, green-black shadows, she visualized the overall effect of the color scheme. Fascinated, she moved closer as if to fix the shades indelibly in her mind. She stared at what she had mistaken for a scrap of discarded cloth. It took several moments for her brain to register what her eyes saw.

In death, the woman's eyes stared in mute terror. The tongue protruding from her slack mouth was blue. One hand, the fingers curled as if begging alms, lay across the pale web her hair spun on the damp ground.

Ann began to scream.

Gradually he became aware of a sound. He cocked his head to listen. Someone running . . . footfalls slapping the path. He grabbed the limp figure under the arms and dragged it behind the tangled web of bougainvillea. Then he ran softly on the balls of his feet, skirting the shrubs and wild grass, until he came to the opening in the stone wall of the deserted property. Chest heaving, he darted behind it and crouched in its shadow. When the running steps came closer, he peered over the top of the wall.

A woman jogged steadily along the road, swinging

around the curve, her blond hair bouncing on the shoulders of her purple sweatsuit.

Mara—?

The woman hesitated, then stopped as she glanced at the thick stand of bougainvillea.

It *was* Mara. He could see her clearly. He stood and took a step toward her. Then without warning she began to scream. He jumped back as pain swelled in his head. Clamping his hands to his temples, he backed away, stumbling over tuffets of grass and hidden rocks, running through the empty lot, scrambling over the wall at the far end, and stumbling down the road. At a house with a high fence that came right to the edge of the street, he stopped to catch his breath. Somewhere above him, a window opened.

"What the hell is going on out there?"

"Don't you dare go out there, Stanley! Call the police—that's what they get paid for."

The window banged shut.

The panic of the nightmare engulfed Ann in a sweeping wave. Branches tipped with magenta blooms reached for her like arms, waving as they dislodged petals which fell on her like grains of sand. She struggled for breath to keep from being suffocated.

Someone grabbed her, pinning her flailing arms. Behind her, a voice said, "Oh my God—"

Ann moved jerkily as the man led her away from the gruesome thing under the bushes. A few yards down the road, he sat her on a low, broken section of the wall. Her chest felt raw and wounded, but the shock was beginning to fade. Ann took a quivering breath as she recognized the man kneeling in front of her. She occasionally saw him when she was jogging, but she'd never met him.

"Don't try to talk yet," he admonished when she opened her mouth. "The police will be here soon." He studied her face with concern, then spoke over his shoulder to the knot of people gathered near the bougainvillea. "Someone get her some coffee."

A woman wearing a robe and curlers in her gray hair broke away and hurried into a nearby house. A bearded young man in running shorts and a sweatshirt emblazoned *Hollywood* motioned the others back. "We'd better stay back. There might be evidence."

Murmuring, people moved to the opposite side of the road. The gray-haired woman returned with an insulated plastic mug of steaming coffee. She handed it to the man kneeling in front of Ann. He coaxed it into her hands.

"Drink some. It will help."

Ann's hands were shaking badly as she clasped the cup. She raised the steaming coffee close and inhaled its warm aroma. "She—she's dead, isn't she?" Her voice was barely audible.

The man said, "Yes."

Ann was relieved that he didn't lie or try to coddle her. The shock was passing, and she knew in a very short time she would have to face the horror of reality. He'd said the police were coming. She didn't have to ask the significance of that. The woman hadn't died accidentally or naturally. She'd been murdered. Ann had never seen a murder victim before, but she'd seen enough movies and read enough to know what a strangling victim looked like. Shaking, she sipped the coffee and closed her eyes to erase the picture of the dead woman's face. When she opened them, the man was peering at her.

She gave him a nervous smile. "I'm all right. Thanks."

"You had a hell of a shock."

"Was—is she someone—who lives—lived—" Ann shuddered at the thought of the dead woman being a neighbor, someone she might have seen or passed on the road. The sound of a siren drifted up the canyon and hung in the damp air. The people clustered across the road milled restlessly, and a dark-haired woman with a small white poodle on a red leash moved away rapidly, as if afraid of becoming involved. As the siren grew louder and a police car appeared, the others hung back, fascinated by the drama in their midst and too curious to leave. Murder. Something you read about in the newspaper, not something that happened in your neighborhood.

The next hour was a blur of activity and commotion. The first officers on the scene were soon followed by detectives, a crime-scene unit, and the coroner's van. The area was roped off with ribbons of yellow plastic and people were questioned, especially Ann, who could tell the detective only that she'd paused because she'd seen the splash of color. To the best of her knowledge, she'd never met or seen the woman before. Several other people, when questioned, knew where the woman lived, alone, and that her name was Sally Dunn.

Nick let himself into the dim apartment. The drapes were always drawn to screen the harsh light that made his head hurt. He was still breathing hard, although he'd stopped running more than an hour ago. It was the excitement of seeing Mara. Knowing she was so close.

He'd found her. He had really found her at last. The other woman was a mistake, or maybe a test to see if he remembered. Oh, Mara, I remember. How could I forget?

He scowled and rubbed his temple, remembering the screaming that had frightened him off before he had a chance to talk to Mara. Pain tightened in a band around his skull, and he began to pace the length of the small room, veering past the television set on its wobbly cart, circling the shabby furniture without seeing it. He'd run from Mara's screams, but he forced himself to go back when people began coming out of houses to see what had happened. They would have noticed if he was the only one going the other way, so he melted into the crowd and went back. He began to shake all over when he saw the man with Mara. Much as he wanted to, he didn't punch the jerk and tell him to stay away from his girl. But neither did he take Mara in his arms and tell her he loved her. He couldn't do it with all those people around. Not that he'd mind, but Mara was too shy. Then when the sirens blared and the red light of the police car flashed so close to him, the ache in his head became unbearable, and he had to slip out of the crowd and make his way back to the car.

He interrupted his jerky, rhythmic stride to yank open the closet door. From the shelf, he lifted down a shoe box tied with purple cord. Cradling it in his arms, he carried it to the armchair near the TV. For a long time, he sat with the box on his knees, his fingers twisting and untwisting the ends of the purple cord. Finally he took a deep breath as if readying himself for a dive and untied the cord with trembling hands. He let his breath out slowly as he lifted the lid, feeling a different kind of excitement as Mara's photograph stared up at him. Beautiful, smiling Mara. Her sparkling eyes spoke to him silently. When he lifted the picture from atop the yellowing newspaper clippings and other objects in the box, the pain in his head began to ease and it was easier to breathe. He smiled at the blond woman in the glossy photograph. Now that he'd found her, his world would be right again. He and Mara would talk . . . and lie on the beach . . . be together the way they used to be. Now that he'd found her, they'd be together again. Always.

Caressing the picture with his fingertips, he leaned back and closed his eyes.

It seemed unreal that the city's life went on without the slightest concern for what had happened on the hill. When the police finished questioning Ann and let her go, she'd been relieved to put the murder out of her mind, or at least crowd it into a niche where it didn't interfere with her work. She finished one of the room layouts and met briefly with Mrs. Hackmer, who was enthusiastic about the sketches and gave Ann *carte blanche* on the project. She spent the afternoon at the Design Center searching for Art Nouveau tables in the precise shade of pink-lavender that the color scheme required. Only once when she held Mrs. Hackmer's swatch of printed cloth against a table did the image of the dead woman in the purple jogging suit superimpose itself. Ann had to steady herself and wait for the dizziness to pass.

On impulse, she went to La Cuchina for dinner alone. She considered calling someone but decided she preferred a quiet, solitary meal during which she wouldn't be drawn into conversation about the murder, which was now news on local radio and television stations. She hoped the crime would be solved quickly so it would fade from the news and her thoughts.

It was dark when she got home. The exposure which usually delighted her and gave the wonderful feeling of spaciousness now seemed indecent, and she drew all the drapes before she turned on the lights. Somewhere in the canyon below, a coyote yipped mournfully, and Ann shuddered. Feeling foolish, she checked every room of the house to satisfy herself she was alone, quite safe. Seeing her reflection in the full-length mirror on the bedroom door, she chided herself for being ridiculous, but she had to admit she felt better. Before she went to bed, she double-checked the locks on the doors and windows.

He came out of deep, black sleep abruptly. He'd set the alarm, but it hadn't rung yet. Squinting at the illuminated face of the cheap drugstore clock, he saw it was almost five-thirty. He sat up and pushed down the button so the alarm wouldn't ring, then lay back to listen to the faint early-morning sounds. It was a ritual he followed each morning, a test to be sure he was back in the city. Los Angeles had sounds all its own: the soft hum of tires on the pavement, the pulse of diesel engines, the whisper of palm fronds rustling in the breeze.

The worn carpet was cold under his bare feet. It was still dark outside, but a yellow haze from the streetlights seeped through the curtains. He shivered and rubbed the stubble on his chin as he crossed to the bathroom. He snapped the light switch and squinted in the glare of overhead fluorescent tube. He turned on the tap, then urinated in the toilet while he waited for the water to run hot. When it did, he washed his hands and face, then worked lather across his chin. He shaved slowly and carefully so he wouldn't nick himself and have to press toilet paper to his chin like some fifteen-year-old kid with his first razor.

When he finished, he left the bathroom door open so he didn't have to turn on another light. He dressed in the gray sweatsuit and running shoes. When he was ready, he checked his pockets methodically: keys, gloves, money for coffee . . . and this morning, an added item, a silver-handled penknife. Then from the bottom drawer of the dresser he got a small pair of binoculars. Satisfied, he let himself out of the shabby ground-floor apartment.

It was chilly again this morning. Fog hung under the parking-lot spotlight like a gray curtain, and he walked briskly to warm himself. Would Mara jog today? Of course she would. She had to. It had been just as cold and damp yesterday. He wouldn't run today, though, he'd already decided that. He didn't want to be out of breath and excited when he talked to her. She didn't like it when he sputtered with excitement. She always laughed and told him to cool it. The out-dated expression was their private joke. "I'm cool," he'd tell her. He'd been excited yesterday with the other woman he thought was Mara, but he had the whole day to think about it, and he knew he could handle it today. Not that he didn't feel excited inside. Just the thought of Mara did that. But he wouldn't let her see. He'd be cool.

He crossed the street to the twenty-four-hour 7-Eleven, where he was the only customer. He filled a Styrofoam cup with steaming coffee and dropped the money on the counter for the night clerk, who barely glanced at him as he scooped up the coins and dropped them into the register. Back in the parking lot, he unlocked his car and got behind the wheel. Setting the binoculars on the seat beside him, he started the engine and sipped coffee while he waited for the car to warm up. It was an old clunker, and the road up into the Hills was steep enough to require second gear all the way. He didn't want to take any chances this morning of the engine stalling. The coffee was half gone when he finally pulled out of the parking lot.

* * *

Ann woke feeling sluggish and headachy, but she forced herself from bed and into her jogging suit. The nightmare had disturbed her sleep again, only this time the falling dirt turned into purple petals of bougainvillea as they covered her screaming face. The dream was a natural reaction to the previous day's events, she told herself. She wouldn't become a hysterical female who imagined the Hillside Strangler waiting for her behind every bush. And she wouldn't allow fear to make her a prisoner in her own home. Outside, she considered avoiding the scene of the murder by going down the hill instead of up, but again she forced herself to confront something she couldn't avoid forever.

The morning was hushed by fog only slightly thinner than the previous day's. Ann caught herself glancing around at every sound. When an owl hooted softly in a tree across the road, she jumped nervously. Annoyed with herself, she gritted her teeth and quickened her pace before she reached the top of the hill. When another jogger appeared suddenly from a side road, she yelped and clutched her chest.

The man smiled apologetically and fell in step beside her. "I didn't mean to startle you. Have you recovered from yesterday's shock?"

She recognized the man who had led her away from the dead woman and calmed her hysteria. He was tall and dark-haired, with deep blue eyes surrounded by laugh lines. She returned his smile. "Not as much as I thought, I guess."

"You shouldn't be running alone up here until the police catch the killer," he said.

She glanced around nervously. "Have they learned anything?"

He shook his head. "Nothing on the early news. They're trying to trace Sally Dunn's background. In most cases, the killer knows his victim."

Ann realized the idea should be comforting. If the killer knew the woman, it wasn't random murder or the work of a serial killer like the Hillside Strangler. And that would mean there was nothing to fear. Still, she felt a faint ripple of uneasiness as she realized none of the other people who were usually out at this time of the morning were anywhere to be seen. Maybe she had been foolish to talk herself into running today. Glancing at the man beside her, her uneasiness stirred as she remembered how suddenly he had been beside her yesterday. She hadn't seen him on the road or heard him approach. Could he have been there all along . . . hiding? She fought a bubble of hysteria. The police had questioned everyone. If they had been the least bit suspicious of him or if they had any doubts—

"My name is Gary Phillips," he said between breaths, smiling again. "I bought the house Frank Sinatra is supposed to have lived in back in the forties. So far I haven't found any music scribbled on the beams."

Responding in kind, she said, "I'm Ann Laurie, and I live in the green house down on the second curve, which was supposed to belong to some actress or other. I think real estate agents make up a history for every house they show."

"You're a cynic. Actually a lot of early Hollywood stars did live up here at some time or other. Are you in show business?"

"Interior decorating. You?"

"A screenwriter. It just happens I'm doing a pilot for a new series on the interesting histories of some of these old places. Lots of fiction added, of course. You know—Sunset Boulevard, Sunset Strip—why not Sunset Hill?" He grinned. "I don't remember seeing you around until a week or so ago. Are you new up here?"

"I moved in a few weeks ago." Ahead, she saw the walled lot and the brilliant color of the bougainvillea. Her chest contracted, even though she knew it was ridiculous to be nervous. Still she was glad not to be alone.

Gary Phillips caught her glance and gave her a reassuring smile. "We seem to be the only ones brave enough to venture near the scene of the crime," he joked.

"Now or never," she said with false bravado. Bits of yellow plastic ribbon which had roped off the murder site lay on the dewy grass. The grass and weeds around the spot where the body had been were trampled, and numerous cigarette butts had been ground into the dirt. Ann sighed audibly when they passed the end of the wall and started down the grade.

Gary Phillips said, "That wasn't so bad, was it?"

"I guess not." She glanced at him. "I don't see you every morning. Are you a regular jogger?"

"Dedicated, but I hate alarm clocks, so I'm not out at the same time every day."

"I haven't thanked you for yesterday."

"Do it by having dinner with me some night. I'll entertain you by giving you the inside story on your house."

"You know it?" She was startled, and for some strange reason, her uneasiness returned. Gary Phillips was a stranger, and she wasn't sure how she felt about his invitation. She concentrated on her breathing for several yards.

"No, but I plan to check it out now that I've met you. What do you say to dinner?"

"I'm pretty busy this week." It was the truth, but it was an excuse, too. He was coming on too fast, too typically Hollywood.

"You have to eat."

"When I work late, I eat at my desk more often than not."

"Terrible habit. You'll get ulcers."

In spite of herself, she laughed. "Let me see how my schedule works out."

"I'll call you. Are you in the book?"

"Yellow and white pages," she assured him.

They reached the place where the road angled down sharply and twisted around numerous sharp curves before it spilled into another road that led to Laurel Canyon. By mutual accord, they swung around the loop of a cul-de-sac and started the return lap. The next half mile of steep uphill grade demanded all their energies, and they were silent except for the sharp bursts of their labored breathing.

He stood screened by a shadowy tangle of vines and the gnarled trunk of an oak tree. When he heard the sound of someone running, he stepped toward the road but stopped quickly when he saw that Mara wasn't alone. He glared at the man jogging beside her. He was tall and dark-haired, young. Wearing a gray sweatsuit just like his own. Confused, he stepped back until they passed and disappeared around the curve of the road. He rubbed his temple. He'd seen the man before. It was the same one who had been here yesterday with Mara. But he hadn't been running with her then. He had come along after she started screaming, Nick was sure of it. Where had he come from? Nick didn't know. Actually, he wasn't sure where Mara had come from, except she'd come along the ridge road. Suppose he was wrong about her keeping the old house? Suppose she lived somewhere with *him*?

Sweat gathered along the collar of his sweatshirt, and he rubbed his hand across his neck. Follow them.

Find out. But suppose they'd turned around and were coming back? He didn't want to meet Mara that way. If she was still angry, she wouldn't give him a chance to explain, to tell her how sorry he was. He'd wait, then follow her home. That way he'd know about the guy, too.

The morning sounds in the Hills were different from those down near the Strip. It was a different world. Birds chirped in the trees, and leaves rustled softly. An occasional fragment of conversation or music told him that people were stirring for the day. Once he heard the almost imperceptible hum of a car engine, so soft it was hardly more than the drone of a bee. Most of all, he heard the silence. Soft, like the fog.

Running footsteps called his attention back to the road. A chubby middle-aged man in red running shorts and a white hooded sweatshirt went by puffing noisily. Then an engine started up not far away, and voices called back and forth softly before a door slammed and the car drove away. A few minutes later, the silence closed in again.

He didn't have a watch, but he was sure at least half an hour had gone by since Mara and the man had jogged past. He was getting worried that they weren't coming back, and he strained, listening. He let out a sigh of relief when he finally heard a soft thumping sound drift up from the lower road. Even though the noise was too far away to be sure it was them, he hunkered down so his light-colored sweatsuit wouldn't stand out against the shadows, and he pulled some branches of the vine in front of his face.

Mara's head bobbed into view. She ran with her face up, like a racer nearing the finish line. The graceful line of her chin and throat flowed to the neck of the running jacket, which she had unzipped a few inches.

She was so beautiful it made his chest ache. He forgot about the man until his image blocked Mara's as they crested the hill. The ache in Nick's chest became a sharp pain.

When they went by, he stepped from his hiding place and moved cautiously to the opening in the wall. The two figures were at a bend in the road that would put them out of sight in a moment. Nick raced along the road until he had them in sight once more. Relieved, he slowed to a soft, easy-paced jog, staying far enough back so they weren't aware of him.

Ann showered and pulled on a bright jumper over a pink body stocking. She ate a hearty breakfast of scrambled eggs and bacon before she carried her coffee into the studio to begin the day's work. She was excited about the Hackmer job despite the unpleasantness of the previous day. Long ago she'd discovered the best antidote for morbid thoughts was hard work. She was eager to coordinate the rest of the accessories for Mrs. Hackmer's rooms, which were taking shape clearly in her mind. She combed price lists, color cards, and sources, making lists so she had everything she needed for her final decisions. When she glanced at the clock and saw it was almost noon, she was astonished at how quickly the time had passed. She took off her jumper, and pulling her exercise mat from the hall closet, carried it out onto the deck.

The morning fog had left a faint haze that gave the sky a metallic look, but the temperature was rising and the day was already pleasantly warm. She stood at the railing looking down the canyon where winter rain had greened the wild hillsides so they were as lush as the well-tended yards. Bright beds of ice plant splashed colorful borders along driveways of houses

on the gracefully curving streets nestled in the canyon. Brilliant aqua swimming pools surrounded by
patio furniture dotted the green valley. Halfway down
the canyon, the surface of one pool rippled as a swimmer turned for another lap. The muted throb of a power
mower reverberated among the hills.

Ann spread the mat on the decking outside the
greenhouse windows of the studio. One problem with
working at home was making sure she got enough
exercise. When she worked regular hours in the
city, she belonged to a health club and worked out
regularly. Now, although she kept her spa bag in the
car, she rarely had time to stop at the club, so she
substituted a routine of daily exercise whenever she
could fit it into the day. Weather permitting, she used
the deck.

Starting with warmups, she went through a series
of stretching and bending exercises, counting and
humming softly as she worked up a sweat. Somewhere in a tree below her, a mockingbird imitated the
staccato throb of the lawnmower, interspersed with
meaningless sounds it had learned elsewhere. Sweating, Ann finally got to her feet for her final series of
body bends.

"One . . . two . . . three . . . four." She blinked as
a flash of light hit her eyes. She sidestepped automatically to get out of its glare. "One . . . two . . . three
. . . four. One . . . two . . . three—" The light flashed
again, and her rhythm faltered. It had to be the sun
glinting on a bit of glass or metal. There was a faint
path where someone had climbed the steep, weedy
hillside in the hollow of the U-shaped curve. She had
never noticed it before. It wasn't anything that would
attract attention. Without the glint of light, she probably never would have given the hillside more than a

casual glance. If someone had gone up there, he or she might have dropped something. A beer bottle or a bit of foil that the sun was striking at exactly the right angle. Or something could have been tossed from the road across the summit. Ann shaded her eyes and studied the sparse hillside. It was one of the few on the road where a house couldn't be built. For the most part, the Hollywood Hills were fairly stable. Even heavy rainstorms created only minor slides or gradual erosion. As a result, houses were built on seemingly impossible property. Below Ann's deck, the lot dropped away sharply beneath a thick bed of Korean grass and succulents that required no care other than regular sprinklings from the automatic rain bird. Building a house in the hills required only enough flat ground to anchor one end. The lot in the bend didn't have it. It climbed steeply from the road frontage; near the summit, it was almost perpendicular. Trying to build a driveway and house anywhere on it would eat into the substructure of the hill and destroy all natural resistance to flood or earthquake damage. A few houses in the Hills had been built on promontories that offered spectacular views, only to have the earth beneath them wash away because the natural contour of the hill was altered when the roads were built. The only salvation then was to cement the entire base of the hill to prevent the houses from sliding down the canyon. The owners of the houses retained their magnificent views while their neighbors got to look at ugly concrete mountains.

The light disappeared again. Ann walked to the end of the deck to study the hillside. She was careful to avoid the part of the railing where raw wood showed that the railing had been broken and repaired. The repair had been less than professional, and having it redone was on her list of improvements for the near future. Now as she squinted at the hillside, she decided that something dropped from the upper road was the most likely explanation for the reflection of light. She couldn't conceive any reason in the world for someone to climb up that steep path.

He had first noticed the path a week ago. It surprised him, because he'd driven the road so often, he would have bet he knew every inch of it. But there was the path on the curve right below Mara's house. It wondered carelessly up a steep bank scattered with loose gravel and spiny bayonet plants and powdery-green sagebrush. The path didn't go anywhere. It vanished halfway up, as if whoever or whatever had made it was plucked from the ground at that point.

Nick remembered the path this morning after he followed Mara down the hill. Just as he thought, the real estate agent had lied to him. Mara still lived in the house. He watched the gate close behind her and, heart thundering in his chest, he jogged by without looking back. When he reached the empty lot and the path, he turned onto it without hesitation. If she came out on the deck she'd see him climbing. For that matter, he'd be in plain sight of anyone glancing out the window of any of the houses on either side of the horseshoe curve, but he couldn't risk going back for the car. It would take him half an hour to get to it and drive back down here. Besides, there was no place to park without blocking the road.

He scrambled up the path, muttering savagely as his skidding feet showered gravel in his wake. At times he had to crouch on all fours to steady himself and pull himself up the steep incline. Once he slipped dangerously but caught himself from sliding all the way down by grabbing a tough sagebrush that miraculously held. Then abruptly the path leveled to a narrow ledge that was invisible from below. Panting, Nick lay flat until he got his breath.

The ledge was a natural formation where the earth's movement in some bygone era had created a shallow depression between layers of rock. It was only a slight concave behind a sharp ridge, barely a foot wide. The moment Nick rolled into it, he realized he was completely hidden from the road and houses below. Smiling, he lay gazing at the sky.

It was perfect. He'd be able to watch Mara from here. He'd know if she left the house and when she came home, and he'd know who was with her. If she didn't pull the curtains, he'd be able to see her moving around inside. The idea excited him, and he covered his eyes with his arm. He could pick the right time to talk to her then. A time when she was alone, maybe even lonely, the way she had been on the beach the day when he first met her. In the narrow gully he was shielded from the breeze, and the heat of the sun puddled like warm rainwater around him. With his eyes closed, he let himself imagine he was lying on the beach at Santa Monica with Mara.

"Nicky, do my back with lotion. I can feel myself burning."

"You don't burn," he'd say, *"you turn to gold."* But he'd reach for the bottle of lotion and pour some onto his palm. Then with long smooth strokes, he'd rub it across her golden back, down her smooth, unblemished thighs, across her calves . . .

He jerked his arm away as he heard a car start. Rolling onto his stomach, he peered over the lip of the gully. The binoculars under his sweatshirt pressed against his chest painfully, but he didn't move until he spotted a car pulling out of the carport two houses beyond Mara's. He let out a long breath. All this would be for nothing if he didn't pay attention. Lying down again, he crawled along the ledge, peering over the edge from time to time until he found a spot where something had gouged a niche in the lip of the ridge, almost like a rifle slit in a fortress wall. He pulled off the sweatshirt awkwardly as he tried to stay as flat as possible. Then he settled like a sentry, his head resting on the folded sweatshirt, his line of vision through the binoculars focused on Mara's house.

He was only vaguely aware of time passing. It was warm in the sun, and his eyes hooded even though he was alert. Once, when he saw a movement behind the greenhouse windows of Mara's sunroom, he shifted position, but when he didn't see the movement again, he settled back.

He was surprised she was staying home all day. Usually she went out soon after she got up. She liked to be on the go, and she kept busy all the time. Maybe it was a new habit, like jogging early in the morning. Or maybe she had a part in a movie and was memorizing lines. He sat up, forgetting for a minute that he'd be outlined against the hillside. When he remembered, he flattened himself quickly.

It would be great if Mara had a really important part. The lead in a big movie, as she always dreamed about. The kind she worked so hard for.

It won't be long until I get my break—just you wait and see, Nicky.

Maybe it had come at last. Maybe she was finally going to have the fame she deserved. The thought made him happy, but it saddened him to think he hadn't been with her to celebrate the news. He'd have taken her out to dinner someplace nice, like the Thai place on Sunset Boulevard or maybe the Old World. Better still, an intimate candlelight dinner at home, just the two of them. Music . . . his arm around Mara . . .

He came alert as one of the sliding glass doors of the bedroom slid back and a pink figure stepped out with something under her arm. He adjusted the binoculars. It took a minute to bring her into focus. He whimpered and tried to get his breath. He studied her lithe body as if it were a statue of priceless value. Raising the glasses to her face, he studied each of her features, marveling at her beauty, which hadn't faded, refilling his mind with fresh images of her full, red, laughing mouth, the incredible midnight-blue eyes the color of grotto pools, the way she lifted her face to the sun, her golden hair falling across her shoulders like sunshine.

He watched her spread a mat, then stretch out and being to exercise. Minutes ticked by while he was hypnotized by the smooth rhythm of her motions, the graceful curving and uncurving of her body, like a sleek animal. His soft moaning sounds drifted into the still day.

Mara . . . Mara . . .

She stood up, stretching like a cat, and the breath trapped in Nick's chest escaped in a soft, painful burst. He followed her with the glasses, watching as she came to the railing and looked up at the hillside as if she were looking right at him. He almost jumped up and waved, but he remembered in time. First he had to be sure she'd talk to him. She was too far away now, so he had to wait. He adjusted the fine focus on the binoculars and stayed where he was. After a few minutes Mara rolled up the mat and went inside. Nick watched the distorted blur of pink behind the windows of the bedroom. She disappeared a moment into the hall, then came back into the bedroom. He couldn't make out her features at this distance, but he could tell what she was doing. At the closet . . . picking out a dress—something pale and summery—and putting it on the bed. Next she went to the dresser and took some things from a drawer and dropped them beside the dress. Then, stripping the pink leotard from her shoulders as she walked, she vanished into the bathroom.

He couldn't see her, but he visualized the room: red-and-white wallpaper, plush red carpeting on the floor. The white marble sink covered with bottles and jars of lotions and creams and a dozen fancy bottles of perfume. The oval-shaped sunken tub in one corner and the huge shower stall in another. Mara emerging from the shower, her body glistening with shimmering drops of water, reaching for one of the soft, thick red towels on the brass rack.

Sweat rolled down his temples and dampened his hands clamped on the binoculars. The eyepieces fogged, and he had to rub them across the sleeve of his T-shirt. His hands were shaking as he raised the glasses again. Mara was back in the bedroom. She had a towel wrapped around her body. Not a red one, some pale color. When she dropped it and began to dress, he saw her skin was pale too. He'd never seen her without a golden tan. For a moment he worried that she'd been sick. Maybe a doctor had prescribed exercise and jogging. Viewing the pale blur of her body behind the window, he tried to assure himself she was well. He should have been here to take care of her.

He was here now, and he'd never leave her again.

Ann heard the phone ringing as she stepped out of the shower. She let the answering machine pick it up. Gary Phillips's disembodied voice floated down the hall.

"Gary Phillips, Ann. You were right, you're in the phone book. I've got a lead on the history of your house. Believe it or not, it really has one. Tell you all about it when you have dinner with me."

He was persistent, she had to give him that. Maybe if the Hackmer job was far enough along by tomorrow she'd accept his invitation. She'd been working hard and deserved a break, and she had to admit Phillips was cheerful company. She was intrigued by his remark about the history of her house. It would certainly give them something to talk about.

She dressed for her two-o'clock appointment at the Inside Gallery, where she was negotiating the purchase of some paintings for clients. Jeff Parker, the owner, was a friend of long standing, and Ann was partial to several artists whose work he handled. In addition to usually being able to find pictures she needed, she thoroughly enjoyed browsing in the unpretentious gallery on Beverly Boulevard for her own pleasure. Often when she was there near closing time, she and Jeff went to Trumps for tea or to a nearby restaurant for an early dinner, but it wasn't a romantic attachment. There was no romantic attachment in her life right now. She was too busy building the business. She didn't consider herself strictly a career woman, but she enjoyed using her talents fully. She hadn't ruled out marriage and motherhood, but neither would she feel unfulfilled without them. Right now her first order of concern was getting established as a decorator of note in a city where interior decoration was an art form second only to show business. After five years of working for established studios, she was on her own. Her game plan called for building a small, exclusive clientele by word of mouth. So far it was working beautifully.

But dinner with Gary Phillips might be fun. She'd see how she felt if he called again. She found her purse in the hall closet, then went through the house making sure the doors and windows were locked before she went out.

He watched the blue station wagon back out of the carport and start down the hill. The window was open, but he had only a glimpse of Mara at the wheel as the car passed below him. She'd done her hair back in a neat chignon, and she was wearing sunglasses. Not the oversized, funky ones she used at the beach but practical ones that made her look very businesslike. But a station wagon? What happened to her convertible?

The station wagon passed the single house built on a wide spot of the curve, then was out of sight behind the five shelf houses on the other side of the curve. It reappeared momentarily at the point, then vanished. It was two miles of twisting, steady downhill road to Sunset Boulevard. He'd never reach his car in time to catch up with her. It made more sense to wait for her to come back. Now that he was certain where she lived, he didn't have to worry about following her again. No matter where she went during the day, she'd be back.

He used the binoculars to scan the exposed windows of the other houses on the curve. Most people were rarely home during the day. A nice quiet neighborhood. When he was satisfied that no one was paying attention, he sat up and tied the sweatshirt around his waist before he scrambled down the slope. It was treacherous, and he had to sit on his rump and slide a lot of the way to keep from pitching headlong. At the road, he dusted himself off again and walked toward Mara's.

There was a silver Mercedes convertible behind the

wrought-iron gate of the carport of the house next to Mara's, but there was no one around and the house was quiet. Mara's carport was empty except for a small pile of fireplace logs stacked neatly in the corner. He glanced at the thick, twisted magnolia tree outside the corner of the patio. Mara hadn't had it removed. Planted long ago, it had grown from a decorative fill-in for the barren corner of the lot to a hazard twenty feet high. The lower trunk pressed against the fence, and the roots would soon create enough pressure to cave in the planking. He'd warned Mara that it would be easy for anyone to climb and drop over inside the patio. He walked on past two more houses before he turned and went back. If anyone was home in the neighborhood, he or she was isolated from him by walls, patios, and lush plantings of trees and shrubbery. As an added precaution, windows that faced adjacent houses were of pebbled, frosted glass. Several homes had fancy iron grillwork over the windows as well, and all had telltale boxes in the carport or on the side of the house that evidenced alarm systems.

In Mara's carport, he studied the alarm box. He smiled when he saw it was the same one. She hadn't changed it. He took a log from the woodpile and braced it so he could stand on it to examine the box. Using his penknife as a screwdriver, he removed the cover and unfastened two wires inside. He replaced the cover and returned the log to the pile. After making sure he hadn't attracted attention, he walked to the front gate and unlocked it with one of the keys from the small chain he'd taken from the shoe box.

He eased the gate shut behind him and looked around the patio. Everything had been painted green, so the patio was a quiet oasis instead of a flashy, cheerful statement of Mara's vibrant personality. He wasn't sure he liked it.

He studied the sliding glass doors and saw the silver tape of the alarm system and the bar securely in place. At the green door, he bent close to read the names on the locks. A Yale and a Schlage deadbolt. She hadn't changed those either. Using keys on the ring again, he had the door unlocked in seconds and stepped inside. Closing the door, he leaned against it, fighting for breath. Mara . . . to be in the house again, to be so near her. He reached out and drew the silky material of the drapes to his cheek, stroking as lightly as Mara's fingertips on his skin. Her presence was overpowering, and he closed his eyes to savor it to the fullest. It had been so long. . . .

When he opened his eyes, he scowled at the cloth he was holding against his face. Dropping it, he examined the draperies that ran the length of the hall covering the glass wall facing the patio. Distastefully, he fingered one of the rose-toned peonies of the pattern. Then with his hand trailing along the draperies, he stepped gingerly along the pale beige carpeting to the living room. He stared at the transformed room. She had changed everything. Why? What had possessed her to get rid of her beautiful things and fill the room with ordinary junk? He circled the room slowly, dismissing the apricot-colored armchair, the pale green sofa, the gleaming wood tables and crystal and brass lamps. Not Mara at all. He wouldn't believe it was the same house if he hadn't seen her come in here. Where was the bamboo table? The hanging wicker lamps? The neon-red loveseat where the two of them had held hands while they looked out at the lights of the city?

Puzzled, he walked through the small dining room. The black-and-white Lucite table and chairs were gone. So were the framed movie posters. The kitchen had been painted white, the red-and-white geometric linoleum replaced by a pale pattern in beige. As if sneaking up on an elusive enemy, he yanked open a cupboard door. Delicate china and cut-glass crystal. He lifted out a stemmed goblet and turned it slowly between his fingers. It caught the light and danced rainbows up and down the virgin wall. Anger burst inside him and he hurled the glass into the stainless-steel sink. It shattered with a tinkling sound that hung in the quiet house a long time.

In the studio, the transformation was even more startling. The long sofa and the ancient theater trunk that served as a cocktail table were gone, along with the fat floor pillows Mara preferred to chairs when she was memorizing lines, and where the two of them had sat and watched television or movies on the video. Now the room had two funny-looking chairs, a desk, a huge table piled with pieces of cloth and wallpaper books, and another table with pencils, sketch pads, assorted bits of cloth, and colored cards all over it. The telephone was white instead of red, but she still had the machine to answer calls when she wasn't home. The greenhouse windows were bare, but now there were green plants hanging on chains and standing on pedestals. He backed out of the room.

The bedroom and bath had undergone complete changes as well. He inspected them in numb confusion. What was wrong with Mara? Why had she done this? He stood at the glass doors looking out toward the hillside where he'd hidden. Something was going on, he was sure of it. But what? He walked back to the studio, concentrating so hard on the puzzle that deep lines formed between his thick eyebrows.

When the answer hit him, he laughed out loud. Of course! It was a role. Mara had a continuing part, probably in a soap. To get in character, she had adjusted her house and life-style to the role she had to play. That had to be it. And it was typical of Mara. She threw herself totally into whatever she was doing. She became the role she played. He sighed with relief. It must be a very good part for her to go to such extremes. But what about the wallpaper and drapery samples? He went to the table and fingered through the swatches of cloth. A piece of bold purple print felt warm to his touch. This was more like it. Mara's colors. Now that she had the role down pat, she was going to redo the house and go back to the colors she liked best, the colors that were Mara. Glancing at the pastel drapes in the hall, he shook his head as he folded the purple swatch and put it in his pocket.

It was five by the time Ann was ready to leave the Inside Gallery. Jeff insisted on dinner, and they went to a small, quiet restaurant a block from the gallery. During the salad course, Jeff brought up the subject of her "friendly neighborhood murder," as he called it, and was astounded when she told him it was she who first had come upon the victim. When she said she preferred not to discuss it, he agreed the best thing was to put it out of her mind. Instead they talked about the paintings Ann had decided on for two clients. As always, Jeff assured Ann her choices would be right on target. He'd also shown her a fourteen-by-seventeen canvas of purple bougainvillea by a new artist and suggested she consider it for Mrs. Hackmer's den. Ann knew the piece was perfect, but the painting revived such vivid memories of the murder she was trying to forget, it was difficult for her to put her own feelings aside. When she finally agreed to take it along, she had insisted on forty-eight-hour approval before she made a decision. The canvas was wrapped and in her car.

Despite her misgivings, Ann was eager to see the

bougainvillea painting against the swatches and color cards. If she was right about the colors, the painting would tie the entire room together. And if it did, the rest of the project would come together ahead of schedule. That was a bonus she could use right now. She'd be able to get started with a new client. One extra job a year would go a long way toward putting the business firmly in the black.

She drove up the hill in a lighthearted mood, the wrapped painting propped on the seat beside her. The afternoon had stayed remarkably clear, and she caught glimpses of the sun glinting on the ocean each time the curving road headed west. It would be a gorgeous sunset. Maybe she'd have a glass of wine on the deck and watch it, in celebration. Humming, she pulled into the carport and lifted out the painting before she locked the car and went inside. Still humming, she carried the painting to the studio and unwrapped it. Propping it on an easel where it caught the late light, she crossed to the work table to get the fabric swatch Mrs. Hackmer had supplied.

She went though the pile of samples a second time, then a third. Frowning, she picked up her portfolio and dumped the contents onto the table. The swatch wasn't there. Annoyed, she went through the samples methodically, and when that failed to produce the length of cloth, she bent down to look under the table and desk. Frowning with impatience, she stood with her hands on her hips, glancing around as she tried to jog her memory. The swatch couldn't have vanished on its own. What in the world had she done with it? Annoyed with herself, she knew it would do no good to get worked up over it. The swatch had to be here somewhere, and she would find it as soon as she relaxed and let her mind clear.

Before she left the studio, she rewound the answering machine and snapped it to playback. There were several messages, and she jotted information on the note pad she kept beside the phone. One call was from a woman who said Ann had been recommended highly and asked Ann to stop by to discuss decorating the house she and her husband were building in Malibu. Ann put that note on the top of the pile for attention first thing in the morning.

The last call on the tape was Gary Phillips again. He repeated his invitation to dinner. He also said he was going to keep calling and leaving hints about the "lurid past" of her house until she couldn't resist calling him. This time he left his phone number.

Laughing, Ann kicked off her sandals and carried them into the bedroom, where she changed to comfortable slacks and a lightweight sweater. She'd have that glass of wine now as part of her memory-restoring therapy. In the kitchen, she reached for a wineglass from the cupboard. The cupboard door was open, and below it in the sink one of her crystal wine goblets lay shattered. Puzzled, she fingered the delicate shards of glass. She was meticulous about closing cupboard doors . . . and closets . . . and dresser drawers. It was as natural to her as breathing. Had an earthquake tremor shaken the door open and jiggled one glass so it crashed in the sink? Stranger things had happened, she supposed. She picked out the larger pieces of glass, then ran the water and turned on the disposal until the sink was clean. From another cupboard, she took a bottle of Sutter Home Zinfandel, uncorked it, and filled another goblet from the cupboard. Turning to set it on the counter while she unlocked the door to the deck, she stopped her hand in midair. For a moment she was totally confused and her mind blanked. When she realized what she was seeing, the wine goblet slipped from her fingers and crashed to the floor, shattering the crystal and spilling blood-red wine across the beige linoleum. On the counter was the missing swatch of purple print cloth. Arranged precisely atop it was a crystal vase, one she had put on the top cupboard shelf for safekeeping. It held two gracefully curving branches of magenta bougainvillea.

The uniformed police officer who arrived an hour later in response to Ann's frantic call was a woman. Ann had cleaned up the broken glass and spilled wine while she waited, then paced restlessly until the police car arrived. Ann was terrified by the knowledge that someone had been in the house during her absence, but the policewoman was unemotional and businesslike.

"Was anything taken?" Officer Bell asked.

"Not that I know of."

"Have you gone through the house? Your jewelry, silver, that kind of thing?"

"I don't have anything that valuable. A few sentimental pieces. I checked. Everything's there."

"It's possible you scared him off. Did you notice anything unusual when you came in, or hear anything?"

Ann shook her head. "Everything seemed just the way it's supposed to be. I unlocked the door—"

"Both locks were fastened?"

Ann nodded. "Yes, and the gate, too. I used my keys the way I always do."

"You're sure about the deadbolt?"

"I'm positive." Ann recounted her actions step by step, her hunt for the swatch in the studio, finding the kitchen cupboard ajar and the broken wineglass, then the vase with the flowers in it. They were still on the counter exactly as she'd found them.

The policewoman looked pensive. "Is there any chance you could have left it there and forgotten?"

"And picked the flowers, too? And pulled out the stepstool to get the vase from the top shelf? Really, Officer, I can be as forgetful as the next person at times, but I'm not apt to erase a whole sequence of events like that."

Officer Bell smiled for the first time. "Sorry, I don't mean to sound patronizing. I believe you, but I can't write up the call as breaking and entering. There's no sign of forced entry. Nothing's missing. What kind of thief leaves a broken wineglass and flowers and doesn't take anything? Does anyone else have keys? A friend, maybe, or cleaning help?"

"No. I moved in less than a month ago. I don't have a cleaning lady."

"Did you change the locks when you moved in?"

Startled, Ann shook her head. "No, I assumed the real estate agent gave me all the keys. You don't think—"

"Was the house on the market long?"

"The agent told me two years. It was tied up in an estate."

"If it was in multiple listing, there could be half a dozen keys floating around. What company handled the sale?" Bell made a note as Ann told her. "It will probably turn out to be something simple. A real estate agent who didn't know the place had been sold. Look around for a card. They usually leave one when they show a house."

"Are they in the habit of snooping through cupboards?" Ann demanded. Then, realizing she was taking her frustration out on a woman who was trying to help her, she apologized. "I'm sorry, but I'm upset. It's scary to think that someone can come in anytime he wants, especially when that woman got strangled just up the hill from here. Suppose—"

Officer Bell drew her eyebrows to an admonishing frown. "Don't torture yourself that way. You have a right to be uneasy, but don't make it worse. I see you have a chain on the front door. Use it, and get a locksmith to come up as soon as possible to change the locks. If someone does have a set of keys, the best way to prevent him coming in again is make sure they don't fit.

"I'll file my report on this as suspected prowler. The division has a car patrolling the area since the murder. The report will flag your house for special attention." She rose and held out her hand. "I'm sorry I can't be more help, but I have to be honest."

"I understand." The cruel thing was she did understand. No crime had been committed, as far as the police were concerned. What could she expect them to do? She walked to the door with Officer Bell, then crossed the patio and let her out the front gate, thanking her again.

Ann tested the gate lock, then slid the bolt. With a glance at the dark-leaved magnolia tree brooding over the corner of the patio, she hurried inside and double-locked and chained the door. Then she made a complete circuit of the house, checking window locks, bars, and deadbolts. In the kitchen, she emptied the water from the crystal vase and carried the stems of bougainvillea out onto the deck and tossed them as far as she could into the growing darkness. When she went in, she locked the sliding door, then drew the drapes throughout the house before she turned on a light.

* * *

From his post on the hill, Nick watched the police car leave. A woman cop. Women shouldn't have jobs like that; they were too dangerous. He always used to tell Mara she shouldn't even audition for a part like that, but she laughed at him and said it would be just another role. She'd take one if it came along, and she'd never give it up just because he didn't like it. He'd pretended to change his mind, but he'd been secretly happy that she never got one.

During the time the lady cop was in Mara's house, he wondered what they were doing. What did Mara need police for? He thought about the broken glass he'd left in the sink. Maybe he should have cleaned it up, but that wasn't anything to call the police about. Most likely the lady cop was a friend of Mara's who'd just stopped by to chat while the taxpayers were paying her salary.

When the police car finally disappeared down the hill, he trained the glasses on Mara's windows again. The sun had gone down, and the hills were already growing dark. Mara hadn't turned on any lights. He couldn't detect anything moving behind the blank panes of glass.

It was getting cold. A sharp breeze was blowing in from the ocean. After leaving the flowers for Mara, he'd gone back to his room for some things. Now the car was parked at the end of a long driveway off a side road on the other side of the U-shaped curve. There was only one house up there, and it had never been rebuilt after fire had destroyed it. The burned-out shell had disintegrated to charred rubble, filling what had been the indoor-outdoor swimming pool. The long curving drive was badly potholed and overgrown with spiky weeds that pushed through cracks in the asphalt. His car bounced dangerously on its worn shock absorbers, but it made it to the top. He parked in a flat clearing littered with fast-food wrappers and broken beer bottles.

Even though there wasn't much chance anyone would go up there in the dark, he locked the car carefully before he walked back down to the road and returned to the spot he'd found earlier. He'd changed from his dirty sweatsuit to brown slacks and a plaid sportshirt with a heavy sweater over it. He also wore a khaki jacket with huge pockets so he could carry everything: binoculars, a bag of trail mix, a canteen of water, a few items he'd taken from the shoe box in his closet, and, of course, his knife and keys. He'd gotten back to his post and settled comfortably long before Mara came home. Again, he considered the idea of waiting in the house for her, but he knew she wouldn't like it. She'd gotten angry with him once before for doing it. This time it was important to be sure she was in a good mood.

He came to attention as one of the sliding glass doors opened and Mara walked out onto the deck. She was still wearing the pale, summery dress, and her slim figure was outlined against the deep shadows of dusk. She had something in her hand, but she threw it over the railing before he could refocus the binoculars to see what it was. When she went back in, she pulled all the drapes before she turned on the lights—living room, dining room, kitchen, bedroom, bath. Only the studio stayed dark, faintly illuminated from the hall so the outlines of the hanging plants made sinister splotches on the greenhouse windows.

He wondered if she liked the flowers. If she tried to guess, she'd know he left them. He had picked an armful of bougainvillea for her once before because purple was her favorite color. He wanted her to know he was back and approved her plans to put the house back the way it used to be. The flowers looked prettier in the black ceramic vase she used to keep on the old trunk in the studio, but he couldn't find it anywhere.

He wished he could see what she was doing. He tried to imagine her sitting in that horrible, ordinary living room but couldn't. Maybe her other furniture was in storage. They could get it out. He'd help her paint and hang wallpaper to get everything back the way it should be. He swung the binoculars across the lighted draperies. He didn't even know which room she was in. She hadn't come close enough to cast a shadow on the windows. Was she listening to music? In his mind, their song played softly. He closed his hand around the cassette tape in his jacket pocket. They'd begin by listening to it together.

A few houses began to go dark, and he wondered what time it was. Mara was usually a night owl unless she had an early call in the morning. None of her lights had gone off yet. Maybe she knew . . . and she was waiting. . . .

It took Ann seven calls to find a locksmith who would come up that night. The price he quoted was more than double what it should be, but she was willing to pay any amount to feel safe again in her own home. Mr. Alpert couldn't set a definite time but promised it would be within three hours.

The wait seemed endless. Ann jumped at every sound. Over and over she told herself it was foolish, that the policewoman was right. Some thoughtless real estate agent had mistakenly shown the house, not realizing it had been sold until he, or she, was inside and saw the definite signs of occupancy. The vase of bougainvillea was an apology. The business card would turn up eventually. It had probably been blown from the counter in a gusting breeze when the door was open.

Darkness pulled over the canyon and hills like a blanket. Even with the drapes closed, Ann felt exposed. She sat in a corner of the living room as far from the windows as possible. She snapped on the radio but found herself straining beyond the music to define small sounds. She turned it off, but the silence was just as bad. It magnified sounds she hadn't noticed: a creak, a tiny metallic ping, rustling leaves, faint music from somewhere down in the canyon below.

She got up and walked to the front door to test the heavy brass chain. Officer Bell was right. No one could break it. And when Mr. Alpert changed the locks, she would have the only keys. For the hundredth time, she glanced at her watch. An hour and twenty minutes had gone by since she called the locksmith. She prayed she wouldn't have to wait the entire estimated time. Or more. The thought of his being late made her shiver, but it was a possibility she had to face. Service people were notoriously off-schedule. What if Alpert didn't show up at all? She remembered the two days she'd waited to have the washing machine and dryer installed. The dispatcher made endless promises that were never kept.

More to keep herself busy than because she was hungry, she fixed a salad and heated some chicken in the microwave. Often she sat at the counter to eat, but tonight the idea of being that close to the windows made her nervous, even though the drapes were drawn. She carried her plate to the living room and balanced it on her lap while she sat in the apricot-colored chair in the corner. When she was halfway through her food, the doorbell rang. She jumped up, almost dumping her plate. She put it on the table and ran to the front door. She pressed the intercom.

"Yes?"

"Miz Laurie? It's the locksmith." His voice came over the speaker in choppy segments.

She started to undo the chain, then hesitated. She pushed the intercom again. "What's your name?"

"Dan Alpert of Alpert Locks."

She unfastened the chain and deadbolt, then snapped back the Yale. Shivering, she crossed the patio and peered through the peephole. A white van with "Alpert Locks" painted in large letters on the side was pulled onto the edge of the carport and walk. The short, sandy-haired man with wire-rimmed glasses standing at the door waited patiently while she looked him over. Ann had the feeling he probably made enough night calls to expect caution, especially from women alone. When she opened the gate and stepped back to let him in, he nodded politely. He was wearing white coveralls with "Alpert Locks" embroidered across the pocket.

She pointed to the front door. "Both locks."

"What about the gate?"

She hadn't thought about it. It made sense, even though a determined burglar would have no trouble getting over the fence. "Yes, that too."

Alpert nodded and set down his toolbox. Opening it, he took out a flashlight and inspected the two locks on the door. Ann edged past and inside. Cool night air spread through the hall from the open door, and Ann pulled a sweater from the front-hall closet and slipped it on. She thought about her dinner but didn't go back to it. She felt safer in the hall watching Mr. Alpert.

She was astonished how quickly he finished. She'd never watched a locksmith work before. She assumed he'd have to disassemble the entire locks, but in a matter of minutes he replaced the cylinders and was done. She wrote his check while he did the lock on the gate. He handed her three sets of keys and was gone in less than fifteen minutes. She made sure the bolt on the gate was in place and the new lock securely fastened. Back inside, she set both locks and the chain, then turned on the furnace to chase the chill from the air. She rewarmed the chicken, finished her meal, and put the dishes in the dishwasher. Normally she'd spend a few hours in the studio before she went to bed, but she was still restless and uneasy. She certainly didn't feel up to dealing with the Hackmer job tonight. She was tempted to return the bougainvillea print tomorrow and find something else, but she knew that was foolish. The print was perfect, and it would be ridiculous to scrap it and start over.

She settled on the sofa with a novel she'd gotten from the book club and hadn't had a chance to read. She'd barely gotten into the first chapter when the doorbell scared her so badly her heart missed a beat. She uncurled from the chair and got up, looking around the room as if she might find some explanation. In the three weeks she'd been in the house, the doorbell had never rung at night, except for Mr. Alpert, whom she'd been expecting. This wasn't a street for casual pedestrians or salespeople. Anyone she knew would call first.

When the bell rang again, she forced herself to walk to the intercom. The bell rang a third time before she pressed the switch.

"Yes?" Her voice was shaking.

"This is Alpert's Locks."

Her hand moved toward the chain, then pulled back. She pressed the intercom again. "What do you want?" She leaned close to the speaker this time, listening intently.

"I found another set of keys."

The intercom distorted voices. Was this the same voice she'd heard earlier? Despite the warm air flowing from the furnace, she shivered uncontrollably. If it wasn't Alpert, who was it? Alpert had come alone. Even if he had an assistant in the truck who hadn't been needed before, Alpert would be out there now. The man had recognized her caution. He would certainly deliver any additional keys himself.

"Ma'am?"

Alpert had called her by name several times. There was no reason for him to avoid using it now. Ann's hand shook badly as she pushed the switch. Her voice was husky with terror. "I'll pick them up tomorrow. At your shop. I—I was already in bed."

"All your lights are on."

She pulled her hand away from the switch as if she'd been burned. She was certain now it was not Mr. Alpert out there, and she was afraid. She forced herself to press the switch and say, "I'm on my way to bed, Mr. Alpert. I'll pick up the keys in the morning."

She moved away from the intercom, hugging the sweater around her chilled body. Whoever was out there knew about the lock company. He had been watching the house. The same person who had entered earlier and smashed the wineglass, then left the bougainvillea? She snapped off the hall light, then hurried to turn off the lamp in the living room and the overhead lights in the dining room and kitchen. Rushing to the bedroom, she turned off the lamp and the bathroom light. She scarcely dared to breathe. Was the man out there the same one who'd come in before? Oh God, it meant there was no real estate agent, no logical explanation for the flowers—

At a soft scraping noise, she pressed her fist to her mouth. So close—the carport directly behind the bathroom. She strained to listen, but it didn't come again. It could have been a branch scraping against the house. Or— Her head jerked around as she heard another sound, a harsh, unmistakably metallic thud, as if someone had bumped into the car. Ann forced herself to move. On tiptoes, she crept to the bed and groped for the telephone on the table. Lifting it, she pushed 911 on the illuminated dial.

"Emergency."

"Someone is trying to get into my house."

"Your name and address?"

Ann gave them quickly and clearly.

"Is he still on the premises?"

"Yes," she said without hesitation. She felt the terrifying presence all around her, the way she had this afternoon when she discovered the bougainvillea in the kitchen. He had never gone away, or he wouldn't know that Alpert had changed the locks. Since she hadn't fallen for his locksmith story, he was trying to find another way in.

"We'll send a car."

She cradled the phone and sat on the edge of the bed hugging the woolly sweater around her shivering body. The faint yodeling of a pack of coyotes was a mournful sound in the distance. Ann tried to picture every detail of the house's exterior. The patio fence and the open carport faced the street. On either side of the house, the ground dropped away steeply only a few feet from the road, and within a yard or two, the slope was already far enough down so no one could reach the house without a ladder. A colony of bees had built a hive under the house while it was vacant, and the bee expert Ann had hired to get rid of them had needed a twenty-foot ladder to accomplish his task.

The only way someone could force an entry to the house was through the patio. Trembling, she got up and tiptoed back to the hall to peek out through the drapes. The night was black velvet with no moon or stars. The patio was thick with shadows that emphasized the degrees of blackness. As her night vision improved, she discerned the outlines of the umbrellaed table and chairs, the twisted branches of the large jade plant she had started to trim but never finished, and the drooping branches of the magnolia tree that hung over the fence. Nothing stirred. No one was there.

Without a key, he'd have to come over the fence. Ann prayed the police would come before he got that far. What did he want? Why had he singled her out? Could he have been watching her and known she was alone, thus easy prey? The worst fear lingered in the back of her mind like a circling condor: was the man trying to get into the house connected in some way with yesterday's murder?

A violent spasm wracked her, and she let the drape fall as she leaned against the wall. Where were the police? What was taking them so long? What could she use as a weapon if the man climbed over the wall and tried to break the glass? She would have the momentary advantage of knowing where he was before he saw her. She'd have to strike quickly, but with what? Something heavy. The Eskimo carving her father had given her as a souvenir of his fishing trip to Quebec. She stumbled to the living room and groped blindly on the shelves of the étagère until her hands closed around the eight-inch heavy stone carving of a seal. Hefting it like a club, she carried it down the hall and stood behind the door, willing her heart to slow its thunderous pounding.

* * *

Why had he lied? Why hadn't he told Mara who it was and asked to come in? *Because he was afraid she didn't want to see him.* He shook his head, then held it between his hands as he leaned against the front gate she wouldn't open and his key no longer fit. No, that *couldn't* be true. Mara would forgive him. It would be like it used to be . . . him and Mara . . . they would start over again and never be separated.

Gradually the pain behind his eyes diminished, and he raised his head and stared into the dark night. He had to talk to her. Face to face, not through the stupid intercom. He had to get inside and talk to her.

He walked back to the road, cursing the bad timing that had brought him down from his perch on the hillside just as the locksmith's truck pulled up in front of the house. He stayed far back in the shadows until it left, even though he knew the man was changing the locks. The truth was, he couldn't think of any way to stop him. So he had read the name on the truck and figured a way to trick Mara into opening the door. Only it hadn't worked. Now he had to find some other way to get inside and talk to her.

His eyes had adjusted to the darkness, and as he saw the magnolia tree outlined against the sky, he considered climbing over the fence. Trouble was, he'd land in the patio, and he knew the inside doors were locked as tightly as the gate. If she saw him, she might not let him in if she was still angry.

He turned and slipped into the carport. As he felt his way past the car, he banged his knee on a fender, because he forgot she had a station wagon now instead of the little convertible. He felt along the corner of the house until he found the telephone wire just below the roofline. Using the snippers from his pocket, he cut the wire. Across the canyon, lights flashed as a car came around the point. He stood very still for a moment, waiting for it to emerge from behind the houses to see if it was coming that far. It was, and as it swept through the horseshoe curve, he saw the unmistakable outline of police lights on the roof. He moved with the agility and speed of a cat. He swung out of the carport and around the corner of the house in a quick motion. He let his feet skid as he hit the ground and flattened his body against the slope. He began to slide down the sharp drop, propelled by his own weight. In seconds he could see the glow of city lights in the space under the house. He folded his arms across his chest and gave a powerful thrust sideways. His downward slide slowed and he rolled under the edge of the house. Flinging his arms out, he grabbed for something to stop him. His fingers scraped rough concrete. With the taste of dirt in his mouth, he ignored the pain in his bleeding fingers as he clung to what he realized now was the concrete base that supported the furnace and air-conditioning units. With tremendous effort, Nick pulled himself up and rolled onto the narrow platform. There was barely enough room for his body alongside the bulky equipment, but he wrapped his arms around an insulated pipe and hung on as he heard the car stop.

Moments later, the beams of two powerful flashlights spilled down the hillside on either side of the house. The ground beside the living room was somewhat flatter than where Nick had just slid down, but it too dropped off sharply within a few feet. The cops played the lights as far as they could reach, but neither of them risked scrambling down the steep slope very far. Nick held his breath as one of the beams hit the equipment he was hiding behind, but a moment later the light moved farther down the embankment to the fifty-foot steel beams set in concrete that supported the front of the house.

Nick lay perfectly still, breathing softly through his mouth, until the flashlight beams swung back toward the road. He hugged the grimy pipe and waited.

After talking to the policeman through the intercom, Ann shoved the hand gripping the stone carving into her sweater pocket as she summoned the courage to open the door. She crossed the patio and looked through the peephole. To her relief, a gray-haired officer wearing a uniform held up his identification for her to inspect. Behind him she saw the readily identifiable police car with its red light flashing. She unlocked the gate. The officer flashed a powerful light around the patio before he followed her inside. A second officer was inspecting the shrubbery across the road.

The story sounded thin as she told it, but the gray-haired officer, whose name was Martinelli, listened politely and made notes. His expression was unreadable when she mentioned the earlier episode of phoning the police, but it seemed to Ann that he became skeptical all at once.

"Have you tried calling the locksmith to see if he came back?" Martinelli asked.

It hadn't occurred to her. She shook her head, feeling foolish. Martinelli went out and said something to his partner. When he returned, he told Ann they were checking it out.

"Now, this man who said he was Alpert, did he try using the key he claimed to have?"

"No—he didn't!" Ann said with a stir of excitement. If it really had been Alpert, he could have unlocked the gate easily!

"Probably didn't want to scare you after you told him you'd pick up the keys tomorrow."

He was implying she couldn't have it both ways. Martinelli wasn't convinced, but Ann didn't need any more conclusive proof that it hadn't been Alpert. Still she said, "I didn't hear his truck. And what about the noises in the carport? Why was he sneaking around out there?"

"It could have been someone's cat or dog. Or a coyote. This area is full of them."

It was senseless to argue. She could no more prove her theory than he could his. And if she persisted, she would be classified as an hysterical female and everything she said would be discounted. At least they had responded to her call. And whoever was out there was gone now.

"We haven't had any other reports of prowlers in the vicinity, but we'll increase the number of our trips up here tonight," Martinelli told her. "We'll pay special attention when we come by here."

It was small consolation, but it was something. Ann nodded. "Do you have a gun, Miss Laurie?" he asked, glancing at the heavy bulge of her pocket.

Startled, Ann shook her head and drew out the stone seal. Martinelli smiled.

"Looks heavy enough to break a skull, but you'd better be pretty sure of your aim on the first try." He took his hat from under his arm and touched the brim as he put it on. "Good night, Miss Laurie."

"Thank you. Good night." She walked to the gate, and when it clicked behind him, she shot the deadbolt. Inside again, she double-locked the door, fastened the chain, and turned off the outside lights. She'd turned on the hall light when Martinelli came in. Now she snapped it off and walked to the living room in the dark. She stood at the drapes looking out until she saw the headlights of the police car sweep around the uphill curve and disappear.

She put the Eskimo carving on the night table when she undressed, then took an over-the-counter sleep aid to calm her nerves before she went to bed. Even so, it was a long time until she drifted off.

The sound of the police car faded, but Nick stayed where he was for a long time. He wouldn't put it past the cops to turn around at the top of the hill and cruise down again. He wanted to be sure they weren't coming back before he went inside to talk to Mara. She must have called them before he cut the line, but he was safe now. She couldn't phone them again.

When there was no sound but the chirp of crickets, he rolled from the concrete ledge and eased himself onto the slope. Because no water or sun reached it, the ground under the house was barren and soft from the original excavation. The slightest pressure sent miniature landslides of loose dirt skittering down the hill. Enough dirt to smother him. It was safer to roll out from under the house. He lay on his back with his arms flat at his sides and waited for the dirt to stop slipping. He took a deep breath and held it as he rolled sideways. He felt himself sliding, but the sideways momentum was equal to the downward pull, and he came out from under the house only a few yards downhill. He crashed into a castor bean plant, and a prickly seed husk stung his palm as he grabbed it. Out from under the house, the ground was firmer where it was held by the root network of weeds and succulents that trapped moisture. He lay breathing the cool night air for several minutes before he let go of the castor bean plant and, still flat on his back, inched downward.

Reflected light from the city and the houses in the canyon created shades of gray in the night. He measured his slow progress by watching the dark outline of the house and deck against the gray sky. The trick was not to make any sudden movements that would cause him to lose control of his speed. He had all the time in the world.

Above him, the sky was a comforting black blanket that shut out the rest of the world. Almost a summer sky, he thought. Like the one he and Mara had lain under at the beach that warm August. A perfect sky, she'd called it. Perfect for being together . . . for making love. For a moment he stared into the past, remembering how it felt to hold Mara in his arms, to press his body against hers. He shivered with longing until he had to close his eyes and breathe deeply to make the pain go away.

Finally he opened his eyes and examined the shadows above him more carefully. The edge of the deck was a sharp line against the deep velvet sky. Without lifting his head, he knew that the concrete pilings in which the steel beams supporting the house were set were within inches of his feet. Palms flat, he moved his leg sideways slowly. A spatter of gravel sounded like thunder rolling down the canyon, but he knew the sound would not be noticed in the house. It would be no more than a spate of dirt dislodged by a fox or coyote prowling in the night. The hills were filled with sounds like that, and they went unnoticed as people listened to the radio or watched television.

The house above him was completely dark. Mara had turned out the lights again as soon as the police left. Occasionally Nick thought he heard a board creak, but he couldn't be sure if Mara was moving around in the dark or if it was only the house settling for the night. As he felt cautiously for the piling, he imagined Mara undressing and getting into bed, but the images made him tremble so violently that he had to squeeze his eyes shut until his body stilled.

He let himself slide down the slope another few inches, then moved his foot again. This time it contacted solid cement. Grinning, he shifted carefully until his soft-soled shoe was against the piling. Then he curled his body and grabbed the block, closing his eyes as sand and gravel splattered over him. He pulled himself up, eyes still closed, and wrapped his arm around the upright beam. Reaching into his pocket, he found a handkerchief to wipe his eyes, face, and nose. Still he felt gritty and he knew his face was streaked with dirt. Depending on where Mara was, maybe he could wash up before he saw her.

He pulled himself up onto the small, rough foundation surrounding the eight-inch round steel beam. For a moment he looked out over the canyon and city, drinking in the cool night air with a sense of being more powerful than all he surveyed. The world was his—his and Mara's! He hugged the beam and swung one arm and leg in a wild gesture of freedom. Then, sobering, he glanced up at the two beams that angled from the base of the upright. It wouldn't be hard to climb in the dark. It was just a matter of moving slowly, never letting go of one grip until the next one was secure. Reaching into his pocket, he found the gloves he'd brought and pulled them on. Heavy leather gloves, perfect for climbing.

He chose the beam that would take him away from the bedroom, so he wouldn't wake Mara. Silhouetted against the night, he was a primal animal moving in its element. Arms and legs wrapped tightly around the metal, he scooted upward inch by inch, his breathing controlled and barely audible. Every few seconds he stopped to rest, gathering strength from the darkness and from the knowledge that he was so close to Mara. He was cool, with only an inner excitement that didn't show. Mara would be proud of him.

Finally he felt his head brush the two-by-eight framework of the decking outside the studio. Arms and legs still wrapped around the beam, he waited until his breathing was normal and he was in control again. Glancing up through the slats, he saw the distorted outlines of deck chairs and potted plants. He recalled seeing some plants on the railing through the binoculars. He'd have to be careful not to knock them over.

When his energy was restored, he reached up to grab the deck. His first grip was too tenuous, and he had to shinny higher on the beam and take off the heavy gloves so he could grasp the heavy wire netting that stretched between the deck and the railing. He twined his fingers tightly in the wires, then unwrapped his legs from the beam. His body swung out over the black void of the canyon. His heart raced and a pulse sang in his temples, but his fingers gripped the wire like steel talons. When the momentum of the swing diminished, he began to pull himself up, knees first, onto the narrow edge of the deck that extended below the protective mesh. He worked his hands up, then threw one arm over the railing while he got one foot, then the other, balanced on the narrow ledge. Again he felt a thrill of exhilaration, like a hawk poised on an air current. The lights of the city twinkled with crystal clarity interspersed with raucous splashes of neon and an occasional blinking radio or television antenna. Hollywood. Mara's town.

Standing slowly, he lay across the rail and drew one leg, then the other across. He was on the deck. Now it was hard to control his breathing. He listened to the soft sigh of the wind, the crickets, the rustle of eucalyptus leaves. The sounds brought Mara so close.

He straightened and listened intently. Mara had gone to bed. The house was quiet and dark. There wasn't even the night light Mara always left burning in the studio. Like a movie set, she told him. When scenes are shot in what's supposed to be a dark room, you can always see everything that's happening. So she always left a low light on, like a movie set.

Not anymore. That was as strange as her changing everything in the house just because she had a part in a picture. He'd have to ask her about that, but not until he was sure she wasn't mad at him. Pain almost doubled him as he remembered how angry Mara had gotten. It had shocked him and hurt him and almost driven him crazy. He couldn't stand her being mad at him. He ran away from her screaming. He no longer remembered all the places he'd gone—scared at first, then growing more and more lonely for her until he realized he had to come back. It had taken him a long time to find her again, but now he'd do anything to make her happy and set things right the way they used to be.

Stepping softly on the balls of his feet, he crossed the deck, avoiding the loose board that he remembered squeaked. He barely glanced at the sliding glass doors of the living room. On a night as cool as this, she'd lock them and drop the bar in place before she went to bed. Same in the bedroom. But one of the louvered windows of the studio would be open a little for air. Most likely it would be one on the far side of the room so the air would circulate toward the bedroom.

The closest streetlight was halfway down the curve, and its light barely intruded on the darkness by the time it reached the deck. Nick moved unhesitatingly, in tune with signals from his mind that had not dimmed in the past two years. At the greenhouse windows, he ran his palm across the metal framework and glass until he found one of the louvered windows open. It was crazy how people who spent a lot of money on burglar alarms, Charley bars, and other security devices paid no attention to louvered windows. In warm climates where slatted glass kept out the sun and let in the air, burglars could get through jalousie windows easier than they could doors.

It took him a few minutes to work the first piece of glass free of the metal strips holding it on either side. He laid it on the deck, well out of his way so he wouldn't kick it accidentally. Within ten minutes, he had the rest of the slats out. With the tip of his penknife and a lot of patience, he went to work on the screen. From time to time there was a tiny metal ping when a thin strand of wire broke under the pressure of the blade, but the faint noises were swallowed by the night. Time meant nothing to him as he worked a small hole close to each of the fasteners. When he had them all, he used the knife blade to turn the holding screws a quarter of a turn each, just enough so he could release the catches. Working from bottom to top, he pushed each one aside, then caught the bottom of the screen with his fingernails and pushed. He grabbed the screen quickly before it fell. He held his breath and listened. When he was sure Mara hadn't wakened, he tipped the screen sideways and pulled it out through the opening. Because it was so light and there was a breeze sweeping up the canyon, he laid the screen flat on the decking so it couldn't blow over.

When he stepped through the narrow opening and into the studio, he felt Mara's presence all around him.

In the darkness lit only by the distant streetlight, none of the terrible things she'd done to the room were visible. Instead he was back in Mara's old studio, sitting beside her on the long white leather sofa, sipping wine, or maybe champagne if she had gotten a good part. He still could hear her soft crystalline laughter and feel the warm pressure of her hand in his.

After a long time he walked to the hall. It was darker as he moved away from the glassed cage of the studio, but his eyes adjusted rapidly and he moved unerringly. He paused in the hall, puzzled by a shadowy piece of furniture he couldn't place. There used to be a silly bench with curved arms. . . . Then he remembered the bookcase he'd seen this afternoon. He made out its rectangular lines, the curved outline of the vase atop it, and another shape, soft and draped. Her purse. Mara had changed the furniture but not her habit of leaving her purse in the most convenient spot near the door.

He felt it like a blind man examining a strange object. Soft leather, with a zippered top and a shoulder strap that was hanging down the side of the bookcase. He gathered it in his hands and held it against his chest so nothing inside would rattle or clank. On tiptoes, he walked to the living room and knelt on the pale green sofa so he could reach behind it and put the purse on the floor, out of sight.

The silence of the house closed around him. He wanted to get everything ready first, but knowing Mara was so close left him weak. He had to see her. He stole to the bedroom door. It was open. He stood against the wall, invisible in the deep shadows, and peered into the room. He made out the outline of the bed and the mound of covers. His heart pounded as he gazed at her golden hair against the satin pillowcase, heard the soft flutter of her breathing, and imagined the rise and fall of her beautiful breasts. It took all his willpower not to rush in and lift her into his arms.

As he passed the studio on his way back to the living room, he felt the draft of cold night air from the open window. He hadn't noticed it before because he was wearing a jacket, but Mara would be cold when she got up. He tugged at the edge of the door, and when it didn't pull easily, he concentrated on a mental image of the studio as he'd seen it this afternoon. Remembering, he bent and lifted aside the stone cat that propped the door open. Then, drawing the door shut, he eased the latch silently before he continued on to the living room.

Despite the mild sedative, Ann slept restlessly. She dreamed in fragments of sound—soft spatters of pebbles, running water, plinking strings of an unmusical instrument. Gradually they were swallowed up by the shadows of the nightmare which began to form a ring around her sleep. She tried to burrow beneath the soft blanket, but she couldn't escape the plaintive quality of distant music that was drawing her deeper into the nightmare. She was once again on the hot, dusty road, and the music was the dry wind scorching her body. Although she couldn't see the canyon walls, she felt trapped by them, as though entombment were inevitable. Part of her mind struggled to waken, but the effects of the sleeping pill cradled her in limbo. Gradually, the music became a tune she thought she should recognize.

A subconscious voice told her if she could waken, she'd break the pattern of the nightmare and free herself from it forever. But she was trapped, hopelessly caught in the hot, dusty sunshine across which the man's shadow had already loomed. Don't look up. If she didn't see him and run, the walls of the canyon couldn't fall on her. She had to will away the unreality she had allowed to become so real.

She burrowed deeper into the pillow and tried to block out the lamenting song. The man's shadow came closer, and Ann squeezed her eyes tightly shut, denying the scene playing in her mind as a child would a horror movie she couldn't bear to watch. It was a dream, a nightmare. It wasn't real, and she wouldn't let it be. *Forever mine . . . can't live without you—*

She woke with a start, bolting up as panic flooded her. For a moment she was convinced she had created a new avenue of the nightmare, escaping the collapsing canyon walls only to find herself in a place more terrifying. Sweat bathed her, and she shivered. The house was dark, but the music was real. It was coming from the other end of the house, from the living room. The same plaintive song that had woven itself into her dream. The radio? Or television? She remembered turning on the radio earlier, but she had shut it off, she was sure. Trying to control her panic, she reached for the telephone and slid under the blanket with it in her trembling hand. Fingering the push buttons, she pressed the three emergency digits. Cupping her hand over the mouthpiece, she waited, so frightened she could scarcely breathe. It took several heartbeats before she realized the phone wasn't ringing. She clicked the plunger frantically, but the line was dead. A sob welled in her throat, and she pressed her face into the pillow.

Someone was in the house. Someone who had cut the phone wire. Someone who had entered with keys earlier and left a calling card of bougainvillea. Someone who was, at this moment, in another part of the house. Waiting.

She was too petrified to move, yet too terrified to shiver helplessly and wait for the intruder to make his next move. She strained in the darkness, listening for some sound that would tell her exactly where he was. Each faint creak of the house cooling in the night air made her breath catch, but she couldn't be sure what she was hearing wasn't only innocent night noises. As her eyes grew accustomed to the dark, she studied the faintly lighter outline of the doorway to the hall. Nothing moved.

Moving her head like a mime acting the part of a marionette, she inspected each corner of the bedroom, the bathroom doorway, the silhouette of a tree branch waving in the light against the drapes. Everything was exactly as it should be, except for the faint musical notes that whispered through the darkness.

Could it be coming from somewhere else? Was it an acoustical trick of the canyon bouncing sound from the hillsides and making it seem contained within the walls of the house? Sounds were distorted and magnified among the hills. That had to be it. It wasn't in the house at all. The nightmare had confused her brain and woven a thread of truth into the fabric of fear. The music that seemed to be coming from her own living room was actually a faint echo from a late party somewhere down in the canyon.

She lay back and pressed the pillows against her ears to block the sound. There was no one in the house but her. The police had checked the house as well as the yard, and she had bolted the door as soon as they left. It was impossible—

The music was there again . . .

She muffled a sob in the pillow. No matter how much she accepted the possibility that music could drift in the quiet night air, she knew that the words couldn't possibly come through so distinctly. She lowered the pillow and stared again into the darkness. Another logical explanation. There had to be one. She bit her lip and forced back tears of fright. A freak electrical phenomenon? A short circuit of some kind? Maybe she only thought she'd turned off the radio. She was so nervous while she waited for the locksmith, she could have been careless.

There was the music again . . .

How many times had the song replayed? No disk jockey would repeat the same song endlessly. As a rule she listened to classical music while she worked, but this was a pop tune. She didn't recognize the artist or melody, only the plaintive quality.

Throwing back the blanket, she felt the carpet with her bare feet until she found her slippers. She pulled on the satin robe that lay across the foot of the bed, then picked up the stone carving before she moved across the bedroom with slow, soundless steps. Clinging to the wall for support, she peered down the hall that ran the length of the house.

She saw immediately that the studio door was shut. Her heart skittered and missed a beat. The door was always open, propped by the stylized onyx Egyptian cat. It was conceivable she might forget leaving on the radio, but she was positive about the door. She'd kept it propped open since the day she moved in. The light that spilled into the rest of the house from the studio was too fantastic to block out. Her mouth was cottony.

It was stupid and foolhardy to walk through the house and increase the distance between herself and the only means of escape. Shaking badly, she sidled across the hall to the front door. Her hand trembled as she inched the slide bolt from the plate and lowered the chain without a sound.

Her purse. She needed the car keys. She reached toward the bookcase and whimpered in panic when her hand encountered only the wood. She always put her purse there when she came in. Always! No, not always—think—she must have put it somewhere else this time!

The song was beginning again. She couldn't control her terror, and her chest constricted painfully. She could no longer delude herself: the music was coming from the stereo speakers in the living room. The melody swept through the house as softly as a throbbing heartbeat. Ann patted her hand across the surface of the bookcase in the vain hope she'd missed her purse, but all she encountered was the sleek, cold bronze statuette of a crouching cougar. She kept a spare set of car keys in a drawer in the kitchen. The thought of going closer to the living room bathed her in cold sweat. But there was no way to get help unless she drove down the hill. She'd never even met her neighbors. The likelihood of anyone opening the door to a stranger in the middle of the night was remote. And if whoever was in the house heard the door open, she didn't have much chance of getting far without being caught.

Where was he? Her gaze searched the dark hall, the faint pale outline of doorway to the kitchen, and the portion of the living room visible ahead of her. When a shadow moved, she bit her lips to stifle a scream and raised the stone weapon until she realized it was a trick of the streetlight across the canyon. Many nights since she had moved in, she'd enjoyed the play of shadows against the walls. Now they were terrifying.

The song ended, and she held her breath. The silence was heavy, with only the papery whisper of a soft wind in the eucalyptus trees humming faintly.

When the song did not begin again, Ann breathed out slowly. She wanted to believe she had frightened herself senselessly, but the iciness in the pit of her stomach would not thaw. Someone had cut the phone line. Someone had closed the door to the studio. Someone had moved her purse. And that same person was somewhere in the darkness, waiting.

Nick sat on the floor beside the flowered sofa. He had washed his hands and face in the small bathroom down the hall. He felt a little cleaner, but he couldn't bring himself to sit on Mara's new pale-colored furniture, or even lean against the wall, when he'd been rolling in the dust and dirt. He'd be more comfortable in the studio even with its changes than he was here. But she'd moved the stereo and TV to the living room, so he had no choice.

He'd recorded the tape from the soundtrack of the movie. Just one song—their song—over and over on both sides of the tape. Someday he was going to buy a tape deck that flipped the tape automatically so he could listen as long as he wanted to without interruption.

It was hard not to close his eyes and slip into the dreams of Mara which had become part of him these past two years. But tonight she was only fifty feet away, at the other end of the house. She wasn't a dream. She was real. She was here. And when she heard the music, she'd know he was here too. She would come to him, and they would be together.

The music ended and the machine clicked faintly. He was sitting close enough to reach up, eject the tape, reverse it, and push the play button. As the first notes of the song began again, he settled down with his gaze riveted on the hallway where Mara would appear.

* * *

An eternity passed before Ann could command her body to obey her mind. She'd taken two steps toward the kitchen when she heard a series of tiny clicks. Suddenly the music began again, and she froze in her tracks and almost screamed. The throaty female voice was singing the pleading love song. The tape had been turned over.

It no longer mattered what was sensible or logical. Terror gripped Ann so totally, she wheeled and ran down the hall, sobbing in panic. She wasted precious seconds trying to yank the door open without letting go of the heavy weapon in her hand before she realized she hadn't undone the snap lock. Twisting it, she yanked open the door. Cold air engulfed her. She raced to the gate and tugged at the deadbolt. She was shaking so hard even the simplest task seemed impossibly difficult. Finally the bolt slid back and she twisted the doorknob.

Before she got the door open, someone grabbed her from behind and yanked her back. The man wedged himself between her and freedom, hunching down as he shot the bolt tight again. She raised her arm and tried to smash him with the stone seal, but he turned in time to ward off the blow with a vicious chop of his hand. The stone image flew from Ann's hand and thudded onto the soft ground near the jade plant.

Breathing hard, the man leaned against the door, wild-eyed. When she opened her mouth to scream, he clamped one of his hands over it instantly. She stared at the pale blur of his face, praying silently and desperately.

"It's me, Nick," he said. "I won't hurt you, Mara." His voice was low and intimate. "Please, don't yell or run. I came to tell you I'm sorry. I didn't mean it. Honest. You know I'd never do anything to hurt you. Please forgive me. You've got to forgive me."

Ann tasted blood where she'd bitten her lip. She was shivering so hard with cold and fear that it was difficult to breathe. His hand gripping her jawbone made her whole face ache. Thoughts tumbled in her mind too fast to sort. He'd called her by another name. He thought she was someone else. He was begging her to forgive him. If he knew the house so well, even had keys, the other woman must have lived here once. Gripped by terror, Ann knew she had to placate him. She forced herself to nod against the vise of his clamped hand. She would tell him he was forgiven. She would tell him anything.

He looked surprised, almost disbelieving. Releasing the pressure on her mouth slightly without taking his hand away, he put his arm around her and led her inside. Still holding her, he walked to the living room, where the mournful love song played on softly.

He let go of her mouth and drew her against his body gently. "Oh, Mara . . ." he said, fighting tears. "I never should have left you. I tried to come back, but they said you were gone, but I knew you'd never leave here." She forgave him. All this time he'd thought she was angry, she had already forgiven him. She was waiting for him to come back, wanting him the same way he longed for her. He smiled lovingly and stroked her face.

"I knew it would be all right all along. It had to be. Something as perfect as our love can never go wrong. Listen—do you hear the song? Our song. I made the tape so I can listen to it all the time. I want everything to be the way it was, Mara. I want us to be together." He ran his fingertips along the curve of her jaw and down her throat.

Ann was rigid with terror but couldn't suppress a shudder as his calloused fingers scraped along her flesh.

He scowled, then hugged her tightly.

"You're cold. I'll light the fire. Sit down." He steered her toward the stereo, then glanced around in confusion, as if the arrangement of the room was not what he expected. He moved her into the apricot-colored chair beside the fireplace and tucked her robe around her legs before he knelt on the hearth. He struck a match and held it to the pyramid of paper, kindling, and wood Ann always kept ready. She loved a fire on a cool night, but now she shuddered as the flames licked up, igniting the dry wood quickly and crackling ominously. The erratic light played on the man's features and was reflected in dark, empty eyes set in hollows of his skull.

She saw him clearly for the first time. He was thin and had a pinched face dominated by bushy eyebrows from under which a wild gaze darted nervously. His muddy blond hair was cut short, and a khaki fatigue jacket hung loosely on his thin frame, giving him the pathetic look of a waif. He was young, under thirty, but had the gaunt, ancient expression of a derelict.

Ann's brain refused to function coherently as she waited for his next move. He still seemed puzzled by the room, glancing around as if looking for something. Finally he stood up and walked to the cabinet that held the television set and VCR. He squinted at the buttons and dials, then turned on both pieces of equipment. From one of the voluminous pockets of the khaki jacket, he took out a videocassette and shoved it into the slot. A late-night talk show came on the television screen, and he flipped channels without hesitation to the one required for video. While the lead-in ran, he turned off the tapedeck, then took Ann's hand and drew her to her feet. With his arm around her, he sat on the sofa and pulled her down beside him.

The television screen sprang to life. It was a wide shot of the ocean and a beach. Accompanying the rhythmic waves, the soundtrack grew louder. Ann recognized the melody of the song that had wakened her, the song that had played over and over on the tape. The shot began to close in on a small figure jogging along the beach wearing a purple sweatshirt over a bathing suit. The girl was blond, young, slim, and very pretty. Her golden hair was pulled up in a ponytail that bounced with each stride. From time to time, she glanced off in the distance across the water. Finally she slowed to a walk, then stopped at a striped beach blanket anchored on the sand by a beach bag and a pair of sandals. She stripped off the shirt as she sank to her knees, then stretched full-length on the blanket, flipping the ponytail from her shoulder and closing her eyes. The camera zoomed to a closeup of her relaxed, pretty face, then panned back to show her stunning figure in the purple bikini. Eyes still closed, she untied the neck straps of the halter top and tucked them down into her cleavage. Her body was bronzed, without any suit marks.

Ann glanced at the man beside her. He was mesmerized by the screen. His expression was one of adoration as he watched the girl. Ann steeled herself not to move as her brain churned in search of the answer to how he had gotten in. She didn't doubt for a second that he had used a set of keys this afternoon, or that he had broken the wineglass and left the bougainvillea. But tonight the doors were locked and bolted with the new locks Alpert had installed. Had this man—what name had he whispered—Dick—no, Nick—really gotten extra keys from Mr. Alpert? Maybe he worked for the locksmith and had access to any keys he wanted. But the chain was on. She had double-checked it and the bars after the police left. If he'd smashed a window, she would have heard the glass shatter even in her drugged sleep. Maybe the sound had wakened her without her realizing it. She suppressed a shudder, knowing that waking hadn't released her from the nightmare. She was still trapped in its terrifying maze of impossibilities and unrealities. Everything was questionable, and there were no answers.

Nick squeezed her shoulder, and she steeled herself not to pull away. He shot her a quick smile, then looked quickly back to the screen.

"Here's where Joe comes along—watch."

On the screen, a handsome, curly-haired young actor strolled along the beach. Ann wondered if she should recognize him, but she so rarely went to movies, she couldn't be sure if she had ever seen him before. In the insolent manner of youth, he eyed the pretty girl, then stopped to stare down at her, his wolfish gaze caressing her curves. When the girl's hand patted the blanket in search of her suntan lotion, the boy bent and plucked it up before she found it. After a few moments, the girl shielded her eyes with her hand and raised her head.

"Looking for this?" the boy asked, still grinning.

The girl held out her hand without answering.

"I'll be glad to put it on for you," he said.

The girl tried to grab the bottle, but he raised it out of her reach, laughing. She looked angry, then her expression relented and she gazed away, taking a handful of sand and letting it sift slowly through her fingers.

Beside Ann, Nick giggled childishly.

"I'll be able to get those hard-to-reach spots," the

boy on the screen went on suggestively.

The girl smiled coyly. Then with a quick motion she grabbed another handful of sand and flung it in the boy's face. He fell back, sputtering and rubbing his eyes. The bottle of suntan lotion dropped to the blanket, and the girl picked it up, uncapped it, and began spreading the oily cream on her shoulders.

Nick laughed with delight. "You sure showed him. God I love that part. He had it coming. They should have cut him out of the picture right there. The creep."

Ann realized the man beside her was totally immersed in the film. It was important to him, and somehow, insanely, it involved her. He was talking to the character in the picture. Ann studied the face of the pretty girl on the screen. Like the actor's, it was not instantly recognizable, not a top box-office star familiar to the infrequent moviegoer. She stared at the glowing colors on the screen, trying to find a glimmer of sense in the nightmare. Why had this intruder— her mind balked at the possibility he was a rapist— brought the videocassette to view? Not just any movie, a very special one, at least to him.

On the screen, the dark-haired youth strode angrily away, glancing back at the girl on the blanket with wounded macho pride and disgust. The girl ignored him completely as she spread oil on her shoulders and arms so they glistened. With languorous motions, she oiled her legs and midriff, then lay back with her eyes closed.

Ann tried to determine how old the picture was by the swimsuit the girl wore, but the bikini was a popular style that had been around for at least ten years. With a sickening lurch, Ann realized the swimsuit was the same color as the bougainvillea that had been left on her kitchen counter. The same purple of the jogging suit the murdered woman had been wearing yesterday.

She felt light-headed and had to close her eyes to keep from fainting. She'd been terrified of a burglar or rapist. It was more likely the man beside her was a murderer. She swallowed the bile that swelled in her throat. Purples . . . blondes . . . it couldn't be coincidence.

The scene on the screen was superimposed by the title and credits of the picture. *Sand Castle*. The producer's and director's names meant nothing to Ann. She waited for the listing of the cast. *Starring Philip Cross and Cecie Anton*. She'd never heard of Philip Cross, but for some reason the name Cecie Anton was vaguely familiar. She watched the listing of other characters without recognizing anyone else. Gradually the theme song swelled again and the girl sat up and put on sunglasses before she glanced at a small cove a quarter of a mile down the beach. A sailboat that had been moored there in an earlier shot was now tacking toward the camera, which returned to the girl as she jumped up from the blanket. She pinned up her hair and walked into the surf. When she was chest-deep, she began swimming with powerful but contrived strokes that kept her face to the camera and her hair and makeup dry.

The camera pulled back for a long shot so the girl became a tiny speck moving seaward. There were other swimmers and several other boats, but none as close as the sailboat the girl had been watching. After a few frames, when she was almost in a direct line with the sailboat, the girl rolled onto her back and floated. Her hair got wet and came loose from the pins, and when she began swimming again, she pushed it back from her eyes. She treaded water and gazed at the sailboat, then began thrashing as if she had tired and suddenly panicked. The camera caught her expression of terror as a wave splashed over her. She came up screaming.

Beside Ann, the man was oblivious to everything but the picture on the screen. He leaned forward, elbows on knees, hands clasped tightly. "I'm coming, darling, hold on—I'm coming—" he said so softly Ann wasn't sure she really heard it. The wild look in his eyes had taken on the fervor of a zealot meeting a long-awaited messiah. On the screen, the actress sank beneath the surface again, then thrashed her way up coughing and struggling.

The man at the tiller of the sailboat shielded his eyes and studied the tiny moving speck in the water. Realizing it was someone in trouble, he yelled to a companion as he heeled the boat sharply and headed for the swimmer in distress. Another shot of the girl struggling, then one of a man in swimming trunks diving cleanly from the foredeck of the sailboat and swimming with powerful strokes to the actress, who sank out of sight before he reached her.

Beside Ann, Nick was breathing with the same measured labor as the man on the screen. He swung his head sideways on each inhalation, imitating the motions of the swimmer. Ann studied his features. There wasn't the slightest similarity to the actor on the screen, yet she had the weird feeling that at least at that moment, the two were one.

Even though she knew her life might depend on it, Ann found it impossible to follow the inane story on the screen. It was a typical low-budget film aimed at teenagers, an overload of California sun, sand, and romance. The girl was rescued and taken aboard the sailboat. Predictably, she revived and thanked her rescuer profusely with words and smiles. The insipid dialogue fascinated the man sitting next to Ann, and he hung on every word. Without paying attention, she knew the direction the story would take. Hundreds of beach pictures like it had been made in Hollywood over the years. They had occasional surges of popularity, as did westerns or horror flicks. What was the fascination of this one for Nick? His absorption with the film was so complete, he seemed to have forgotten Ann's existence. He no longer had his arm across her shoulders. He was leaning forward with his hands clasped as he stared at the screen.

Ann studied his rapt expression. Could she escape while he was engrossed in the film? Cautiously, she shifted position, and when it didn't disturb him, she edged farther from him on the sofa. He glanced at her with annoyance, and Ann quickly riveted her attention on the screen as if she were enjoying the picture. From the corner of her eye, she saw him turn back to the movie.

If she tried to bolt, he'd catch her before she could reach the door. He had already demonstrated his strength and agility, and she was no match for them. She needed an advantage of some kind. The stone seal was gone, and he had already bested her in physical attack.

The scene on the screen shifted to a plush office. The girl, dressed in a casually revealing sundress and looking pure and wholesome, was seated across a desk from the man who had rescued her. In a three-piece suit of impeccable white linen, he was the perfect executive. He pressed the intercom on his desk and spoke to an unseen secretary.

"Set up a screen test for Miss De Long this afternoon." He broke the connection and sat back in the russet-colored leather armchair. "I'm sure we can fit it into this afternoon's schedule. In the meantime, would you like to look around the studio lot? I'm tied up, but I'll have someone give you the grand tour. And as soon as the test script is ready, I'll have a messenger bring it to you. You're sure you don't need more time to study it?"

"No, I'm a very fast study." She smiled engagingly at him. "I can't thank you enough, Mr. Fallon. You've been just grand. First rescuing me, now arranging this screen test. If you knew how hard I've worked and tried—"

"Saturday was a fortunate day for both of us, Mara," he said. "I'm happy to give you a chance, but you have to prove yourself."

"I will, I promise. Thank you."

Ann stared at the actress's lips without hearing the dialogue. The actor had called her Mara. *Mara.* It was the name Nick had whispered when Ann pretended to forgive him. Mara was a *character,* not a real person. Mara was make-believe, and the man sitting beside Ann, the man who more than likely had killed the woman in the purple jogging suit and who had broken into the house, was living in the fantasy world of a grade B picture.

Glancing at him again, Ann knew she was right. It was the screen character he loved, the screen character from whom he sought forgiveness. For what? Was his transgression real or imagined? Was it possible he was in the picture? She looked back to the screen, not at the major characters now, but at the dozens of minor ones and extras who moved in the backgrounds of shots. If Nick had taken part in the picture, it might explain the reality of it for him. But she didn't spot anyone remotely resembling the man sitting next to her on the sofa. She wished now she'd paid closer attention to the opening titles and seen what year the picture was made. If it was old, Nick could have changed considerably. She might not recognize him even if she saw him on the screen. Another thought struck her. He might have *worked* on the picture as a grip, or an electrician, a makeup man—anything. But he must have had some connection with it for him to believe so completely in one of the characters.

She moved nervously, and Nick gave her another impatient glance. "Watch. Your screen test is coming up. The part where you show them all how great you are."

Ann swallowed the dryness in her throat. "I'm thirsty. I want something to drink."

"I can't leave now!"

"I'll get it," she said quickly. "Do you want anything? A glass of wine maybe?"

He scowled. "I promised you I'd never drink again. You called me—" He darted a glance at the television screen to be sure he wasn't missing anything and didn't finish the sentence. "I don't drink anymore. You didn't think I'd be able to keep my promise, but I have. Not a drop, I swear."

Ann moistened her lips nervously. "I'll make some tea—"

"Takes too long. You'll miss the good part."

She stood, her hands clasped tightly so he wouldn't see them shaking. "I've seen the picture a million times. I'm going to put on the kettle. I want a cup of tea." It was risky, but if he was so infatuated with Mara and had once displeased her badly enough to need forgiveness, he might worry about the anger in her voice.

For a moment, fury glinted in his dark eyes and his

thick brows knit. Then obviously exerting control, he nodded sullenly. "Okay, but come back while the water's heating."

Ann's feet were leaden as she walked toward the kitchen. She felt his gaze follow her but didn't turn. In the kitchen, she turned on the light over the sink, then filled the kettle to the brim with cold water. The longer it took to boil, the more time she had to think out her next move. She had bluffed him momentarily, but could she keep it up? Maybe she was wrong not to watch the picture. Suppose the clue to Nick's behavior lay somewhere in the story line? Suppose Nick was a character in the story too?

"Come on, Mara, it's the screen test!" Nick yelled from the living room.

Ann turned on the burner and went back to the living room. She tried to sit on the other side of Nick, closer to the front hall, but he grabbed her wrist and pulled her back to her former seat. A knife—she should have grabbed a knife! Numbly, Ann tried to catch up with the movie. The girl, Mara, was emoting before a camera crew. She obviously had some talent but was untrained and hardly ready for the competition of a big studio. The expressions of the professionals on the set clearly showed her screen test was doomed to failure.

The kettle hissed, and Ann jumped up. She hurried to the kitchen before Nick could stop her. She dumped tea into the pot and filled it with boiling water. She took a tray from a cupboard and started to get out cups and saucers, then left them in favor of two mugs similar to the one the girl had drunk from on the sailboat. *Play the part,* she told herself. Keep him in the fantasy so he thought she was Mara, at least until she found a moment to catch him unaware. Rattling the mugs on the tray to cover the sound of opening a drawer, she reached for the extra set of car keys, but they weren't there. She pulled the drawer open farther and searched desperately. The keys were gone. How could he have known? She stifled a sob as she eased the drawer shut.

Did Mara take milk or sugar? If she made a mistake, would he notice, as he'd noticed her slip about the wine? Ann drank her tea plain. She'd chance it. Actresses were notorious dieters, so unless there was some reason for the character in the story to do otherwise, the actress's preference would probably be followed.

She set the teapot on the tray. Heat radiated from the ceramic pot filled with scalding water. If she threw it at him, she'd have a few seconds. She opened the knife drawer. Her hand hovered over the long carving knife, but she had no place to hide something that size. She'd have to use a smaller one—

"I'll carry it." Nick had come up behind her soundlessly. Ann jumped and leaned against the drawer to shut it. She shoved her shaking hands into her pockets and smiled nervously as he picked up the tray and motioned her toward the living room. He set the tray on the polished rosewood coffee table, then poured tea into one mug and handed it to her. He pushed aside the tray so it didn't block his view of the television and settled comfortably, taking one of Ann's hands as he concentrated on the screen again.

His fingers were like steel clamps on her flesh. An image of the murdered woman under the bougainvillea flashed in her mind. Strangled by these iron hands. A sour taste pitted Ann's tongue. Her stomach knotted, and she felt tremors begin in her middle and spread. The woman jogger had been strangled so swiftly that no one in the vicinity had heard her cry out. The police theorized the murder had taken place only minutes before Ann discovered the body, yet no one had seen or heard anything.

It was possible the murderer had not run away at all but stayed and blended into the crowd. Most runners, like herself, knew only a handful of the people they saw irregularly. Some might know their immediate neighbors, but she was sure no one knew everyone that had gathered at the murder site. Ann glanced at Nick's profile. Had he stood among the crowd? She didn't remember seeing him, but in her state of shock, she doubted she had noticed half the people who were there. The only one she remembered clearly was Gary Phillips. If only she had answered his call! Gone out to dinner with him!

Nick squeezed her hand and pointed to the screen. Ann looked in time to see the blond Mara being dismissed from the set as the screen test ended. She stood offstage watching the director and cameramen, her face a study in hope. Again, Ann found it impossible to follow the action or story. Somehow she knew that the solution, the answer to the riddle of Nick and Mara, lay not within the picture itself but with Nick's fascination with it. If she searched every face that appeared on the screen, Nick would not be there. Nick had the zealous expression of a fan, but he had fallen in love with a character, not the actress. Mara was alive in his mind. The real actress didn't matter.

Actress. A thought struck Ann like the aftershock of an earthquake. An actress had owned this house. According to the real estate agent, the reason the house had stood empty two years was that it had been tied up in the woman's estate. No mention had ever been made of how she died. Or of her age. Not terribly interested at the time, Ann had assumed it was an actress from Hollywood's heyday and the story was a sand castle built on a few grains of truth. She recalled wondering at the time why the real estate agent hadn't mentioned the actress's name, but she chalked it up to the woman's no-nonsense approach to business. Actually, Ann had respected her for it at the time. The celebrity-fan syndrome created a ready market for numerous houses in the Hollywood Hills, Bel-Air, and Beverly Hills. It was part of the same phenomenon that attracted droves of people on bus tours to "See the Homes of the Stars," but it could be a terrible bore when you wanted to talk plumbing and price.

Was it possible the girl on the screen was the former owner? Ann dredged her mind for the actress's name in the opening credits. Cecie Anton. It had seemed vaguely familiar; now she knew why. Cecily Anthony was the woman from whose estate Ann had purchased the house.

Had Nick confused the girl on the screen with the flesh-and-blood woman who'd lived here? The keys . . . his ability to watch the house and her without being seen . . . his determination when she'd thwarted him by having the locks changed . . . He was still living his fantasy. First Cecie Anton, now Ann, had become the fictional character he was watching with such adoration. Ann was Mara to him now.

She fastened her attention on the screen with an intensity equal to Nick's. Her salvation, if there was to be any, would come from Mara. She studied the actress's mannerism, movements, and voice. The part was the typically innocent ingenue caught between her own burning ambition and the evils of Hollywood. Obviously Mara was willing to use guile to help her cause, and her fake drowning had gotten her a screen test.

Now she undoubtedly would run afoul of lecherous men with evil intentions, but in the end she somehow would triumph and find true love. The story didn't matter. Ann had to find a clue in Mara's character that would give her control over Nick.

Sweet and innocent. If it were daylight, Ann might come up with half a dozen excuses to go outside, but Nick would never let sweet, innocent Mara wander around in the dark alone. Did Nick recognize the guile and hard edge of ambition showing through Mara's character? His anger had dissipated quickly when she insisted on the tea. He didn't want her mad at him. It was a slim hope, but it was the only wedge she had.

She sipped the tea and tried to devise some kind of plan. The phone didn't work. She'd have to entice him outside, but how?

"Nick," she said with as much encouragement in her voice as she could muster. When he glanced at her, she smiled. "I've seen the picture so many times, I'm tired of it. Let's go somewhere."

His gaze flicked to the screen, then back to her. "You love this picture."

"Sure," she said quickly, "but I'd like to see something else. Let's go to a movie."

He turned away petulantly. "It's too late. Drink your tea."

She realized she'd made a mistake. It was almost midnight. Only all-night porn movies on the seedy end of Sunset played at this hour. She watched him side-long while she held the hot mug close to her mouth. What other excuse could she invent for going outside? No movie, no drinks, no walk on the beach. What else would Mara do?

Of course!

She set the mug on the table and got to her feet. Nick tried to grab her, but she pulled away with a show of impatience. "I have to go to the bathroom. I'll be right back." He let go.

The half bath was at the end of the hall near the studio. She walked as naturally as possible, wondering if he was watching her. At the powder-room door, she reached in to snap on the light before she went in. As she closed the door, she glanced at the front door almost directly across the hall. The chain was hanging loose the way she'd undone it. In the faint light, there was no way to see if either of the locks was on. Had he snapped them when they came in? She shut the bathroom door so the light wouldn't make him suspicious. She couldn't remember about the locks. She had been too terrified then to notice anything. No, that wasn't true. She clearly recalled him slamming the bolt on the gate. Her hopes soared. The chain was undone. There was a very good chance the deadbolt wasn't fastened either. The snap lock was the only one she had to worry about. If she had set it open, it wouldn't lock automatically when he shut the door.

How much time would she have? Ten seconds, maybe fifteen. She'd have to be out the front door and get the gate open fast. How far could she get before he covered the distance between them? She was trembling violently; she was afraid her legs wouldn't hold her. She'd go down the hill. It was easier. If he caught her—

She glanced around the tiny room in desperation. Her pale, frightened face with huge dark circles under the eyes stared back at her from the mirror over the sink.

Hurry, she told herself. Hurry before he gets suspicious. If only she'd left a pair of jeans or slacks in here. It would be easier to run in pants than in a long housecoat. It couldn't be helped. She flushed the toilet and was about to run water in the sink in case he was listening. To her astonishment, the sink was streaked with dirt. She'd washed her hands here when she was trimming back the jade plant, but that had been three days ago, and she had scrubbed the sink to a shine afterward. She trailed a finger through the gritty sand and found it was damp. *He* had washed his hands here! So close to the bedroom. She was weak at the thought that she had no idea how long he'd been in the house before she wakened.

Staring at the brown trails on the white porcelain, she knew she had to make a run for it while she had the chance. She couldn't go back to the living room. She pulled open the cabinet drawer and sobbed with relief when she saw the garden shears she'd used to cut the thick, soft branches of the jade plant. She slipped them into her pocket with her hand gripping the clasped handles. Turning out the light, she turned the doorknob and inched open the door. *Now.* She stepped across the hall, not daring to glance toward the living room to see if he had noticed her. As she reached to snap open the Yale lock, Nick's voice spoke close behind her.

"What are you doing?" He was standing in the bedroom doorway. His jacket was gone, and the sleeves of the plaid shirt were rolled up to his elbows.

Ann let out a startled yelp. "I—I was just making sure the door is locked." So close! Tears stung her eyes, and she blinked rapidly.

Nick took a step toward her. "I'll do it."

Ann flattened her back to the door. "I can do it!" She heard the note of hysteria in her voice and took a sharp breath. "Go back and sit down. I'll be there in a minute."

He didn't move.

"Go ahead," she coaxed in an imitation of the screen character's ingenuous voice. "Pour me some more tea."

He was silent a moment, then said, "Okay. You sure you don't want to watch the rest of the movie?" He was almost pleading.

Ann gave him a tremulous smile. "Tell you what, rewind to the beginning of the screen test. Let's watch that part again. You know it's my favorite."

He nodded eagerly. "It's my favorite, too." He hurried down the hall.

The moment he was out of sight, Ann opened the door and slipped outside. She ran to the gate and got the locks undone and opened it. She was outside then, running down the road past the dark neighboring houses. The heavy shears in her pocket banged against her hipbone, and she pulled them out and clenched them in her fist.

"Mara!" The scream behind her was full of rage and pain.

One of Ann's soft slippers flew off, and she whimpered as the cold, rough asphalt stung her bare foot. The two houses next door were dark, their gated carports vacant. The long, empty curve stretched ahead. She'd be out in the open. The flying pink housecoat spotlighted her in the darkness. Ann risked a glance over her shoulder. She saw only an indistinct blur of movement on the dark road behind her, but she knew it was Nick, out of the house and running after her. Despite the good condition she was in, fear was constricting her chest, so she was gasping for breath. He would overtake her in minutes if she stayed on the open road.

The beginning of the long curve started past her second neighbor. Then there was a lengthy stretch without houses, where one side of the canyon wall rose sharply and the other dropped precipitously, unfit for anything but jackrabbits and coyotes. But it was her only hope, her last chance.

She raced past the second house hugging the inside curve. Her decorator's eye recalled the bed of ice plant in colorful bloom adjacent to the house. She veered abruptly, praying that Nick was still far enough behind not to see, and plunged down the hill. She lost her footing immediately as her slippers tangled in the thick plants. The clippers flew from her hand as she skidded in the wet ooze from the broken leaves of the succulents. She fell to her seat, then to her back as her speed increased. She grabbed desperately, but the soft plants snapped and did little to slow her. Sobbing, she spread her arms to create as much resistance as possible. Finally she came to a stop when the ground changed pitch.

She lay where she was, choking down her sobs and listening for anything on the road above her. Were the thumps his running footsteps or her own pulse pounding? No lights had come on in either of her neighbors' houses, but the glow from the canyon and the city gave the hillside a deep gray gloom that, once accustomed to, was not impenetrable. Why couldn't the freakish fog have lasted one more night?

Then suddenly she heard him on the road. Going past! He hadn't seen her! She watched his moving figure against the darkness as he raced around the curve. Then, abruptly, he stopped.

Ann realized he could see all the way to the next bend. There were no houses on the steep side of the road, and only one on the other. There was nothing to obstruct his view, and he had just realized she couldn't have gotten that far ahead of him. She imagined his puzzled, angry look as he turned and raised his hands to his eyes. With a sick feeling, she realized he had binoculars!

There was no way he could miss the huge, pale splotch of her pink housecoat, even in the dark. Ann didn't wait for him to spot her. She stumbled to her hands and knees and began to crawl through the tangle of ice plant. Succulents so wonderful for retaining moisture throughout the dry months now crushed under her weight and became a greased skid. She slid dangerously downhill with each attempt to move crosswise on the steep ground. Then the bed of ice plant ended abruptly and she was dragging through dust and spiny wild plants that stabbed and cut her flesh.

"Mara!" Nick's wounded cry rolled down the canyon and bounced among the hills. "Mara!" Coming up the hill, car headlights swept the road. Nick looked around in confusion, and when the approaching headlights outlined him clearly, he crouched and leaped out over the embankment.

There was a dull thud as he landed. He curled into a ball and rolled, spinning toward Ann as though some desperate inner radar directed him. Sobbing, Ann scrambled as fast as she could. Her palms and knees were raw, and cactus barbs dug at her flesh like needles. Dust choked her, and she coughed painfully, no longer making any effort to be quiet. If she had the breath, she'd scream, but it took all her energy to keep moving.

She was in line with the house next to hers but some fifty feet down from the edge of its deck. No matter how hard she tried, she kept skidding downhill. Finally she let herself slide. It was her only hope. There was no way she could get back up to the road. She tried to increase her speed by running, but she fell headlong down the steep grade. She was too dazed to do anything but bounce and spin downward, crashing through tough sagebrush and banging against rocks. Remembering Nick's image tumbling toward her, she managed to curl up the way he had and roll. She came to a jarring stop against something that stabbed her shoulder painfully.

She lay facedown inhaling dust. Her body ached all over, but she found she could move. She turned her head. She had rolled into a gully where rainwater and dew gathered enough moisture to permit a thick stand of bamboo to survive. In the faint, eerie glow of light, the wide path she had painted down the hillside was clearly visible.

Gradually she realized another light was coming from above on the road. It swept down the hill in a scanning arc, searching. Nick was on the hillside somewhere behind her. Someone else was shining the light. As she watched, a spotlight came on, this one from the curve where Nick had stopped running when he realized she wasn't ahead of him. The two beams swept and crossed, crisscrossed, and finally pinpointed the moving figure about twenty yards above her and less than five from the stand of bamboo. Ann clamped her hand over her mouth to choke back her sobs and screams.

"You down there—don't move or we'll shoot!" a voice boomed through a bullhorn.

Pinned in the glaring lights, Nick crouched in the dust and broken shrubs. His head swiveled from one light to the other. Then, without hesitation, he started downhill again with leaping strides, like a bounding mountain goat. He crashed through the bamboo. The powerful lights followed him.

Ann crawled out of the thicket, terrified of being

caught in the crossfire. She waved her arms frantically.

"Mara!" Nick screamed and plunged after her.

Sobbing, Ann clawed the ground, too weak to run. Nick came toward her like a madman, hands groping and teeth bared in an insane grimace of love and hate and obsession. He was the macabre madman of her nightmare. Around her, the ground slipped and crumbled when she tried to move. Nick loomed over her.

Mara . . . The name screamed inside Ann's head. She felt loose dirt squeeze between her fingers as she scooped up a handful and flung it in Nick's eyes.

"Aaagh!" He fell back, crashing into the bamboo. He made another sound that could have been a moan or could have been a desperate attempt to call Mara's name once more. Then he was still.

Her cuts, bruises, and stings treated, Ann gratefully accepted Gary Phillips's offer of a ride home from the hospital emergency room. She'd refused the sedative the doctor wanted to give her, and although she had stopped shaking, she was still keyed up with nervous energy.

Gary settled her comfortably on her sofa, then sat cross-legged on the hearth while he coaxed the dying fire back to life. Ann didn't know where to begin. She started with "Thank you." The medics who had carried her up the steep embankment to the ambulance had told her that Gary had called the police.

Next she said, "I'll go crazy if you don't explain all of this. I still feel as if I'm trapped in a nightmare."

He glanced up, and the firelight danced across his pleasant features. "The nightmare's over now."

"How in the world did you know what was happening? What made you call the police?"

He grinned. "Elementary, my dear Watson. I called the police because as I drove up the hill after my lonely meal and bottle of wine to drown my sorrows of rejection, I thought I saw someone leap down the side of the hill. I was ready to blame it on the Bordeaux until I saw your front door wide open. I ran in to rescue you, but all I found was the movie *Sand Castle* playing to an empty house. I'd spent at least twelve minutes earlier this evening writing one of the most dramatic and enticing phone messages ever to be left on an answering machine. It was guaranteed to get results, but when I phoned, your line was dead. Now suddenly the house of mystery was emanating mystery again." He tossed a log on the burning kindling and watched to make sure it caught.

"But my phone wasn't working—"

"My car phone was. You forget, you're dealing with a man of distinction. The open door, the empty house, and thinking I saw some lunatic jump down the hill got me thinking about Sally Dunn and about the unsolved murder that happened in this house two years ago—"

Ann bolted up. "What unsolved murder?"

"I won't tell you the story unless you follow the doctor's orders. Now lie down and relax." He poured Zinfandel into the two goblets he had brought from her cupboard and handed her one.

When she had settled back again, he told her the bizarre tale he had uncovered when he researched her house in order to convince her to have dinner with him.

Cecie Anton had lived in the house two years. She was a moderately successful actress who was relegated to minor roles or the lead in dreadful quickies like *Sand Castle*. Though she excelled in the kind of beauty that captured ingenue parts, she was vicious and aggressive in pursuit of her career, so much so that she had gained a reputation in the industry as a difficult bitch. At age twenty-seven, her career was going downhill because producers and directors refused to work with her. She was unpopular with her neighbors, too, because she was given to late and loud entertaining.

After a particularly noisy night, a neighbor noticed a broken railing on the deck. When he looked down the hillside, Cecie Anton's body was lying half covered by dirt about a hundred yards down the hill. She had been strangled during a violent struggle and had fallen or been pushed over the railing. No one had seen the killer, nor was the crime ever solved.

"There were vases of bougainvillea all over the house, and the video hadn't been turned off, even though there wasn't any tape in it. The studio had given a copy of the tape to Cecie Anton. The picture never made it to video any other way," Gary said. "It was missing after the murder." He sipped his wine and watched her over the rim of the glass.

Ann paled. "He murdered her and took the tape?"

Gary nodded. "I'll write the scene with him losing control when Cecie Anton, the bitch, flies into one of her typical rages and tries to throw him out. His idol is destroyed and his mind flips. They fight. His hands—" He stopped when he saw Ann's face pale. "They may never get the whole story, but that seems the most likely bet. The police are trying to run down his history. No one knows where he's been the past two years or how he got to know Cecie Anton. There's a good chance he really didn't know her at all, but either conned or forced his way in that night the same way he did tonight. They're checking through R&I for similar crimes. The only real evidence they have so far is his obvious obsession with a pretty girl he saw in a movie."

Ann shuddered. Nick had said he'd been looking for her a long time—for Mara. He'd mistaken Sally Dunn for Mara as well, just as he'd once believed Cecie Anton was the fictional character with whom he'd fallen in love. A character who didn't exist, and when flesh-and-blood women didn't fulfill his fantasy, he destroyed them in rage.

"It was your luck to buy the house that was part of his fixation. I told you the place had a lurid history." Gary smiled again and winked.

"What's going to happen to him now?"

"The DA doesn't have much of a case. He'll probably get Nick committed to Atascadero on the basis of what happened here. If they ever think about letting him out, he'll have to stand trial for Sally Dunn's murder." Gary glanced at the burning log in the fireplace and closed the screen. Then he lifted the crystal wine goblet to touch Ann's. "If you were an actress, I'd see that you got cast for the lead when we shoot the story on *Stand-in for Murder*."

"No thank you," Ann said, shuddering. "Show business is too dangerous for me. I'm going to stick to decorating."

"And this house, I hope?"

Ann sipped her wine, smiling. "Yes, it's perfect now that the nightmare is over." And it was. She knew she'd never dream the horrible dream again.

THE HOUSE OF CRIME
VINCENT McCONNOR

As everyone knows, show business is an insecure way of life. The public's taste is fickle, and as actors grow older, once-promising careers suddenly can look less than secure. As a result, Los Angeles is filled with former actors making their livings in all kinds of ways. Scot Carddo, in Vincent McConnor's "The House of Crime," is one of them. Now he runs a mystery bookstore, knowledgeably advising his customers on the latest arrivals or overlooked classics of detection. Until one day a real murder convinces him to turn detective.

* * *

SCOT Carddo drank the last of his cooling coffee, pushed the Spode cup and saucer to one side with his plate.

He'd enjoyed his customary weekday breakfast of two small baked sausages, toasted granola muffin with one sparse spoonful of imported confiture—it had been apricot this morning—and a single cup of black coffee.

Reaching for his morning paper, as usual, he glanced across the sunny terrace toward the deep canyon beyond his pool and saw the ridiculous towers and rooftops of Hollywood far below.

The only sounds were the cooing of pigeons and chirpings of wrens.

He could barely hear Nicholas singing to himself in the distant kitchen.

His houseman had been featured in hit Broadway musicals, back in the thirties when he first came over from London, and he still had a pleasant light baritone. His repertoire consisted of songs from the past. Mostly Gershwin, Kern, Rodgers and Hart. At the moment it seemed to be Kern, although he couldn't be certain.

Opening the *L.A. Times,* Scot squinted at the new leaves on the eucalyptus trees along the south side of his property, watched them shiver in an invisible breeze. Another beautiful spring morning.

He only glanced at the front page. Another bombing in the Middle East, a new political scandal in Washington, and more problems with pollution in California. Put the first section aside and pulled out the three sections he always read immediately. Metro, View, and Calendar. Local crime news, book review, and show biz. Unfolded the Metro section and spread it open.

A headline jumped at him as he recognized a familiar face in the accompanying photograph.

Judith Morgan? She had worked with him, years ago, in television.

ACTRESS EIGHTH VICTIM
OF THE TWILIGHT MAN

He read the brief story quickly. The facts were few, the story shocking.

Judith Morgan, age thirty-two—she was possibly older, because actresses always cut at least five years from their age—had been killed with a single shot in the head, last evening, as she left her car in the parking lot of an apartment complex, where she made her home, on Havenhurst Drive.

The police believed her killer was the Latino known as the Twilight Man who, in the past year, had killed seven women. He had been given the name because he struck just before lights were turned on in parking areas of most apartment buildings. It was believed he waited for his victims, hidden in shrubbery or in his car. They were always attractive young women whom he raped, robbed, and shot.

There was one difference in the murder of Judith Morgan. Her purse was missing but she had not been raped. A spokesman for Hollywood Division claimed the investigating police believed her killer was scared away before he could complete his usual pattern of operation. A neighbor had seen a black Toyota pull out and speed off as he parked his own car at the rear of the parking area.

The driver was a Chicano with long black hair, mustache, and beard, wearing a black shirt. This neighbor had identified a composite portrait drawn by a police artist of the Twilight Man as the person he saw fleeing the scene. There was a brief biography of

Judith Morgan that would be expanded in later editions.

Scot let the paper fall onto the patio table.

What a way to die. A casual killer, waiting for his victim in the twilight. He'd read every story, from the first, about the Twilight Man. Clipped and filed them.

Judith Morgan had shown considerable talent when he worked with her. An attractive, intelligent actress. She'd been on Broadway for several seasons, in respectable productions, before coming out to Hollywood. As the paper said, she had been featured in a dozen minor films before getting an important and continuing role in the successful television series *The Hills of Beverly* for the past three years. Ronald Temple had the lead and Judith Morgan was featured.

"Something wrong, sir?"

The inquisitive British accent made Scot look up to see his houseman peering at him, holding a silver tray on which he was about to remove the breakfast debris. "It seems the Twilight Man has killed again."

"Has he, indeed?" The trained actor's face registered shock.

"This time his victim is an actress."

"Someone we know?"

"Judith Morgan."

"Ah, yes. I've never met the young lady but I see her every week in *The Hills of Beverly*. One of my favorite shows. She plays a bitchy neighbor who lives up the canyon next to Horace Hill and his snobbish wife. Always causing trouble for both of them. The character appears to have had a rather lurid past. I suspect, when she was younger, she might have had a brief fling with Horace Hill. The women in his past are constantly turning up."

"I've never seen the show." Rising from the white patio table. "Better do my exercises. Shave, shower, and get to work. Don't pack lunch for me today. I'll get a bite somewhere."

"Will you be driving the Mercedes or the Rolls?"

"I think the Chevy might be better."

"Very good, sir."

"Less conspicuous. I just might get involved in this Twilight Man investigation. After all, I am an honorary cop." He secured his shantung robe as he headed for the house. "As well as actor and bookshop owner."

Driving down Laurel Canyon, easy on the curves, Scot continued to consider the improbable death of Judith Morgan. The first person he'd ever known, personally, to be murdered.

Turning the Chevy left on Melrose, he continued on, through heavy morning traffic, toward the bookshop.

Questions darting through his mind. And quotations. "Other sins only speak; murder shrieks out." "Murder cannot be hid long." "How easily murder is discovered."

Speeches remembered from his classes, long ago, at RADDA.

Was murder easily discovered? Could he find this Twilight Man the police had been hunting for the past year?

Solve a murder! Such an idea had never occurred to him before.

He glimpsed the neat sign hanging above the entrance to his shop.

Scot Carddo's
HOUSE OF CRIME

The sign had been created by an artist friend. With an ivory skeleton, garlanded with flowers, holding an armful of books. The sign always made him smile, with pride and pleasure.

He turned the Chevy up Edinburgh Avenue and swerved into the alley behind his shop.

He'd bought this property because of that cross street. His mother had been born in Edinburgh. He had changed his name to Scot Carddo when he became an actor in London. That had seemed better for the theater than John Carddoni.

As he parked the Chevy next to Jimmy Matsuda's motorbike, he realized that Havenhurst was only half a dozen blocks away. It started at Sunset and came to an abrupt end at Santa Monica.

The murder had taken place last evening, at twilight.

He had left the shop before six. Closing time was seven, but he rarely remained on the premises that late.

He got out, locked the Chevy, and went in through the rear entrance, into the white-painted storage room, between cartons of books waiting to be unpacked. Opened the door and went into the shop. Paused there, unnoticed, looking down the length of the handsome room toward the display window on Melrose. His bookshop.

Two customers. A middle-aged woman and a young one. He'd never seen either of them before.

The older woman stood at a table displaying new detective novels by British writers, with the latest P. D. James conspicuous in the center. The girl was at a table offering novels by California writers. They looked like browsers who wouldn't buy.

Jimmy Matsuda was perched on his stool at the cashier's desk, reading, sneaking glances at the two potential customers through his black-rimmed spectacles. Hidden speakers were whispering Scarlatti—

Landowska at the harpsichord—to soothe the sleeping books.

Each of these thousands of books was his friend, and he gave them a peaceful home until someone took them away.

The air was always fresh here, air conditioner turned low, because of small No Smoking signs scattered through the shop.

He saw that Jimmy had become aware of his arrival and was leaving his book on the desk, beside the cash register, and hopping down from the high stool.

Scot moved forward and went into his private wood-paneled nook, where he sank into a comfortable brown leather armchair near the marble fireplace that was always lighted in cold weather. Unfortunately it was only a gas fire. He'd tried to install a real fireplace but discovered there was a law forbidding one in a shop crammed with inflammable books. At the moment there were pots of amaryllis blooming on the hearth. There was, at least, a small bar for when old friends dropped in for a visit. He looked up as Jimmy joined him, wearing an eternal oriental smile in the center of his round face but his eyes troubled behind the spectacles.

"You read about that murder, boss? One of our regular customers!"

"I did."

"Can't believe Ms. Morgan's dead. Never to buy another book! She was in last week and bought two."

"Death is certain for all of us, I'm afraid."

"Such a nice lady!"

"I worked with her, years ago, on some long-forgotten television show, and I've talked to her many times, of course, in the shop. But I've no idea what sort of person she was." He hesitated. "An adequate actress.

Not great. One successful series can make an actor famous these days. Talent or no talent." He sighed. "Anything new this morning?"

"The usual bookie-lookies. Three phone calls. All coming in later to pick up books."

"I won't see anyone this morning, or take any calls. Want to think about this latest Twilight Man murder. Try to solve the puzzle in my head, at least. Why he would kill Judith Morgan? Perhaps make a few phone calls. Ask questions."

"Yes, sir."

"What time does Vikki come in today?"

"Twelve o'clock. Irving couldn't make it until three. I'll go out for lunch at one, if that's okay."

"I didn't bring lunch today. I'll handle the shop while you're out. May slip off for a bite, after the lunch crowd's gone."

"Is anyone here to take my money?" Woman's voice from the shop.

Scot laughed. "You've made a sale in absentia."

Jimmy hurried back toward the front.

Scot relaxed in his armchair as Scarlatti changed to Bach. There was no door to this spacious private nook, but customers rarely came back this far and he had complete privacy, but at the same time he was able to hear every sound from the shop. He could see one rear corner at an angle, but those shelves were nonfiction, books on notorious criminals and famous detectives, which only attracted writers.

From his armchair he could see those books on their carved oak shelves and one of the large framed photos of a scene from some old film in which he had starred as a detective. It always pleased him when a customer remembered those early movies. The framed stills were hung between the ranks of shelves with a small armchair under each.

He glanced at the pair of telephones resting on his Victorian desk. The white phone was an extension of the one in the front, the black phone was his private unlisted number. Both were within reach of where he sat.

He couldn't put Judith Morgan's death out of his mind. An honest-to-God murder. Involving a personal acquaintance. Not a friend, but an acquaintance.

What did he really know about Judith Morgan? Very little.

Starting with the week they spent working together on that series. Couldn't recall the name of the show. He'd done so many. And that was only a one-shot. He'd played an American and had had several scenes with Judith. He was impressed by her talent but they hadn't become friendly. That seldom happened when you met an actor for the first time working in television. He hadn't, really, talked to Judith that week, between scenes, and didn't see her again until she came into his shop. Perhaps two years ago.

She had told Jimmy Matsuda they were friends—in Hollywood everybody was your friend if you only said good morning—and Ron had called on the extension to tell him Ms. Judith Morgan was in the shop and asking for him. Jimmy was always impressed by a pretty face.

He hadn't recalled the name but, as usual, went into the shop to greet her. There were several women looking at books and he didn't recognize any of their faces. Jimmy, at the desk, whispered which was Ms. Morgan, and he joined her at a table piled with a display of classic mysteries. He pretended to remember her but was at a loss to recall where they had met until she mentioned that series they had worked on together.

He had no idea what they talked about that day.

Judith bought a big book containing all five of the novels written by Dashiell Hammett.

The next time she came into his shop she opened a charge and he learned she lived on Havenhurst. After that she dropped in several times a month—always bought books—and became quite friendly. If he was free he would chat with her. He did that with all the regular customers. Enjoyed hearing how they liked the books they had bought on their previous visit or if they didn't, why not?

He had many such conversations with Judith Morgan—you learned a great deal from a person's reactions to a book—but was told little about her personal life.

The morning paper said she was born in Philadelphia thirty-two years ago. More likely thirty-five or even thirty-seven. Say thirty-five. That would be 1950.

He was already in Hollywood that year. He'd been here several years and, like his pal Ray Milland, was playing American as well as British parts. Had made more than thirty features, in addition to doing many radio shows, especially those based upon successful films. Television was new then.

Judith claimed to have worked in little theater, before leaving Philadelphia, as well as off and on Broadway in New York. That must've been in the sixties, when Broadway was already on the skids.

She'd come to Hollywood in the middle seventies and signed with an agent who got her small parts in television and feature films and, eventually, a running part in *The Hills of Beverly*. That series had been an instant success—in the top ten—from the first show.

She must've gotten an enormous salary, because recently she had talked about buying a beach house in Malibu. Had mentioned an inheritance. "From the past," she had said. Probably a rich relative in Philadelphia was leaving her the money.

He wondered if she'd bought that property before she died.

Was it possible he could solve her death? Find some clue or bit of evidence that would lead to the capture of this Twilight Man?

The police had been after him for months. It was presumptuous to imagine he would be able to find the killer—even if he was an honorary member of the LAPD. Lieutenant Scot Carddo.

He glanced up at the framed scroll hanging, in a place of honor, above the fireplace. It had been presented to him by Chief Gates in recognition of the countless detective roles he'd played in films, radio, and television. The inscription said it was "for his ability to always catch the criminal." He'd suspected, at first, it was a stunt to publicize a feature film he was making but learned that the police had arranged for their own publicity people to offer him the honor.

Since then he'd met many detectives from Hollywood Division and had made one real friend among them—Harry Danihy, Lieutenant Henry Danihy, who worked out of Burglary-Homicide. They dined together at least once a month, and Harry dropped by the shop every week to buy the latest paperback detective novels. Anything but police procedurals, which reminded him of his job.

Scot picked up the novel he'd been reading yesterday, opened it to the pages separated by a bookmark—one of those included with every purchase at the House of Crime—and slipped on the spectacles he kept on his desk. He found it difficult to pick up the story again, because his mind was occupied with Judith Morgan and the Twilight Man.

Had the bearded Latino killer in his black shirt been

waiting when she pulled into her drive? He wondered what make car she drove. Did the guy shoot her as she turned and saw him? That other car pulling in—the neighbor who'd glimpsed the killer—must've scared him away. Before he could rape his latest victim.

The book didn't hold his interest. Even yesterday, when he wasn't thinking about a real murder, he'd been unable to become involved. The characters were too predictable, and he didn't like novels that had so many dead bodies. Explanations became too involved and it took too long to tie up the loose ends. He liked a novel with three or four murders. This one already had seven.

Scot closed the book and laid it on his desk. That would be one of those he never finished and would never recommend.

He wondered what Hollywood Division had turned up on Judith Morgan's death. In the past the Twilight Man had left no clues. Except the bullets removed from his victims' heads. Did the bullet from Judith Morgan's skull match the others? The autopsy might be under way, at this moment, downtown.

He pulled off his spectacles and set them on the desk. Why not call Harry Danihy? Find out what he knew about the Twilight Man's eighth murder? It would be impossible to solve Judith's murder unless he had every fact known to the police.

Harry was usually in his office around noon. No matter where he'd been during the morning, he liked to return to check over his notes and go over reports from other detectives working on his current jobs. There would be extra men assigned to this Twilight Man investigation.

Maybe invite Harry out to lunch. That way they could talk, for at least an hour, without interruption.

He would call Hollywood Division after twelve. Either Harry would be in his office or they would know when he might be back.

A phone buzzed on his desk. Each had a different sound.

He picked up the white phone. "Yes, Jimmy?"

"Boss, Ms. Winston's here."

"I'll be right out."

He put the phone down and got to his feet.

Alicia Winston was one of his oldest and dearest friends. He and his wife had known her since their early days in New York. Now Alicia was a widow and he was a widower.

He left his private nook and stood, briefly, inspecting the shop. Sunlight flooded through the display window from the street, and there was soft light from shaded lamps scattered on small tables throughout the shop.

Alicia was standing at a table piled with the latest novels. As he walked toward her, his steps silent on the blood-red carpet, he saw that nobody was aware of Alicia's presence. One of the top stars, but her simple spring suit, flowered scarf, and white hair gave no indication of her fame. She wore white gloves and no jewelry. As he approached her he saw that she was still—she must be eighty—one of the most beautiful women he'd ever known. Her hair was simply arranged; the sand-colored linen suit made it seem silver. Her face didn't show a wrinkle and she wore no makeup. In fact, she looked exactly as she had when he first saw her in that big musical at the Ziegfeld Theatre.

She looked up, sensing his presence. "Scot, love!" Holding her face up to be kissed.

He touched her cheek gently with his lips, aware

of the same floral scent she had always worn. "Dear friend . . ."

"We're driving up to Ojai, and I realized I was out of books. What do you suggest? As usual, not too much blood, please."

"There's a new Dell Shannon and a fine Julian Symons."

"I'll take both! Where are they? I don't have my specs, as usual."

He picked up a copy of each. "Then there are two new writers I like very much. One mystery set against a Broadway background. Late forties."

"I would like that. We were there, both of us."

He reached for the two books. "This other one's about young American tourists in Paris. Great fun and a real mystery."

"I haven't been to Paris in years. Books remind me how beautiful it used to be."

"Then there's a very good anthology of mystery novellas. Famous authors." He took a copy from a tall pile. "I'd never read any of them before."

"That looks too heavy to read in bed, but I'll try. Well! These should keep me out of mischief for a bit."

He walked beside her toward the cashier's desk.

"I suppose you read about that actress in the morning paper? Shot by that disgusting Twilight Man."

"Certainly did." He handed the books across the counter to Ron. "I worked with Judith Morgan several years ago."

"Did you?"

"One week in some forgettable television play. Never got to know her until she came into the shop."

"She was one of your customers?"

"For the past two years. Her apartment's on Havenhurst."

"I never heard of Havenhurst before."

"Only a few blocks from here."

Jimmy returned the books across the counter to Scot, neatly wrapped with a loop of cord to carry them.

Alicia smiled one of her famous smiles. "Thank you, Jimmy."

"My pleasure, Ms. Winston."

"Los Angeles is very dangerous at night. I never venture out. Only in the car with my chauffeur, and Eric's getting a bit old to protect me from Twilight Men."

"I'll take you to your car." Scot walked beside her, with the parcel of books. "How is beautiful Ojai these days?"

"Recovering from the spring floods and preparing for the summer fires. But I wouldn't live anyplace else. Except my hotel suite in Beverly Hills."

"How long have you had the house in Ojai?"

"Thirty years. And it will take more than fires and floods to make me move."

Scot pushed the door open and followed her across the sidewalk, where the uniformed chauffeur, tall and white-haired, was opening the rear door of the Rolls. "How are you, Eric?"

"In the pink, Mr. Carddo." Reaching for the package of books.

Scot leaned down to kiss the actress on her cheek again. "Take care of yourself, dear lady."

"I always do." Holding out her hand for the chauffeur to assist her into the Rolls. "See you, love, when I get back. Why don't you drive up to Ojai for a weekend?"

"Well . . ."

"You can leave your precious bookshop for one weekend. I still have the same wonderful cook, and you have my phone number up there."

The chauffeur closed the door and, touching his cap to Scot, circled the shiny black Rolls to the driver's seat.

Scot was smiling as he watched the big car nose into traffic and silently move away. None of the passersby had noticed that enchanting face. Too busy looking at the Rolls.

Alicia Winston was one of the last of the great stars. There were a dozen minor ones among his clients, but she was one of the all-time box-office greats. Nobody in the shop ever recognized her.

He turned back into the bookshop, where Jimmy was adding the just-purchased books to Alicia Winston's account. "Don't put any calls through for ten minutes. I'll be on the private line."

"Right, boss."

As Scot walked through the center aisle he wondered what he would say to Harry Danihy.

"Pardon me, Mr. Carddo . . ."

"Yes?" He faced a young man, a regular customer, whose name he could never recall.

"That lady you were talking to just now. Wasn't that Jeanette MacDonald?"

"No. It wasn't."

"Face looked familiar. Thought it was Jeanette MacDonald."

"Miss MacDonald died several years ago."

"I didn't know that."

"Excuse me." He continued on to his office nook. Sat down and picked up the white phone. Dialed a familiar number.

"LAPD—Hollywood Division."

"Is Lieutenant Danihy available at the moment?"

"Who's calling?"

"Scot Carddo."

"Don't believe the lieutenant's in, sir. Let me check."

He glanced at his wristwatch. Only five after twelve. Should have waited until twelve-thirty.

"Mr. Carddo?"

"Yes?"

"Lieutenant Danihy went out early this morning and hasn't returned. Nobody seems to know where he might be or when he'll come back."

"Tell him I called. I'll be at my bookshop all day."

"I'll do that, Mr. Carddo. S'pose I should say Lieutenant Carddo. I was there that night when the chief presented you with a scroll."

"Did we meet?"

"Not in that mob of greedy cops! All after your autograph."

"We'll have to meet one day. Thanks." He set the phone down.

Now, to pass the time, he would work the shop. Mingle with the customers. Talk to them and sell a few books.

He enjoyed that, as long as complete strangers didn't ask too many personal questions. When they acted as though they had every right to know about his private life, he made a fast retreat to the nook.

Scot pushed himself up from his armchair and stepped out into the bookshop. Several customers moved among the tables displaying new books and along the shelves covering the walls, running the length of the shop, front to back. Two were standing before the notice board where recent reviews of mysteries were displayed. Jimmy was making change for a young woman but looked up, saw him, and nodded, accustomed to his working the floor in the middle of the day.

The street outside was bright with sunlight. Melrose had been widened a few years ago and the side-walks were so narrow they always seemed crowded during the hours people were window shopping.

Vikki would arrive at twelve and Jimmy would go to lunch, return at one, and work until four. Irving Kritzer would come in at three today, instead of two, and partner Vikki until closing. They were treasures, along with the cleaning woman—a Guatemalan mother of four—who arrived at nine every night to remove all evidence of the day's activities. The four of them had been with him since he opened the House of Crime and he hoped they would never leave him.

And he hoped Harry Danihy would call and tell him what the police had learned about the murder of Judith Morgan. Was that her real name? All he knew was she came from Philadelphia.

"You're Mr. Carddo, aren't you?"

He looked around to see a pale young woman with a Botticelli face and long blond hair. "That's right."

"You don't have any secondhand books?"

"I'm afraid not." He moved closer, drawn by her beauty, aware that her clothes were shabby.

"I adore mysteries, but I can't afford to buy new ones."

"There's a large section of paperbacks."

"I prefer hardcover. But they're so expensive."

"We don't have secondhand books—I don't like to call any book secondhand—but there's one section of books . . ." Motioning toward the east wall. "They're from my personal library. After I read a book, if I don't keep it for my private collection at home, I add it to these shelves. I like to call them used books, not sec-ondhand. To me no book is ever secondhand."

"I agree." She smiled as she moved toward the shelves. "Good books are old friends. I never throw one away unless it falls apart."

He followed her, interested and amused, curious to

see which book she would select. "There are some treasures here. Many were duplicates I replaced with new editions. Although I keep all first editions of my favorite writers."

"Here's a Josephine Tey I've never read. *The Singing Sands*."

"I replaced that in my library when I found a copy of the 1952 British first edition. Splendid book!"

"I'll take this. If it's not too expensive."

"All these books are half price, or less."

"Thank you, Mr. Carddo. You're one of my favorite actors."

"How nice of you to say so."

"I'll be in again."

He watched her carry the novel to the desk as he moved around the shop, making himself available to any customer who wanted advice or information. He enjoyed meeting them, learning their tastes and guiding them to more interesting writers. Introducing them to Simenon, Raymond Chandler, or the Gideon series by Marric.

He worked the aisles, happily, until Vikki arrived in flowered blouse and tailored slacks. He nodded as she carried her purse and several parcels toward the back room, where each of his staff had a locker for personal belongings. After a moment, he returned to his nook, sat back in the armchair, and waited for her.

Vikki came from the storeroom, primping her bright red hair. "Here I am! Ready for anything. And more than willing."

Scot laughed.

She lowered her tiny body into the other armchair, resting a large handbag on her lap. "What do you have to say about that Morgan girl? Getting herself killed by the Twilight Man!"

"I've absolutely nothing to say."

"Why would he kill her? Such a nice young lady."

"He obviously picks his victims at random. Like all serial killers."

"When I was a girl, 'serial' meant the movies I saw Saturday matinees in Brooklyn."

"Today it's a killer who continues to operate again and again, using an identical method of murder and never leaving a clue. Which makes him almost impossible to apprehend."

"Any theories about this one?"

"None."

"All those detective novels you've read!"

"Novels don't tell you how to catch criminals. What about all the books you've read? Who do you think shot Judith Morgan?"

"I wouldn't hazard a guess."

"You see!" He realized she was frowning, as though she was remembering something. Vikki was a tiny woman with shrewd eyes, in her late sixties. He knew nothing about her personal life, only that she had for many years worked in the box offices of the finest theaters in New York and Los Angeles. She knew many of the stars from the years she'd sold them theater tickets and had come out of retirement to work at the House of Crime, running the operation with Jimmy and Irving. She took complete charge of the books, both bookkeeping and the ordering of books from publishers, as well as paying all bills. She lived in a small Hollywood apartment with an ancient Yorkie, Cary, named for her favorite actor.

Her voice was vintage New York, with a Brooklyn accent like pure steel. She had been talking to a customer at the desk last winter and—without raising her voice—said, "Take that book out of your pocket and put it back on that shelf." Two customers had done so, at once, and scurried out of the shop.

Vikki had been his wife's idea. One of her best. A kind of legacy. Josie had died two weeks before he opened the House of Crime.

"I've just thought of something."

"Yes, Vikki?"

"About Judith Morgan . . ."

"Oh?"

"We always had a little chat when she stopped by my desk with the books she was buying. She would talk while I added them to her account. I learn surprising things when customers stop at my desk. Complete strangers! It's as though the atmosphere of our shop allows them to say things they'd never say at Dalton or Brentano's."

"And what did Judith Morgan say?"

"I can't recall, exactly, when she told me this. Whether it was the last time she was in, or the time before that. But I do know it was within the past two months."

"And what, in God's name, did she say?"

"She was having trouble with two of the men in her life."

Scot straightened in his armchair.

"One was a fellow who turned up, unexpectedly, from the past. She implied that she'd known him when they were very young. The other man was a waiter, and she was trying to avoid him because he was much too persistent."

"Did she tell you their names?"

"Only the waiter. And I've been trying to remember, all morning, what it was, but I can't. She was afraid he might eventually cause trouble, but she would be able to avoid him. She planned to move out to Malibu and he didn't have a car."

"She told you all this at the desk?"

"You'd be amazed what the customers tell me!" She

pushed herself up from the armchair, clutching her handbag. "I'd better get to work." Hesitating, her eyes on his face. "You know, love, you ought to find Judith Morgan's murderer."

"Why do you say that?"

"You've read more novels of detection than anybody who comes into your shop. The police have been after that Twilight Man for months. They'll never find him, unless he walks into Hollywood Division and gives himself up."

He was smiling as she hurried toward the front of the shop, greeting customers on her way to the cashier's desk.

So Judith had been involved with at least two men.

A waiter who was being a nuisance.

Could that be the murderer? Was he dark, with long black hair and a beard like the Twilight Man?

Did the police know about this waiter? How could they? Who would tell them?

And who was the man from Judith's past? Someone she'd known in New York?

He nodded as Jimmy hurried toward the rear to get his motorbike and take off for lunch. The motor sputtered then faded away.

"I've remembered his name."

Scot looked up to see Vikki again. "Whose name?"

"That waiter I told you about. His name is Jean-Claude. I knew it would come to me."

"Jean-Claude?"

"Find him and maybe you'll have the Twilight Man." She hurried back into the shop.

Scot frowned. Jean-Claude meant the too-persistent waiter was French. Must be a hundred young French waiters in Los Angeles. . . .

* * *

The sidewalks on both sides of Melrose were busy with early-afternoon shoppers peering into the smart display windows, mostly elegant women in pairs carrying Gucci purses and men, in sport clothes or business suits, looking relaxed after lunch.

Scot had left Vikki in charge at the House of Crime, Jimmy unpacking new books in the storeroom. He was heading for his own favorite lunch spot, Chez Henri, in the block west of Edinburgh Avenue.

The sun was hot on his bare head and the shoulders of his light tweed jacket. A glorious spring day: clear blue sky overhead with puffy white clouds that seemed to have been hung there by a window decorator.

Cars parked, bumper to bumper, at the curb. He passed two Mercedes and a white Rolls. Only a rock star would buy a white Rolls.

He stepped out of the sunlight into the air-conditioned restaurant and saw several empty tables. The lunch crowd had departed and he could eat in peace.

Henri appeared from the depths of the dim dining room, smiling and bowing. "Monsieur Carddo!"

"*Bonjour,* Henri."

"Your usual table is waiting." He led the way.

As Scot followed he remembered the first time he'd come here for lunch and had asked if the restaurant was named for the old Henri's on East Fifty-second Street in New York. This Henri had never heard of the other.

Henri paused at the banquette table. "Would monsieur care for an apéritif today?"

He slipped in and sank onto the black leather seat. "A glass of the house Chardonnay."

"*Plaisir, monsieur.*" He headed for the bar.

Scot glanced around, eyes adjusting to the soft glow coming from hidden lights edging the ceiling. Pairs of people lingering over coffee, discussing business or making plans for the evening.

Small French restaurants always relaxed him. Paris, New York, or Los Angeles. Their quiet intimacy and good food were comforting on the most difficult day. He and his wife had found many such restaurants in Paris. On side streets most Americans never explored. Josie had eaten here only once. The night when the interior of the bookshop was complete and all the shelves were filled with books. He had brought his wife for a final inspection of the shop and, afterward, surprised her with this restaurant. "I suspect it will become our private hideaway," she had said. "We will never tell anyone it's here." They had enjoyed a perfect dinner, and the following week that specialist had told him Josie would be dead in two months. She had never eaten here again, but he still felt it was their restaurant.

"*Bonjour, monsieur.*"

He looked up to see Louis, his usual waiter, with a glass of wine on a small silver tray. "I'm not interrupting your lunch?"

"I never eat lunch, monsieur." Placing the wineglass in front of him. "Later, perhaps, some bread and cheese with a glass of beer."

"What should I have today? What's left?"

"There's a cold cream of leek soup."

"Excellent. But only a cup."

"And there's a quiche with mushrooms and fresh asparagus."

"Sounds perfect." He had a sudden inspiration. "Tell me, Louis. You know many of the young French waiters in Los Angeles. . . ."

Louis shrugged. "Twenty or thirty."

"Do you know one named Jean-Claude?"

"Jean-Claude? I think not."

"I suspect he may work in the neighborhood."

"I do not recall any waiter named Jean-Claude. Is he in some trouble, this Jean-Claude?"

"Nothing like that. A friend mentioned his name and I wondered where he worked. My friend neglected to tell me which restaurant."

"I will bring the soup."

As Scot tasted the wine he wondered if his asking about another French restaurant had annoyed Louis.

It would seem, at least, Jean-Claude did not work in this area. Judith Morgan could have met him at a restaurant in Beverly Hills. His mind continued to raise questions about the actress as he ate his soup. Was Judith Morgan her real name? Who was this man from her past who had turned up in Los Angeles?

He wondered whether he should tell Danihy about the two men in Judith Morgan's life when he phoned. Perhaps he had learned of their connection to the dead woman and already questioned them.

Louis removed his empty soup cup and placed a slice of quiche in front of him, bubbling from the broiler and fragrant with Parmesan cheese. "Looks and smells delicious."

As he ate, Scot resumed his line of thought about the dead actress. Was it possible the police were on a wrong track? The murderer was not the Twilight Man but someone who looked like him. In Los Angeles there were hundreds of Latinos with long black hair, mustache, and beard, who wore black shirts and trousers like uniforms. Was it possible this waiter, Jean-Claude, looked Chicano? Many Frenchmen from the Riviera had Spanish or Italian blood. He'd seen them in Cannes and Nice.

"Was told I'd find you here, pal."

Scot looked up at the bulky silhouette of Lieutenant Henry Danihy against the sunny entrance. "Harry!" Held out his hand and felt it engulfed in the detective's muscular paw. "Tried to reach you."

"I got the message."

"Sit down and have some lunch."

"Don't mind if I do." Sinking onto the banquette, facing him, as he unbuttoned his sport jacket. "I haven't seen food since an early breakfast. Stopped by your shop and Vikki told me you were here. What's that thing you're eating?"

"Quiche. And the cold leek soup is excellent." Turning as the waiter joined them, he ordered the same lunch for Lieutenant Danihy as he himself had had.

"Something to drink, Lieutenant?"

"Bottle of beer."

"Yes, sir."

"Strange your phoning me, Scot. Been thinking about you all morning."

"I called because I was interested in this latest Twilight Man murder. I knew Judith Morgan."

"Was wondering if you might."

"Knew her casually. We acted together in a television show."

"When was this?"

"Must be two years ago. We didn't become friendly until she started coming into the House of Crime."

"She read detective novels?"

"Five or six every month. She opened a charge account. If I'm in the shop I always have a chat with her. She's an attractive young woman—or was. Extremely intelligent."

"What can you tell me about her friends? Especially the men."

"Nothing, I'm afraid." Better not mention that French waiter or the man from her past. "She was always alone when she came into the bookshop." As he talked, the waiter set a small bowl of cold soup in front of Danihy. "I knew, of course, she lived on Havenhurst because of her charge account. So who do you think killed her? That's why I phoned you. Was it this Twilight Man?"

"We think so, but as usual, there's not a damn thing to prove it. This soup's pretty good! A neighbor claims he saw a Latino taking off in an old black Toyota. Could've been delivering an order of food from the nearest Taco Bell."

"The *Times* said he identified the man from a police composite of the Twilight Man."

"Several people have done that in the past. Happens every time there's another murder."

"The paper said her purse was missing but she wasn't raped."

"He never took a purse before! Only the money. This time with a car pulling in he didn't have time to open the purse. So he snatched it. It'll turn up. Probably in a corner mailbox."

"So he has her keys. To her car and her apartment."

"Lot of good that'll do him. We've impounded the car and there's nothing in her apartment. We searched it last night and again this morning. Not a damn thing of any interest. Man from latent prints checked every surface. Only prints he found were the victim's."

"What about the bullet? Did it come from the same gun the Twilight Man used in the past?"

"He's never used the same gun twice."

"I'd like to see that apartment."

"Be my guest. We're not sealing it, because the murder happened outside and I want to have another look around myself this afternoon."

"You mean that? I can see the apartment?"

"Why not? You're an honorary cop. No reason why you shouldn't check out your friend's place. Parking space nine. Same number as the apartment. I'll tell the manager to give you a key. You'll have a fresh eye. Maybe find something we've overlooked."

"Perhaps I'll go there this evening." He looked up as Louis removed the soup bowl and set a slice of quiche in front of the detective, with an opened bottle of beer and an iced glass.

Danihy stared at the bubbling cheese and golden crust. "Now that looks mighty tasty." Picking up knife and fork as the waiter departed. "Why don't you join us on this investigation, pal? Help us catch the Twilight Man. God knows I'm getting nowhere, and I've been on the case for months, along with a constantly increasing number of assistants. Two more men from Homicide Special joined us today. I spent all morning questioning everyone involved in that television series—*The Hills of Beverly*—actors and crew. They'd known Judith Morgan for three years but couldn't tell us anything personal about her."

"Actors don't get involved with each other off the set. They see enough of their fellow actors during the day, so they keep their personal lives apart.

"So I learned." Chewing as he talked. "What did you say this thing is?"

"Quiche."

"Pretty damn good. Have to tell the wife about it."

"Off the record, Harry, who do you think this Twilight Man is?"

"If I could tell you that, pal, eight murders would be solved and he'd be behind bars. We haven't a clue to his identity. This is the decade of the serial killer.

Last year it was the Night Stalker. Took months to track him down. Now it's the Twilight Man. Serial killers are the toughest to catch. I'd be grateful for anything you come up with. The smallest clue or suggestion. The chief might even give you a promotion!"

Scot slowed the Chevy down Havenhurst through the fading twilight. Because of the trees the street seemed dark, although there were several street-lamps.

This street held many pleasant memories. The old Garden of Allah Hotel had occupied the left side of Havenhurst below Sunset. Famous stars lived there. Hotel and stars long gone. Here was the big apartment complex—five or six stories high—where Joan Blondell lived in the fifties. He recalled going to a dinner party at Joan's, he and his wife—remembered the laughter. Joan told wonderful stories about Jimmy Cagney and Walter Huston while her dogs scampered underfoot. He slowed past the number he sought and parked in the first free space, got out, and walked back, past new buildings he'd never seen before.

Scot hesitated as he reached his destination. He stood on the sidewalk looking up at the three-story complex. Not a new building. Today they wouldn't put up a high wall in front, an arch in the center, shrubbery and flowers planted between wall and street.

That wall would make the lower floor dark. Then he realized there was no ground floor, only parking spaces.

He walked up the incline of the entrance drive to the dark parking area. Most of the spaces were occupied. Many small sport cars. Which meant the tenants were young. Probably aspiring actors.

The entire area was dim. Small bulbs, high on the

walls, gave a minimum of light. A deep stone planter, in the center front to back, with tall cypress trees that would make the apartments more private.

A lighted sign said ELEVATOR but he saw no steps. Raising his head, he checked the apartments and saw that each had a terrace. He moved along the parked cars until he came to an empty space and saw NINE lettered on the wall in white. There was no lighted bulb. In fact, it was quite dark here.

He walked slowly, the length of Judith's space, but could see no stains to indicate where she died. They would've been washed away by now.

He found the elevator in an alcove and took it to the second floor. There was a long open balcony lined with numbered doors. The first door said MANAGER. Scot pressed the bell button and heard immediate footsteps.

The door was opened by a plump gray-haired woman wearing too much makeup. "Mr. Carddo! How very nice. Been expecting you."

"Lieutenant Danihy called?"

"He dropped by, in person. Said I should give you the key." She held out her hand with a dangling key. "Number nine."

"Thank you." He took it from her fingers. "I may stay for several hours. So I'll leave it in the apartment. Then I won't disturb you again."

"Whatever you say. I've plenty of duplicates, and there's no telling how many others are floating around. Judith had them made for her friends. You don't remember me, do you?"

He knew what that meant. "You were in some picture with me! Which one? There've been so many."

"It was thirty years ago. You were the detective looking for David Niven. I had a lovely bit. Two scenes.

Unfortunately they weren't with you."

"Did Judith have many visitors? Friends . . ."

"I never watch my tenants. Only see them when they pay their rent or have a complaint. She was a lovely girl. Never gave any trouble. Such a terrible thing to happen! The police tell me it's that Twilight Man again. I do think they could catch him."

"I'm sure they're making every effort. Now, if you'll excuse me."

"It's the next floor."

"Thank you." He escaped to the elevator and rose to an identical long balcony with more numbered doors.

Finding number nine, he slipped key into lock and opened the door. A surge of cold air hit him as he stepped into the apartment.

What did he hope to find here? Something important? Or nothing?

He fingered the wall, located a wall switch, and snapped it. A small antique chandelier blazed above a shallow foyer. Scot stepped inside and shut the door. The foyer walls were covered with framed glossies of Judith Morgan. Some were from New York stage productions but most were stills from Hollywood films and television shows.

He moved on, into the inner room, snapping more wall switches. Shaded lamps revealed a large and attractive living room. The only sound was the hum of the air conditioning. He peered around, feeling uncomfortable at being in somebody's apartment uninvited. A dead person's apartment.

Judith Morgan had liked fine antiques. He identified a Chippendale sofa and a Hepplewhite bookcase, two of his favorite periods. Elegant sofas and comfortable armchairs with convenient lamps on low tables holding personal treasures. He noticed a white phone on a table near one small sofa. Next to the phone was a silver-framed photograph of a young man with curly black hair but no beard. He was so handsome he must be an actor.

The entire wall, straight ahead, was a glass window facing across a terrace toward those tall cypress trees in the center of the parking area. So that window faced north.

He found the cords at each side and closed the floor-to-ceiling striped window curtains. Moving back into the center of the room, he saw that the east wall was a solid mass of bookshelves. He wondered how much of their contents had come from the House of Crime.

There was a marble fireplace in the west wall that held several pots of white geraniums, a door to the left of the fireplace, and a large dining alcove to the right with a continuation of the glass wall facing the terrace. Comfortable French Provincial dining table, chairs, and a sideboard displaying fine china.

Scot closed the curtain as he continued on toward the single door in the dining area. Posters of stage productions, identically framed, hung in a row.

The door opened into more darkness. He snapped a wall switch and a compact kitchen was revealed with smaller windows facing the cypress trees. The kitchen was neat, everything in order.

He returned to the living room, passing the fireplace to the only other door. Another dark room. Snapping a wall switch, he found himself facing Judith's bedroom. Now he really felt he was intruding.

Hesitating on the threshold, he realized this room had no windows. He wouldn't care to sleep in a windowless room. Could be claustrophobic.

The bedroom was more feminine than the living room. Its dominant color was a kind of soft apricot:

walls covered with dark apricot silk, armchair, chaise, and tufted bedspread in pale apricot satin. A large television screen faced the foot of the bed. There was a solid wall of closet doors. He slid one back and saw rows of dresses, suits, and coats. Dozens of pairs of shoes. Two brown leather makeup cases in a corner on the floor.

He opened the door beyond the television set and snapped more wall switches. Light came on in a dressing room with an elaborate makeup table, surrounded by bulbs, and a tufted armchair. Beyond an archway was an elaborate bathroom with a sunken tub and flowered porcelain fixtures the actress must have had installed.

For the next hour he played detective and went over every inch of the apartment, aware that several real detectives had done the same thing earlier. No matter! He had to check everything himself, see what he could find out or deduce about the dead actress. At the end of the hour he had learned only that Judith Morgan had very expensive tastes.

He hadn't, really, expected to find anything that would connect her with the murderer or reveal his identity.

The lower part of the bookcase turned out to be a desk with partitions for envelopes and letter paper. A silver tray held pens, and there was a gold box for postage stamps. One small drawer held rubber bands and paper clips. A larger drawer contained manila envelopes and everything that might be required for letter writing. Nothing personal, except for several unpaid bills. Another drawer had file folders with paid bills and canceled checks but no bank statements.

Finally he closed every drawer and left the desk as he'd found it. He switched off the lights in all the rooms, then opened the living-room curtains and, sliding back the floor-to-ceiling window, stepped outside and walked to the parapet facing the cypress trees. He couldn't see the cars parked below or those on the far side.

Impossible to glimpse anything of the opposite tenants. These apartments had complete privacy.

Tall bamboo fences separated the terraces, and the actress had covered hers with growing vines. She had liked plants. He'd noticed several in the living room, and among the white patio furniture were more.

This terrace, like all the others, would be invisible from below. It had been easy for the Twilight Man to hide down there and appear, suddenly, when Judith parked her car and was preparing to go up to her apartment. He wondered if there had been many muggings and robberies down there.

This might be a good place for him to wait. On the terrace.

He had a strong hunch the murderer would return tonight. He had taken Judith's purse. That other tenant had driven in before he could remove the money and he had fled with it to his car, which would be parked nearby.

Scot picked up one of the white patio chairs, a padded armchair, and set it with its back against the bamboo fence next to the open window. Sitting there, hidden from inside by the bunched-together curtains, he could look into the apartment without being observed. Eyes adjusting to the dark, he glanced around the terrace and up at a sky quivering with stars.

No blaring television sets or loud voices disturbed the silence. Most of the windows would be closed, because every apartment would have air conditioning.

Decent of Danihy to tell that manager to give him

the key. Otherwise she could have detained him for half an hour asking stupid questions, even though she recognized him.

Would Harry be upset if he caught the Twilight Man tonight? After all, he hadn't been able to find the guy in a year. Hollywood Division wanted to close the investigation. Harry knew he wouldn't seek publicity if he was lucky enough to catch the murderer. And it would, certainly, be luck.

A faint glow of light came from inside the apartment. Scot, slowly and cautiously, got to his feet, wishing he'd brought a gun with him. That pistol the police had given him, along with an official permit, when they made him an honorary detective lay in a polished rosewood box, looked at countless times, but never touched. The small box of shells remained unopened. He'd never fired a gun but, at this moment, would feel more comfortable with one in his hand.

A dark figure was coming into the living room from the foyer. Scot moved closer to the edge of the curtain and saw that it was a woman. She snapped a switch and all the lamps lighted in the living room.

He saw that she was peering around, looking for something. She was an attractive blonde, possibly in her late twenties, wearing a flowered blouse over gray slacks, bare feet in sandals.

"Mr. Carddo?"

His name startled him.

"Where are you, Mr. Carddo?"

He stepped through the window, into the light. "Who the devil are you? And how'd you know I was here?"

"Olivia Pancoast, the manager, told me."

"Did she, indeed?"

"Said you were working with the police."

"Damn."

"'Judith has mentioned you many times. I've bought books at your shop, but you were never there."

"And what are you doing here?"

"I'm Miriam. My apartment's toward the back. I knew Judith would want me to water her plants. Let me get some water."

He watched her go through the dining area and disappear into the kitchen. Waiting impatiently, facing the kitchen door, he wondered how many other people had gotten keys from that stupid manager today.

"I've always been a fan of yours, Mr. Carddo." She returned with a large plastic pitcher and, moving briskly, watered the plants. "I loved your features, especially when you played a detective. They're my favorites. I read at least two detective novels a month. People used to sneer when I told them. Not anymore. Everyone seems to read them now." She moved from the living room to the terrace, Scot following, where she splashed every plant. "You're British, aren't you, Mr. Carddo?"

"I was born in Scotland."

"Then you're Scotch?"

"My mother was. My father's family was Italian. They owned a famous circus, years ago, in Italy. Most of them were acrobats. My father was their star performer. He was a clown."

"A clown?"

"I grew up in London, where my father, Aldo Carddoni, performed in the music halls with a trio of acrobatic cousins. Unfortunately, I had no interest in the circus. At an early age I wanted to be an actor and the family insisted I study with the best. RADDA and, later, with a wonderful actress. Martita Hunt."

"Did you?" She left her pitcher on the terrace. "I've finished here. Sorry I interrupted you. Whatever you were doing . . ."

"Not at all." He followed her inside.

"I'll drop over every evening and water Judith's plants. So they won't die." She turned to face him as she reached the foyer. "Who do you think killed her?"

"The police say it was the Twilight Man."

"I read that in the paper. Poor Judith. Well, I'd better go. It's been terribly exciting, meeting you."

Scot watched her leave, then snapped off the lights in the foyer and all the rooms. Finally, when the apartment was dark, he stepped out onto the terrace, returning to the silence and the stars overhead. Sunset Boulevard was only half a block to the north, with its noisy flow of traffic, but no whisper of sound reached down here.

He was beginning to think he shouldn't have come here tonight, wasting an evening when he could've been reading a new mystery, matching wits with the writer, solving a fictional murder. But this wasn't "who killed Roger Ackroyd." It was "who killed Judith Morgan." Fact, not fiction. Blood, not ink.

There was something he was missing in Judith's apartment. Some object. A letter? Bankbook?

There had to be something here in her apartment. Something that would reveal the identity of her killer.

That was, of course, if it wasn't the Twilight Man. And he had a gut feeling it wasn't. After all, he hadn't raped her and he had taken her purse. The Twilight Man always raped his victims but never took their purses.

If the killer did return tonight it wouldn't be until much later. Not until the neighbors retired and the last car had been parked below. He turned abruptly and went inside. He snapped each switch and lighted the lamps. Then, slowly, starting with the foyer, he searched every inch of the apartment once more. He looked behind each framed picture, under every rug, beneath all the pillows on sofas and bed. He lifted lids and peered into everything, brought out each hanger, shook and felt every garment. He looked in her shoes. After opening every piece of luggage he sank, exhausted, onto the bed. He had remade it after stripping it and turning the mattress over.

Sitting there, feeling deflated, he accepted his defeat. There was nothing here to reveal the identity of the murderer. Apparently, Judith Morgan had no secrets.

He got to his feet and turned out the lights in the bath, the dressing room, and the bedroom. Moving through the apartment, he switched off every light. In the living room he noticed the antique clock on the marble mantel showed nine-thirty.

He'd taken longer than he realized to go through the apartment a second time. No matter. He'd done a thorough job.

Scot turned off the foyer chandelier, returned to the dark living room, and stood facing the big window open onto the terrace. There seemed to be a blue glow of light from the night sky.

Then, suddenly, he remembered two things he hadn't examined.

Those brown leather makeup cases! The smaller one was for casual jobs and the larger was designed for lengthy jobs—a week or even months—when an actor worked on location for a feature film or many weeks on a television series.

He had glanced at the two expensive leather cases in a corner of the cupboard but hadn't bothered to pick them up or open them.

Had the police done the same thing?

A makeup case was the perfect place for an actor to hide something important. It was carried everywhere and nobody noticed it. Only an actor knew that.

THE HOUSE OF CRIME

He turned, suddenly, in the dark, bumping against a chair. Heading back toward the bedroom, he snapped on the lights and went straight to the cupboard. He slid a door back and reached down for the leather cases.

The larger one seemed heavy. He carried them to the bed and snapped both cases open, surprised that they weren't locked.

There were gold locks on each, but no keys. Judith would have kept them on a key ring, which the murderer would have found when he opened her purse. But he wouldn't know what any of the keys would fit.

The smaller case contained only a few basic makeup items. The other one had everything an actor might need if he wanted to redo a job some careless makeup person had botched. There were expensive perfumes and lotions, matched jars and bottles in fitted leather compartments so they didn't touch and couldn't break. No wonder the case was heavy.

This was the most elaborate makeup case he'd ever seen. He'd never owned one himself, except that battered black tin box he'd used, years ago, in the theater.

The only possible hiding place would be in the lid of the larger case. He leaned down, feeling the lining, searching for a zipper. His fingertips lifted a long strip of leather that revealed what he was seeking. In a matter of seconds he had the zipper open on three sides of the lid and pulled the stiff lining back like the cover of a book. Inside the space was a flat package neatly wrapped in a towel so it would not move when the makeup case was carried.

So Judith Morgan did have a secret! And he had found it. He lifted the towel-wrapped parcel and rested it on the quilted satin spread. Sat beside it and unfolded the towel.

Two unmarked file folders were revealed.

He set each folder, separately, on the spread. The first contained three clippings. The top one had been cut from a Philadelphia paper dated 1969. A review of an amateur production of *The Glass Menagerie* given by the Philly Players. The local critic was enthusiastic about the production and praised the three actors who performed the leading roles.

The second clipping was dated the following year.

BANK TELLER QUESTIONED IN
CASE OF CHILD MOLESTATION

The teller, George Warren, had been questioned about a recent molestation, in West Philadelphia, of a fourteen-year-old girl. The victim's name was withheld by the police. George Warren, age twenty-six, lived with his parents across the street from the girl and had recently been seen walking with her. Warren had not been arrested. His employer told police his reputation was excellent. Young Warren had, last year, received favorable publicity when he acted in a Philly Players production of *The Glass Menagerie*.

Scot checked the first clipping and saw that George Warren was one of the actors praised in the review.

He wondered briefly if one of those two actresses might have been Judith Morgan as he picked up the third clipping.

GEORGE WARREN DISAPPEARS
FOLLOWING POLICE INQUIRY

After questioning by the police, the week before, George Warren had not been heard from by his family or anyone at the bank where he had worked for several years as a teller. A detective who had questioned him about a case of child molestation had told the pa-

THE HOUSE OF CRIME

per that Warren had withdrawn his savings from another bank prior to being questioned. There was no suggestion that money had been stolen or embezzled. Police refused to say whether Warren was believed to be guilty in the molestation case.

The second folder contained a checkbook and monthly statements, for the past two years, from Judith Morgan's bank in Los Angeles. He turned to the last statement and checked her current balance.

The amount was surprising: more than a hundred thousand dollars. No wonder she was planning to buy herself a house at the beach.

Did this mean she'd received that inheritance she had mentioned? He checked her deposits and saw she had made a regular deposit of two thousand seven hundred dollars every week. That would be her fee for *The Hills of Beverly* series, less ten percent to her agent. He also noticed she made monthly deposits of another five thousand dollars.

He went back through all the statements and saw she'd been making that five-thousand-dollar deposit every month since the end of 1985. At least eighteen months. Eighty thousand dollars!

Scot frowned. Judith Morgan had been blackmailing somebody.

Could it be George Warren? Had she discovered him, somehow, in Los Angeles? Using a new name, maybe vice-president of her bank? Stranger things were possible.

There was a faint click behind him and a surge of music. He got to his feet as the television screen came alive. Loud music, crude colors. Scot moved toward the big screen as he saw golden letters against an aerial shot of green hills and blue sky: THE HILLS OF BEVERLY.

"Good evening, ladies and gentlemen!" The baritone voice was unctuous. "Welcome to another visit with your favorite family—the Hills of Beverly! Horace Hill and his incredible circle of relatives, friends— and enemies. With Ronald Temple as handsome Horace Hill. The man you love and hate! Grace Lansing as his patient but vengeful wife, Hildegarde. And Judith Morgan as their neighbor on the next hill, the beautiful but conniving young divorcée Gwen Golden . . ."

Scot reached down and snapped off the television set. What bad taste! Didn't they know Judith Morgan had been murdered?

The damn set had turned on automatically, scheduled by an invisible timer to come alive when Judith would be relaxing in bed, waiting to see the weekly telecast of her series. Had she done that every week? Reclined there and . . .

A faint sound whispered through the bedroom. Scot turned toward the open door as lights came on in the living room. Someone else was in the apartment!

He strode to the door without hesitation and saw the intruder.

The whispering sound came from green tissue paper around a large bouquet of white roses held by a young man with black hair, standing in the center of the living room, looking straight at him. His face was the one in that photograph near the phone.

Scot walked toward him. "You are her friend Jean-Pierre."

"And you are her friend Monsieur Carddo. Yes, I am Jean-Pierre—Jean-Pierre Laurent. I brought these roses for her. As soon as I finished work. Pardon. I must put them in water." He carried the bouquet across the living room. "Do not disturb yourself, monsieur. I know where to find everything." He crossed the dining area and went into the kitchen.

Scot stopped in the center of the room and waited.

So the Frenchman had a key to her apartment. His hair was black, but it was short and curly and he had no mustache or beard. He looked nothing like the Twilight Man in that police drawing. What's more, he didn't have the air of a killer. Who was it—Spilsbury of Scotland Yard?—who, repeatedly, claimed that murderers were always arrogant?

Laurent returned with the roses in a tall glass vase, which he set on the table near the phone. "I recognized you, monsieur, from films I've seen. My friend Louis said you were asking about me, this afternoon, at Chez Henri."

"So Louis does know you!"

"He phoned me at Maison Colette, where I work, in Santa Monica. Told me you were having lunch with an American *flic*."

"Lieutenant Danihy from Burglary-Homicide. An old friend."

"Do the police think I killed her?"

"They don't know you exist. And I haven't told them."

"You are very kind, monsieur. Who do you think is the killer?"

"I'm not sure. I've spent the evening here looking for clues."

"I adored Judith. In spite of many arguments . . ."

"Did she ever mention a man named George Warren? A man from her past?"

"No. She didn't talk about the past. I am desolate over her death. We had wonderful plans. Judith arranged for me to meet people who might invest in the restaurant I hope to have, one day, in Beverly Hills."

"Your own restaurant?"

"That is my dream. If, ever, I can get backers. I am a graduate of a Swiss school of restaurant management. I came to Los Angeles without money, which is why I am a waiter, and Judith was the first person to introduce me to wealthy men and women who might invest in my future. But so far, none of them have done so."

"Why did you quarrel, you and Judith?"

"Because she wanted me to be an actor. Her agent wished to handle me. But I have no desire to act." He looked down at the white roses. "I loved her, monsieur, but I could not ask her to marry me. Not until I had a successful restaurant. I detest being a waiter. But then every French waiter in Los Angeles survives because he dreams of opening his own restaurant. Forgive this intrusion, monsieur." He turned abruptly and headed for the foyer.

"How many others have keys to this apartment?" Scot asked.

"I've no idea, monsieur." He looked back and shrugged. "I hope I am the only one, but I shall never know. *Bonsoir,* Monsieur Carddo."

Scot waited until the door closed, then hurried back to the bedroom. He gathered the file folders and wrapped them in the towel, then stuffed them into the shallow hiding place and zipped it shut. He pressed the strip of leather over the zipper and closed both makeup cases, setting them in the corner of the cupboard again. Then, moving quickly, he snapped off every light in the apartment.

That done, he crossed the dark living room to the open window. He had found Judith Morgan's secret. She was blackmailing someone. Probably George Warren. But where would he find George Warren?

He would, of course, have to tell Harry Danihy what

he'd found here. That would send the police on a search for the missing Warren, who had disappeared with a molestation charge hanging over him. He must have taken another name and started a new life. Maybe had a wife and children.

Standing at the open window, he was aware of perfume coming from the roses. Danihy would be able to trace those blackmail checks. Or did the victim pay with cash?

Scot went outside, to the edge of the parapet. Streaks of light on the cypress trees from some of the apartments. Music, very faint, in the distance. He wondered if any of the tenants were watching *The Hills of Beverly.*

He sank onto the white patio chair again and made an effort to relax. He would stay here—at least until midnight—on the chance that the Twilight Man had found the door key in Judith's purse and returned to rob her apartment.

But was the elusive Twilight Man her murderer? He had a strong feeling it was someone else. Somebody who looked like the Twilight Man.

Forcing himself to relax, Scot thought of more pleasant things. The bookshop. His dear wife. Alicia Winston this morning.

His wife had adored Alicia. Incredible that she survived. Looking as beautiful as a young girl.

He seldom thought of sex anymore. Unless, as this morning, he was with a beautiful woman like Alicia. Aware of her perfume.

There couldn't be another woman like Josie. He'd never considered a second marriage. It was love that was important, not sex. And it was love that endured. He remembered that aged painter, years ago in Paris, who'd claimed sex was two hours of persuasive conversation, ten minutes of ecstasy, and half an hour of dull conversation. He had probably never been married.

Love was an instant urge, half an hour of ecstasy, followed by sweet golden sleep.

That's how it had been with his beloved. Josie had given up a promising career in opera to marry him and move from New York to Los Angeles. With never a word of regret. She'd had a lovely lyric soprano— he'd read her reviews many times—had sung Cherubino, Mimi, and Sophie with the smaller opera companies but never made the Met or sung in Europe.

Sunday afternoons, when Nicholas went off to a movie and dined at his favorite British pub in Santa Monica, he played one of three operas on his record player. *La Bohème, Nozze,* or *Rosenkavalier.* There were certain arias which made him weep because it was Josie's voice he heard.

She had persuaded him to open a bookshop and sell nothing but mysteries because those were the only books he read for pleasure. The shop had saved his sanity, given him a reason to continue living alone. And the House of Crime was now making a profit, although he didn't need the money. His business manager assured him he had more than enough for the rest of his life.

Had Josie suspected she was dying, long before those specialists told them? He would never know.

Was that why she had urged him to open the bookshop? Knowing it would give purpose to his life after she was gone. . . .

They had both realized there would be no great film roles coming up in the future. That acting had become a bore for him.

He closed his eyes and, immediately, saw her lovely face.

Josie would be amused if she could see him tonight. Playing detective.

She had enjoyed reading novels of detection as much as he. At least once a month he would find an especially interesting one and, after he had read it, would suggest they read it aloud. Each would read an alternating chapter, and Josie would try to guess the identity of the murderer. She frequently succeeded, but he wouldn't tell her she was right and they continued on to the final revelations. . . .

Scott came awake with a start. Surprised that he had been asleep. Couldn't have been for long.

Some noise must've wakened him.

He had a feeling it was a door closing. Somebody in the apartment? He pushed himself up from the metal chair and stood, hidden by the folds of curtain.

Mustn't move an inch beyond the edge of that curtain or he would be visible from inside.

Was someone in the apartment, or had he dreamed he heard a door close?

A thin beam of light was moving across the living room.

It was the murderer! Anyone else would turn on the lights.

Scott moved back, against the bamboo fence.

The flashlight beam kept darting nervously around the living room. Pausing briefly, then going on. It found the white roses, and they seemed to glare in the light. Then the beam of light moved on.

The intruder was getting his bearings. After all, he'd never been here before. Everything was strange. He had to see where he could walk without sending something crashing to the floor. Should he wait until he went into the kitchen or the bedroom, then step inside and switch on the lights? Wait for him to return?

He saw the beam of light moving toward the foyer

again. It found the wall switches just inside the living room. A black-gloved hand appeared in the circle of light and snapped all the switches. The room blazed with light.

Scot stepped back instinctively, as light reached out across the terrace. But not before he glimpsed the killer. Long black hair, black shirt, black cord trousers, and black boots.

It was the Twilight Man!

His back was turned, so it was impossible to see his face.

Should he step inside and surprise him? What if he had a gun? Surely he wouldn't fire a shot! Afraid a neighbor would hear it. But nobody had heard that shot last night, when he killed Judith Morgan. Perhaps no one was home at that hour.

Scot knew what he must do. He moved forward suddenly and stepped through the open window into the room.

The man whirled. Scot saw his face. A Latino. Dark-skinned, black mustache, small beard.

The Twilight Man was so startled his mouth dropped open. Scot realized that he'd been recognized. He could tell from the man's eyes. An unmistakable look of recognition. Must've seen his films or television shows. Maybe that would prevent his shooting him. He took several steps toward him. "You are the Twilight Man."

"*Sí, señor*. That's what they call me." He smiled arrogantly.

Spilsbury was right. Murderers were arrogant. "You killed Judith Morgan last night."

He shrugged. The flashlight was still lighted in his leather-gloved hand.

"You must've read her name in today's paper, or heard it on the news."

"That's right, señor."

"And you've come back to see what you could find in her apartment. The keys were in her purse."

"*Sí, señor.*"

"I keep expecting you to pull a gun and take a shot at me."

"Why would I do that, señor? I do not have a gun."

Scot felt a surge of relief. What should he do now? What move could he make? The phone was too far away, on that low table, for him to reach it quickly. The killer could knock him down. His shoulders looked massive and his torso was muscular under that tight black shirt.

"What you doin' here, señor?"

Why the devil did he end every sentence with "señor"? Like a bad actor playing a Mexican part. "I've been waiting for you. Certain you'd show up tonight."

"And the police? Where are they tonight?"

"At home, asleep, I presume. They went over this apartment today but, apparently, found nothing important. Nothing to implicate you. You've probably never been here before. They say you pick your victims at random."

"That is right, señor."

"What will you do now? Now that I've seen you. Know you have the key to this apartment."

"Maybe I get the hell outta here, señor. My car's round the corner. Nobody seen me come in an' nobody gonna see me leave."

Scot moved toward him, as they talked, but the man didn't seem to notice. "I suppose you couldn't be persuaded to give yourself up to the police?"

"I would be a fool t' do that, señor!"

"You can't go on like this, killing innocent women." Moving closer, he saw that an inch or so of bare flesh exposed between the black leather gloves and the cuff of the shirt was not the dark bronze of his face.

"Nothin' you can do, señor. You got no way t' hold me here."

"Perhaps not." Now he could see brown pancake streaked on his neck and, at once, knew who this was. "You're not the Twilight Man."

"What, señor?" He looked startled. "What you say?"

"You forgot to put makeup on your arm."

He lifted an arm and stared at the exposed pale flesh.

"You're George Warren."

There was a brief moment of silence. Neither man moved.

"I used to be George Warren. A lifetime ago." There was no longer a fake Mexican accent. "How could you know about George Warren? How'd you find out, Mr. Carddo?"

"Judith Morgan left newspaper clippings hidden here. I found them tonight."

"That's why I came here. To find them." He sank onto a chair and began to peel off his gloves, revealing the blue-veined hands of a middle-aged man. "She's been blackmailing me. Five thousand dollars every month! Recently she's asked for more. To buy a house and invest in some restaurant. I knew it would never stop. I had to get rid of her. To protect my wife and children. Thought I'd worked out a perfect disguise. The Twilight Man who killed women he'd never seen before." He avoided Scot's eyes as he talked. "I had the wig made, the beard and the mustache . . ."

"That makes it premeditated murder."

"Seemed the perfect way—the only way—to eliminate Judy from my life. That was her name in Philadelphia. Judy Hopkins."

"You acted in *Glass Menagerie* together. She left one of the reviews with two other clippings. The police questioning you for child molestation. Your disappearance."

"Judy was an ambitious bitch. Even in those days. To think I encouraged her to go to New York and become an actress. Had no idea she'd turn up. Years later." He sighed. "I suppose you have to hand me over to the police."

"I'm afraid so. Yes." Scot glanced at the phone beyond the vase of white roses.

"So the masquerade's finished."

He turned to see Warren removing the black wig, revealing a fine head of silver-gray hair. Then the mustache and beard. The face now revealed was familiar. "You're Ronald Temple."

"When the producers were casting *The Hills of Beverly* I was told they were considering an actress named Judith Morgan. I met her but didn't recognize her. After all, we hadn't seen each other in fifteen years. Her face had hardened and the color of her hair was different. I never did recognize her until the day she revealed who she was and demanded money to keep silent about the past. We had worked together for a year before she recognized me. I'd had plastic surgery, on my face, when I worked as an actor in New York. Thought nobody would ever discover my past. I don't regret killing her." Gordon suddenly buried his face in his pale hands and began to sob. "There was nothing else I could do. . . ."

Scot turned and slowly walked toward the telephone.

He had solved his first murder, but he hadn't caught the Twilight Man.

As he approached the table he became aware of the perfume coming from the roses.

If only he could tell Josie about tonight! His wife would be proud of him.

He was smiling as he picked up the phone and dialed.

PIRATE'S MOON
WILLIAM F. NOLAN

L*ike any large American city, Los Angeles is a melting pot of many diverse ethnic groups with their own special customs and traditions. Its Oriental and Mexican populations are only two of those renowned for their contributions to the city's vitality. In William F. Nolan's "Pirate's Moon," a paranormal investigator working with the L.A. Sheriff's Department happens on a much more obscure group—one whose customs seem to be adding less to the city's vitality than to its mortality.*

ALTHOUGH we'd never met, Dwight Robert Lee and I shared the same beach. Separated by several miles of sand, but with the same blue-green Pacific waters washing over us both. Me, wind-surfing near the Santa Monica pier, trying to forget a rough day with my tax accountant, using the ocean as personal therapy—until it got too dark and cold to stay in the water. Him, a few miles further up the coast, at Pirate's Cove, doing nothing in particular, loose-limbed, just rolling with the waves, letting them take him where they would. Neither of us was in any hurry to go anywhere.

By the time the moon came out, riding clear of a massed cloudbank, I was home, wrestling a bachelor's steak onto my backyard charcoal barbecue. Dwight Robert Lee was still at the beach. Stretched out on the cool sand in the sudden wash of moonlight. He wasn't going home that night. Not in his condition.

For one thing, his head was missing.

Naturally, I read about the discovery of his body in the *L.A. Times* the next morning. But I didn't personally get involved with the case for another week. Not until the afternoon Mike Lucero decided that he needed my help.

Mike is a close friend, so I'd better tell you about him. He's a homicide detective working out of the Malibu Sheriff's Station. Built like a weight lifter. Big, slab-muscled, with a wide grin that buries his eyes in sun wrinkles. Miguel Francisco Lucero. Oldest of nine children. He grew up on one of those small mountain villages in northern New Mexico where they believe in witches and *mal ojo,* the evil eye. (Helps him put up with me!) After he left the University of New Mexico with a degree in psychology, he headed for California. Wanted to be a cop. And since there's always a need for bilingual officers in the L.A. County Sheriff's Department, Mike got signed up fast.

He lives in Woodland Hills, in the western San Fernando Valley, with his wife, Carla, and a loud pair of twin five-year-old daughters. He's a good man and a good detective.

I met Mike three years ago, when he attended one of my psychic seminars. As a cop, he figured it would help if he could develop his psychic ability. We all have it, to one degree or another. Some more, some less. Just a matter of self-development. I'm into the world of the paranormal; it's what I do for a living. I teach, write, investigate, conduct seminars, hold personal consultations—the works. I don't expect everybody to believe in all the stuff I deal with (I'm still mentally struggling with a lot of it myself), but I do ask people to keep an open mind about our incredible universe and what might or might not be in it. In outer *and* inner space—the space inside our being. You, me, and the cosmic universe. A big package.

Anyhow, after listening to some of my ideas, Mike figured I was a certified nut case and we didn't see each other again for a year. Until the body of a teenage girl was found in Topanga Canyon with her throat cut. No clues. No suspects.

Mike came to me, reluctantly, and asked if I could help him crack the case. Brought along a ring found on the body. "You're the psychic," he growled, "so tell me what happened."

I couldn't. My psychic powers are quite limited. I sent him to a woman named Brenner in Pasadena. She "read" the dead girl's ring, and her mental visions eventually led Mike to the killer. Doesn't always work that way, but this time it did. Lucero was impressed.

We talked. Had dinner together. By evening's end, he gave me that slit-eyed grin of his and said, "Damn if I don't think we're friends. What do you think?"

Over the next two years I helped Mike on half a dozen cases. Not all of them were solved, but I gave each one my best shot. Which is why I'm an official Sheriff's Consultant—with a shiny badge to prove it.

So here was big Mike Lucero, on a foggy coastal afternoon in May, sprawled across my living-room couch, sipping from a can of Diet Pepsi, talking about the dead man found under a pirate's moon.

"This guy was one bad dude," Mike declared. "They called him Stomper. That's because he enjoyed putting the boot to people he mugged." Mike took a swig from his Pepsi. "Dwight Robert 'Stomper' Lee. A sick-minded sadistic shit. Believe me, he was no loss to society."

I was across the room in a chair by the fireplace. Wasn't fire weather; it's just my best chair. "How come you know his name when the corpse was stripped and his head was missing? How'd you make the ID?"

"Body tattoo. Skull and crossbones on the right side of his chest. Which told us he belonged to the Henchmen."

"That outlaw cycle gang?"

"Right. Every member of the Devil's Henchmen has to carry a chest tattoo."

"Even their women?"

"You bet. On the right tit. Anyhow, we figured he'd have a record and ran his prints. Bingo. Computer told us all we wanted to know about him."

"Except who killed him."

"Yeah." Mike nodded. "Not that I personally give a damn. Whoever did it rates a medal—but I happen to be a cop and he happens to be a murder victim. So you play the game." Mike shrugged his heavy shoulders.

"Why come to me on this one?" I asked him.

"Because we're zip on it. Absolute dead end. And because it's weird." He gave me his slitted grin. "You know I always bring the weirdos to you, Dave."

"So what's so weird about finding a cycle freak with his head missing? Maybe he ripped off another Henchman's chick and they stomped the Stomper. Or it could be the work of a rival gang who kept his head for a souvenir."

"Whoever did it took more than his head," said Mike.

I raised an eyebrow. "More?"

"The scumbag's heart was missing. Cut right out of the body." Mike reached into his jacket and handed me an object sealed in clear plastic—a beaded feather, with a complex pattern of bright threads wound through it. "We found this at the beach near Lee's corpse. You know something about Indians, so I brought it here."

I'd told Mike a lot about my childhood—about my early years in Arizona on the Hopi Reservation. My parents worked there for the U.S. Bureau of Indian Affairs. After they died—in a desert flash flood when I was six—I grew close to an old, half-blind Hopi medicine man who became a father figure to me. He gave me my first real taste of the spiritual world when he taught me the metaphysical Hopi view of life. Later, at the University of Arizona, I expanded my knowledge by studying Indian lore from a wide variety of tribes.

So Mike was right. I know something about Indians. I carefully examined the feather, turning it slowly in the air.

"Well?" Mike growled impatiently. "What tribe is it from?"

"None," I said.

"Huh?"

"I mean it's not from any Indian tribe in North America."

"Where then?"

"You got me. I've never seen one like it. How do you know this is connected with Lee's murder?"

"I don't," Mike admitted. "It could have washed up on the beach the same way he did."

"Have you tried a psychic?"

"Sure. a couple. The two you put me onto—the Brenner woman and that bearded guy in Santa Monica, Dorfman."

"What did they tell you?"

"A lot of nothing is what they told me." He scowled, scrubbing a hand along his cheek. "Claimed they couldn't get any kind of clear reading on it."

"Then maybe the feather's *not* related to Lee's death," I said, handing it back. "Could have been tossed into the ocean by anybody."

"Yeah." Mike sighed. "Who the hell knows?"

He put his empty soda can on the coffee table and stood up. "Well, thanks anyhow."

"Going already?"

"Have to. Carla's got dinner in the microwave. I promised her I'd be home early."

"Tell her I said hi."

"Sure." When he reached the door he turned to level a hard look at me. "When you gonna get married again?"

"Whoa, pal! Give me some time. The divorce papers have barely cooled."

"Don't shit me," growled Mike. "You need a woman. Living alone is no damn good."

And he was gone before I could think of a snappy reply to that one.

* * *

A month later, in late June, Lucero contacted me again. I'd been out of state, conducting a mind-expansion seminar outdoors in Arizona, and I got back to find Mike's recorded growl on my answering machine. His message was brief and to the point: "Another murder. And another damn feather. Call me."

When I reached him by phone at the station he seemed edgy. " 'Bout time you got back. Where the hell were you?"

"In the Arizona desert earning my living," I said tersely. "You know, I'm not paid to be on call to the Malibu Sheriff's Department."

His tone softened. "Okay, okay . . . I'm out of line. But this has been a crappy week."

I eased back on the couch, the receiver cradled against my shoulder. "So tell me about the second feather."

"I'd rather show it to you. Can you come down to the station?"

"I guess so."

"Then I'll be waiting." And he rang off.

The ocean sun was laying its usual late-afternoon strips of hammered gold over the surface of the Pacific when I turned off the Coast Highway and rolled my little red CRX Honda into the parking area at the Malibu station.

Mike looked sour and angry when I walked into his office. Obviously, the case was at a standstill. He nodded toward a battered leather chair facing his desk. I took it.

"How'd your outdoor seminar go?"

"Could have been better. It rained both days."

"Manage to expand any females?"

"Is that supposed to be funny?

"Just friendly concern."

Mike settled behind his work-cluttered desk, a scarred oak relic that looked like a thrift-shop reject. In fact, Mike's office was something less than sumptuous. It smelled of mildewed files and stale cigar smoke. But he'd fought a lot of wars here and wasn't about to change anything.

I put out a hand. "Let me see it."

He gave me the second plastic-sealed feather. It was almost identical to the first. Bright with beads and intricately threaded.

"What about the body?" I asked.

"Same MO. Head missing. Heart cut out."

"Tattoo on his chest?"

"No. This guy was no scummy biker. He was a real celebrity. Athlete. Olympic runner. Had his picture on the cover of *People* last month. They called him the California Iron Man."

"Eddie Lansdale?"

"Yeah, him." Mike took a cigar from his desk and ran a match flame carefully around the tip. "He was easy to identify. Had a missing thumb on his right hand. Born that way." He let out a deep sigh. "The newspapers are gonna have a field day with this one."

"Where was he found?"

"Santa Monica Mountains. Couple of honeymooners were backpacking into the area when their mutt ran into this cave and began digging like crazy. Lansdale was buried there—*with* the feather. We still don't know what the hell it means."

His cigar had gone out and he was running a fresh flame over it.

"I'd like to take both feathers to someone I know. An anthropologist. He might be able to help." I looked at Mike. "What do you say?"

"I say they're the only clues we've got. I'm not supposed to let them out of my sight." He hesitated. "But go ahead, *take* the damn things. See what you can find out about 'em."

He opened his desk again and gave me the other feather.

"I'll be careful with your only clues," I said.

Mike grunted. He was still looking sour when I left his office. But at least he had his cigar going.

On-campus parking at UCLA is usually a hassle, but I got the CRX stashed neatly on a lot close to my target: Haines Hall. Home of Sidwick Sims Oliver, B.A., M.A., Ph.D. And the chairman of the Department of Anthropology.

Sid looked more like a Texas linebacker than a university professor, with his wide shoulders and bulky torso, but a pair of thick-lensed tortoiseshell glasses testified to his bookish character.

"Kincaid! Happy to see you!" He greeted me in his usual expansive manner with a crushing bear hug. (He never called me David.) Then he stepped back, frowning. "My God, are you trying out for Wild Bill Hickok?"

He referred to my fringed-buckskin shirt, Levi's, silver Indian belt, and tooled-leather boots.

"I'm a desert critter, remember? Sun and sand and cacti. Haven't been in a suit since my Uncle Jack was buried. And that was three years ago."

Sid chuckled, a bass rumble. "To each his own!"

We were standing in the hall, flanked by shelves of native artifacts from a dozen world cultures. He waved me into his office. Which was as neat as he was. A place for everything and everything in its place. With all his papers in neat little piles. Freud would have called him anal retentive.

"I need your expertise," I told him as Sid handed me a minicarton of fresh carrot juice from his office fridge. He selected mango juice for himself. We sat down facing one another.

"You helping the police on another case?"

I nodded. "Yeah. The Sheriff's Department. This one involves two headless corpses found in the Malibu area."

"*Two!*" Sid pursed his thick lips. "I read about the headless cycle gentleman. But . . . *another!*"

"It'll be in the papers by tonight," I said. "With all the gory details. Well . . ." I corrected myself. "Not *all* the details. It won't mention these."

And I produced the two feathers.

He took the plastic-covered objects gingerly into his large hands, peering myopically. The sun from the window fired the beads to points of brightness.

I leaned toward him. "Can you identify them?"

"Of course I can," he said, raising his head to me. "They're from Papua New Guinea. The threading and the beads are ceremonial. Stone Age stuff."

I blinked at him. "What are feathers from the Stone Age doing next to dead bodies in Malibu?"

"I didn't say they were actually *from* the Stone Age," Oliver grumbled. "It is simply that tribal customs in New Guinea have remained constant since that era. As to their connection with your two corpses, that is up to you and your police friends to determine."

"Can you tell me what specific tribe these are from?"

"No. That would be extremely difficult for me to ascertain. I'm no expert on New Guinea. But I know someone who is."

"Here in the department?"

He shook his head. "A freelance professional journalist. Kelly Rourke's done research in the mountains of Papua. You could talk to Rourke."

"Sounds good."

Oliver flipped through the cards in his Rolodex, scribbled on a notepad, tore off the page, and handed it to me. "Rourke has an apartment in the American Comic Book Company building on Ventura. That's Studio City."

I scanned the note page. "Phone?"

"No, Rourke hates phones. Just go on over. Say I sent you. Odds are you'll get your information."

"Sid . . ." I clapped him on the shoulder. "I owe you a lunch."

"Solve the case and we'll celebrate. You can buy me champagne."

"For *lunch*?"

"Brunch. A champagne brunch."

And I had to submit to another crushing bear hug before I got out of there.

I took Sunset from UCLA, passing all the giant show-biz billboards along the Strip, gaudily promoting rock groups with names like Shiva, Orange Love, and The Little Big Men, then turned left on Laurel Canyon and made my way up and over the twisting snake of road that divides Hollywood from the San Fernando Valley. The little CRX danced through the curves like a prima ballerina and I got to Ventura Boulevard in jig time.

The American Comic Book Company was on the second floor. I climbed the carpeted steps, with a jagged red lightning bolt painted on the wall, to a wide landing with two doors facing one another. The first was open, and I peered into a comic fiend's paradise. Wall-to-wall superheroes in multicolored underwear.

The second door was closed. On pebbled glass, lettered in black, were the bold words: GO AWAY. I

317

DON'T LIKE STRANGERS. AND IF YOU'RE SELLING ANY-
THING—DIE!

I hoped Sid was right about my getting cooperation.
Mr. Rourke didn't seem the friendly type.

I rapped on the glass. A red-haired knockout in a
tight black turtleneck and thigh-hugging plum stretch
pants opened the door and glared at me. "Can't you
read?"

"Must have the wrong office," I said. "I'm looking
for Mr. Rourke. He's a writer."

"You're looking at him," she said. "Only I'm a *her.*"

"You certainly are," I said.

She smiled at my lewd enthusiasm. "My mother's
maiden name was Kelly. She planned on giving it to
her son, but I came along instead. I'm always surprising people."

"You sure surprised me," I admitted. "I'm David
Kincaid. Sid Oliver sent me here. He said I should
talk to you."

"About what?"

"A double murder that may extend back to the Stone
Age."

That one got me inside.

". . . and when I needed more data, Sid suggested
you. So here I am."

"Let's see the feathers," she said.

I gave them to her. Their glowing colors contrasted
with the dimness of the room. Kelly told me she kept
the curtains drawn because she could think better that
way; raw sunlight bothered her when she was writing. Well, as Sid would say, to each his own.

Her place was neat and comfortable. Big-pillowed
sofas (we were sitting on one), antique chairs, oil
paintings of ocean sunsets, and a cabinet of painted

plates behind glass. Plus books. Lots of books. Writers have books like alley cats have fleas. Comes with the territory.

After she'd examined the feathers, Kelly walked to a shelf, selected one of the books, brought it over to me. The title was in red: *Tribal Customs of Papua New Guinea.* By Nigel somebody.

"New Guinea's part of Australia, isn't it?" I asked.

"Used to be, but they got their independence in 1975." She flipped the book open. "Look at these."

The photos were in full color, showing gaudily painted natives with bones through their noses jumping up and down inside a big bamboo hut of some kind. And they all wore feathers.

"That's a Purari ceremonial dance," said Kelly. "The masked dancers in red and black represent ghosts of the dead, and that tall character, the really ugly one in the middle, he's a witch doctor. Chases away evil spirits. Check the feathers he's wearing."

She placed one of Mike's murder clues next to a close-up photo in the book. "Notice the pattern—the way the beads are threaded into the main body of the feather."

"Yeah . . . they're the same."

"And your missing heads and hearts tie right in."

"To what?"

"To their tribal customs." She gave me a steady look. "The Purari were cannibals."

I let out a long breath as Kelly continued.

"They severed the heads for luck. Or what *we'd* call luck. Sleeping on a skull at night was considered strong magic."

"And the hearts?"

"They devoured them. In order to absorb the victim's *mana*, or life force. Eating the heart was supposed to give them the victim's strength."

I leaned back into the pillow, turning one of the feathers slowly in my right hand.

"Could these be fake? I mean, not the real McCoy?"

"Nope," Kelly said flatly. "For one thing, the thread pattern is far too subtle and complex."

"Meaning what?"

"Meaning that only a real Papua New Guinean would know how to make these. Most likely a tribal witch doctor."

"We don't have cannibal witch doctors in L.A.," I said.

"They don't have them in New Guinea, either. Not anymore. Cannibalism has been extinct there for a long time."

"Then how do you explain all this?"

"I don't. But I think we should go talk to the Australian consul general."

"We?"

"As a writer, I want to follow through on this. Might get a piece for *The New Yorker* out of it. Okay with you?"

"I never say no to a beautiful woman."

Kelly smiled sweetly. "Bullshit," she said.

The abstract stained-glass tower of St. Basil's Cathedral speared its long shadow across Wilshire Boulevard, darkening the marbled entrance court of Paramount Plaza. Kelly and I walked through the tall doors of an elegant twenty-story stone-and-black-glass office building and took the elevator to the seventeenth floor.

Above an impressive continental shield, featuring an embossed kangaroo, the words AUSTRALIAN CONSULATE GENERAL were gold-leafed on the door of Suite 1742.

We went in. Several pale orange couch chairs faced a wall of shelved reference books. A framed painting of Queen Elizabeth II, in royal regalia, was on the wall next to a large contour map of Australia.

Kelly walked over to a stiff-faced lady in a glass-fronted reception booth and told her we were here to see the man himself, Sir Leslie Fraser-Shaw.

"Do you have an appointment with Sir Leslie?"

"I called in. He knows me. He's agreed to see us."

The stiff-faced receptionist verified this on her intercom, then ushered us into the sanctum sanctorum.

As we entered, Fraser-Shaw rose like a white-suited Buddha from a desk the size of a polished iceberg. He was a wide-bodied man in his sixties, with a florid complexion and deeply pouched eyes. He gave us a political smile.

"Ah, Kelly, my dear . . . safely back from the untrammeled wilds of Mongolia, I see."

"Yep, two weeks ago," she said.

"Splendid!" Fraser-Shaw swung his puffy eyes in my direction. "And you are . . .?"

"David Kincaid. From the untrammeled wilds of Malibu."

"Ah, yes." His smile wavered. He led us to a long white sofa. "Please make yourselves comfortable."

Sir Leslie settled down next to us, folding his small pink hands across the bulk of his stomach.

"Now, my dear," he said to Kelly, "just how may I be of service to you? Planning another Australian trip?"

"No, not this time," she said. "Mr. Kincaid is assisting the police on a homicide. Two of them, in fact. The murders may involve tribal Papua."

"How very peculiar," said Fraser-Shaw.

"Our purpose in coming here," I said, "is to find out what you can tell us about people from Papua New

Guinea who may now be living in the Los Angeles area."

"This is the *Australian* Consulate," Sir Leslie said firmly. "We have no legal ties to Papua New Guinea."

"I realize that—but since there is no New Guinea consulate . . ."

Fraser-Shaw shifted in his chair, tenting his delicate pink fingers. "Of course there are many Australians here in Southern California, but I really don't believe there are any residents from Papua New Guinea. At least, not to my knowledge."

"There was a ceremonial feather left at the site of each murder," I said. "From Papua."

"They're definitely authentic tribal feathers," Kelly declared. "Very much the real thing."

"Your murderer could be a collector," said Fraser-Shaw. "He could have purchased the feathers in Papua—leaving them as, one might say, his personal calling cards."

"That's possible," I admitted.

Sir Leslie checked his watch and stood up, letting us know the meeting had ended.

"I do wish I could spend more time discussing this matter with you," he said, "but I am victim to a crowded schedule."

"Appreciate your seeing us, Sir Leslie," said Kelly, smiling at him.

He put a fleshy paw on her shoulder. "You are most welcome, my dear. And if I can be of any further help, do not hesitate to call on me."

"We just might do that," I said.

He nodded toward me. "Good luck with your enquiries, Mr. Kincaid."

I said thanks to that.

After a late dinner, I dropped Kelly off at her comic-book address, promising to "keep her in the picture" as the case progressed—*if* it progressed. Then I phoned Mike Lucero and filled him in on the Papua New Guinea angle. He was, to say the least, highly skeptical about the possibility of Stone Age cannibals in Los Angeles.

"But it explains the feathers," I told him.

"Sure it does," he said. "Now all we have to do is find a *real* explanation. Just bring 'em back to me in the morning, okay?"

"In the morning," I said.

I drove home under a full moon, turning off Malibu Canyon Road at Las Virgenes and aiming the CRX up the mile-long climb past the Hindu Temple to road's end near the Cottontail Ranch. I eased the Honda down the curving gravel drive fronting my place, got out, and took a deep breath—inhaling the sweet scent of pine, sage, and oleander. And even this far inland a sea wind brought me the faint iodine smell of the Pacific. There are worse places to live, and I was smiling as I keyed open the front door.

Inside, I experienced a neck-prickling sensation that told me I wasn't alone.

I spun from the door as three tall, heavily muscled figures came for me, brandishing wicked-looking knives and spears. They had bones in their noses. The moonlight played across naked chests and painted faces, and all I could think of was how goddam surprised Mike Lucero would be to see his ole buddy being attacked at home by three frothing Stone Age cannibals.

I dropped into a defensive crouch as a bamboo spear whistled past my left ear to bury itself in the wall. I figured it was time to make all those painful hours of karate practice pay off.

I took out the first guy with a *yoko-geri*—a powerful side kick to the neck with the outside edge of my right boot. He went down like chopped timber.

I pivoted toward the second guy, into a *mawashi-zuki*, thrusting my left fist forward in a roundhouse half-circle from the hip to the side of his head. He crashed backward, taking a lamp table down with him.

The third guy was the biggest, with a long raised scar puckering his right cheek, and he was charging in with a raised blade big enough to impress Jim Bowie. I ducked under the glittering arc of his knife and put the elbow of my right arm hard into his ribs— the always-effective *empi-uchi*. One of his bones cracked, like a dry twig breaking. He grunted and dropped the knife, staggering, his eyes wild, lips pulled back from the pain.

I was gearing up for more action when the three of them decided they didn't like my magic. The knife-wielder scooped up his blade and the spear-thrower retrieved his spear. Then, like three night shadows, they left the way they'd come in, sliding through the living-room window and instantly vanishing into the thick brush and trees.

When Mike Lucero answered the phone his opening words were fogged with sleep. "Yeah . . . who . . . who's calling?"

"Kincaid."

"*Dave?* Christ, it's late! Don't you ever go to bed?"

"Being attacked by cannibals tends to keep me awake."

He was really pissed now. "You call me in the middle of the friggin' night because you're having a friggin' dream about cannibals?"

"No dream, Mike. These three boys were the genu-

ine article. Feathers, body paint, bones in the nose—
like they stepped right out of a Stone Age time machine."

"I thought you didn't do drugs," Mike growled.

Now *I* was pissed and allowed the anger to edge my
voice. "I don't, and you know it. I'm telling you
straight—when I got home tonight three painted savages with knives and spears were waiting for me. They
damn well tried to *kill* me. Without my karate training I would have bought the farm."

"Okay, okay . . . I'll take your word about the attack. But whoever they were, they weren't Stone Age
savages."

"Who were they then?"

"Could've been three of the Henchmen, playing native. To go with the feathers they planted on the two
bodies. Trying to freak you off the case."

"You think the Henchmen are responsible for both
murders?"

"I'm not ruling out the idea. I questioned as many
of those slimeballs as I could round up—and they're a
mean bunch of mothers, lemme tellya. They could be
using all this New Guinea savage crap as a smoke-
screen."

"But *why*? What's the point of it all? If they wanted
to snuff the Stomper and the Olympic guy for some
reason, why not just kill them outright, with no frills?
Why the big masquerade?"

"Could be their sick sense of humor. These people
are *twisted,* Dave."

"I don't buy it," I said firmly. "It's just too bizarre."

"Look." Mike sighed. "Let's talk at the station. I gotta
get back to sleep or I won't be worth shit tomorrow.
I'm just glad you're okay." He hesitated. "You *are* okay,
right?"

"I'm fine. Not a scratch."

"Then can we talk about this in the morning? You can file a full report."

"Sure. In the morning."

And I rang off.

When I woke at ten, the sun was hiding out. A fog had blown in from the ocean, making everything gray and cobwebby. Which was how I felt. I showered, dressed, and fixed myself Swedish pancakes for breakfast. Whenever I get depressed I treat myself to Swedish pancakes. Stomach therapy.

I was in no hurry to talk to Mike Lucero. We'd said all there was to say at this point, and I figured I'd rather look into Kelly's deep green eyes than Mike's scowling cop's mug. So I phoned her.

She seemed delighted to hear from me. "I was going to call *you*," she said. "I want to take you someplace special today. To see a bloke I know."

"A *bloke*? That's Aussie talk."

"It's the only clue I'll give you," she said. And she laughed.

Forty-five minutes later I picked her up in front of her comic-book building in Studio City and asked where we were headed.

"For Yuppie Heaven," she said. And her green eyes glinted.

I knew where that was: the oh-so-hip area of neoned "in" shops and cafés stretching for several blocks along Melrose, below Hollywood. With names like the Last Wound-up, Indiana Joan's, and the Big Bravo. Where all the young, upwardly mobile couples twitter over the latest craze in clothes, videos, records, collectibles, and books.

On the way over I told Kelly about my violent brush

with the Stone Age. She was shocked when she realized I wasn't kidding.

"Mike figures they were cycle freaks, coming on as
natives," I said.

"He's wrong," Kelly declared. "From your description, I'd say they were real."

"Real *savages*?"

"Not in the sense one associates with the term. But
definitely people from Papua New Guinea."

"But Fraser-Shaw told us there aren't any people
from New Guinea in L.A."

"He said he didn't *know* of any. Well, I do."

"Yesterday you didn't."

"That was then and this is now. I did some phoning.
That's why we're going where we're going. You'll see."

"Okay, but I'm running out of patience. Where the
hell *are* we going?"

"The Down-Under," said Kelly.

The place is owned by a female pop singer from
Australia. When you go inside there are dozens of
framed pictures of her along the walls. And near the
back there's this big screen with constantly running
footage of her performing but with no soundtrack. It's
kind of spooky, watching her sing with no words coming out.

"It wouldn't be appropriate to our overall atmosphere."

That's what the manager of Down-Under told me
when I asked him why we couldn't hear the singer
singing. He was the Aussie "bloke" Kelly had taken
me to meet. Derek Newcombe, a tall string bean of a
guy. Seems his parents used to work with the natives
in Papua New Guinea before the big split with Australia.

He was standing behind the planed-wood "Aussie Milk Bar" (in red neon letters) as Kelly and I perched on two high stools at the counter.

"What'll it be, mates?" Derek asked.

"Vegemite, and a Blue Heaven milk shake," said Kelly.

"I'll just go with the Blue Heaven," I said. And turned to her. "What's Vegemite?"

"It's great! Everybody in Australia has it for breakfast. Highly nutritious, too."

When her order arrived, with the Vegemite spread darkly over buttered wheat, it looked exactly like cinnamon toast. And I *love* cinnamon toast.

"Want a bite?" she asked.

"You bet," I said.

"Chew it thoroughly," advised Derek.

I bit into Vegemite-covered toast and began chewing. "Gah!" I sputtered, barely able to swallow the stuff.

"I don't think he cares for it," Derek said to Kelly.

She nodded. "It's an acquired taste." And she dug into her order with sickening enthusiasm.

"What the hell's it *made* of?"

"Yeast, mainly."

"Yech! No wonder."

Two big stuffed kangaroos flanked the bar, and I would rather have bitten into one of them.

Then Kelly got to the point of our visit.

"Derek, on the phone this morning, you told me that you know for a fact that there are at least two to three dozen people from Papua New Guinea living in the Los Angeles area. We've come here to find out about them."

Newcombe compressed his lips and scratched his head, looking like Stan Laurel. And he also had Laurel's sad eyes. "Well . . . maybe I spoke out of turn."

"What's that supposed to mean?" I asked him.

"These people . . . they're very private. Keep to themselves. They don't like to mix with outsiders."

I nodded. "With anyone who isn't from Papua New Guinea, you mean?"

"Right, mate. Exactly right." He even had Laurel's high, piping voice—but with a thick Aussie accent. "I wouldn't advise attempting to make contact with any of them. If that's what you had in mind."

"Really?" I said. "Well, three of 'em sure tried to make contact with *me* last night."

"I don't follow you, mate," said Derek.

"Forget it," I said. "Just tell us where we can find these people."

"I'm not sure . . . if I should. . . ." Newcombe looked uncertain.

"C'mon, Derek, what's the problem?" Kelly demanded. "We just need to ask them a few questions. It's no big deal."

"All right then, luv," said Newcombe. "Go down to Third and San Pedro. There's a bar on the corner— the Imunu. That's where they congregate. Kind of a meeting place for them."

"How do we know when they'll be there?" I asked. "Or what they look like?"

"My father goes there to drink with them sometimes," said Newcombe. "He told me that this tall bloke from Papua named Dibela works there days as a bartender. He might answer whatever questions you have. But I wouldn't count on it."

"How do we recognize Dibela?" asked Kelly.

"That's easy. Bloke has a right fierce scar along his cheek."

I did a double take on that one. Jackpot! The spearthrower!

It was time to move.

"Thanks, mate," I said, steering Kelly toward the door. She was still nibbling Vegemite on the way. "Be sure to give Olivia our best next time you see her."

When we left, the singer was still performing soundlessly on the screen.

I phoned Mike Lucero and told him to meet me at the Imunu in an hour and that I'd explain why when he got there. Then we took the Hollywood Freeway into central L.A. I parked the CRX in a lot a half-block east of the bar. The afternoon sun was gradually sliding down the edge of the western sky, lengthening our shadows as we moved along San Pedro.

Walking through this seedy, down-at-the-heels area, passing the battered, grimed storefronts, decorated by dopers, winos, grifters, pimps, and prostitutes, was a depressing business. This was another, darker world, full of poverty and violence and smashed lives. Derek had it right; we didn't belong here.

The Imunu was a typical product of the area. A soot-blackened COORS sign flickered in dying neon behind a grease-filmed window. The bar's name had been painted on a strip of peeling wood above the front door, but the last two letters had flaked away, leaving only IMU on the weathered board.

Inside, the air reeked of sour tobacco and spilled beer. "This place would give Count Dracula the creeps," I muttered to Kelly.

It wasn't crowded. Perhaps a dozen drinkers huddled over their glasses at tables and booths, regarding us with suspicious eyes as we crossed the smoke-dimmed room to the bar.

"Shouldn't we wait for your cop friend?" Kelly asked me. I'd told her about the scar. "This Dibela guy might go for you again."

"Not in public," I said. "And not without his pals. I just want to make sure he's the same bird before Mike gets here to put the cuffs on him."

"Okay." Kelly shrugged. "We'll play it your way."

The guy behind the bar was tall and black and mean-looking, but he *didn't* have a scar on his cheek.

"What you want?" he demanded, with a glare.

"Does a man named Dibela work here?" I asked.

"Maybe."

I slid a ten-dollar bill across the counter. He closed his hand over it like a shark's jaw, not looking at the money. He kept glaring at me.

I waited. "Well?"

"He took off early today—couple of minutes before you came in. Said he had something special he had to do. Might still be able to catch him." The bartender flicked his head toward the rear of the building in a quick gesture. "Got an old Ford pickup truck. Keeps it round back. If it's there, he's there."

"Thanks," I said, and hustled outside with Kelly. We sprinted for the lot behind the building. Dibela was just getting into the pickup—rusted-orange, with dented fenders and the rear bumper missing. We got a side flash of his scarred face as he climbed into the truck.

"Is that the guy?" asked Kelly.

"Yep. Only his spear is missing." I looked around, the muscles in my jaw tightening. "Where the hell's Lucero? Guy's gonna be long gone in another two seconds!"

Then Mike's unmarked car rolled up to us. Talk about the nick of time! He waved from the window. "Saw you hop around the building. What's going down?"

I climbed into Mike's car, pulling Kelly in after me. I'd introduce them later. "See that guy in the Ford?"

It passed us, pulling onto San Pedro.

"Yeah, so what?"

"So follow him—but don't let him know he's picked up a tail. He's one of the three weirdos who attacked me. I figure he could lead us to the others."

"You've been a busy little bee since last night," Mike declared, moving out into the traffic flow.

"You packing your .38?" I asked.

He patted his coat. "Always."

"Good. We just might need it."

Dibela had no idea he was being tailed, but Mike was careful anyhow, staying far enough back to keep out of his driving mirror. Our boy cleared downtown L.A. and got on the Ventura Freeway, with us right behind him.

As we drove I told Mike all about Kelly and Derek Newcombe and filled in details of the night attack.

"And you're a hundred percent sure the guy we're after was one of them?" he asked.

"Hundred percent," I said. And told them about the scar.

He nodded, smiling faintly. It was the kind of smile I'd seen on his face before, when a tough case was coming into focus. "Sounds like you two are really on to something."

Kelly leaned toward him. "Then you're ready to believe us now—about the New Guinea tie-in to the murders?"

"I'd be a fool not to, at this point," he said. "Wacko as it seems, you've got me convinced we're chasing a goddam cannibal down the Ventura Freeway!"

And we all grinned.

Dibela took the off ramp for Malibu Canyon Road, heading toward the coast. He didn't give any indication he'd seen us as Mike made the same turn, three cars behind the pickup.

The road twisted through rolling hills the color of lion pelts, with the lowering sun tinting the distant horizon.

"When you didn't show up at the station this morning, I began feeling guilty," Mike said.

I looked at him. "Why guilty?"

"The way I put you off last night, right after you'd practically been killed. As if my getting some extra shut-eye was more important than what you had to tell me."

"Hey, Mike, there was nothing you could have done. I just wanted you to know what happened."

"I still feel guilty about it. Then today, when you didn't show or call in, I began to worry—that maybe those three creeps had come back for you. So I drove over to your place to check it out. When you didn't answer, I forced a window to get inside, but you were gone."

"I meant to call you earlier, but Kelly took me under her wing."

"I have very soft feathers," she said.

Mike chuckled deep in his throat. "Seems you two make a good team. And if I do say so, a damn handsome couple."

I could see where this was heading, with Mike Cupid trying to set up a new soulmate for his ole buddy Dave. Another ten miles and he'd have us married.

The road now sliced between Malibu Canyon's sheer walls, with steeply rising sun-shadowed cliffs of tumbled granite to our left. California can look like many states, and right now it looked like the canyon country of Arizona. Hard to believe, at this moment, that a big blue ocean was waiting just over the ridge.

There was only one car between us and the Ford pickup when Dibela swung abruptly off the highway onto a narrow dirt trail leading into the mountains.

The sudden route change took Mike by surprise, and we skidded over some rough ground before reversing to complete the turn. By then the Ford was out of sight around a twist in the trail.

"This is no road," Mike grumbled. "Where the hell's he *going*?" He lifted his head, eyes slitted against the sky. "Nothin' up there but trees and rock. It's all raw wilderness."

"You found the second body in the mountains," I reminded him. "Maybe these New Guinea boys have some kind of headquarters up here."

"Makes sense," said Kelly. "This terrain is a lot like the mountains of Papua. Probably makes them feel right at home."

The dirt trail looped and bumped us upward, full of deep cuts and half-buried stones. Fit for coyotes, not cars. We were following the Ford's dust cloud, so there was no way Dibela could spot us behind him.

When the dust thinned, Mike slowed to a crawl, knowing Dibela had stopped somewhere just ahead. He drove off the trail into heavy chaparral, shielding the car.

"We walk from here," Mike said. "Stay right behind me, and keep to the trees. We don't want to be seen." He slipped the .38 from its clamshell holster, checked the load. "No telling what we'll run into."

With Mike leading, we proceeded cautiously through the trees paralleling the dirt trail. The sun had now dropped below the horizon, and an early-evening chill, blown in from the ocean, was settling over the mountains. We were moving through scented stands of eucalyptus, oak, and sycamore. There were king snakes and rattlers in these mountains, and I hoped we wouldn't be stepping on any. Or on a mountain lion's tail.

"You okay?" I asked Kelly.

"Sure." She nodded. Her hair was like rubbed brass in the sunless twilight. "Just glad I'm not wearing high heels."

We were into a screening mass of tangled chamisa when Mike raised a warning hand. "Keep your heads down. We're coming up on something."

We arrived at the edge of a large clearing—and from our hiding place in the brush we saw Dibela's rusted-out truck parked behind a long roughly constructed board shack.

"He's probably inside," said Mike, keeping his voice low. If there were any guards around, we didn't want to attract their attention.

At the farther side of the clearing was a second structure, much larger than the shack, raised from the ground on a platform of thick wooden stilts and made of what I guessed was thatched bamboo.

"Do you recognize that?" I asked Kelly. "Looks native to me."

"It is," she said softly. "A tribal ceremonial house . . . called a House of Skulls."

"Sounds cozy," I said. "Just the place for a family picnic."

"What kind of ceremonies go on in a joint like that?" asked Mike.

"Different kinds," Kelly replied, "but they all center around tribal magic."

"Something's sure going on in there right now," I said, as a rhythmic pulsing of drums began, backed by chanting voices. That's when we saw the door of the shack open and our boy Dibela emerge. Dressed just the way he was when he attacked me—a loincloth around his waist and his dark-bronze flesh daubed with colored paints. He had a bone through his nose, with a mass of feathers decorating his head. And he carried a spear.

"Holy shit!" breathed Mike.

"Dibela is more than a bartender," said Kelly. "He's also a tribal witch doctor."

We watched him cross the clearing and enter the House of Skulls. The chanting inside changed pitch, becoming more intense, almost frenzied.

Mike swung his head toward Kelly. "What would you guess they're up to?"

"Impossible to say from here."

"Then it looks like we go have ourselves a gander," Mike declared.

We scanned the area for guards. It looked safe. Guess they felt secure up here in the middle of nowhere. With Mike leading, we sprinted across the clearing, ducked between stilts, and crouched in the dry mustard grass beneath the House of Skulls.

Directly above, the platform juddered under pounding feet—and the sound of the drums and chanting voices washed around us, a sea of alien sounds.

We crawled to a better vantage point. Through a wide opening in the platform we could see more than two dozen natives, wearing wigs of fiber and bark, and necklaces of teeth, their dark bodies decorated with shells and colored seeds.

Many of the dancers carried bamboo spears and bone daggers, their skin painted in bizarre patterns, feathers weaving as they swayed to the throbbing drums.

The interior walls were crowded with painted wooden shields and grotesquely carved tribal masks—and, of course, with skulls. Lots of skulls, with gaping, eyeless sockets and hanging jaws of yellowed bone. I figured a couple of them had been lopped off the bodies of Stomper Lee and Eddie Lansdale. God knew where the others came from.

Then I heard Mike draw in his breath sharply. "Jesus!" he whispered. "They've got a guy tied up in there!"

He was right. At the far end of the platform, on a makeshift altar, we could see their latest victim, a young man stripped to the waist with his hands and feet securely bound. His neck rested on a crude wooden block, and it was obvious they intended to behead him. *And* cut his heart out.

That's what this damn ceremony was all about. This was the "something special" Dibela left work early for. Another ritual murder.

"Here, take this," Mike said, handing his .38 to me. "I'm going to the car and call for some backup. We gotta stop this before it's too late."

"I'm no good with a gun," I protested. "You might need it if you run into trouble."

"I'll be okay," Mike declared. "If they begin the main action before I get back—the head and heart bit—then start shooting. They can't stand up against bullets with the weapons they have."

"And what happens when I run out of bullets?"

"Cops'll be here by then."

And he ducked away from us, running low across the clearing in the direction of the car.

Lucero didn't get far. Two big natives who were rounding the shack spotted him, and loosed their spears. One missed; the other didn't.

Mike was down with a bamboo spear through his right shoulder.

"Bastards!" I muttered, and brought up the gun. I was ready to fire when Kelly grabbed my arm.

"Don't!" she warned. "Save your bullets until they're really needed. If we reveal ourselves now, *nobody* has a chance."

"Okay . . . I guess that makes sense." I lowered the .38, sweating. The palms of my hands were slick and my jaw muscles ached. This case was no longer colorful; it had turned deadly and frightening. I was shaking with tension.

The two natives dragged Lucero to his feet, and one of them jerked the spear loose. Mike let out a cry of agony. The spear point had gone through the soft flesh of his upper shoulder, and there was a lot of blood coming from the wound. Plus a lot of pain. But he was not seriously hurt.

Not yet.

Kelly and I ducked back into the shadows beneath the platform as the two natives passed us, forcing Mike ahead of them into the House of Skulls.

Inside, a wave of hostile cries was directed at Mike. Dibela danced around him, shaking his spear, teeth bared like a hungry wolf.

Then another native emerged from the clearing. He hurried into the House of Skulls, spoke intently to Dibela. The witch doctor left for the shack, remained inside for a few moments, then returned to the ceremony.

"Something's going on at the shack," I said.

"What should we do?" Kelly faced me, her green eyes shaded with concern. "Should one of us try for the car?"

"No," I told her. "They'll be posting new guards now that Mike's been spotted. We have to stay right here."

Sure enough, just as I finished speaking, three painted natives, armed with spears, left the ceremonial house and began prowling around the clearing.

"I'm sure they won't think of looking under here," whispered Kelly. "We'll be safe for a while."

"Yeah," I muttered, gripping the .38 tightly in my right fist. "For a while."

"They're putting Mike on the altar with that other guy," Kelly pointed out. "That means—"

"I *know* what it means."

We watched and listened in shock as the drums began a faster beat; the dancing intensified, and the chanting mounted in volume. Things were heating up.

Dibela approached the altar. He'd replaced his spear with what was obviously a ceremonial blade. He waved it in the air, and the frenzied dancers let out a howl.

"Shit, he's gonna do it!" I told Kelly. "He's gonna lop off Mike's head!"

"Then I guess . . . it's time for you to start shooting," said Kelly.

My hand was shaking as I brought up the gun, aiming at Dibela through the gap in the flooring.

Now I had the .38 in both hands, trying to steady my aim, when that bronzed devil raised the blade full above him, ready to bring it down on Mike's neck. His eyes gleamed and a smile puckered his scarred face. The chanting was really crazed.

"Dave!" Mike yelled. "Shoot the sonuvabitch before he *kills* me!"

My finger was about to squeeze the trigger when three loud shots, like popping firecrackers, stunned the dancers into silence.

Dibela slowly turned from the altar, blood gouting from his head and chest. His glazed eyes were already dead as he dropped the blade and sprawled forward across the floor.

"It's Fraser-Shaw!" I gasped.

The rotund, white-suited consul general was standing in the doorway of the House of Skulls, a thin spiral of blue-gray smoke curling from the barrel of the big .45 automatic in his right hand.

Kelly and I lost no time in making our presence known. We scrambled from our hiding place and ran into the ceremonial house like two happy kids.

Fraser-Shaw had introduced himself and was cutting Mike and the other victim loose, with both of them babbling their thanks, when we arrived on the scene. The natives, utterly silent, had drawn back against the walls. I swung the .38 toward them, but they didn't seem to offer any threat. Their sick little show was over.

"Ah," said Fraser-Shaw, turning to face us. "Miss Rourke and Mr. Kincaid. I had no idea you were here."

"That goes double for us," I said. "Where did you come from? And how did you find this place? Are you alone?"

"Please." He raised a hand. "One question at a time, Mr. Kincaid. First, we must inquire as to the condition of these two gentlemen."

"I'm okay," said Mike. "Not much feeling in my right arm, but a lot of the bleeding's stopped."

Kelly was using her neck scarf as a makeshift bandage. I handed the .38 back to Lucero, glad to be rid of the damn thing.

"And what about you, young man?" Fraser-Shaw asked.

"I'm still . . . kinda . . . shook-up," he answered.

"That's quite understandable," said Fraser-Shaw. "However, let me assure you that there is nothing more to fear. Now that I have killed their witch doctor, these people are rendered powerless. Their magic has been lost."

"Who are you?" Kelly asked the young man.

"McCammon," he said. "Ben McCammon. I'm an assistant track coach at USC. These freaks kidnapped me from the athletic field last night. Man . . ." And he shook Fraser-Shaw's hand vigorously. "I'm just glad you showed when you did!"

"I'm going to call for backup," said Mike. "The rest of you stay here and keep an eye on these characters."

And Mike took off at a fast trot for the car.

Huddled close to the walls, the natives watched us silently.

Fraser-Shaw faced me. "Now, Mr. Kincaid, let me answer your questions. Your visit to my office yesterday roused my personal curiosity about the possible existence of a New Guinea cult in this area. I began an investigation and discovered that such a cult did indeed exist. The two recent murders were obviously the result of a brutal reversion to ancient tribal customs. Using my official status as a representative of Australia, I was able to locate one of these cultists. I found out he was going to attend some sort of ceremony."

"*This* ceremony?" I asked.

"Precisely," said the consul general. "I had no idea of its nature when I followed him here earlier today. Had I guessed it was another blood ritual, I would have brought along the authorities. I was, please understand, still operating from theory. However, shortly after I arrived here, I was discovered. I was taken prisoner and tied up in the shack. Eventually I managed to free myself. I recovered the weapon I'd brought here with me, and was fortunate enough to intervene before more blood was spilled." He smiled at me. "It's as simple as that."

I stared at him. "You're a remarkable man, Sir Leslie. Really remarkable."

"Why, thank you."

"It's not a compliment," I told him—spinning abruptly on my left heel and karate-kicking the .45 from his hand. I scooped up the automatic and leveled it at his fat gut.

Kelly and McCammon were staring at me as if I'd gone round the bend.

"Dave!" Kelly protested. "What's *wrong* with you? He saved our lives!"

"He was just trying to save his own. Trying to keep himself out of jail—but he didn't quite make it. Did you, mate?"

Fraser-Shaw glared at me, eyes frosted, lips compressed. "When the police arrive, I'll have you arrested for assault," he said tightly.

"Sure you will," I said. And smiled.

Of course, there was no assault charge. Sir Leslie Fraser-Shaw was the one they arrested. For murder. When the shack was searched, no binding ropes or tape or handcuffs were found—but the sheriff's deputies *did* find the carved wood spirit mask and body robe worn by Sir Leslie when he participated in the blood ceremonies.

He'd come here to share McCammon's death, and was in the act of preparing himself for the ceremony when Mike's capture abruptly changed his plans. That's when he called Dibela to the shack and instructed him to proceed with the ceremony. Now that the cult's latest victim was a homicide cop, Fraser-Shaw realized things had gone too far. It was time to bail out. Dibela had been the only one who could identify the consul general; the others had seen him *only* in his masked role as a spirit of the dead. Therefore, with the death of the witch doctor, any evidence connecting Fraser-Shaw to the cult would vanish. So he decided to play "hero" and save Mike's life by shooting Dibela.

And it had almost worked.

"What I don't understand is how you knew the consul general was lying about being held captive," Kelly said.

"Noticed his wrist when he was holding the gun," I told her. "If he'd been bound and had struggled to free himself, the skin would have been chafed and raw. It wasn't. And that white summer suit of his—not a wrinkle or a smudge on it. So I knew he had to be lying."

Kelly shook her head. "I still can't figure why a man like Sir Leslie would involve himself in a blood cult."

"He was more than just involved," said Mike. "We got a full confession out of him. He was the guy behind the whole thing."

The three of us were in the Valley, sitting at a table at Jennifer's, another Aussie joint Kelly had discovered in Woodland Hills.

"That's right," I told her. "Fraser-Shaw began all this out of a sense of personal guilt. He felt the Aussies had mistreated the natives, including the ones in Papua New Guinea. Tribal cultures had been disrupted and destroyed. Then he found out about this core group from Papua. They'd immigrated to Los Angeles after independence. He began working with their leader, Renagi Dibela, to restore the ancient tribal customs. Even financed the building of the ceremonial house. But the situation got out of hand with the reversion to cannibalism."

"Yet he went along with it?" Kelly asked.

"Yeah." Mike nodded. "The creep admitted to us that he actually began to *enjoy* that aspect of it. Gave him a real power lift. And damned if he didn't *eat* part of those missing hearts!"

"Oh, wow!" said Kelly with a grimace.

"Couldn't have tasted worse than Vegemite," I said.

She gave me a dirty look.

"Private joke," I told Mike.

Lucero stood up. "Well, I gotta split. Lots of paperwork waiting for me at the station." He looked down at Kelly and me. "Like I said before, you guys make a handsome couple!"

And, with a wide grin, he left the restaurant.

"Mike's an incurable romantic," I told Kelly. "Since my divorce, he's been trying to link me up with the right woman."

"I've got a great idea," said Kelly.

"What's that?"

"Let's go to your place and link up."

She was right. It *did* turn out to be a great idea.

DING-DONG, THE LIZARD'S DEAD

RAY RUSSELL

The era of the old Hollywood studio system has passed forever, and along with it the legendary breed of studio moguls who built the fledgling industry from scratch. MBAs and market research have replaced the crude but effective showmanship of the Golden Age. But were the days of the Selznicks, the Zanucks, and the Warners really the good old days? When Lieutenant Garcia of the LAPD is called in to investigate the death of the last of the great Hollywood patriarchs, in Ray Russell's "Ding-Dong, the Lizard's Dead," he finds that the good old days concealed some unpleasant secrets.

* * *

345

GARCIA found himself humming the old tune as he turned off Doheny onto Pico and drove deeper into West Los Angeles. Old tune, but revised words. Not "the witch is dead," but "the lizard's dead." That's the way it was being sung the past few days by all the registered smartballs in town. Garcia was tired of it, but he couldn't keep it from running through his head.

On his left, he noted the kosher eatery owned and operated by Steven Spielberg's mother; on his right, where shops used to be, was the discreetly walled enclosure of an oil company's slant-drilling operaion, always smelling faintly of unrefined petroleum. (Progress!)

Just the day before, one of his younger colleagues, Jameson, had been trying to tell him that the world was getting better. He had snorted at the presumptuous pup and said, "Better? Are you nuts? Have you seen the latest numbers on narcotic addiction? Have you waded through your phone bills since they busted up Ma Bell? Do you know how many people are dying of AIDS—a disease that hadn't even been *invented* when I was your age? Don't give me 'better.' The world is the *pits*. And it's getting worse every day."

"Come on, Garcia," Jameson had persisted. "When you were my age, a black dude like me wouldn't even be on the same payroll with you." Garcia had refrained from responding that there hadn't been many Garcias or Gomezes or Rodriguezes on the strength back then, either, and there still weren't enough to suit him. The black man had continued, "When you were a kid, I bet they didn't even have TV. Now, guess what I bought yesterday? I went out and got myself a VCR."

"Great," Garcia had groaned. "Now you can rent

Casablanca for more than I paid to see it first run on the *big* screen."

"*Casablanca!* That old thing? I can rent X-rated stuff, and me and my little honey can watch it together."

"Exactly! The pits, like I said. You and your little honey will probably end up with herpes."

"From a *cassette*?"

It was well before noon, but the Southern California sun was already threatening to turn the car into a potter's kiln, even with the windows open. He closed them and turned on the air conditioner as he passed the green, woody fragrance of Rancho Park golf course on his left. Garcia put pressure on the gas pedal and picked up speed. He didn't want to be late for the show.

Because that's what it would be. A show. A display. He didn't expect to accomplish anything this morning, do any business, conduct any interviews. Wrong time, if not wrong place. All he could do would be to study the . . . cast of characters. He touched his chest and felt the crinkle of paper in the inside pocket of his jacket.

He passed Twentieth Century–Fox—now shrunken to a wraith of its sprawling former self by a real estate sell-off to developers. Garcia, a native Angeleno, was saddened by such changes. A big blue bus of the Santa Monica line roared past him, leaving behind a black cloud of diesel flatulence. He was glad he had closed his windows.

He passed the warm Spanish architecture of St. Timothy's: a reminder that he hadn't been to confession for . . . he couldn't remember how long. He let his wife take care of all the religious stuff. Well, what the hell, what did *he* have to confess? *He* didn't shoot dope or watch X-rated filth with a little honey. But he made a mental note to visit the confessional box anyway. Tomorrow. Or over the weekend, at the very latest. It couldn't hurt.

His destination was almost on top of him, and he quickly moved into the next lane without signaling, luckily avoiding any traffic mishaps.

As he drove under the giant arch bearing the letters O-Z, a uniformed guard stopped him with an authoritative gesture. Garcia lowered the driver window, and before the guard had a chance to speak, he flashed his ID and said, "I'm looking for Stage Twelve."

"Straight ahead, then turn right. Just follow the rest of the parade."

Parade. Nice word for it. Garcia drove on, slowly trailing the stately procession of long, costly sedans and limousines. His eyes narrowed in the sunlight as he watched the huge sound stages go by his car window.

It had been a long time since he'd been on the "Oz" lot, as it was often called by people who liked to be considered in the swim. But the real insiders called it either O-Z or just Oracle, short for Oracle-Zodiac Pictures. The company had been formed, decades earlier, by a merger of two studios, Oracle and Zodiac.

The string of cars came to an end at Stage Twelve, its colossal doors open wide. Garcia parked as best he could, climbed out, and watched the collection of notables do the same. Stretch limos, stretch jeans. The people were of both sexes and all ages, and many of the faces were familiar to him. Some he had seen all his life on the screen. He tried to blend in with them as he sauntered into the cavernous interior of the soundstage.

There, pinned like a rare butterfly by the dramatic beam of an overhead spotlight, was an ornate open coffin banked by floral wreaths. Organ music—recorded, Garcia assumed—softly cushioned the assembled mourners. Inside the coffin lay the mortal remains of the studio's late production head, Baruch Isaac Gross. Mister B.I.G. The Lizard of Oz.

"He ruled his kingdom, Oracle-Zodiac, with despotic genius," the newspaper eulogy had said. "A man of clashing contradictions, he could one minute be crassly commercial, and the next minute he might approve an experimental project by a bright young student fresh out of cinema school. A brilliant if untutored armchair psychologist, he knew what made his employees tick, and that knowledge was power. Crude, forceful, admired by few, hated by many, he countered accusations of 'grossness' by responding: 'You know what Gross means? It don't just mean the grosses. Gross means Great! Look it up.' And, in his way, B. I. Gross was indeed great, the last of the old-style tyrannosaurs that once were wont to do battle with each other in the primeval jungles of Hollywood. . . ."

Dead, he didn't look much like a lizard, Garcia thought. You needed to see the teeth when he smiled that mirthless smile; you had to shrivel before those glittering eyes moving under the canopylike lids.

"Yep," a man standing next to Garcia whispered, "Gross was absolutely right. Look at this turnout, will you? Like he always said, 'Give the marks what they want and they'll line up like sailors at a whorehouse.'" The cynic was a burly middle-aged man with sandy hair going gray and thin.

"You mean," asked Garcia, "all these people are glad he's dead?"

"Well, you don't see any tears, do you? Except from one or two crocodiles, maybe. They all hated him, every one of them, the whole ball of wackos."

"You could be right. Pardon me, you're . . . ?"

"Hammond."

"Buck Hammond, the cameraman?"

"Cinematographer," Hammond corrected with an ironical grin.

"Right. I'll be talking to you later. You live up in Bel-Air, don't you?"

"Talk to me about what?" asked Hammond, with a scowl of suspicion.

"The death of Mr. Gross."

"Who the hell are you?"

"Name of Garcia. Lieutenant, LAPD." Garcia smiled. "Homicide Division. Nice to meet you, Mr. Hammond."

Earlier that week, a lawyer named Creeley had phoned and asked Garcia to drop by his office. The office was located in one of Century City's twin triangular forty-four-story high-rises, a cold structure like an upended ice cube tray, in a synthetic "city" without houses, without litter, without children, without dogs or cats; a place avoided by most birds, where even the severe platoons of trees, though real, seemed to be clever plastic fakes; where all the parking was hidden underground, and nothing was permitted to exist that did not turn a large profit.

In years gone by, the 180-acre complex had been the backlot of the Twentieth Century–Fox film studio. It could be argued that the long-gone fabulous backlot had been no less relentlessly commercial in its goals than its rigid, frigid successor. Certainly it had been far more tawdry. But to be tawdry, Garcia reflected, is to be human. He hated Century City.

When he had complied with the request and visited Creeley's office, the attorney had handed him a sealed gray envelope addressed in longhand to Sergeant P. Garcia, LAPD.

"From my client—well, my former client, the late B. I. Gross," Creeley had said. His eyes were about the size of poppy seeds. "It was among his effects, to be delivered to you upon his death. If you *are* the correct Garcia, that is. This says 'Sergeant,' but my secretary announced you as Lieutenant. . . ."

"I was still a sergeant when Mr. Gross and I met some years ago. A little scrape his son got into. Nothing serious. I wasn't in Homicide then."

Garcia had thanked Creeley and had declined to open the letter there in the office, despite (or possibly because of) the attorney's obvious curiosity.

At a taco and hot dog stand well away from Century City, Garcia had avoided the tacos as being a desecration to the memory of those his mother had made with such care and authenticity and settled for a hot dog with sauerkraut. Chewing his lunch and washing it down with diet root beer, he had opened the letter and read it. Written in Gross's hand on heavy, rat-gray personal stationery, it said, in effect, that if the writer were to die from causes other than natural, certain people were to be investigated because they all wanted him dead. A list of nine names followed.

Garcia, fighting back the threatened eruption of a volcanic root-beer belch, had put down his hot dog half-eaten. Causes other than natural? Gross had died of barbiturate poisoning. Accidental? Suicide? Murder? Suddenly this letter had made murder the odds-on favorite. A much closer look into the matter was in order. A more thorough search of the dead man's house. And a microscopic examination of the nine suspects.

That was when Garcia had assigned a team to the house and had made it his personal business to attend the funeral service that was held, with typical B. I.

Gross showmanship, on one of his own soundstages. Among those in attendance, the lieutenant noted with interest, were all nine of the people on the Lizard's list.

He had researched all of them, and in the week following the burial of Gross, he sought out and interviewed them, one by one.

First, he interviewed the one he already knew: the dead man's son, Martin. The sullen, delicately pretty young man of twenty-seven lived in a tastefully appointed little house in that part of the Hollywood Hills sometimes known as the Swish Alps. He opened the door himself.

"Hello, Martin," said Garcia.

"Do I know you?" Martin blinked and seemed the worse for drink, an assumption enhanced by the alcoholic odor that radiated from him like a halo.

"You were only eighteen when we last met. Lieutenant Garcia, LAPD."

"Oh, sure, the *cop*! Come on in, friend."

Declining the offer of a drink, Garcia got right to the point. "Your father left me a letter," he said, "naming several people I should investigate if he died."

"And I'm one of them?"

"I'm afraid so."

Martin Gross laughed. "Love it! I *love* it! What's my motive supposed to be?"

"You tell me," Garcia suggested.

"Oh, no. That's what *you're* paid for."

"Well," Garcia said casually, "I know you're gay, and your father knew it, too . . ."

"And hated the idea, yes indeed, but that's a motive for *him* to kill *me,* not me him."

"What I started to say was, I know you're gay because of that little scrape when you were still a high school senior, when you tried to pick up that fellow in the bar, and he got all uptight about it and swore out a complaint against you . . .”

“I'm eternally grateful to you, Lieutenant, for smoothing that over and convincing my father it had something to do with pot. Bad enough in his eyes, the devil's weed and all that, but if he had found out the *truth* . . .”

“He did find out later, though, didn't he?” said Garcia. “It's only gossip, of course, but the way I heard it, he caught you and another man—”

“*In flagrante delicto,* or do I mean *delicious*?” Martin laughed. “Yes, he certainly did, Lieutenant.”

“And he couldn't take that. So, for appearances, he forced you to marry some starlet under contract to his studio . . .”

“As you say, for appearances. But also ‘to make a man of me.’ Can you imagine the naiveté of the old fool? To think that marrying me off to some tart would ‘cure’ me? The marriage didn't last, of course. Oh, I never blamed *her,* the poor little bubble-brain. She'd been servicing the old man for years, and most of his friends as well, like that spic Montoya . . . oh, sorry about that! . . . but anyway, I was just another assignment to her.”

“The story goes that the whole experience turned you into a lush. Sorry about *that,* Martin.”

“Oh, I *am* a lush. I've been a lush for simply *years.* But it wasn't the marriage to little Charlaine that did it. Good grief, that was only a bore. And an inconvenience. What made me a lush was being the son of that unspeakable pig!”

“Then you hated him?”

“Of *course* I hated him! Who didn't?” Martin began to sing: *“Ding-dong, the lizard's dead . . .”* He broke off, and said, "My stepmother hated him, too. Why don't you talk to her?"

"I will," said Garcia. For she was on the list.

It was not Martin's stepmother Garcia visited next, however. The next name on his list was Fawn Blake, and in order to interview her, he had to drive into the San Fernando Valley. He wisely resolved to schedule his further interviews more efficiently, to cut down on driving time.

He eased his car across Sunset Boulevard and kept driving north on Highland until that avenue obligingly became the Hollywood Freeway, conveying him smoothly into the Valley. Fawn Blake. . . . Garcia smiled as he recalled her pictures with affection. . . .

Signaling right, he drifted deftly across the lanes and made it to the off ramp just in time, curving gracefully down onto Lankershim Boulevard and leaving only one angry horn honking in his wake. "Same to you, buddy," he muttered to his steering wheel.

He found Fawn Blake at Universal, on the set of a top-rated television series, where she was doing a guest appearance.

"As an aging actress," she said sweetly. "But it's a job. Come, Lieutenant, let's take a break in my dressing room. They won't be needing me for a while."

The dressing room was only a trailer, but it contained the necessities of television life, as well as the thick, cloying odor of makeup. "Sit down somewhere," said Fawn Blake, easing off her shoes, "and tell me what this is all about."

She had always been, if not a great beauty in the classic sense, the epitome of girl-next-door innocence and sincerity. Much of this essence still clung to her.

Garcia perched himself precariously on a small

folding chair and told her about the list. She smiled. "That's just dear Biggie making trouble for everybody," she said. "Doesn't mean a thing."

"Biggie?"

"B.I.G. A lot of us called him Biggie. Of course, *some* called him the Lizard of Oz or even worse. The killer will probably turn out to be somebody not even *on* the list."

"Maybe," Garcia admitted. "But you did have a motive, Miss Blake."

"Do tell." She smirked, not unattractively.

"Well," said the lieutenant, "the characters you played in your films . . ."

"Movies," she said primly. "I made movies. We all made movies in those days. It was when they started making *films* that they began to lose the public."

He nodded. "Anyway, you always played—how should I put it?—wholesome ladies . . ."

"Pure as the well-known driven snow," she added.

"Right, both on and *off* the screen. Not a breath of scandal. Never in the gossip columns. Your private life was spotless. You were held up as some kind of ideal, by church groups and so on."

"You have a good memory, Lieutenant."

"You were my mother's favorite actress," said Garcia, and when he saw her face begin to harden, he quickly added, "Mine, too."

"On your dear mama's lap? Very well, I was the original Mrs. Clean. Where is all this leading?"

"The inside story is that although you were a big star, very popular—especially after you made that picture about St. Therese—you worked for low pay under contract to Mr. Gross—"

"Peanuts," she snapped. "I wasn't a very good businesswoman."

"You worked for low pay," Garcia continued, "because Mr. Gross possessed the only existing print of a one-reel movie you made when you were fifteen. The kind of movie they used to call a stag film and that was shown only at men's smokers. Today, movies like that are shown in theaters, rated X, big screen, color, stereophonic sound. But not then."

"Rumors, Lieutenant," said Fawn Blake, "just rumors."

"The film was in Mr. Gross's wall safe," said Garcia. "As part of this investigation, I screened it. It pretty much supports the rumors, Miss Blake. They say you moved heaven and earth to have all the prints destroyed, but Gross had the last remaining copy, and he held it over your head."

"And I killed him because of that? After all these years? Don't be silly." The warm crinkle of her eyes took the sting out of the admonition.

"It's a valid motive," Garcia insisted.

Fawn Blake shook her head. "You're barking up the wrong lady, Lieutenant. Oh, I admit that I used to be terribly afraid of that little strip of celluloid. But that was back in the old days, when people took things like that very big. Now?" she shrugged. "Frankly, my dear, I don't give a damn—as Clark said in the movie." She giggled. "What a stir that caused! When he said 'damn.' And today they say anything they please. Well, *autres temps, autres moeurs.*"

"I'm sorry?"

"Never mind—just a French proverb I picked up from Charles Boyer. As for that little old one-reeler of mine, you can book it into all the trendiest theaters in Westwood, for all I care. I only wish my last two pictures were as good as that one!"

"It certainly doesn't have any dull moments," Garcia conceded.

"You saw it, you say?" Garcia nodded. Fawn Blake sighed wistfully. With a faraway gaze in her still-innocent wide eyes, she said, "I had great tits in those days, didn't I?"

The next name on the list took Garcia back to the O-Z lot and the office of Sidney Warren, executive vice-president of the studio. He was a crisply tailored, gray-haired man, well into his sixties, thin and angular as a praying mantis. A hint of lime-scented aftershave lotion clung to him.

"Is this sort of thing really necessary?" he asked. "Wasting people's time . . . bothering them in their hour of grief? I thought these days the police solved crimes in the forensics laboratories."

"We do, some of them," said Garcia. "And our police labs here in L.A. are among the best in the country. But I guess I'm old-fashioned. Also, it so happens that the Justice Department, not too long ago, completed a three-year study of local, state, and federal crime labs. Know what they came up with, Mr. Warren?"

"I haven't the faintest idea," said Warren, bored.

"Fully *half* of the labs couldn't identify dog hair. Thirty-four percent couldn't tell three kinds of paint apart. Twenty-two percent couldn't differentiate among three different metals. Thirteen percent couldn't analyze which guns bullets came from. So, yes, this sort of thing really *is* necessary."

Glancing at his watch, Warren said, "I have a full agenda today, Lieutenant. I can allow you five minutes."

Garcia told him about the list, adding, "You were Mr. Gross's second-in-command here, isn't that right?" Warren nodded. "That means you're first in line for the top-dog position, now that he's dead."

"It seems likely," said Warren.

"The talk around town, though, is that you never had his showmanship or daring, and he didn't have much respect for your opinions."

"I'm surprised you listen to 'the talk around town,' Lieutenant," Warren responded. "Actually, Baruch and I got along very well."

"He called you the Accountant, I understand."

"I *was* an accountant when we first met."

"He made fun of your cautious attitudes."

"And I criticized his lack of caution. It was a nice check and balance."

"They say," Garcia went on, "that a long time ago, when you were a young employee at a credit-reporting agency, he came to you with a proposal. If you would fiddle with the files and give his financially shaky company, Zodiac, a phony triple-A credit rating so he'd be in a better position to merge with Oracle, he'd reward you with a large slice of stock and a position in the new company."

Warren said, "I've heard that story. But whether or not it's true, it doesn't give me a reason to kill him."

"No, it doesn't," Garcia agreed. "But the other things do. The resentment, the desire to be main man . . ."

Warren looked at his watch again. "Your five minutes are up. If you'll excuse me?"

As long as he was on the O-Z lot, Garcia figured he might as well visit Barry Birmingham, who was acting in a picture being shot on Stage Four. He was one of the people on the list. The handsome leading man was not to be found on the soundstage at the moment, however, and Garcia was directed to his bungalow.

There, resting between acting chores, Birmingham was dressed in a burgundy velour robe and, presumably, nothing else. His tanned bare feet and ankles seemed aggressively casual, particularly in light of the fact that he was not alone. With him in the bungalow was a handsome, if glassily brittle, woman in elegant early middle age—forty?—dressed exactly the same as Birmingham. His and Hers matching robes? wondered Garcia. Her toenails were tinted tea-rose pink. Her face seemed faintly familiar to Garcia, but he couldn't place her.

"What can I do for you, Lieutenant?" the actor asked amiably after Garcia had identified himself.

"Actually, Mr. Birmingham, I'd like a few words in private."

"You can speak in front of Mrs. Gross," Birmingham assured him. Now Garcia recognized the former Regina Thayer, who had been a minor contract player at O-Z until Gross had married her some fifteen years before. Garcia had noted the widow's veiled presence at the funeral service, as she had been helped from her limo by a black chauffeur. "We have no secrets from each other," said Birmingham. "Right, Regina?"

The woman drawled, "If that's the way you want to play it, Barry."

Birmingham smiled. "What does the Bard say? 'Man and wife are one flesh . . .'"

"We're not married *yet*, darling," Regina Gross reminded him. "There has to be a decent interval between the death of one husband and marriage to the next."

"True," said Birmingham. "'The funeral baked meats' mustn't 'coldly furnish forth the marriage table.'"

Regina smiled wryly at Garcia. "Don't mind all that Bard stuff, Lieutenant. Barry has been boning up on Shakespeare, now that my late lamented has croaked."

Birmingham winced. "Please, dear," he said. "Not 'croaked.' 'Shuffled off this mortal coil.'"

"Whatever." She sauntered over to the refreshments table. "Something to drink, Lieutenant?"

"I'm on duty," said Garcia, "but maybe some of that Perrier water? It's a hot day."

As she handed him the icy drink, Garcia apologetically said, "I guess I'm a little slow, but I don't get the connection between Shakespeare and the death of Mr. Gross."

Barry Birmingham replied, "Biggie always kept me trapped in pretty-boy roles. But I'm meant for better things. Dramatic parts. The classics."

"I see. Then I guess that's one reason you're on the list, Mr. Birmingham."

"List?"

Garcia explained, adding, "That gives you a pretty good double motive for murdering him. Better parts, and Mrs. Gross's inherited fortune, if you marry her."

Birmingham frowned hammily, in a jocose mockery of malevolence. "Aha, so I'm cast as a villain . . . a 'bloody, bawdy villain . . .'"

"Barry, for Christ's sake, knock it off with the *Hamlet,* will you?" Regina pleaded. "Lieutenant, believe me, he's a pussycat. Wouldn't hurt a fly."

Garcia asked, "What about you, Mrs. Gross? You're on your husband's list, too."

"Not exactly an exclusive club, is it? What's my motive?"

"The money," said Garcia. "A say in studio business. The freedom to marry Mr. Birmingham. Plus you hated Mr. Gross. Your stepson says so. And you certainly had plenty of opportunity."

"So did the butler, the gardener, the chauffeur, the maids. Why don't you grill *them?*"

"I'm going to," said Garcia. "One of them is on the list, in fact." Turning back to Barry, Garcia asked the actor, "Are you sure I can talk about anything at all in front of Mrs. Gross?"

"As I said," Barry replied, "no secrets."

"Okay," said Garcia, "then you had another motive, too. A reason for fearing B. I. Gross—and for him hating you."

"You mean because I was banging his wife?"

"That, too. But mainly because you were banging his son. He caught you and Martin together. He couldn't stand the thought of a son of his being that way, and he forced the boy to marry a starlet. He punished you by locking you into insipid parts. You might have wanted Gross dead not only because of the money and the classic roles, but also because he knew you were gay and he could spill the beans about it."

Birmingham laughed. "Spill *what* beans? Everyone knows I'm AC/DC. I swing both ways, Lieutenant, and give equal satisfaction to both genders. Ask Regina. Ask Martin. They've never complained." He rolled his eyes skyward. "To be or not to be a pederast—who *cares* anymore?"

Maybe *I* care, Mr. Pretty Boy Birmingham, Garcia muttered to himself that evening. Maybe I care that *cabrones* like you are committing adultery, sodomy, screwing other people's wives and sons and *dogs,* for all I know!

"What are you mumbling about, Pablo?" asked his wife as she put an aromatic platter of *carne asada* on the table. She was a bright-eyed, energetic woman in her fifties, with a remarkably Aztec profile. She had kept her svelte figure and peppery personality through a quarter century of marriage and two children, both now grown, married, and in the process of producing the lieutenant's first grandchildren.

To his wife's question, Garcia replied, "Nothing. Just talking back to Barry Birmingham—in my own mind."

Serving him the meat, she said, "I don't care very much for him. Seems too stuck on himself, at least on the screen."

"You wouldn't like him any better in person."

"Who are you going to interview tomorrow?" she asked as she sat down.

"I think I'll talk to Kleinbaum first."

"Who's he?"

"A composer. Writes movie music."

"Songs?"

"I don't think so. The music that goes on behind the action."

"Never heard of him."

"He was supposed to be fairly big back in the old country."

"Why did Gross put him on the list?"

Garcia shook his head. "Maybe he figured Kleinbaum hated him."

"Why?"

Garcia chewed his meat thoughtfully. "The story is, Kleinbaum barely made it out of Vienna during the Nazi days, but not before having some pretty nasty experiences with the Gestapo, and losing some family members, like both parents and a sister, in concentration camps. When he got over here, he got a job at Oracle-Zodiac, in the music department. . . ."

"Then he was luckier than most. So?"

"So B. I. Gross used to think it was a lot of fun to sneak up behind him and yell *'Heil Hitler!'* in a loud German accent—making Kleinbaum jump about three feet in the air and come down shaking like Jell-O for half an hour."

"What a terrible thing to do!" she said, appalled.

Her husband shrugged. "That's the kind of guy he was."

She shuddered. "I'm surprised he stayed alive as long as he did."

"Pass the tortillas, please."

Kurt Hermann Kleinbaum's study was a small, restful, cluttered room in his Pacific Palisades home. He lived there alone—"with my memories," he said, perfectly straight, as if unaware that it was a hackneyed phrase.

A bust of Bach occupied a focal place on a bookshelf. A musical score stood open on the gleaming mahogany piano. Photos of dead friends glowered from the walls. Kleinbaum introduced Garcia to them: "Erich Korngold . . . Arnold Schönberg . . . Anton Webern . . . Alban Berg . . . I knew them all, Lieutenant, in Europe. And some of them over here, as well. Korngold wrote music at Warner Brothers, for Errol Flynn pictures. Schönberg taught at UCLA. They named a building after him."

"Oh, *that* Schönberg," said Garcia.

"And I . . ." He laughed sourly. "I worked for the great Gross. Do you know, I was the one who told him that the German word *gross* means 'big' or 'great'? As in Beethoven's Great Fugue, the *Grosse Fuge*. He repeated that again and again, to everybody—'Gross means Great!' He loved it. But he kept me writing monster music."

"Monster music?"

The old composer nodded. "I wanted to write the music for important films, beautiful films. After all, in Vienna I was considered a serious artist. I wrote symphonies, operas, concertos. But Gross assigned me to such stuff as *The Shrieking Dead* . . . *The Snake*

Woman . . . Return of the Snake Woman . . ."

"Must have been quite a comedown," said Garcia.

Kleinbaum's eyes narrowed. "I see these young ones today, with their rock scores, their electronic sounds, their computerized music . . . I see them winning Oscars, making millions of dollars . . ."

"Hard to take," Garcia suggested.

"Hard? No, Lieutenant. Easy. Because next year their trash will be totally forgotten, replaced by other trash. There will be rust on their Oscars. But my work, my *real* work—my *Rhapsodic Symphony*, my Double Concerto for Viola and Harp, my opera *Abraham*—these will *live*. They will live forever!"

"Sure," Garcia said. "But even so, you must have resented Mr. Gross."

"I deplored his taste, his manners, his ghastly sense of humor. I was also very sorry for him."

"Sorry? Why?" wondered Garcia.

"He was a man who had nothing. No friends, no loved ones. His own wife and son hated him. He was desperately unhappy. But I had friends, and the respect of my colleagues, and the talent God gave me. That is why he envied me. That is why he played his pathetic, sick little jokes on me, and kept me writing music for monsters and maniacs. That is also why he put me on his list. . . ."

To himself, Garcia said: I'll be the judge of that.

Doretta Mulvane also lived in the Palisades, so when Garcia left Kleinbaum's house, he sought out the home of that madcap star of yesteryear.

"Yes, Lieutenant, I've heard about your list," said the stately *grande dame* who bore scant resemblance to the light comedienne of so many screen romps. A veritable mist of lavender aroma surrounded her, as if she had bathed in cologne.

"News travels fast in this town, Miss Mulvane," said Garcia.

"It's like Gilbert and Sullivan, isn't it?"

"Pardon?"

She chirped a tune: " 'I've got a little list . . . they never will be missed . . .' And am *I* on the little list?"

"I'm afraid so, Miss Mulvane."

"One wonders why. I had no motive for murdering the old boy."

"Mr. Gross seemed to think you did. Something about your whirlwind romance with Arturo Montoya, maybe, and your marriage to him."

"But that was *ages* ago, Lieutenant!"

Garcia nodded. "I think Mr. Gross figured you hated him because he busted up the marriage."

"I did hate him for that," she declared. "I was very much in love with Arturo. Gross was always messing about with people's lives. Forced that boy of his to marry that silly little bit of candyfloss. Forced me to divorce Arturo. Not that Arturo minded, the scamp! He only married me because he'd got me preggers. People *did* that in those days, you know. Got married *before* having babies. Now it's the other way round, more often than not."

"The baby was stillborn, I read," said Garcia.

"Yes," she said softly. "A little girl, they told me. I never saw her."

"Why did Gross disapprove of the marriage?" Garcia asked.

"He *said* it was because the public wouldn't accept a popular romantic idol like Arturo being married. Bad for box office. But the *real* reason was because *he* wanted me."

"Gross?"

"None other. He had a very high fever for me. Kept after me all the time. But I never let him take liberties. That made him furious! And that's why he hated me and broke up the marriage."

"Why are you on the list but not Montoya?"

Doretta Mulvane shrugged. "Search me. Ask Arturo."

On his way to Arturo Montoya's Malibu beach house, Garcia thought about something Fawn Blake had said: "The killer will probably turn out to be somebody not even *on* the list. . . ."

Like Montoya?

It was cooler near the ocean, and almost completely smogless. Garcia parked near Montoya's house, but he didn't walk up to the door immediately. He watched the Pacific waves breaking for a minute or so, inhaled the salt tang of the air, and appreciatively eyed a coven of high-school-age girls in bikinis that seemed to be constructed of dental floss. If they had dressed that way when *he* was a teenager . . . He shook his head, not so much in disapproval as in wonderment—wonder at changing times and at the beauty of the sea, the sun, the lithe young bodies of these unashamed kids. He had to get out to the beach more often, he told himself.

Despite the ocean breeze, the sun was beginning to draw glistening droplets of moisture from his forehead. Or was it those near-naked girls who were doing it? he pondered. Dabbing his face with a handkerchief, Garcia turned away from the pleasant scene and walked up to the beach house's door.

His knock was answered by a stunning black woman whose smooth chocolate flesh was in bold contrast to the French-cut maillot that clung to her like a coat of lemon-yellow paint. The one-piece swimsuit was, in its way, even more enticing than the all-but-nude models displayed by the girls outside, for the hip-high leg holes, waist-deep neckline, and porthole sides revealed easily ninety percent of a vibrantly healthy, trim, yet ample female body. A short beach robe of the same yellow shade hung, open, from her shoulders.

"Yes?" she inquired. After Garcia had identified himself and his mission, she invited him inside, saying, "I'm Mr. Montoya's secretary, Trisha Jones. I'll tell him you're here. Oh . . . and this is Mr. McCoy," she offhandedly added.

A casually dressed, tow-headed young man with glasses crouched over a coffee table, script and pen in hand. He looked up and nodded as the provocative Trisha left the room. "How's the investigation going?" he asked.

Garcia made a noncommittal gesture. "Slow but unsure," he said, studying the young fellow. "McCoy . . ." he muttered. "Are you Jack McCoy?"

"That's right."

"The director?"

McCoy nodded. "Heard of me, have you? That's a switch."

"Sure. You're up and coming."

"Was," said McCoy.

"Why was?"

"Ding-dong, the lizard's dead," McCoy recited, rather than sang.

"I know Mr. Gross signed you up right out of film school," said Garcia. "Let you direct some small stuff, then just recently gave you the green light on a major project. . . ."

"*The House of Atreus*. Greek tragedy, updated to the contemporary world. But Sid Warren will cancel it for sure. Too risky. Too big a budget, too small a director. Iffy subject matter."

"So now you're working on something with Montoya?"

"Just a favor. Helping him with a guest spot on a TV show. A little dialogue coaching on his lines."

"Sort of ghost-directing him?"

"In a way. I think they tried to get Cesar Romero for the part, but he was unavailable, so they settled for Montoya. Trish asked me to do it." McCoy smiled. "I'd do anything for her."

"She's a beautiful woman."

"I know. I'm crazy about her. So is Montoya." His face clouded. "No contest. He's a 'star,' and I'm the youngest has-been in town."

"Isn't he a little old for her?"

"He sure is. But she's blinded by his so-called Latin charm."

"Careful what you say about Latin charm, Mr. McCoy. My name is Garcia, remember."

Trisha Jones reappeared with her employer. He was clad in an immaculate blue-and-white running suit. The actor, his dark virility not entirely ravaged by the onslaught of time, flashed Garcia a brilliant smile and offered his hand.

"Lieutenant, a pleasure," said Arturo Montoya. "How can I help you get to the bottom of this terrible thing?" The Hispanic accent had remained intact over the years, Garcia noted, although the dazzling teeth were probably capped at the very least, and the curly hair was surely dyed that raven hue.

"Miss Mulvane suggested I talk to you," said Garcia.

"Doretta? Such a lovely lady, no?"

"Mr. Gross left a list of people he thought would be glad to see him dead. Miss Mulvane is on the list, but you're not. I wondered why."

Montoya looked dubious. "I do not believe that Doretta wished the *jefe* to be dead. She did not like him, true, because he broke up our marriage . . . but to desire him to be dead? That is a bad thing, a sin, no? Not Doretta . . . a sweet girl . . . no, no . . ." He shook his head.

"And you, Mr. Montoya, did you like him?"

Another flash of teeth. "I got along marvelously with him. We played cards, we got drunk, sometimes we swapped girls. We understood each other. He called me Wetback!" Montoya's brown eyes twinkled.

The term didn't sound like an endearment to Garcia. "What part of Mexico are you from, Mr. Montoya?"

"I am not Mexican, Lieutenant. I am from Bolivia."

"Oh," said Garcia. "I guess that explains the accent. It doesn't sound Mexican. My parents came from Mexico. Oaxaca."

"Well, we are both Latinos, eh, *amigo*?"

"Yes, sir. Didn't you hate Mr. Gross when he broke up your marriage?"

Montoya shook his head. "I understood Jefecito's reasons. Sound business reasons, from his point of view. He was not a sentimentalist. And . . . well, to tell you the truth, I was a restless young *muchacho* and did not really want to be tied down." He turned and looked lovingly at Trisha. "Not *then,* that is."

Trisha returned the loving look. "So you see, Lieutenant," she said, "Arturo has no motive. That's why he's not on the list."

"None of you are," Garcia told her. "Not you, or Mr. Montoya, or Mr. McCoy. But I had to ask, because of the old connection with Miss Mulvane."

"We understand," said Montoya, with a sympathetic smile.

"How many more on the list?" asked Jack McCoy.

"Two," said Garcia. "A cameraman and a chauffeur. I'll see them tomorrow."

"Chauffeur?" asked Trisha. "Mr. Gross's chauffeur?"

"That's right. Duncan Jones." Reflectively, Garcia repeated the surname: "Jones . . . it's a common name. . . . I don't suppose you're related to . . . ?"

"Yes," said Trisha, her voice hushed with concern. "He's my father."

"What are you doing here?"

"I have to talk to you before that cop does."

"Cop?"

"Garcia. If he starts to grill you, everything might come out."

"Why should it? No percentage in that for me."

"You might get careless . . . rattled . . . the pressure . . . he might scare you."

"Hmm . . . true enough. I *might* let the cat out of the bag, at that."

"You can't!"

"It sure will be hard keeping my mouth shut under all that *pressure,* like you say . . . unless I have a good reason to keep quiet."

"I'm already giving you plenty of good reasons—with pictures of presidents on every one of them. Have been for years!"

"But I want more."

"How much more?"

"As much as it's worth. Or else I'll tell."

"No!"

"And I'll tell the *other* thing, too. . . ."

"Other thing?"

"That's right. The thing even *you* don't know. Believe me, you're not going to like it when you hear it. You're not going to like it one little bit. . . ."

Garcia had scheduled the last two interviews for the same morning, to save himself unnecessary driving.

Both men lived in the gracious northerly reaches of Bel-Air, Buck Hammond in a rambling ranch-style house, Duncan Jones in quarters over the ample multiple-car garage of the B. I. Gross estate. The lieutenant visited Hammond first.

The bulky cinematographer was on his knees, tending the roses in his garden. They exuded an oppressively sweet perfume that reminded Garcia of a funeral parlor.

"My wife loved roses, but they don't do so well in this dry climate," he said. "They like it wetter than this. Oregon. England. That's where they thrive."

"But these look great," said Garcia with admiration.

As Hammond led him inside to his den, he said, "I do the best I can with what I've got to work with."

"Just like your movies."

"That's right," Hammond agreed, pushing his thinning hair out of his eyes. "Even if the script is a load of manure and the actors are about as animated as those guys on Mount Rushmore, I try to make everything *look* good."

"You've certainly got the Oscars to prove it," Garcia said, indicating several burnished Academy Award statuettes on the mantelpiece.

"Well, I learned from the best. Jimmy Howe, Gregg Toland . . . Can we get down to business?"

"Sure, Mr. Hammond. You didn't like B. I. Gross very much, did you?"

"I didn't have to. He paid me to do a job and I did it. Liking him wasn't part of the contract."

"I mean, I remember some of the things you said when you and I were standing at his coffin."

Hammond grinned. "Well, I didn't know you were a cop or I would have kept my mouth shut."

"What exactly did you have against him?" Garcia asked. "He assigned you to some big pictures. You might say he made it possible for you to win those Oscars."

"Yeah, you might say that." Hammond sighed and lit a cigarette. "I'm a widower," he said, after exhaling a double lungful of acrid smoke. "About a year ago, my wife and I planned to take a long trip, just the two of us. Call it a second honeymoon. We both knew it would be the last trip we'd ever take together, because she was terminally ill. So we made all our plans, got all the reservations, and then Gross said he needed me on an important picture. 'But she's dying!' I told him. Know what he said? 'We're all dying. You'll be better off working and getting your mind off your troubles. It'll be better for her, too.' So Sally and I never took that trip."

"And you hated Gross for that?"

"Yep," Hammond admitted. "But, you know, the old bastard was probably right. Better to keep working, carry on a normal life. I couldn't see it that way at the time, though. . . ."

Hammond's phone rang, and he grabbed it, barking, "Yeah?" Then he handed it to Garcia. "For you."

"I gave the station this number." He took the phone. "Garcia speaking."

The voice of Sergeant Jameson crackled in his ear: "Hey, my man, you better get on up to the Gross place. There's been a shooting. We just got the call. You're near there, aren't you?"

"I'm on my way."

"And we've got some other late-breaking news, too, but that can wait," Jameson added.

"News about what?"

"The Lizard's choice of reading matter, for one thing," said Jameson.

When Garcia arrived at the Gross estate, Duncan Jones was being lifted into an ambulance on a stretcher, and a body bag was being stowed into another vehicle.

"Who's in the bag?" he asked the nearest officer.

"Some actor."

"Actor? *What* actor?"

An older policeman, closer to Garcia's age, supplied the name: "Arturo Montoya."

"What?"

"Yes, sir. He shot the chauffeur and then killed himself. A .455 Webley in the mouth. Took the top of his head right off."

"Christ!" Turning to a paramedic, Garcia asked, "How bad off is the chauffeur?"

"Pretty bad," said the paramedic. "He may not make it to the hospital."

"I've got to ride with him. There are some things I need to know." Garcia followed the paramedic into the back of the ambulance, where Duncan Jones lay, connected by plastic tubing to an IV bottle. The paramedic closed the doors and the ambulance rolled, siren blasting.

Garcia peered into the pain-dimmed eyes of the chauffeur. "Why did Montoya shoot you?" he gently asked.

"Name . . . not Montoya," whispered Jones, staring straight up.

"Then what *is* his name?"

"Arthur . . . Montrose. Light mulatto from Louisiana. Been passing for white all these years . . . fake accent . . . nobody knew . . . but Mr. Gross found out . . . and I knew . . . and Montoya *knew* that I knew . . ."

"How did he know, Mr. Jones?"

Duncan Jones seemed reluctant to answer.

"*How* did he know?" Garcia repeated, adding casually, "You were blackmailing him, is that right?"

Jones nodded. "When you said . . . you were going to talk to me today . . . he got scared . . . thought it would all come out . . . about him being black . . . so he offered me more money . . . but I wanted even more than he offered . . . or I'd tell the *other* thing. . . ."

"What other thing?"

The chauffeur's eyes glazed and he licked his lips. The siren relentlessly split Garcia's eardrums as the ambulance sliced through traffic. "*What* other thing, Mr. Jones?"

"Something Montoya didn't even know . . . until just this morning when I told him. . . ."

"Go on," Garcia urged.

"The way Mr. Gross found out Montoya was a black man . . ."

"Yes?"

"Because Miss Doretta's baby . . . Montoya's baby . . . was black . . . real dark . . . took after Montoya's grandpappy or something. . . ."

"Happens that way sometimes," said Garcia.

"Mr. Gross paid off the doctor, the nurses . . . to say the baby was born dead. . . . Miss Doretta didn't never know no different. . . . Montoya never knew different, neither. . . ."

"The baby wasn't stillborn?"

"No, sir. . . ."

"What happened to the child?"

"Mr. Gross gave the little girl to me and my wife to raise . . . we didn't have no children of our own. . . ."

"Then you mean *Trisha* is—"

"Montoya's daughter. And lately she's been . . . been . . ."

"Sleeping with him?" Garcia suggested.

"Yes, sir. When Montoya found out who she really was . . . he went crazy . . . said *she* mustn't ever find out she's his daughter, she'd die of shame. . . . That's when he pulled out the gun and . . . and . . ."

A long, hissing sigh emptied the lungs of the stricken chauffeur.

"I guess we don't need the siren anymore," said the paramedic.

"Jonesy sure must have done a whole lot of talking before he cashed in," said Sergeant Jameson. "And with those slugs in him! He must have been one big tough brother."

Jameson and Garcia were having a couple of beers at a bar near the station. "He was in pretty good shape for his age, all right," said Garcia. "But Lester Gillis weighed in at only a hundred and twenty-five pounds, soaking wet, and he took seventeen hits from an FBI agent with a submachine gun, then got up to live six more hours, kill that agent and two others, plus a couple of cops."

"Awesome," Jameson agreed. "Who was Lester Gillis?"

"Better known as Baby Face Nelson," said Garcia.

"*Him* I heard of. But getting back to modern times, I guess there wasn't any murder after all, huh?"

"Sure there was. What are you talking about? Montoya murdered Jones before he killed himself."

"I meant Gross," said Jameson.

"No, Gross wasn't murdered. You saw that report from the team we put on his house. Those books they found locked in the secret compartment of his desk . . . what were the titles again?"

Jameson pulled the report from his pocket and unfolded it. "*Justifiable Euthanasia: A Guide for Physi-*

cians, by Dr. P. V. Admiraal . . . *Let Me Die Before I Wake,* by Derek Humphry . . . *Commonsense Suicide: The Final Right,* by Doris Portwood . . . *How to Die with Dignity,* by—"

"That's enough," said Garcia. "And his doctor started prescribing sleeping pills for him a whole year ago, but he probably never took them, just saved them, maybe till he worked up the nerve to overdose himself. 'We're all dying,' he told Buck Hammond a year ago. That must have been when he first learned he was terminal."

Jameson frowned. "Yeah, but then why did he make that list?"

"To stir up trouble, probably. 'That's just dear Biggie making trouble for everybody. Doesn't mean a thing.' That's exactly what Fawn Blake said. And, you know, I think maybe Gross had a pretty good idea that things might turn out the way they did, or close to it." Garcia sipped his beer. "Well, one good thing has come out of all this," he said. "Trisha's stopped bedding her own father."

"Yeah, that's an improvement," said Jameson, "specially for McCoy, but you really think old man Gross could have foreseen that?"

"Maybe not. But he was a shrewd son of a bitch, and like that newspaper article said, he was a good amateur psychologist, he knew what made his people tick, how they'd react in certain situations."

"But what beef did he have with his chauffeur?"

"The kid Martin filled me in about that. Seems Duncan Jones was blackmailing Gross, too, not only Montoya."

"Blackmailing Gross? About what?"

"His son being gay. Gross didn't want that spread around."

Jameson shook his head. "Not a very nice dude, Jonesy."

"A lot of not very nice people in this mess," said Garcia.

"Beginning to think you're right about the world getting worse and worse," Jameson said glumly.

"No, I was wrong about that," Garcia admitted. "The world is getting better."

"Say what?"

"Well, look at all the fuss these old-timers had to put up with about being black or white or passing. Or being gay. Or having a porno skeleton in the closet. Or romantic stars not getting married because they thought it was bad for box office. All that crap, causing all that unhappiness and blackmail and loused-up lives. Today, it couldn't happen. Black, white, gay, married, unmarried, so what? No, the world is slowly getting better, believe it or not. Not much, but little by little. It's like an old movie I saw on TV a while back. William Powell is at a party and some drunk is bending his ear about how great it was back in the good old days. Powell tells him, 'Don't kid yourself. *These* are the good old days.'"

"Hey," said Jameson with a chuckle, "next thing you'll be getting yourself a VCR, just like me!"

"Why not?" said Garcia. "My wife has been after me to get one. And the first movie I'll rent will be *Gone with the Wind*."

"That old thing?"

"Yeah," Garcia said, smiling. "I still get a kick out of the way Gable says, 'Frankly, my dear, I don't give a damn.'"

ABOUT THE AUTHORS

Jon L. Breen is the author of mystery novels, of which the most recent is *Triple Crown,* and over fifty short stories for *Ellery Queen's Mystery Magazine* and other periodicals. Two of his reference works, *What About Murder* and *Novel Verdicts,* have received Edgars from the Mystery Writers of America. With his wife, Rita, he edited the recent anthology *American Murders.* He lives in Fountain Valley and is a professor and librarian at Rio Hondo College in Whittier.

D. C. Fontana is best known for her television work, which includes over one hundred credits on such series as *Star Trek, Streets of San Francisco,* and *The Waltons.* Ms. Fontana and her husband, special effects cinematographer Dennis Skotak, live in Los Angeles, where she is currently working on a period mystery novel.

George Fox is a novelist, author of the best seller *Amok,* a short-story writer whose fiction and nonfiction have been published in *Playboy, Esquire,* and *The Paris Review,* and a screenwriter. The last time he used Los Angeles as a setting was as co-author of the film *Earthquake,* which reduced the entire city to flaming rubble. He still lives there anyway.

William Campbell Gault is the prolific author of hundreds of mystery stories and novels, including a series of popular mysteries featuring the characters of Brock Callahan and Joe Puma. His first mystery novel, *Don't Cry for Me,* received an Edgar Award from the Mystery Writers of America. Almost all his stories and novels have been set in Southern California, including his most recent Brock Callahan novel, *The Chicano War.*

M. (Marilyn) R. Henderson is the author of more than fifty novels and made her debut in psychological suspense fiction with her widely acclaimed chiller, *If I Should Die.* She is a former regional vice-president of the Southern California Chapter of the Mystery Writers of America. She has lived in Los Angeles since 1972 and says she is irresistibly drawn to the "haunted aura" of the Hollywood Hills above Sunset Boulevard, the setting of her story "Dream House" and her most recent novel, *By Reason of.*

Vincent McConnor, mystery novelist and short-story writer, also has had a distinguished career in radio—

his first radio script starred a young actor named Orson Welles—and television, where he was the first writer to have three original scripts telecast by the networks in one week, and where he was the first editor-producer in TV on *The Web* suspense series. He is now working on his tenth mystery novel—his most recent was the widely praised *I Am Vidocq*—and says he plans to move soon from L.A. to a small town in the Topa Topa mountains "where Shangri-la is waiting."

William F. Nolan, a Los Angeles resident since 1953, has had work selected for more than 125 anthologies, including *Best Detective Stories of the Year.* He is the author of *Logan's Run* (best-selling novel, MGM film, and CBS TV series), as well as 44 other books, over 600 magazine contributions, and 30 film and television scripts.

Ray Russell has lived in Beverly Hills since 1961. His fifteen books include *The Case Against Satan, Sardonicus, Incubus, Princess Pamela,* and *Haunted Castles.* His work has appeared in fifty magazines, including *The Paris Review, Midatlantic Review, Ellery Queen, Alfred Hitchcock, Twilight Zone* and *Playboy,* of which he was the first executive editor. He has been published in ten languages.